D0273251

JENNIFER L. ARMENTROUT

Cursed

**HODDER &
STOUGHTON**

First published in the United States of America in 2012
by Spencer Hill Press

First published in Great Britain in eBook in 2013
by Hodder & Stoughton
An Hachette UK company

First published in paperback in 2014

1

A CIP catalogue record for this title is available from the British Library

Paperback ISBN 978 1 444 79794 7
eBook ISBN 978 1 444 78148 9

Typeset by Hewer Text UK Ltd, Edinburgh
Printed and bound by Clays Ltd, St Ives plc

Hodder & Stoughton policy is to use papers that are natural, renewable
and recyclable products and made from wood grown in sustainable
forests. The logging and manufacturing processes are expected to
conform to the environmental regulations of the country of origin.

Hodder & Stoughton Ltd
338 Euston Road
London NW1 3BH

www.hodder.co.uk

For my friends and family

I

Something soft and warm—definitely hand-sized—settled on my chest, and then moved to the right, headed uphill. I wasn't sure why I expected to be looking into the baby blues of some hot guy when I opened my eyes. Maybe it was because I'd just had the best dream of my life. But I certainly didn't expect to be staring into washed-out, ghostly blue eyes.

There was a hamster perched on my chest, its white-and-brown fur covered in grime. Specks of dirt covered my night-shirt, and bits of gravel clung to my bedspread.

I screamed.

Startled, the hamster scurried off my chest and disappeared under the covers. I jumped off the bed, almost face-planting into the worn-out carpet in the process. I ran from the room, wanting to scream again. My heart was still thumping when I slowed outside my little sister's bedroom. Her door hung cracked open, and my gaze fell first to her bed. Finding it empty, I scanned the room. Early morning light spilled into the bedroom, casting shadows over Olivia's slight frame.

With her back to the door and head bowed, Olivia sat on the floor. Crimson curls curtained her face. Stepping into the room, I tripped over one of her baby dolls. I forgot about the hamster as I stared down at the doll. One of her arms had been twisted off. Olivia had taken a Sharpie to the doll's face, marking out the eyes. Then, in the ultimate act of weirdness, she'd scribbled the word "SEE" across the doll's forehead.

My palms felt sweaty. "Olivia . . ."

She stiffened. "Ember? I did something bad this morning. You're gonna be so mad."

Dreaded words from a five-year-old, but I already knew what she'd done. I moved around the bed even though I wanted to turn and run. There were times Olivia scared the crap out of me. "What did I tell you, Olivia?"

She tilted her head and stared up at me. Her green eyes were wet with tears, shining like glittering emeralds. "I'm sorry." Her lip trembled. "Squeaky got scared when I brought him back in the house. He ran off before I could stop him."

Somehow I managed a smile as my eyes fell over her nightgown. Brown flakes of soil spotted the crisp cotton, and dirt sprinkled her little arms and chubby fingers. The shoebox in her lap was covered in filth.

The very same shoebox I'd used to bury Squeaky in the backyard last night.

I squeezed my eyes shut, mentally stringing together as many cuss words I could think of. I should've known she'd do this. A violent shiver went through me.

Olivia just couldn't let dead things be.

"I'm sorry," she whispered. "But Squeaky loves me and he needed me."

I skirted around her and dropped to my knees. "Squeaky didn't need you! Olivia, you can't do this every time one of your pets dies. It isn't right. It's unnatural." Like it hadn't been natural to bring back the dead pigeon she'd found in the driveway the other day. Or Smokey, the cat she'd discovered alongside the road.

"But . . . I did it to you," Olivia insisted.

I opened my mouth, but what could I say? Olivia *had* done it to me two years ago, and I was just as unnatural as Squeaky. Even more so . . . "I know, and trust me, I appreciate that. But you can't keep doing this."

She flinched back. "Don't."

I glanced at my hands, unaware I had reached for her. Frustrated, I let them drop to my lap. "When things die, it means it's their time to go. You know this."

Olivia jerked to her feet. "You're gonna take Squeaky away from me."

The scent of death clung to the shoebox, invading my senses. Horrified, I wondered if I smelled like that. The urge to sniff myself seemed too strong to pass up.

"Please don't take Squeaky," she went on, getting ready for an Olivia-sized breakdown. "I promise not to do it again. Just let me keep Squeaky! Please!"

I stared.

Olivia stopped moving, but her nightgown still swung around her knees. "Ember, are you mad at me? Please don't be mad at me."

"No." I sighed. "I'm not mad, but you have to promise me you won't do this again. And mean it this time."

She bobbed her head eagerly. "I won't! So you'll let me keep Squeaky?"

"Yes. Just go get the stupid hamster." I stood, sighing. "He was under my blankets."

A bright, beautiful smile broke across her face as she whirled around and took off toward my bedroom. I trailed behind her, my skin crawling as I glanced at the twisted doll. The door to my bedroom hung haphazardly on its remaining hinge.

This house was old, like Civil-War-era old. Everything sagged or slanted at crooked angles. Paint peeled off the walls in sheets like snakeskin. Nothing stood straight. The air smelled of death and decay.

Almost like the house had died two years ago.

Turned out that Squeaky was still under my covers, doing God knows what. Olivia held the squirming ball of fur close to her face. "I get to keep you!"

I clasped my hands together to keep them from shaking. "Put Squeaky in his cage and get ready for school, Olivia. We'll . . . pretend this didn't happen, okay? And go brush your teeth." I paused. "And don't even think about wearing your princess dress to school today."

She stopped in my doorway. "But I *am* a princess."

"Not at school. Go." I pointed toward her bedroom, ignoring the way my stomach was churning.

Olivia skipped down the hallway, completely clueless to how messed up both of us were. "Normal" didn't have a place on my list of words describing us. I wasn't even sure "human" would get a vote.

Alone in my bathroom, I stared down at my shaking hands, at the charcoal smudge on the tips of my index finger, and ordered myself to pull it together. I couldn't afford to lose it. Olivia needed me to be strong. I glanced at my reflection and forced a smile. It was broken.

And I also had the hugest zit ever on my temple.

Awesome.

After a quick shower, I padded out to the bedroom, yanked on the first clean pair of jeans I found, and grabbed a cardigan off the back of my desk chair. A slinky top would have been so much prettier, but the scars patchworking across my arms would have been visible. Apparently Olivia's healing touch didn't fix everything.

In gym last year, one of the girls—Sally Wenchman—had seen the scars while I'd changed. Sally had called me "Frankenstein," and the nickname had stuck ever since.

I snatched my sketchpad and shoved it into my book bag. On the way out, I grabbed the flesh-colored gloves off the chair and slid them on. The long-sleeved shirt hid most of the gloves, and the kids thought I was trying to hide the scars.

It was partly true.

"Are you ready?" I yelled, stomping down the steps. "We have, like, twenty minutes."

"Yeah," came the muffled response.

Following the sound of her voice, I found Olivia at the table eating cereal . . . in her princess dress. Dammit. The kid was weird enough without wearing the same damn dress every day. "Olivia, what did I tell you?"

She hopped up from the table and dumped her bowl in the sink, turning back to me with an impish grin. "It's too late for me to get changed."

I stared at her, dumbfounded. "You're such a brat."

She came to my side, a tentative look on her face. Slowly, she reached out and wrapped her fingers around my glove-covered ones. When I nodded, her grip tightened and all was right in her world.

Two years had passed since I'd been able to touch Olivia without some sort of barrier between her skin and mine. When she fell and scraped her knee, I couldn't kiss it and make it better. If she cried, I couldn't hold her. I couldn't even remember what the closeness of someone else felt like. This whole super-special-touch-of-death crap sucked.

Olivia was currently on this kick where she thought she had superhuman strength or something, so I pretended to let her pull me through the house and out to where my Jeep was parked. The dull, black paint gave it a world-weary look, and it needed new tires and brakes. Still, it was my baby. I could caress its smooth, outer frame and roam my hands over its soft interior all I wanted. My heart fluttered to know it wouldn't keel over and die from my toxic touch.

All the way to school, Olivia obsessed over a new toy she had seen. It took everything for me not to beat my head against the steering wheel. Before jumping out in front of her elementary school, she leaned forward for her obligatory air-kiss. Up close, we were undeniably sisters—with the same deep, auburn curls and freckles.

"Be nice to the other kids today," I reminded her. "And, please God, don't touch anything dead."

She sent me a rather adult look before racing across the walkway in a flurry of pink and glitter. I sat there for a moment, watching as she disappeared among the other pint-sized people. Dad used to say that Olivia had an old soul in her, and I hadn't really understood that until lately.

I glanced at the clock in the dashboard—five minutes to make it to homeroom without getting another tardy. Collecting tardy slips had become sort of a hobby of mine. One day, I would have a pretty collage of pink paper with angry red writing. I'd hang it on the fridge for Olivia. She dug pink things.

Ten minutes later, I slid into my seat with another late slip in my hand and a disgruntled look on my face.

"Again?" whispered the tawny-haired boy beside me.

I sent him a haughty look, only to be met with a broad grin. "What does it look like, Adam?"

He shrugged, still grinning. "Maybe you shouldn't oversleep?"

Adam Lewis was the only person in Allentown High who hadn't stopped talking to me after the accident. Sandbox love— that was what we had—but it wasn't like I could tell him I was late because my little sis had dug up her dead hamster this morning and brought him back to life. I kind of wanted to keep him as a friend.

Adam gave me a puzzled look. He was cute in that nerdy kind of way, but nothing other than friendship lay between us. There couldn't be more. Ever.

Our teacher narrowed her eyes, her lips drawn in a tight line. Mrs. Benton had a no-talk policy during homeroom, which added to her unpopularity among the students. I turned back to my notebook and started scribbling, waiting for the first period bell to ring. I kept thinking about what Olivia had done while I started to sketch the old oak tree outside our classroom window.

My version of the tree looked nothing like the one outside. Maybe it was the fact I'd opted for thick clouds in the background and turned each branch down so the edges were jagged, instead of capturing how the early morning sunlight illuminated the red and golden leaves.

My sketch lacked life. Like me.

I had no idea how Olivia could bring back the dead. For all I knew, she could've been born this way, but it had taken a careless driver and the twisting of metal to spotlight her unique talent two years ago.

I had died in the car, along with Dad.

Those new-age people totally lied. There was no bright light at the end of a dark tunnel. No angels waited to cart me off; no dead family members lingered in the shadows. There was nothing, absolutely nothing . . . until I felt *something* tugging on me, pulling me back into my body. It didn't hurt, but I felt strangely empty—almost like a part of me had stayed in the black abyss. Maybe I'd left my soul somewhere in the hereafter.

When I'd pried my eyes open, I'd seen Dad first. He'd looked a mess—really dead, and Olivia couldn't reach him. The paramedics, the doctors—none of them had had problems touching me. I remembered thinking maybe I'd dreamed about dying.

When I'd gotten home, when everything was so jacked up and felt surreal, I'd realized I hadn't dreamt crap. Sushi had been the first victim. With his smashed-up nose and one eye, the cat happened to be the ugliest thing I'd ever seen, but I loved him. I picked him up, and he died about sixty seconds later. Several dead houseplants later, I realized something was wrong with me—very wrong.

I stopped touching things. Just like that.

Oddly enough, Olivia's ability to bring back the dead had vastly different outcomes depending on what she used it on. Animals ended up with eyes like mine, but they didn't carry the death-touch like I did. I wasn't sure if that would be the same with anybody else she'd bring back, and I really didn't want to find out.

The shrill sound of the first bell drew me out of my thoughts. I gathered my stuff and followed Adam into the crowded hallway.

"So why were you late this morning?" he asked.

I shrugged. "I overslept. It happens."

He sent me a doubtful look, and I felt terrible lying to him. My gaze dropped from his face to his shirt. It read: I BELIEVE IN TROPHY WIVES. Nice.

I changed the subject. "Do you think we'll have a quiz in history?"

He nodded, eyes a bright blue behind the wire frame glasses. "Yeah, did you study?"

I shuffled out of the throng of students, smiling up at Adam. "What were you saying?"

Adam rolled his eyes. "Did you study?"

"Oh. Olivia was being especially needy last—"

"Freak," said Dustin Smith, varsity football captain and all-around douche bag.

"You dated her," cut in another boy. "She's *your* freak, Dustin."

The "dated her" part was sad, but true. When I was fifteen, popular, and still could touch people, we'd had a thing. Dustin and I had kissed . . . *a lot*. Then I'd turned into the black widow. So the chances that I'd die a virgin remained pretty high.

A freak and a virgin—couldn't get any better than that.

"Man, I'm trying to forget that part of my life," said Dustin. "Can you not bring it up?"

My fingers curled around the strap of my bag as I stared at the dirty floor. *Keep staring at the floor*, I thought. *Looking up only makes things worse.* But I never listened to the sane, reasonable voice in my head. Almost against my will, I lifted my head and glared at Dustin.

He jumped back, throwing his hands up as if he wished to ward me off. "Jesus! Don't look at me with your dead eyes, you freak!"

"Hey!" yelled Adam, stepping around me. "Don't talk like that to her."

Dustin lurched at Adam like he was going to hit him, but it was fake. I knew it, and Adam knew it, but we both winced. The crowd around Dustin burst into laughter, the word "freak" still being tossed around as they made their way down the hall.

"What an asshole," muttered Adam. "God, you know what?"

"What?" Hot tears burned my eyes, threatening to spill over, and I hated myself for letting a jerk like Dustin get to me.

"You know he's gonna be pumping our gas one day. He thinks he's Big Shit now, but he'll be working at his father's gas station until he dies." Adam slammed his locker shut, his face softening. "Em, don't let him get to you like that. You're better than him and all his friends."

I blinked furiously. "Are my eyes really that creepy?"

Adam swallowed and it took him a few moments to answer. "No . . . they aren't creepy, Em. They're just different, that's all."

I sighed. Who was he kidding? My eyes *were* creepy. The funny thing was they used to be a shade of boring brown, but after the whole dying thing, they'd changed. Now they possessed the palest shade of blue possible—kind of like the color of the sky on an overcast day, when the world appeared dull and diluted. People thought it was the trauma from the accident or something.

"Em?" he said. "Wanna hang out tonight? We can order pizza. Your favorite this time—no pepperoni—just peppers and mushrooms."

"Sure." I cleared my throat, forcing a smile. Adam never questioned why I didn't like to be touched. He just accepted it—*accepted me*. He made life here tolerable. "I have to pick up Olivia after school and get some groceries, but you can come over."

Adam smiled, visibly relieved. "Good—"

The second warning bell went off, drawing a groan from Adam. He had biology next. Today he'd be dissecting frogs. I pushed away from the locker, about to send him a sympathetic smile when, out of the blue, that line from Macbeth popped into my head: *Something wicked this way comes*. I twisted my neck and peered over my shoulder.

My eyes found him at once.

He was tall—even taller than freakishly tall Adam.

Deep brown hair fell over his forehead in wild waves. His face was arresting and intriguing, with broad cheekbones and a determined mouth. Not conventionally handsome, but universally alluring. Even from where I stood, I could see his eyes were so dark they were almost black.

There was something eerily familiar about his face, like I'd caught glimpses of him in a crowd before. He looked up, and our eyes locked. The intensity in his gaze forced me to step back, almost knocking into Adam.

"Em? You okay? What you staring at?"

I whirled around. "You don't see that guy?"

Adam frowned. "What guy?"

Turning back around, I blinked. The spot where the boy had stood was now empty. The hall was long and narrow. There was no way he could've just disappeared. And it was obvious that Adam hadn't seen the boy in the first place. Was I going crazy now, too? Imagining a sexy new guy standing beside our sparse trophy case?

I guess it could be worse, I admitted. If I was going to hallucinate, then at least it was some hot dude instead of something gross.

2

I was obsessed with Hot Dude for the rest of the day, which was pathetic. My brain must have felt sorry for me, so it'd created the only type of guy I could touch—a fantasy one. When Sally had knocked my English book off my desk, I'd barely raised a brow. When I was confronted by Dustin and his cronies after lunch, I was too caught up in trying to remember all the elements of Hot Dude's face to pay them much attention.

Adam reappeared at my locker at the end of the day, minus his glasses. "What happened to your glasses?" I shoved everything except my trig book back into the locker. It never failed—I always had trig homework.

"What do you think? Dustin the douchenozzle took them in gym class." He switched his bag to his other shoulder.

For a brief second, I entertained the idea of ripping off my gloves, rushing down the hall, and jumping on Dustin's back like a psychotic monkey. I knocked my locker door shut, sighing. "How many has this been?"

"Fourth pair since school started. Mom's going to kill me."

We started toward the back doors. "It's not your fault."

"Try telling her that. She acts like every pair of glasses is a child lost." He held open the door, letting me slide past him. "Alert the police! Another one gone missing!" he cried, clutching his chest. "Someone put my glasses on the back of a milk carton, STAT."

An image of Mr Potato Head's glasses and nose popped in my head, causing me to giggle.

Adam beamed. "So, we still on for tonight?"

"Only if you don't think your mom is going to freak out that badly." I stopped beside Adam's beat-up Ford Taurus. He had a prime parking spot, right in the first row. Since I was always late, I was way back in the section of the parking lot reserved for potheads and students one step from dropping out. I glanced at him, frowning. "You sure you can drive without your glasses?"

He pretended to be offended. "I'm not blind. It's just signs, cars, and people I can't see."

"Nice."

"Anyway," he opened his back door and threw his book bag on the backseat, "Mom will be cool by the time I sneak out of the house. You sure you don't want help at the grocery store?"

"Nah, I'm good." I started off before he could insist, which is what he did every time he knew I had to do the family errand thing. "I'll text you when I'm done."

He gave me a quick, two-finger salute before climbing behind the wheel. I winced and hurried out of his way, muttering a prayer under my breath.

My legs burned by the time I tossed my bag in the back and peeled out of the parking lot. Thankfully, Olivia's school let out an hour after mine, which gave me some free time. Before the accident, I would've headed off to the mall or movies. Now I went the one free place no other kids my age would go—the Allentown Public Library.

Three minutes later, I pulled in front of the squat, two-story building and grabbed my bag. Cool, stale air greeted me as I pushed open the glass doors. Mrs. Compton was where she always was, standing behind the circulation desk. A friendly smile pulled her lips up as she saw me. Shoving a pen into her gray bun, she leaned a plump hip against the counter.

"How was school, Ember?"

"Blech."

She laughed, shaking her head. "One day, when you're my age, you'll look back at high school and wish you were back there. Trust me."

Not likely, but I smiled as I headed to my spot by the window. Curling up on the overstuffed chair that had seen better days, I pulled out the worn copy of *The Picture of Dorian Gray*. I hoped to get a chapter or two done for my essay before I'd have to leave to pick up Olivia.

I thumbed the book open, preparing myself for the bizarreness that was Oscar Wilde. Only ten or fifteen minutes had passed before a shadow blocked the sunlight streaming through the window behind me. I lifted my head and my heart stuttered.

I was hallucinating again, because Hot Dude was standing in front of me.

The sun cast a halo around him, making him appear surreal. His arresting mouth formed a crooked grin and one lock of brown hair, tinted red by the light, fell over his forehead. I blinked, but he didn't vanish.

"Hi," he said in a deep, soft voice that sent a pleasant shiver down my spine.

I looked around, checking to see if anyone else had noticed him, but there was no one near us. My gaze returned to him. Up close, he was actually sort of breathtaking, with his tousled hair and olive skin. His sooty eyelashes had to be the envy of every girl he crossed paths with.

He ran a hand through his hair and rocked back on his heels. The awkward silence stretched out, and I suddenly became painfully aware of how different I was from two years ago. I'd always had something witty and flirty to say. Now I just stared up at him like an idiot. A fierce blush stole over my cheeks, spreading down my neck.

"Uh . . . I've seen you around here a couple of times," he tried again, staring at the book I held. "'*I had come face to face with some one whose mere personality was so fascinating that, if I allowed it to do so, it would absorb my whole nature, my whole soul, my very art itself.*"

I stared. "What?"

His lopsided grin spread into a full one, and it felt like someone had socked me in the chest. "It's a quote from Oscar Wilde's *Dorian Gray*. It's one of my favorite books."

Hot *and* smart. And apparently he was a real-life boy. I was still staring. Snapping out of it, I shut my book and shoved my hands under my crossed arms, hoping to hide the gloves—as pointless as that was. "I've never seen you here before. I would've noticed you."

His gaze landed on my face, eyes dark and warm. "You would? That's flattering."

I kind of wanted to hide under the table—or at the very least, hide my flaming cheeks. Embarrassment and confusion triggered my flight response. I shoved my book in my bag and moved to stand.

"I was just teasing." He held up his hands. "I'm sorry. I didn't mean to embarrass you." He nodded at the chair across from me. "Do you mind?"

I gripped the strap on my messenger bag as I stared up at him, caught between wanting to bolt and to stay here with him. Boys, except for Adam, rarely spoke to me. Well, unless it was to hurl an insult in my face. "I . . . I have to leave soon."

He smiled fully then, momentarily stunning me into further stupor. He slid into the chair and leaned on the little table separating us. "You come here often, don't you?"

"Yeah." I dropped my hands to my lap, hoping he hadn't noticed the gloves. "I . . . I saw you at school today."

His dark brows rose as he leaned back in his chair, folding his arms across his chest. "You did?"

"Yes. You were standing next to our trophy case." Accusation unintentionally colored my words; my social skills were sorely lacking. I tried to make up for it. "Are you transferring to the school?"

"I was checking it out."

My lips pursed. That hadn't been an answer. "You're new to this town."

"Must be a small town for you to notice me." He tipped his head to the side, his gaze so intense that I knew he was studying me. "I'm from a small town, too. By the way, I never introduced myself. Hayden Cromwell."

"Hayden Cromwell?" His name rolled off my tongue smoothly. I realized he was waiting for me to tell him my name, and I started to, but my cell took that moment to bounce around the table as the alarm went off in vibrate mode. Jumping to my feet, I snatched the phone. "I'm sorry. I have to go."

He stood fluidly, shoving his hands into his pockets. "Walk you out?"

The girl inside me screamed and did a happy dance, but I quickly smacked her upside the head. I started backing off. "No. Uh, no thank you. There's no reason. My car is just right outside."

Disappointment flashed across his face, but he covered it with a quick smile. Shoving my hands under my arms, I turned away before he could say anything else. I felt a little sad about not being able to stay and chat longer, but what was the point?

"It was nice talking to you, Ember."

My legs stopped moving as a shiver tiptoed down my spine. I slowly turned around. "I never told you my na—"

He was gone.

I scanned the narrow stacks and aisles for him. The guy was well over six feet tall; there was no way he could just disappear like that. I felt pretty confident I hadn't made "Hayden Cromwell" up. And I'd never once mentioned my name. That was twice he'd disappeared as if he'd been sucked into a vacuum.

More than a little creeped out by that, I hurried out of the library without saying goodbye to Mrs. Compton. Thick, gray clouds had rolled in, warning of an early fall thunderstorm. I hurried to the side of my car, daring a look over my shoulder.

My gaze went right to the window where I'd been. A dark shadow stood there, tall and lean. I took a step back, bumping into the car door as my heart sped up. He stood there, watching me.

Hayden Cromwell.

I shuddered as I whirled around and climbed into the Jeep. Another shiver danced over my skin. I knew without looking that he was still standing there. Lurking—that's what my mom would've said, if she still talked to me. The dude was *lurking*. All the tiny hairs on my body rose in response.

Hot or not, I was officially skeeved out.

Even if I could still touch a guy and actually get knocked up, I wouldn't have kids in a million years – dealing with Olivia had taught me that. My little sis was in one of her moods—a dark, demented mood. Nothing I'd done from the moment I'd picked her up from school was enough.

Olivia wanted a toy she'd lost *five months ago*.

Then she wanted McDonald's.

Then she wanted to go to the zoo, for crying out loud.

And she sure as hell didn't want to go to the grocery store. All her crying and throwing herself on the porch—in front of the neighbors—was over the damn grocery store. Her sudden animosity toward shopping was very odd. Olivia loved to go and throw crap we couldn't afford into the cart when I wasn't looking. It was like a pastime of hers.

She stared up at me, her lip trembling. "I don't want to go!"

Very gently, I grabbed hold of her arm and lifted her to her feet while our nosy neighbor, Cat-Lady Jones, watched through parted blinds. As soon as I let go, Olivia collapsed on her knees again. I should've gone straight from her school to the store, but I'd left the stash of money in my desk drawer in my bedroom.

"Olivia!" I hissed. "Get up. You're embarrassing me."

Fat tears rolled down her round cheeks. "We don't have to go!"

I popped my hands on my hips. "Then how are we going to eat, Olivia? Who's going to buy the groceries? Mom?"

She stared up at me, her brows lowered and lip jutting out. "I don't want to go."

"Oh, come on!" I reached for her again, but she took one look at my gloved hand and stuck her tongue out. I closed my eyes and counted to ten. "Seriously, I'm going to leave you outside if you don't knock it off."

Olivia latched onto my leg at that point, howling.

"Fine," I muttered, limping forward as my evil sister held on. I dug out the keys and managed to get the door open. It was like pulling a forty-pound sack of potatoes. "Olivia, come on. I'd really like to have Adam come over tonight. That's not going to happen if you keep acting like this."

She continued to sob like I'd pulled off all the heads to her Barbie dolls—which I had done once, when she'd ripped apart my sketchpad because Squeaky needed new bedding.

But damn, the kid was strong. She held on all the way to the kitchen, letting go and plopping down on the warped tile only after I pulled a juice box out of the fridge.

"You want this?" I shook it in the air, just out of her reach.

Her eyes narrowed as she swiped at it.

"Okay. You can have this and a package of cookies of your choice if you stop crying."

Olivia whined, wiggling her fingers. "Can't we go tomorrow?"

"No." I peeled off the straw and unwrapped the plastic. Slowly, I stabbed the straw into the top and took a sip while she whined some more. "Mmm, this is really good."

"All right!" she shouted.

Triumphant, I handed over the juice box. "What's your deal, anyway?" I asked as I went over to one of the cupboards.

"I just don't wanna go. I have a bad feeling, Emmie."

I rolled my eyes as I yanked open the cabinet. The handle popped off in my hand. Fabulous. I scanned the sparse shelf, dropping the handle on the scuffed counter. "We need to get food, like now." I reached inside, frowning. "All we have is generic mac and cheese and canned green beans."

"I like beans."

"We can't just have green beans for dinner, Olivia." I moved onto the fridge. The leftover vegetable soup was gone, meaning Mom had decided to feed herself at some point today. That was a step back into the land of the living, right?

While Olivia sulked at the kitchen table, I scribbled down a quick and dirty grocery list. I'd kill for some Doritos, but the budget only allowed for that or milk.

Olivia liked milk.

I made her some mac and cheese, which she took into the living room so she could watch cartoons. Probably wasn't the best pre-dinner snack. The sound of children laughing and singing lulled me to a blissfully blank state of mind while I washed the dishes from last night. Hopefully Olivia would be in better spirits before we made the trip to the store. I wasn't in the mood to pull a screaming child through the produce section.

Sighing, I dried my hands and went upstairs to get the cash, trying not to let the everyday worries creep up on me. I didn't want to think—not about Dad or the life I'd lost since the accident, or how Olivia had been able to bring me back, or why I couldn't touch anything. I didn't want to give too much thought to being the sole caregiver for a little girl who surely deserved better than me. She deserved a mother—a real one. But all she had was a sister who couldn't touch her and a lifeless shell of a mother hiding in her bedroom.

Sometimes I wanted to do what Mom was doing—say "screw it" and just waste away. Who'd blame me? But then, who'd take care of Olivia? Out of nowhere, I thought of Hayden Cromwell.

Hours after the weird library incident, I was pretty sure I'd imagined him standing by the window.

No one that good-looking had a reason to be that creepy.

A quick check of Mom's room induced the same urge I felt every time I looked in on her—the rampant need to throw something at her sleeping head. She sprawled across the bed, a broken, beautiful doll with deep red curls and porcelain skin. Mom was utterly useless. Was it even humanly possible to sleep as much as she did? Maybe she just pretended to sleep so much. I really didn't know. Each day that'd passed after the accident, my mom had simply faded further away. Just like the memory of my dad's face.

I approached her bed, folding my arms around me. "Mom?"

Silence.

"Mom, if . . . if you're listening, Olivia really needs you."

Nothing.

A burning kicked up in the back of my throat, and my chest felt like it was weighed down with cement. "She deserves better than this. She needs you to be her mom."

Still nothing.

I whipped around and left her bedroom. The heaviness in my chest lingered as I pulled out the cash, separating just enough to cover the bare essentials.

We were running out of money. Dad's life insurance would be gone within the next year. What would I do then? College was out of the question. Hell, finishing my senior year might be out the window if I needed to get a job sooner than I'd planned.

Downstairs, Olivia waited for me; her face stained with the remnants of her earlier tears. I looked away, feeling like an epic failure. "You ready?"

Tipping her chin down, she shrugged her tiny shoulders. She didn't talk to me the whole way out to the Jeep. While she buckled herself in the backseat, I eyed the needle on the gas gauge and mentally counted the leftover funds.

"Emmie?"

I glanced over my shoulder at her. "What?"

Her eyes were wide, a vibrant jade color. There was something in them that gave me pause. Unease unfolded in the pit of my stomach, making my hands tremble.

"I have a really bad feeling," Olivia said, picking at a patch of glitter on her dress. "Like the one I had before . . . before Daddy died. Do you remember? I have that feeling again."

Of course I remembered *that feeling*.

But Olivia had been three at the time of the accident, and I'd barely paid attention to any of the babble that'd come out of her mouth.

I still remembered, though.

She'd leaned across the backseat and grasped my arm. "Something bad is going to happen," she'd whispered.

And I'd frowned at her and ripped my arm away, annoyed because our parents had been arguing again—arguing about her. Shaking myself out of those memories, I rubbed my forehead, feeling a headache starting in.

"Emmie?" Olivia gripped the back of my seat.

I forced a smile for her. "Nothing bad is going to happen. I promise you."

She looked doubtful, and it was like a punch in the gut.

"We'll be in and out, and then Adam will come over later. You like Adam, right?"

She let go of the seat, falling back. "Yeah."

"Okay. Good," I whispered.

Since Olivia had successfully freaked me out, the trip to the store took longer than before. I was extra-wary of stoplights and other drivers. I breathed a sigh of relief when we pulled into the back of the packed parking lot.

Rain clouds had darkened the sky, causing several of the street lamps to flicker on. Fat drops splattered the dense woods surrounding the parking lot. I glanced at the clock on my cell, surprised to find it nearly seven o'clock.

Olivia hopped out the back, trailing behind me. "Can I push the cart?"

I welcomed the change in the mood. "Promise me you won't run over any old people this time and it's a deal."

Olivia giggled as she wiggled between me and the shopping cart. There was no deal. She was death on wheels behind a shopping cart, but it helped me keep an eye on her and it would prevent another epic breakdown.

Old people, watch out.

Her head barely reached the bar as she inched the cart through the automatic doors. The place was packed for a Thursday, full of women in heels and men frowning at shopping lists.

Olivia rammed the display of bananas and then the back of my legs when I stopped to grab a bag of apples. "Beep! Beep! Beep!" She shrieked as she backed the cart up.

Limping over to the bread, I grabbed a loaf. My cell vibrated in my back pocket. Sticking the bread under my arm, I slid the beat-up thing out and flipped it open. It was a text from Adam. **Any news?**

Still at store. Will text u when done, I sent back.

Not even five seconds later I received, **U SUCK. OK. Text me**.

I grinned and headed back to the cart. I didn't know what I'd do without Adam. It was hard to even think about it. I dropped the bread in the cart. "Olivia, what's all over your face?"

She turned away quickly. "Nothing."

"Whatever. There's white powder all over your lips and—oh, my God!" I glanced around quickly, thankful no one was around us. "Did you eat the doughnuts again? They're not free, Olivia!"

"No!"

"You're such a little liar." I knelt down in front of her, wiping off her lips with the sleeve of my cardigan, trying not to laugh. "I can't believe you did that."

"They shouldn't put them out if they're not free."

My mouth dropped open, and then I cracked up. "You are so rotten."

Giggling, she squirmed out of my grasp. There were no more eating food incidents, thank God. I got everything on the list, and Olivia had chosen a bag of Oreos as her cookies of choice. That made me pretty damn happy as I could already taste them. A whole row already had my name on it.

I groaned as I spied the lines at the register. "It's going to be— Olivia!" Too late. She lost control of the cart, smashing it into the back of a brawny-looking man. I grabbed the cart, blushing furiously as I yanked it back. "I'm so sorry! My sister didn't . . . crap."

Dustin Smith stared back at me, rubbing the back of his leg with one hand and holding a case of soda in the other. His brown eyes bounced from my sister to my face. "You should get better control of the brat."

Anger rushed to the surface. It was one thing talking smack about me, but my little sister? I stepped in front of Olivia, blocking her. "Don't talk about my sister like that."

He smirked. "I can talk however I want to."

I itched to take off my gloves. "Not about her."

"This is rich." Dustin laughed. "What are you going to do about it? Throw your food stamps in my face?"

I *wished* we qualified for food stamps, but I still flushed. "You're a jerk."

"And you're a frigid freak," he spat.

So many witty comebacks floated to the surface. None of them would be appropriate for five-year-old ears. I turned to grab Olivia and just walk around Dustin, but she dodged my gloved hand. She walked right up to Dustin, her little hands balled into fists.

She kicked him in the shin.

So shocked by the pint-sized terror, Dustin dropped the case of soda. Brown liquid exploded off the tile, fizzing and streaming in dirty-looking rivulets. The right side of his pants was drenched with sticky liquid. We hadn't drawn any attention up to that point, but several customers turned and stared at the mess.

Part of me knew I should yell at Olivia for kicking Dustin, but the other part, the really immature one, was secretly gleeful for the red stain rapidly spreading across his face.

"Smooth," I said. "Got beat up by a little girl? Wonder what your friends would think about that?"

Before Dustin could respond, I ushered Olivia and the cart to the register furthest away from the mess. I bit my lip to keep from smiling as I knelt next to her. "Olivia . . ."

Her cheeks were ruddy, eyes bright. "He was mean to you."

"I know, but you can't kick people who you think are mean." *Even if they did totally deserve that and more*, I silently added.

"Why not?"

I inched the cart up. "Because kicking people is mean, Olivia. And you don't want to be a mean person like him, right?" She folded her arms, pouting. "No."

"So, no more kicking?" I stood, pulling items out of the grocery cart. "Yeah. Okay." She wiggled between the cart and a display of candy bars. "Can I have my cookies now?"

I shook my head, smiling. "In the car."

Olivia smiled and giggled at the middle-aged woman ringing up our groceries, behaving like a precocious child instead of the ninja-child who'd kicked Dustin. That was my sister. She went from one extreme to the next within seconds.

I took over cart duty and pushed our groceries out to the back of the parking lot. It had poured while we were in the store, and Olivia insisted on jumping through every one of the huge puddles on the way to the car. I had her sit inside—with the package of Oreos—while I put the groceries in the back. She gabbed on about what she'd learned at school, something to do with words rhyming. It was dark and desolate in our corner of the lot by the time I shut the hatch and wheeled the shopping cart back to a nearby return.

I checked my cell, groaning when I saw the time. Olivia would need to go straight to bed when we got home, and I doubted Adam would still want to come over this late, especially when I had math homework.

As I shoved my phone back into my pocket, a tall, thick shadow stepped out from behind a large truck parked beside my Jeep.

I halted, my heart leaping into my throat.

Dustin stood between me and my car, the leg of his pants still soaked. For a second, I didn't know what to do, but I decided to walk around him and ignore him.

"You think you're funny, don't you?" he called out, his voice hard.

I kept walking, my stomach filling with knots. Just a few more steps—that's all.

"Hey! I'm talking to you, freak!"

I whipped around. "My name is not 'freak.' It's Ember. You know that."

Dustin laughed. "You're whatever I call you. Freak? Bitch? Whore? Whatever."

"I'm frigid *and* a whore?" I rolled my eyes, turning away. "So very clever, Dustin."

A second later, Dustin grabbed my arm and spun me around. "I must've been on something when I thought you were worth my time, you know that?"

I yanked my arm free. "Is that supposed to insult me? Seriously?"

"You think you got one over on me in the store? You're going to be sorry. I'm going to make every day hell for you." He laughed. "You can trust that."

"Whatever." I let my gaze drop. "Did you pee yourself?"

His arm struck out so fast I hadn't even seen him move. My

back slammed into the passenger door of the truck. Shock knocked the air out of my lungs.

"Emmie?" I heard Olivia's soft cry from inside the Jeep.

Dustin got right in my face, a vein throbbing at his temple. "You're nothing more than a scarred-up freak. Yeah, Sally told me how you're all cut up." He sneered. "You're disgusting."

It shouldn't have hurt, but it did. Tears burned my eyes as I pushed off the truck and started around him again. I would not let him see me cry. Absolutely—

He grabbed my arm again as he dug into his pocket. "How scarred up are you? Sally said your whole stomach was covered." Pulling out his cell phone, he laughed. "How about we do a little show and I tell the school? Better yet, how about I take some pictures?"

Over the blood rushing in my ears, I could hear Olivia crying out for me. "Don't!" I wrenched back, but his grip tightened.

It was too late. Dustin grabbed the hem of my shirt, shoving his hand under it. Part of me wondered, in that brief second before his flesh touched mine, when Dustin had become such a bastard. He hadn't always been *this* bad.

But then his hand was against my stomach, against my scars. The first time another human being had touched me in two years, and I wanted to puke.

His eyes popped open. The phone fell from his limp fingers, cracking when it hit the pavement.

Everything slowed down. A shiver slithered down my spine and coiled in my stomach. The sick sense of dread seeped into my veins like venom, familiar yet unwelcome. It reared, poised to strike, and then its sharp fangs bit deep. It was the same sensation I'd had right before I'd died.

Time seemed to stop.

Dustin's eyes flared as the first wave of pain crashed into him. He went down on one knee, veins bulging in his forehead as his mouth worked in a silent scream. His hand was still against my stomach, as if he couldn't let go.

I grabbed for his arm, but he started jerking like he was having a seizure. His normally tan skin turned sallow, and his hands spasmed.

When his eyes rolled back into their sockets, he fell backward like a puppet whose strings had been cut.

I stood over him, breathing heavily. "Dustin?"

He didn't move.

I wrapped my arms around my waist, but that did nothing to stop the violent trembling. I knelt down, staring at his chest. One second passed. Five seconds, and then twenty, and his chest still hadn't moved. My stomach rolled, almost forcing me to my knees. I backed up quickly, shaking my head.

He was dead—Dustin was dead.

And I had killed him.

3

I don't even remember getting back in my car, but I was sitting behind the wheel, staring out through the windshield. The keys bit through my gloves into the fleshy part of my palm.

"Emmie?" Olivia's voice trembled.

I'd killed Dustin. Something shifted in my stomach again, which I found strange, because I hadn't eaten dinner. Every muscle in my body seemed to lock up. Then I heard the door being unlocked in the back. I twisted around in the seat. "Don't! Don't open that door, Olivia!"

She froze, her lower lip trembling. "What's happening?"

My hands shook as I turned back around. "Nothing . . . nothing is happening."

Olivia let out a sob. It was little and soft, but so heartbreaking. "Emmie, I'm scared."

I was terrified, too. I'd just killed someone—a classmate, a guy I used to date. Dustin had a mother and a father, a little brother, and friends. People who loved him and would miss him.

Part of me knew I needed to do something about this—call someone, go to the police. Tell them what had happened. Then what? I'd be sentenced, but I doubted jail would be in my future. A research facility sounded more likely. What would happen to Olivia? She'd go into foster care, and that was enough to give me nightmares. I couldn't let that happen, but I couldn't just walk away. My gaze dropped to my gloved hand. Desperation welled up, choking me from the inside out.

What had I done?

Something knocked against the window. Olivia let out a muffled shriek. Startled, I jumped in my seat. A man peered in through the driver's window, possibly in his late twenties or early thirties.

"Open the door," he commanded in a voice that said he was used to people obeying him.

I stared at him wordlessly. Was he a cop? He didn't look like a cop, unless cops had started wearing long dusters and cowboy hats in Pennsylvania. I might've laughed.

His mouth was a hard line, jaw locked. "Open the door, Ember."

My heart did another crazy leap. I slammed my hand down on the lock before the guy could yank the door open. There was no reason this stranger should've known my name. Just like Hayden in the library. Two strangers in one day who knew my name didn't seem likely.

The man hit the window, shaking but not shattering it.

Olivia was getting worked up in the back seat, snapping me into action. I shoved the key into the ignition, hands shaking.

"Don't!" The man pulled on the door handle like he intended on ripping the door open. "Ember!"

The instinct to flee overpowered me. I turned the ignition and slammed on the gas. I caught a glimpse of the man jumping back before the tires ate a speed bump and curb.

We hit the main road, and I drew a shaky breath.

Olivia sniffled. "Emmie, what's going on?"

I gripped the steering wheel. "I'm sorry, Olivia. I'm so sorry."

She started crying again, and I think she knew what'd happened in the parking lot. Perhaps that was what she'd sensed earlier. Something bad *had* happened. Olivia had warned me, but I hadn't listened.

"I'm sorry," I said again.

Olivia only cried harder.

*   *   *

Numbness had taken over by the time we got home. I put away the groceries blindly and ordered Olivia to go to bed without looking at her. I sat down in the living room, ignoring Adam's text messages. With the sound of every car that passed the house, I expected flashing red and blue lights. Any strange noise from outside had me peering out the window, expecting to find the cowboy or the police bearing down on our house.

Hot tears burned my eyes but didn't fall as I stared at my cell. Several times I'd reached for the phone, fully intending to call the police and turn myself in. They had to have found Dustin's body by now, and even though my touch hadn't left any visible mark on him, his death could not be ruled natural. But then I thought of Olivia . . . and Mom. It wasn't so much the question of who would take care of them, but the fact that I couldn't leave them.

At some point during the night, Olivia came downstairs and crawled up on the couch. Carefully, she placed her head in my lap. The tears came then, coursing down my cheeks as I kept my hands shoved under my arms.

I tortured myself the rest of the night with images of me accidentally touching Adam, or worse yet, Olivia. I replayed my encounter with Dustin over and over again. Had there been time for me to move before he'd touched my skin? Was there something different I could've done?

Sleep didn't come for me that night. Not that I deserved any sort of rest. When it was time for Olivia to get ready for school, I gently roused her. She lifted her head, her corkscrew curls all over the place.

I made myself smile. I had to act normal while I decided what I needed to do . . . or until the police hauled me off to jail. "Time to get up, sleepy head."

Olivia scrubbed her eyes. "You're still here."

My breath caught. "Where else would I be?"

Her gaze dropped from my face to my hands. "Can we stay home today with Mommy?"

God, I wanted nothing better than to stay home, but I needed things to be normal for Olivia, at least until the world fell out from underneath us. "Not today, Olivia. You need to go to school."

She didn't argue like I'd expected her to. We went upstairs to get ready. There was no bouncing or humming today. I went through my morning routine like a zombie, barely paying attention to anything I was doing. There wasn't even anger when I poked my head into Mom's bedroom—just profound sadness.

I crept to the side of her bed. "Mom?" Holding my breath for a response—anything—I sat on the edge of the bed. My eyes started to leak. "Mom, please. I don't know what to do. I didn't mean to hurt him. I promise. It just happened."

My mom gave a little sigh.

And my heart broke. "Olivia isn't the only one who needs you. I do, too. I need you. Please come back."

Today was no different to her. She didn't respond, and I didn't have any more time to wait. Dragging myself from the bed, I wiped the back of my hand under my eyes.

Olivia was silent on the way to school and squeezed my arm before she climbed out of the backseat. My stomach twisted in raw knots by the time I arrived at school. I expected to see police cruisers there, or at the very least, clusters of somber students mourning the loss of a friend.

Everyone was acting like they normally did, talking and laughing, pushing one another, or making out by their lockers. The halls were a study of controlled chaos, but there wasn't a single teary-eyed face. And there were no deputies waiting to speak to students.

I kept my head down as I shuffled down the hall, stopping at my locker long enough to switch out my books. Slamming the door shut, I turned around and saw Adam's concerned face.

"God, I've been so worried." An old pair of glasses—with

thicker frames than the wire ones he usually sported—made me think of owls.

"What happened last night?"

What happened last night? *I accidentally killed the guy who stole your other pair of glasses.* That's what happened.

"Hey," he leaned in. "Are you okay? You look like crap, Ember."

"I . . . I don't feel very well." It wasn't a lie. I felt like I was going to hurl.

"Did you get sick last night?"

I nodded. "Sorry. I should've responded to your texts."

"Nah, it's okay." He waved his hand. "Do you think you should be here?"

Looking back, I wasn't so sure if that had been a bright idea. My legs felt weak as I murmured something and trailed after him. The warning bell went off, causing most of the groups in the hall to scatter. Adam kept casting worried glances in my direction while I squeezed the strap of my messenger bag so tightly I knew my knuckles were turning white.

We slid into our homeroom seats without drawing any attention. Today it seemed that Adam and I were like ghosts in the high-school caste system. No one paid attention to us—to me, except to make my life miserable. I stared at my gloved hands for what felt like the millionth time since last night, waiting for the sword to drop.

Nothing happened.

No one talked about Dustin. His absence from biology hadn't raised any suspicion, but I was still a mess of bundled nerves throughout the day. Adam made me promise that I'd call him if I needed anything. When I arrived at Olivia's school to pick her up, I felt weak and dizzy. The lack of sleep and food wasn't a good combination. I'd skipped the library and waited with the buses in front of her school.

A final bell sounded, and crowds of kids spilled out of the school, loading onto buses and approaching moms in minivans. I watched, trying to spot Olivia in the throng. It was slow to dawn on me that she wasn't among them. Something heavy dropped in my stomach as I pulled the keys out of the ignition and climbed out of the car. I crossed behind the last bus, stumbling up the curb.

"Are you okay, miss?" a teacher called, clipboard on hand.

"Yeah," I breathed, rushing inside. My hands shook, and I dropped my keys as soon as I stepped inside the front office.

"Can I help you?" the receptionist asked, eyes wide in alarm.

"I'm looking for my sister. Her name is Olivia McWilliams. She's in kindergarten. She's five and—"

"Yes," she cut me off, pulling a pencil out of the pile of gray hair. She was obviously in a hurry to leave for the day. Her purse and coffee mug were on the desk. "I know who she is."

"Okay. Good." I took a deep breath and leaned over the counter, the keys' jagged teeth digging into my palm. "She wasn't outside. I—"

"Of course she wasn't," she said. "Her mother picked her up this afternoon."

The room tilted to the side, spinning around me. "What?"

"Her mother picked her up right after lunch. I'm sorry. What was your name again?"

Almost in tears, I slammed my hands down on the counter. "My mother wouldn't have picked her up!"

The old woman huffed before drawing herself up to her full height, which was shorter than me and that wasn't saying much. "Miss, we just don't let anyone come into school and take our children. It was Ms. McWilliams who picked up Olivia this morning. Now, what is your name?"

Rage flooded through me like a hot wave in my veins. The urge to react surged. I wanted to reach out and wrap my hand around her fat fingers. I wanted to *touch* her.

"Miss, what is your name?"

"How could you?" My voice sounded eerily calm. "That wasn't our mom."

The woman blinked rapidly, shaking her head in denial. "No. She's listed in our system, and she signed her out! Who are you?" she demanded. Other people were starting to come out of smaller offices. "Are you a family member?"

I backed up, clenching my hands into tight fists. There was nothing else to say. Spinning around, I took off. I'd go home next. There was a chance—a small chance—that it'd been Mom. I'd have a better chance of waking up and discovering the last twenty-four hours had been a nightmare, but the small sliver of hope was all I had. Desperate, I clung to it. My throat constricted when our house came into view. Mom's beat-up station wagon was parked in the front of the house. It hadn't moved since Dad's funeral. The old wooden swing swayed on the front porch, sending darts of panic shooting through me.

There was no breeze.

Heart pounding, I climbed the steps and flung open the front door. The extra set of keys sat on the table by the door.

"Olivia?" I called out. "Olivia, where are you?" I went into the kitchen, then the living room, and finally rushed upstairs. "Olivia! Answer me now!"

Still, there was no answer.

Her bedroom was empty. "Oh, my God."

I didn't know what to do. I had no idea how long I stood there, staring at her empty bed. Nothing seemed real anymore. Only the blood rushing through my veins and slow desperation spiraled inside me. A sob rose in my chest.

I was supposed to take care of Olivia.

A sudden noise, like someone knocking into a piece of heavy furniture, raised the tiny hairs along the nape of my neck. Swallowing down icy fear, I wheeled around and stepped back into the hallway. I pulled off my gloves, clenching them in one hand. Could I kill again—on purpose?

Yes, if Olivia was in danger.

Sunlight spilled out into the hallway through my bedroom door. The room appeared to be safe, inviting even. Had I left my door open this morning? I couldn't remember. Slowly, I inched toward the open door. For a moment, I thought the room was empty.

It wasn't.

He stood in front of the door to my bathroom, wearing the same duster jacket from the night before. A mane of blond hair stuck out from underneath a cowboy hat. The sudden image of a lion crouching, waiting for its prey to stumble into its sight, flashed before me.

I realized a split second later I was the prey.

The lion sprang before I even had the chance to release the scream building in my throat. He didn't say anything, but the look of fierce determination as he moved toward me, arms outstretched, said it all. Panic quickly turned into something else as I jerked back against the wall. Fury and desperation welled, spinning and bubbling over.

He reached for me.

Instead of touching him, I grabbed the lamp off the bedside table and hurled it at him. The base of the lamp struck his head, making a sickening thud and knocking off the cowboy hat.

The cowboy fell to the floor, unmoving.

"Well . . . that wasn't necessary," drawled a deep voice that tugged at my memory.

I shrieked and spun around.

Standing in my hallway was Hayden Cromwell. He held his hands out in front of him. "I don't mean you any harm, Ember. I'm here to help you."

"Help me?" I stepped back, brushing against the man's leg. My stomach turned over as I looked at him. The cowboy hat lay beside him. Blood matted his blond hair. When had I become so violent? Had I always been this way?

"Don't look at him, Ember. Look at me."

It was like being compelled. I had no choice but to look at him. "Where is my sister?"

"Everything is fine. Your sister is safe. We have her—"

All I heard was the last three words. I lunged at him. He didn't even move out of the way. He simply caught my hand in his and squeezed gently.

The act knocked the air and common sense right out of me. This—*this* was what I'd been yearning for. A simple touch, a brushing of skin without hurting someone, and it was everything I thought it would be. Strength. Warmth. Humanity.

All in one simple touch.

"I don't understand," I whispered hoarsely. My gaze locked on his hands. His fingers were long and graceful-looking. They were strong.

"I'm absorbing your gift," he said. "I'm like you, Ember. Gifted."

I lifted my eyes, and saw the proud lines of his face tense. Hayden's fingers left my hand and slid under the cuff of my sweater. His touch was scalding, and my skin tingled wherever his fingers went.

Dizziness swept through me, and Hayden seemed to sway. The room spun. I blinked, but everything still moved. Panic squeezed my heart as I tried to pull my arm away, but he held on.

"What are you doing to . . .?" I couldn't remember what I was saying.

"I'm sorry, but this is the only way," Hayden said, sounding like he truly was. "We're going to help you." He placed his other hand on my cheek. "It's going to be okay. Trust me, Ember."

My name was the last thing I heard. The world went black, and then there was nothing.

4

I knew I needed to wake up, but my eyelids felt like they'd been glued shut. Slowly and with much effort, I peeled them open. Dazzling sunshine flowed in through the lace-covered windows.

Curtains?

There wasn't a single curtain in my entire house. Not that I had anything against them, but I could never figure out how to get the damn rods up. Woozy, I pushed myself onto my elbows and glanced around. I was in a bed much bigger than the one I was used to. Gilded frames decorated the buttery yellow walls. A flat-screen TV sat on a cherry oak dresser that looked like something hand-carved in the nineteenth century. A matching desk stood beside the dresser, with a slender, expensive-looking laptop perched atop it. French doors led to what appeared to be a balcony and on the other side of the room, another set of doors led to a bathroom . . . and a walk-in closet.

Okay, this was definitely not my room.

I sat up, biting my lower lip as a rush of dizziness threatened to push me back into the soft comforter. The events leading up to this fuzzed in my brain, but I remembered enough to push down the nausea the headache was causing. I swung my legs off the bed and stood. The room spun for a couple of seconds before righting itself.

The bedroom door opened, revealing a man with neatly trimmed, dark hair and a tailored business suit. I stepped back, bumping into the bed.

"Good. You're awake. We were getting worried. Hayden's gift can pack quite a punch," he said pleasantly. "My name is Jonathan Cromwell. You are in my home."

"Who . . . where is my sister?" I asked hoarsely.

He folded his hands behind his back. "Olivia is here, and she's been asking for you. I can take you to her. Then, you and I must talk."

I placed a hand to my thumping temple and winced. "Talk about what?"

"I think you should see your sister first, Ember. It would ease her anxiety tremendously to know that you are well."

Concern for Olivia urged me forward, but suspicion pinged my thoughts. "How do I know this isn't a trick . . . or something?"

A patient smile formed on his lips. "I know you have a lot of questions, but you must put them aside. Olivia needs you, Ember."

Olivia needs you. Those words had always provoked an instantaneous need. I nodded and scrunched my face up in pain. My head felt like it was going to explode.

Mr. Cromwell stepped aside, motioning for me to follow him. I kept a safe distance between us as we made our way down the wide hallway, passing several closed doors. Instead of stopping at the last one like I expected, he went down a winding staircase. Below, I could see two more levels. Everywhere I looked, there were various paintings of Greek and Roman gods on the walls. Anatomically correct marble statues stood in the corners.

We stopped outside a door on the second floor. Childish giggles radiated from the room, pulling me forward like a moth to light. I'd recognize the sound of her laughter anywhere. I stepped around the guy and pushed open the door.

Relief flooded me. Olivia, her hair subdued into two little pigtails, sat in the middle of a large bedroom, surrounded by a ridiculous number of toys, stuffed animals, and . . . Mom. My mother sat in a chair, wearing an oversized sweater and slippers. Her face was as blank as ever, but she wasn't in bed.

This had to be a dream.

Olivia twisted around and erupted in high-pitched shrieks. "Em! Em!" She was on her feet, rushing at me like a mini-tornado. "I've missed you! Emmie! Em!"

"Olivia," I choked out.

She wrapped her arms around my legs without hesitation. I wanted nothing more than to pull her into my arms, but my gloves were gone. My hands hovered above her curls as if they had a mind of their own. I squeezed my eyes shut and inhaled sharply.

"Em!" She tugged on my jeans. "Look!"

I opened my eyes. She broke away from me, pointing at the cage atop the dresser. "They let me bring Squeaky. And look! This is Mr. Sniffles!" She rushed toward a large tabby cat I'd thought was a stuffed animal.

"That's nice." My eyes fell to Mom. She occupied a rocking chair that I imagined belonged in a nursery room. "Mom? It's me." I took a step forward.

She blinked slowly, but it was like a soundproof wall prevented her from hearing me.

"Em, what have you been doing?" Olivia asked, drawing my attention back to her. She'd dropped the cat and moved on to a baby doll. "I wanted to see you, but Mr. Cromwell said you needed to rest."

I glanced over my shoulder at the dark-haired man. "Yeah, I've been sleeping."

Olivia held the doll by one arm, swinging it around and around. "You've been sleeping for days."

For *days*? "Um . . . well, I was really tired."

Skipping up to me, she seemed to accept my excuse. "I like it here, Emmie."

"Really?" I felt dizzy, faint. God, was I going to pass out again?

She nodded impishly and then twitched her chubby index finger at me. It was a habit of hers whenever she wanted to tell me a secret, so I bent closer and lowered my head. "What?" I whispered, ignoring the white specks of light dancing across my vision.

Leaning in, Olivia whispered near my ear. "Mr. Cromwell says I'm gifted."

"Oh. Okay," I whispered back, my brain reeling. Olivia jumped away and twirled across the room. "Squeaky likes it here."

"Ember," Mr. Cromwell said.

I nodded without looking back. "Olivia, I need to talk to Mr. Cromwell. Are you okay up here?"

"Yep. Mommy and I are playing with my new toys."

Against my will, I looked at my mom again. She turned her head and smiled down at Olivia. Just seeing her provoked so many emotions. I tried to remember what she'd been like before the accident, but her current state overshadowed those memories.

I shook my head and turned to where Mr. Cromwell waited, a patient expression on his face.

"We can talk in the kitchen," he said. "I'm sure you must be hungry."

Before I could pull myself away from the room, I heard Olivia speak. "Mommy?"

I stopped. My heart fluttered in my chest. I just wanted to hear her voice, that's all. Then: "Yes, baby?"

"Why don't you talk to Emmie? It makes her sad."

There was a moment of silence. "Baby," Mom said softly, "I can't talk to her. Ember's in heaven with Daddy."

We sat in the type of kitchen my mom would've given her first-born child to have before she had lost her mind.

"Your mother is very ill, Ember. Possibly one day her memories will resurface." Cromwell frowned. "It must be hard for you to have your own mother believe that you're dead."

I rolled a can of soda between my palms. It felt weird to be around people and not have my gloves on. Untouched plates of cold cuts and cookies sat between us.

"How have you managed to take care of her and your sister? You were only fifteen at the time of the accident."

My irritation level rose, as did my suspicions. "How do you know about the accident?"

Cromwell smiled. "We know a lot of things, Ember."

My appetite dried and shriveled up. "How do you know so much? Why am I here? And where *is* here, anyway?"

His blue eyes seemed to shine in the bright kitchen. "You're in Petersburg, West Virginia."

A hysterical laugh bubbled up and broke free. "Where? I've never even heard of Peterstown or whatever."

"Petersburg," he corrected. "Not many outside of this state would. We are at the base of Seneca Rocks."

I stared blankly. Was I supposed to know what that meant?

His expression was one of parental patience, but it was off somehow—wrong even. "You're remarkably calm."

"Oh, trust me. I'm freaking out inside." I glanced up and met his eyes.

"Maybe I should start at the beginning." He leaned back in the chair, crossing his arms. "I think that would help you understand there is nothing to fear."

I seriously doubted that.

"There are two kinds of people in this world, Ember. There are ones who are mundane, ordinary. Those people are like outsiders to us."

"To us?" I said, wanting to laugh again.

The patient look didn't fade. "Yes. You're different. Just like your sister."

Lying was like second nature. I didn't even think about it. "There's nothing different about Olivia."

"Ember, you and I both know better than that. Like I said,

there are two kinds of people in this world: outsiders and the gifted. You and your sister are far from normal." Mr. Cromwell leaned forward and rested his hands on the table. "Look at what happened to that boy. He died from simply touching you."

Ice coated my insides. I opened my mouth, but nothing came out. A rush of cold air went down my spine.

"It was an accident. I understand that," Cromwell said gently. "But it's a shame for someone so young to perish."

Tears clogged my throat and burned my eyes. "I didn't mean to . . . to kill him."

"I know."

"What happened to his . . . body?"

"It's been taken care of."

"But this isn't right." I squeezed the can so hard the sides dented, spilling soda over my fingers. "I need to turn myself in. I should be punished or something. I need to be pun—"

"What has been done is done. And I cannot allow you to turn yourself in." He leaned back, folding his arms. "Your . . . touch would expose all who are gifted. We cannot risk that."

I stared at him, reeling. This man knew I was capable of killing—had killed—and he was more worried about me exposing people than what I could do to him? He was insane. I was insane for sitting here, listening to him.

"No one will ever find out about the unfortunate accident. Everything that has happened is in the past now. You're safe here."

"No. That man . . . the one in the cowboy hat wanted to hurt me."

Cromwell clucked his tongue. "Kurt meant you no harm. He can be rough around the edges, but he's a good man. I trust him with my life and that of my son."

The urge to laugh came again. "So he's not dead?"

"No. You gave him a good knock on the head, but he survived."

I guessed I should feel good about that.

"Ember, I want to help your family. Your sister has gifts that need to be controlled, but we have to be honest with each other and not play games."

My eyes narrowed. "I'm not playing games. I don't even know who you are. You kidnapped us."

"You also tried to kill Kurt and my son," he replied bluntly.

"Your son? Hayden? He was stalking me! And he hurt me! His touch or whatever did something to me."

"Hayden is unique. His touch drains the power of others, if he wills it. Such a remarkable boy. But even as gifted as he is, your touch would've still affected him if he hadn't used his gift."

I rubbed my forehead. None of this made any sense to me. I needed to be plotting a way to escape from this lunatic.

Cromwell rested his elbow on the table and cupped his chin. "We have been tracking you and Olivia for two years."

I choked. "*What*?"

"To be able to bring back the dead . . . Then you? There was nothing about you which indicated your gift until Olivia brought you back."

The whitewashed walls seemed to spin around me again.

Cromwell sighed. "Ember, when someone dies, they don't come back the same. You know this, don't you? Some would say it's unnatural. Wrong."

I started to stand, but sat back down. My heart was thundering in my chest. *Unnatural. Wrong.* Those words cut through me like a hot knife.

"I don't mean to be so blunt, Ember. But you must know what you can do is only a product of your death, and of your sister's natural gift. You brought something back with you—an ability even rarer than your sister's."

"I'm not bad—I'm not evil," I blurted out. But then it hit me. Maybe I was. Good people didn't kill.

He smiled evenly, but something about it made me shudder. "I know, my dear. But what happened was inevitable. It could've been Olivia or a boy who got too close to you. Your friend, for example—what's his name? Ah, yes. Adam. It was bound to happen. Truth be told, I should have intervened long before this. The incident could've been prevented."

I was confused and scared, really freaking scared. This man knew about everything, even Adam. And what he'd said was true. It could have been Olivia or Adam.

"There are other people here like your sister. Others who are gifted in a way the world could only fantasize about. Here," he said, "she is not alone."

I sank a hand into my curls and pulled them off my face. "I don't understand what you're trying to tell me."

"I know. Things are terribly confusing for you," he said. "You're worried about Olivia, about your mother. Why a strange man would bring you into his home."

I laughed then. It sounded a bit rough. "No, really?"

"But you don't have anything to worry about anymore. We'll take care of your sister. And we'll try to take care of you."

I looked up, trying to sound braver than I felt. "Do you even understand how creeptastic this sounds? You're a complete stranger to me. You keep talking about gifts and stuff that makes no sense."

"I can help your sister, Ember. Her gift of giving life and healing needs cultivation. And she needs to be around others like her—others who will understand." Cromwell drew in a deep breath, and his eyes met mine. "Then there is you, and frankly, I'm not sure what to do with you."

Tiny hairs on my neck stood up. "What do you mean?"

"When I was Olivia's age, I had no one looking out for me. I've made it my life's mission to make sure no other gifted children face what I did." A dark look stole away the warmth in his eyes. "Both you and your sister are valuable for different reasons.

There are people out there who would seek to manipulate what your sister can do, and abuse what you can do. I intend to make sure that doesn't happen."

"Really?" I glanced around the kitchen for an exit. "That really didn't answer my question."

"Your sister belongs here, Ember. For that reason alone, I am willing to take a risk on you."

There were a lot of doors—escape routes—in the room, and Olivia was upstairs, but I was a weapon of mass destruction. I could take the weirdo. "Is that so?"

"This is your new home," he said like it explained everything, like he wasn't a delusional, kidnapping freak holding my family prisoner.

"Huh?" I looked at him.

"You will be staying here from now on."

Needing no other reason than that, I shot across the table. The edge of the oak table cut into my stomach for a nanosecond, and then I was flying backward. My sneakers skidded across the floor. A second later, an unseen force pinned me against the wall.

Cromwell's expression didn't change, but he sighed. "That's enough, Gabriel. Let her go."

I hadn't even noticed someone else was in the kitchen. He stood in the archway—a boy about my age, maybe a year younger, with a head full of blond curls and the prettiest face I'd ever seen on a guy. He had his hand raised in front of him; a look of concentration wrinkled his brow.

"Gabriel," Cromwell said again. "Let her go." Gabriel looked like he'd rather toss me through the air some more, but he lowered his hand.

I slid down the wall, stumbling to the side.

"She was going to touch you," he said, his voice surprisingly deep. "This was a mistake."

Cromwell pushed away from the table and stood. He turned to the boy. "Gabe, is there something you need?"

Gabe finally pulled his eyes off me. "Where's Hayden? He didn't wait around after class. I figured he came right home, like he has every day since you brought *her* into the house."

"He's not in the kitchen, now, is he?"

Gabriel narrowed his eyes at me.

"It's okay. Go. If you happen to find my son, please tell him I need to speak with him."

Gabriel rolled his eyes. "All right, but if she kills you, I warned you." With that, he turned and left the kitchen.

"Oh. My. God," I whispered, heart racing.

"Gabriel is one of my children. There are several kids here your age. They're a bit concerned, but don't think they cannot protect themselves."

I frowned. "I don't run around touching people for the fun of it."

He smiled tightly. "I know this is a lot for you to take in, but I will not tolerate you attacking anyone. Do you understand me?"

I pushed away from the wall. I didn't reach for him, even though I wanted to. God knew what other superpowers he had hidden in this house. "You can't be serious. This can't be legal. There have to be laws against this."

"This isn't against any law," he replied calmly. "Your mother is here with you and Olivia. We did not remove you from her guardianship. And need I remind you that *you* have already broken the law by not reporting what happened to that boy?"

I ignored that. "Like my mom can even make those kinds of decisions." My self-control cracked and shattered. "I don't even understand why you're doing this!"

"I'm doing this to help your sister, Ember. To help you."

"How is this helping me?"

His hands dropped to his sides. "You're seventeen and playing mom to a child. Who, by the way, deserves a life far better than what you can provide for her."

Ouch. That stung all the way to my core, mainly because he was totally right.

"You're a guest in my home," he continued. "As are your mother and sister. But if you think of leaving, or if you harm anyone, I can no longer consider you a guest."

My heart skipped a beat as I stared at him. "Are you threatening me?"

"I'm just telling you how it will be. The others are already wary of you being here. Don't do anything to add to that."

"Why did you even bring me here?" I yelled. "Because really, you don't sound like you want me here."

"Because your sister is gifted, and I have no desire to split her from you. I'm doing you a huge favor. There are places you could go to, Ember. Places—"

"You don't have the right to do this!"

Mr. Cromwell slammed the palms of his hands on the edge of the table. He spoke through clenched teeth, and, like a mask slipping from his face, coldness filled his expression. "I have all the right, Ember. This is my town."

Everything stopped as I stared at him.

"We have only your best intentions in mind. Nothing can be changed now." Another perfect smile graced his lips. "We have already taken all the necessary steps to ensure your transition will be as smooth as possible. You will have the weekend to adjust and on Monday, you will start school."

Just like that, I lost control of my life. Bile rose into the back of my throat.

"I expect that you understand I'm placing a lot of trust in you. Do not make me regret it. Even though I have no wish to separate you from your sister, if you give me reason to, I will." He stood. "You're excused."

5

Upstairs, I struggled to gain control over the heady mess of emotions I was feeling. I wanted to cry and scream. I wanted—I didn't know what I wanted to do.

I stopped in front of the desk. My outdated, beat-up cell phone was plugged in next to the shiny laptop. I made a move for the phone, and stopped short. A brand-new set of charcoal pencils lay on top of my sketchpad, next to the phone. I cringed at the idea that someone had looked through it. My drawings were, well, private. No one would understand the dark twist everything took on when I sketched.

I guessed dying kind of warped my artistic flavor.

Unwillingly, my gaze fell back to my phone. I wanted to call Adam, but what would I tell him? I had no idea. So I took a shower, a really long, scalding hot shower. I washed my hair twice. Even after I'd scrubbed myself raw and ruddy-colored, I still had no idea what to tell Adam—or what to do.

Wrapped in a fluffy red robe that clashed horribly with my hair, I stood in front of the closet. Cautiously, I opened the doors . . . and then stared in open wonder while the girl in me squealed.

Mingled in with my old clothes were various shirts, dresses, jeans, and sweaters that I could never have afforded in a million and two years. Shoes and boots filled the closet floor, next to what appeared to be a new backpack—one that wasn't as dirty and ragged as the one Dad had gotten me before the accident. I searched for it, but the one thing tying me to Dad was gone.

Feeling numb, I grabbed a pair of sweats and a bulky sweater. After changing, I picked up my phone, the sketchpad, and a new pencil. As I opened the balcony door, the breezy perfume of pine and earthy rich soil filled me. I took a deep breath and shivered. It was cooler, much cooler, than the last time I'd been outside.

Paying no attention to how the air attached itself to my wet curls, I took in my surroundings. The balcony appeared to wrap around the side of the house, but I wasn't brave enough to explore where it led. I approached the railing and looked over. A strong sense of vertigo pushed me back. I hated heights, absolutely despised anything taller than me.

I planted myself against the wall before I looked around again. Trees and, well, more trees surrounded the house. Some were ancient-looking pines, and others looked like oak and maple, but I could never tell the difference between them. It wasn't the trees that caused my grip to loosen around the phone, however. Rising up into the sky like a jagged set of uneven fingers was a mountain the color of sand and granite. The sheer size of the thing cast deep and unforgiving shadows over most of the thick forest, turning the woods into something desolate and intimidating. I could easily imagine people going in there and never being seen again—getting lost and then eaten by a bear or something.

I swallowed down panic and flipped open the cell. Several missed calls and voicemails greeted me. I dialed Adam's number.

He answered on the second ring. "Ember! Where in the hell are you? What happened to you? I've called you a million times. Hey! Are you there?"

"Yeah," I croaked out. "I'm here."

A sigh of relief was audible. "Damn, Em, where are you? You disappeared from school on Wednesday—Wednesday, Em. Without so much as a heads-up. And I haven't seen you since."

"I'm sorry."

"Sorry?" He paused, and I could picture him staring at the phone dumbfounded. "Em, what's going on? Are you okay?"

The words just tumbled out. "No. I'm not okay."

"What do you mean? Em, what is going on?"

"I'm in this place, Adam. With these people I don't know, and I don't know what to do."

There was a stretch of silence. "Em, have you been kidnapped or something?"

I started to laugh, because it sounded ridiculous, but what came out sounded more like a sob. Then I was crying, the kind of deep sobs that stole my breath and hurt. I never cried, not like this and not in front of Adam.

"Em, tell me where you are. I'm going to call the police," he said in rush. "Just tell me where you are."

"You can't call the police. You don't understand, Adam," I said, running my hand over my face. "You never knew. I never told you."

"Knew what? You're not making sense. Are you in danger?"

"I don't know. Yes. No. Probably. But you can't call the police, Adam. You have to promise me."

There was another long gap of silence. "Okay. I won't call the police. Where are you?"

"Um, in some place called the Dark Forest."

"Come again?"

I laughed weakly. "It's a town called Petersburg. I'm in West Virginia, Adam—West 'by God' Virginia."

"*What*?" he shouted.

"You know the place where that movie about the incest hill-billies was filmed? Remember, they like ate people or something. You said the one guy with the gross hands reminded you of our gym teacher?" I took a deep breath. It caught in my throat.

"Em? Are you still there?"

"Yeah."

"What's going on, Em? I went to your house. Everything is gone. The place is empty."

Everything was in that house. The paperwork to the bank accounts. Pictures of Dad, of us together, before the accident were all there.

"Everything is gone?" I whispered.

"It's like no one lived there. Ever," he said. "It was the freakiest thing I'd ever seen."

Cromwell hadn't been joking when he said everything had been taken care of. Even if I did find a way to go back, there was nothing to go back to. No way to buy food, to pay for stuff, to do anything. How could I take care of Olivia or my mom now? My legs felt weak. I slumped down on the balcony floor and pressed my forehead against my bent knees.

I was trapped.

"Em? You still there?"

"It's my mom," I said finally, choosing the one lie I had always relied on. "She's worse. I'm with friends of the family." He didn't respond. The silence stretched out for so long I thought he had hung up the phone.

"Adam, are you there?"

"Yeah." He cleared his throat. "How long are you staying there?"

"I don't know. I may be here for a while."

"You're joking," he said. "Right? Because people just don't up and leave without any sort of warning."

A sudden tightness clamped down my chest. "Adam, I'm not joking."

"I don't understand." His voice sounded strained, choked.

The vise-grip spread to my throat and my eyes started to burn again. "I have to stay here for a while, Adam. I don't want to, but I have to."

"That doesn't make sense, Ember." He took an audible breath, and I could hear him moving around. Probably in his room—he was always in his bedroom. "What friends of the family? Whose house are you staying at?"

"Jonathan Cromwell," I told him.

"I've never heard you mention them before."

I closed my eyes and clutched the sketchpad to my chest. "Yeah, I know. Adam, please don't worry. Everything is okay."

"You don't sound okay, Em."

"Really, I am. It's just been a . . . rough couple of days. I'm sorry I freaked you out and I haven't had a chance to call. Look, I need to get off here. I'll call you soon."

"Ember, don't hang up!" he yelled. "Something isn't right. You don't sound right."

I shook my head, sending damp strands of hair against my cheeks. "I've got to go. I'll call you later. I promise. Okay?" I stopped abruptly, having to take a moment. "Just don't worry. I'm okay. Everything is okay."

"Ember—don't hang up the phone. Please! Just tell—"

I snapped the phone shut, and after a few seconds, I turned it off. I knew Adam would call, and if he did, I *would* answer. Then I would break and tell him I'd been kidnapped by the neighborhood Friendly Freak Association. I had a feeling that wouldn't end well—not for me, my mom, or Olivia.

Olivia.

What would happen if I made a run for it? I couldn't leave Olivia here, but what would I be taking her to? There was nothing out there for us now. Staying here meant I'd have to trust Cromwell. Could I trust a stranger? But I knew the answer. I'd do anything for Olivia.

I'd even put my fate—my future—in Cromwell's hands.

6

I sat, staring blindly at a blank page. I started with one line—the horizon, but as I continued, the line became ragged and broken by tall elms with points as sharp as needles. I pressed harder, giving the shadows more depth, more secrets. The drawing wasn't working, but I couldn't stop. Smudged lines flowed across the page.

"What are you doing?"

I snapped the pad shut and twisted toward the voice. Hayden. In the sun, his hair shone a dozen colors of red and brown.

He took only one step closer, pulling his hands out of the pockets of his jeans. "Ember?"

I jumped to my feet. "Don't come any closer."

Hayden stopped. "I'm not going to hurt you. I just want to talk to you."

"Not going to hurt me?" I backed up, successfully trapping myself against the wall. "You said that right before you knocked me out for three days."

"I'm really sorry about that." He looked away, drawing in a deep breath. "I know you, Ember. You're a fighter—"

"You don't know me. We only talked for five minutes in the library."

A lopsided smile pulled at his lips as he turned toward me. "Since the accident, we've checked in on you. Sometimes I came with my father. I saw enough."

A fine shiver coursed through me. I wrapped my arms around me, but it didn't help. "Saw what?"

He looked away again, staring off at something I couldn't see. "How hard it was for you. The way those kids at school treated you. How you managed to survive when there was no one there to help you." The striking lines of his face turned hard. "I know you're scared, but you don't have any reason to be now."

"Really? Because you tell me so, huh? And this is coming from a boy who has been stalking me with his father. Not to mention the fact that you guys have kidnap—"

"I wasn't stalking you, Ember, and we didn't kidnap you." He faced me once again. "We just . . . relocated you."

"So Olivia can be among her 'kind'." I rolled my eyes. "Are you serious? I don't have a 'kind', and neither does Olivia."

"But you do." Hayden moved fast. I flattened myself against the wall as if I could somehow disappear into it. I held the pad between us. It made for a weak, stupid barrier. "Jonathan Cromwell really isn't my father, did you know that? My parents—my real parents—didn't want anything to do with me. They were scared of me. When I was young, I couldn't control it."

A voice inside my head screamed at me to shut up and run, but I didn't. "Control what?"

Hayden's lips twisted. "I'm what they call an 'enerpath.' I can drain energy from just about anything there is, including the air around us. With people, I can drain a little of their energy. Or I can take it all. It works the same with people who are gifted."

"And what did you mean about the air?"

"I could bring this entire house down if I wanted to."

My mouth dropped open.

"I was in foster homes for several years. If Jonathan hadn't found me, I don't know where I'd be now. He told me what I was and taught me how to control it. Never once did he ask for anything in return. I owe him my life, Ember. As does every kid he's ever saved." His eyes flicked up. "I've scared you, haven't I?"

"I . . . that's . . ." I shook my head, "freaky?"

Silence stretched out between us while he studied me in a way that made me feel transparent. His brown eyes shifted to a much darker color, almost black. Then he moved away, going back to the railing.

"I'm sorry." I found myself apologizing without even knowing why. "I didn't mean—"

Hayden threw up his hand, cutting me off. "It's okay. Being called a freak by you is sort of a compliment."

Was that an insult? "What happened when you touched me? I mean, for a few seconds nothing happened. No one—nothing can touch me."

"I can touch you for a minute or two. It's like a buffer, Ember. I can handle small portions, but it would overwhelm me if you held on and I didn't drain your touch."

"But you knocked me out, like, hard-core."

Hayden ran the tips of his fingers over the railing. "That's what happens when I drain your touch. With others, it just stops whatever they are doing. If someone is telekinetic—can move things with their mind—my touch would stop them from doing so. If I drain just a little, it can take the edge off some of their gifts. For some reason, with you, it just knocked you on your butt." He looked over his shoulder at me. "Maybe it's because your gift is so tied to your life-force now. I don't know."

"So we can touch, but one of us ends up . . . hurt?"

A slow smile spread across his lips. "If we aren't careful, yes. Anyway, how did you discover it? I—we never saw that."

I remembered how I thought he'd looked familiar when I first saw him. I *had* caught glimpses of him.

"Ember?"

"After the accident," I said finally, "I had a cat named Sushi."

"And?" He pushed off the railing, coming to stand in front of me again.

"I picked it up." I took a deep breath and looked away. Part of me didn't even know why I was sharing this, but it felt liberating telling the truth for once. "It died, right then and there. Then I tried to hug Olivia."

"Whoa," Hayden murmured. "Poor kid. Poor kitty."

"Yeah . . . well, I told Olivia the cat ran away. That was before I understood what she could do. I mean, *really* understood." My cheeks were hot, but I kept going. Diarrhea of the mouth, I supposed. "I quickly learned plants and animals pretty much keel over right away. People are different. My touch hurts at first, then . . . well, you already know what happens."

"It was an accident," he said without hesitation. "And *he* touched *you*."

"Does it really matter how it happened? He's dead because of me."

"It's not the same thing." He appeared to want to say something else, but shook his head. "Why were you upset earlier? Was it the phone call?"

Lying would be pointless. The lump in my front pocket was obvious. "I had to call my friend and let him know I was okay."

"Did you tell him where you are?"

A frown tugged at my lips and I lied, sort of. "No."

Hayden seemed to relax. "We can be ourselves here. Outsiders are rarely trusted. My father wants it to be different. Being the mayor has helped."

"He's the mayor?" Cromwell's words came to back to me. *I have all the right. This is my town.*

"Not illegally or through manipulation." He stepped back and leaned across the railing, crossing his long legs at the ankle. "Outsiders just love the man. Everybody does."

"Great." I started chewing my lip. "Does he think I'm going to run around and kill people now, because you know, that's how I roll? Is that why he brought us here?"

Hayden tipped his head back and laughed, really laughed. It was a nice sound. Rich. "No. I don't think he believes you want to kill anyone."

I zeroed in on his word choice. *Want* to kill people versus kill people by accident. I sighed again, feeling uncomfortable in my own skin.

His dark eyes flickered over me. "You're not a freak. None of us are. And maybe I—we can help you get control of it. All you have to do is trust us."

Just trust us.

Trust was a two-way street that usually didn't start with being kidnapped.

I weaseled my way out of dinner even though Olivia threw an epic tantrum. She didn't understand I needed time alone to think all of this through, to figure out what the next course of action should be.

So I skipped dinner, but still had no idea what to do. Now I was freaking starving. When I was pretty sure I was going to start gnawing on my arm, I sucked it up and tried to find my way back to the kitchen.

The hardwood floors didn't creak under my sneakers and the paint was an array of soft, welcoming colors. It was nothing like our worn-down home in Allentown. I kind of missed that old place, no matter how sad it had been for the last two years. It felt like us, and this house didn't.

Eventually, I found the right hallway, but the kitchen wasn't empty like I'd hoped. I lingered outside the entrance, torn between running back to my room and busting in on the obvious family meeting about . . . *me*.

"You can't be serious? She's been awake for a couple of hours and she's already tried to attack you."

"She's scared out of her mind, Gabe. She woke up in a complete stranger's house. Think if we'd done that to you. Or to Parker and Phoebe," Hayden said, his deep timbre recognizable.

"I'd throw you across the room, not kill you with my touch!"

"Knock it off. She's staying. For now." Cromwell sounded like he was accustomed to the two arguing.

Something slammed down. "You're letting her go to school with us on top of it? What if she hurts someone?" Gabe said.

"She's not going to run around and touch people on purpose," Hayden snapped. "She went two years without hurting a single person."

"She killed a boy!" said Gabe.

"That was an accident," Hayden responded. "The asshole attacked her! *He* grabbed *her*. It wasn't her fault."

Nice of him to defend me. Squeezing my eyes shut, I leaned against the wall.

"If she hurts someone, or if I think she will, then I will handle it," Cromwell said. "I'll turn her over to the Facility."

"What?" That was Hayden. "You can't be serious! You know what they'll do to her there."

"Better than what she'd do to us," Gabe spat.

"You have no idea what it's like there," Hayden said. "I do. She doesn't deserve that. We could try to work with her."

"Hayden," Cromwell said, clearly exasperated.

"What? We could try to control her gift."

"She's not gifted."

I didn't recognize the voice, but his words were cold.

"The damn girl is a freak of nature, and if anyone belongs at the Facility, she does. Her sister is one thing. That little angel has a gift, but Ember doesn't." There was a pause, and then the man laughed. "Oh, for the love of God, Hayden, don't look at me like I just kicked a baby. I'm just stating the truth."

"Kurt, you're an ass," Hayden said. "She should've hit you harder."

My eyes snapped open. The lion man—the one in the cowboy duster—was here.

"Whatever. At least I'm not the one hung up on the Grim Reaper," Kurt retorted.

A string of curses erupted. Behind my head, the wall trembled. I jumped back, staring at the wall. It writhed like a snake for a second, then stilled. Plumes of plaster floated down from where the wall met the ceiling.

"Hayden, don't!" Cromwell ordered sharply. "She stays for now. It's done, and I refuse to continue to argue it. And Hayden, stay away from her."

Someone snorted loudly. I'd put my bets on Gabriel.

"I know you think you can help her," Cromwell said. "And I know you want to help her, but I won't have you risking your life for her. You have no experience with a gift like that. I know what will happen."

"Father—"

"I won't lose everything I have worked for—I won't lose you for anyone. If you push this, then I will remove her from this house."

Out of the stark silence that followed Cromwell's warning, Hayden finally spoke, "That won't be necessary, Father."

Wishing I hadn't eavesdropped, I pushed away from the wall. My heart thundered in my chest as I crept down the hall, feeling sick to my stomach. What was this place called the "Facility," and did he really think I'd let him turn me over to them?

I roamed the many rooms until I stumbled upon my sister and two people I hadn't seen yet. They looked so much alike I knew they must be siblings.

The guy was handsome in a cold, methodical way, like he'd been chiseled out of stone and someone had forgotten to give him a touch of warmth. He didn't look up, although he stiffened when I entered the room.

The girl was playing dolls with Olivia. She was stunning, with black hair, bright green eyes, high cheekbones, flawless skin, lush red lips, and a body I'd kill for. She was the kind of girl that I wanted to look like and knew I never would.

Olivia shot to her feet once she spotted me in the doorway, screeching my name loud enough to make me cringe.

The guy glanced up from the book he was reading. His stare wasn't hostile, but I wouldn't call it friendly. The girl, on the other hand, stood and motioned to the guy. They left without saying a word to me.

Sitting down beside Olivia, I tried to ignore their reaction to me. I picked up one of the dolls and realized it was the one Olivia had been whining about for weeks.

"Emmie? Did you know that Parker and Phoebe are twins?" She pointed at the door the siblings had used. "I like the people here."

"You do?" I made the doll walk over to hers.

She bounced her head up and down. "And Liz is nice. She plays dolls with me when Mommy is sleeping."

"Who's Liz?"

"She lives here."

I dropped the doll on the floor, irate by the idea of some stranger buddying up with Olivia. "Has Liz been with you since you got here?"

"Yes. She came to the school when we left home and got me a Happy Meal." She picked up my doll.

Happy Meals—the unofficial way to a child's heart. How devious of this *Ms. Liz*.

"Everyone is nice," she went on, dancing the dolls between us, "to me and Mommy."

Hearing that just pissed me off, and I knew it was stupid, that I should feel relief that everyone was so damn nice to Olivia. I stood, scanning the huge room for a window to throw open or break.

"Don't you like it here, Emmie?"

"It's great." I frowned down at her bowed head. "But this isn't our home, Olivia."

"Ms. Liz said it was our home now."

Oh, did she? I was really starting to dislike this woman.

"And Emmie . . . I like it here," she said in a small, tentative voice.

Of course Olivia liked it here. All the toys in the world to play with, and Liz, who could pick her up and hold her hand.

She dropped the dolls. "I wanna stay here."

I kicked one of the dolls, sending it clear across the room. It hit the wall and the head fell off in the process. "We can't stay." My stomach turned. "This isn't our home."

Olivia watched me, eyes wide and lips trembling. "But I like it here."

"I know." I pulled a hair tie off my wrist and yanked my hair up into a messy bun. The back of my neck felt damp. So did my forehead. "But these people are strangers, Olivia. We can't trust them."

"I trust Ms. Liz." She climbed to her feet, her hands balling into little fists. "They're nice to me. They said I'm gifted—"

"I don't care what they say—dammit!" I dropped down in front of Olivia. "I'm sorry. I'm just tired . . . and I don't know what to do."

She took a step back, eyes wide.

I let out a sigh. "Olivia, I know you like it here. They have all this stuff to play with, but this is not our home. Our home is in Allentown."

Olivia's cheeks puffed out, a sure sign she was about to have a major throw down again. She picked up one of her dolls, a porcelain one with pink-painted cheeks. I so knew what was coming next.

"This is our house!"

"No," I said quietly, coming to my feet. "This is a nice house, but—"

"No!" she screeched as she launched her doll across the room. The face cracked and a leg fell off. "No! No!"

I winced and rubbed my temple. "Olivia, knock it off. My head is pounding."

"No! I don't wanna leave! Ms. Liz—"

My temper snapped. "Ms. Liz isn't your mom, Olivia. Your mom is upstairs! And if I say we have to leave, then we have to!"

Like a mini-volcano, Olivia erupted into a fit of screams and tears. For someone so small, she could make a lot of noise. Seeing her like this didn't make me feel good. I felt terrible, like some kind of evil creature hell-bent on destroying all her dreams.

She hit the floor, stomping her feet.

I tried to get her to stop, but not being able to touch her complicated the whole process. So I stood by helplessly, hoping she'd just tire herself.

"Is everything okay? Sounds like a freight train coming through the house."

A slender, dark-haired, and neatly-polished woman stood in the doorway.

It seemed a switch was thrown; Olivia's temper tantrum shut off. Now on her feet, her eyes fastened on the woman. "Ms. Liz! I don't wanna leave."

Liz smiled fondly. "Honey, you don't have to leave. I've told you already. This is your home as long as you want it to be."

I snapped. "Shut up! Stop telling her that. This isn't her home. You aren't her mother!"

She blinked, taking a step back. "I'm not trying to take your mother's place, Ember."

"Bullshit." Anger and something akin to hatred boiled through me. I stalked across the floor.

Olivia darted in front of me, cutting me off before I could reach Liz. She held out her arms, wiggling her fingers. In one quick swoop, Liz cradled Olivia in her arms.

I froze mere feet from the two. Olivia reached up and wrapped her arms around Liz's neck. A hot, fierce emotion cut through me and stole my breath. Betrayal. I recognized the stupidity behind the emotion. Olivia didn't know what she was doing, but whatever fight I had left burned out.

"What's going on in here?" Cromwell asked, standing behind Liz.

"Ember wants to leave," Olivia said. "Do I have to leave?"

Cromwell stepped into the room, resting his hand on Olivia's back. "No. You don't have to leave. Ember is just tired and confused. Perhaps she should make it an early night. I'm sure she'll feel better in the morning."

Olivia pushed her head into the crook of Liz's neck. She mumbled something, but I couldn't hear her. There was a buzzing in my ears, a sick feeling in my stomach. Head down, I darted around them. I walked down the wide hallway, and then bolted up the stairs. My heart felt as if it would shatter into a million pieces.

Once inside my bedroom, I slammed the door shut behind me. Once. Then twice. Doing that always made me feel better whenever I'd gotten into an argument with my parents.

I didn't feel better now.

Slowly, I slid down the closed door and gulped in air. I'd lost control of Olivia to complete strangers in a matter of minutes. And they hated my guts and planned on shipping me off to some godforsaken place the moment I made the wrong move.

7

I hardly slept—big surprise there.

The sun had barely crested the mountains when I climbed out of bed. Unsure of why, I'd searched the quiet house for the room my mom had been placed in, my hands shoved into the front pocket of my hoodie.

She sat in a rocking chair, staring out a large picture window overlooking the front yard. Limp curls hung around her pale face. The vibrancy in her hair seemed to have dulled since yesterday. Beside her was an untouched glass of water.

Ignoring the raw ache in my chest, I crossed the room and sat down cross-legged next to her, resting my chin in my hand. "There's something wrong here." I stopped and laughed wearily. "Besides the obvious. But he has these kids here and they hate me. And I think they all can do things."

Silence.

"This lady wants to make Olivia her own daughter. That should bother you, Mom. She's cramping your space."

Mom blinked.

I wondered if that was some form of communication—like Morse code or something. "They've been watching us for two years. It's really creepy."

I liked to think Mom agreed.

"Olivia doesn't want to leave. She practically picked sides last night. I know she doesn't understand, and all she sees are new toys and people who can touch her."

She let out a little sigh.

I looked up at her, frowning. "I don't know what to do. There's going to be no way I can get Olivia out of this house, and even if I did, where would we go? Everything is gone, Mom."

Still, there was no response.

I sighed again. "Mom, you know I'm not dead, right? I did die, but I'm not dead. I'm sitting here, right in front of you, and . . . and I don't know what to do. I don't know if I should stay here or try to make a run for it with Olivia. I don't even know where the damn keys to my car are, or if my car is even here."

She rested her head back and closed her eyes, humming the same song Olivia did.

"And Olivia really does like it here. She's getting so much attention and I've never seen her happier . . ." I trailed off, closing my own eyes. "I'm sorry for picking seafood that night. I knew you wanted to go home. I was so mad, because you and Dad were arguing. If I'd just kept my mouth shut, none of this would've happened."

Mom stopped humming, but didn't respond.

I pulled my knees up and rested my head on them. Giving up on the one-sided conversation, I stayed quiet. After a while, I headed downstairs. I really had no idea where I was going. Hunger gnawed at my stomach, but I was afraid someone would be in the kitchen again. So I found myself staring at the front door. Freedom seemed just a doorknob-turn away.

When I did open the door, freedom didn't wait—a half-naked Hayden did.

Damp hair curled around his forehead and flushed cheeks. He was shirtless. Absolutely naked from the low-hanging jogging pants up. A music player was attached to one of his biceps, and a low hum came from the earbuds.

Hayden pulled the earbuds out, smiling. "Hey. You're up early."

My throat felt dry. "Yeah."

"Were you going outside?"

Instead of answering, my eyes dropped. He was an obvious runner. Skin stretched over taut muscles, slender hips, and a very hard-looking chest—and wow, it was a nice chest. My cheeks suddenly felt hot.

"Ember?"

I forced my eyes up. He was smiling that lopsided grin. "What?"

"Were you going outside?" He slid the music player off his arm and started to wrap the earbuds around it. "This early?"

"Yes. I thought . . ." I inhaled. Huge mistake. Autumn leaves and something wild teased my senses. He smelled wonderful. The sudden urge to touch him hit me hard.

"You thought what?"

What was I thinking? I couldn't touch him. And I didn't want to. "You're not supposed to be talking to me."

He frowned. "What?"

"I overheard you guys last night. You're not supposed to be talking to me or whatever."

Hayden folded his arms across his chest. "You're not really good at eavesdropping. I was never told not to talk to you."

"You were told to stay away from me."

"That can be construed in many ways. Anyway, you're not planning on running away?"

"No." I stepped to the side. "I just wanted to go outside. I'm not allowed to go outside?"

He shadowed my movements, blocking the door. "You are allowed to do whatever you want."

"Except leave?"

"Except that, but it's for your benefit," he said. "You'd get lost out there. You saw it yourself yesterday. We're surrounded by woods, and there's about fifteen miles between here and town."

Irritation spiked. I tipped my chin as I met his eyes. "I'm not as stupid as you must think I am."

"I don't think you're stupid at all." Hayden stepped forward. He was close, way too close. The tips of his sneakers brushed mine. "Never once did I think you were stupid. You wouldn't have lasted as long as you did caring for a five-year-old if you were."

"How would—" I stopped myself. Of course, he had been watching *us*—*me*.

Impossibly, he seemed to have moved closer. My back hit the doorframe. "When you returned to school after the accident, the kids were assholes about you wearing gloves. You always wore long sleeves, even during the summer. But I'm not sure if your friends abandoned you, or if you pushed them away."

I nearly choked. "They abandoned me."

Hayden tipped his head down and locks of damp hair fell over his forehead. "Within weeks you stopped everything. You were a cheerleader before. You wanted to go to college—Penn State? To become a doctor like your father." His voice dropped to a whisper. "All of that stopped. Olivia became everything to you. Instead of going to the coffee shop before school like all the other kids did, you were dropping her off at a babysitter."

My hands fell away from my body, hanging limply at my sides. His words were oddly compassionate, tender almost—and very creepy.

"I saw you once, outside of a bank in town. You were upset. It was the first time I could remember seeing you cry. I wanted to . . ." He trailed off, lips forming a hard, tight line.

I knew what day he was talking about. It'd been only a month or two ago. The money from the life insurance had been running low for weeks. I knew there was some in the savings, but the bank had told me they needed my mom's signature to transfer the money over. Mom hadn't held a pen since the accident.

"Why were you guys watching so much?" I asked, genuinely curious. "Why didn't you talk to me before the day in the library? Then this wouldn't be so . . . messed up."

His dark gaze settled on my face. "I couldn't, Ember. I . . . wasn't supposed to keep going back, but . . ."

"But what?"

A door opened somewhere in the house, followed by the sound of footsteps.

Hayden reached out and brushed a curl off my cheek. My heart stopped. His hand hovered there. "Don't roam off too far." Then he walked off, leaving me standing in the open door.

In a daze, I stepped outside. The air smelled strongly of pine and maple. The sun was still warm for a late September morning. Tiny beads of sweat dotted my forehead as I made my way around the sprawling house.

It was ridiculously huge. The main part of the house stood three stories high. Single-story wings spread out from the middle, flanking each side like a cloverleaf. Only the long, winding driveway and small patch of front lawn remained clear. Everything else was nothing but shadows and thick, imposing trees.

Isolation.

Did Cromwell pick this house because of its location? I could scream and no one would hear me. I shuddered and forced myself to keep walking. A large garage sat at the edge of the woods, kitty-corner from the house. Inside were two Porsches—both black and shiny coupes. Behind them towered a really nice SUV and two more absurdly expensive cars.

Sitting beside the cars, my poor Jeep looked like a sad, unfortunate creature. For the first time since I woke up, a smile broke out across my face. I didn't care if it looked ugly. It was mine—my way out.

I started toward it, but the sound of tires crunching over gravel drew my attention. Curiosity propelled me back to the front of the house. Was it the cowboy man? The boy who wanted to toss me around the kitchen? My steps slowed considering the options.

What I hadn't expected to see was Mrs. Lewis' Toyota creeping up the driveway. The Camry rolled to a stop; the car door swung open before he killed the engine.

I broke out in a dead run. "Adam? What are you doing here? How did you—what are you doing?"

Adam stepped out of the car, his glasses crooked, shirt wrinkled. He gave me a goofy smile. "Google Maps, Ember. It wasn't hard to find Petersburg. Apparently, it's well known for those rocks." He pointed to the monster in the sky. "I've been driving all night. Had two energy drinks and a coffee, probably grounded for life, but I'm here. Alive."

I stared at him, and then burst into laughter. "Adam, you're in so much trouble. When your mom finds out, she's gonna kill you."

He shrugged. "Look, I needed to make sure you were okay. I tried calling you, but you turned your damn phone off. I thought you'd been kidnapped and stuck in a one-room shack in the mountains of West Virginia. Apparently, I was wrong." His eyes squinted at the house behind me. "You're stuck in an eighty-room shack."

God, I wanted to hug him. I also wanted to strangle him. "Adam, how did you find this house?"

"You told me the guy's name. I Googled Jonathan Cromwell, and found out he's the mayor. So I asked for directions at the gas station over on some hick road named Patterson," he explained, clearly proud of his investigative skills. "Anyway, this is what friends do. They watch out for each other. Mom will just have to suck it. She can't ground me forever."

"Oh, Adam," I whispered, and then inhaled deeply. The scent of detergent and familiarity washed over me. Sandbox love—nothing was stronger.

"Em, something is wrong with all of this. You can tell me you're okay all you want. I know you're not."

I wasn't okay. "It's complicated."

His brows went up and his glasses slipped further down his noise. "Try me. Some say I'm smart. I just may understand."

"Adam, I just don't know how to explain this. I'm not even—"

"Ember, step back now."

The authority alone in Cromwell's voice forced me away from Adam. Except Adam didn't recognize the tone, or he just didn't care. Because he knew I didn't like to be touched, when Adam stopped me, he grabbed my sweater-covered arm.

"Who is that?" His eyes were glued above my head.

"Uh, that's Mr Cromwell. Adam, you should probably—"

Adam frowned. "The mayor is *that* young?"

"Huh?" I turned around and froze. I hadn't mistaken the voice. Cromwell stood on the porch, but it was Hayden whom Adam was staring at. "No . . . that isn't the mayor."

"Ember, what's going on?" Cromwell came striding down the steps.

Adam dropped my arm and stepped in front of me. "My name is Adam Lewis. I'm Ember's friend."

I should've been paying attention. Instead, I stared at Hayden. Gone was the strangely compassionate boy who had stood next to me in the doorway. In his place was someone who was as hard and cold as one of those statues inside.

"Adam," I whispered. "You should probably leave."

He snorted. "I'm not leaving. Shouldn't he invite me in? He *is* the mayor. Shouldn't he be friendly and inviting?"

"Adam, that isn't—" I stopped. The cowboy was here—Kurt. Like a tumbleweed, he had come out of nowhere.

Cromwell smiled. "How did you find your way here, Adam?"

"The internet," he responded dryly. "So you're a friend of Ember's family? That's kind of funny since I've known her forever, and she's never once mentioned you."

"Adam, please—"

Kurt propped himself against the hood of Mrs. Lewis' car. "She obviously told him where she was, Jonathan."

"Get off my mom's car, man. I get a dent in the hood, I'm dead." Kurt grinned.

"Does your mother know where you are, young man?" Cromwell asked.

"Who wants to know?" Adam was frowning at Kurt.

"He knows too much, Jonathan." Kurt pushed off the car.

"What?" My heart thrummed. "He doesn't know anything."

"I know enough," Adam cut in. "Enough to know you're all a bunch of freaks living in the middle of nowhere."

"Adam, shut up!" I yelled.

His gaze flickered at me as he started digging in his pocket. He pulled out his cell. "Em, is Olivia really here? I'm calling the police."

Several things happened at once.

"Wipe him," Cromwell ordered with an almost sad shake of his head.

A second later, Kurt had Adam by the front of his shirt. Adam didn't even get the phone open.

"No!" I rushed forward, only to be stopped. Arms like bands of steel captured me around the waist, holding me back.

"Don't," Hayden whispered in my ear. He started pulling me back, away from Adam. "You need to go inside, Ember. Now."

"No. She needs to see this. To understand I will not have our kind threatened." Cromwell's eyes met mine. "I take no pleasure in this, Ember. I asked you not to let me down. You've left me with no other choice."

"Father?" Hayden had a catch in his voice. "You can't—"

Cromwell's face hardened. "This is not your call."

"Wait! What are you doing?" I struggled, but Hayden's grip was unbreakable. I couldn't get my hands up. Touching him was out of the question.

Adam stayed rooted to where he stood, eyes wide with fear. "Em? What's going—?"

Kurt touched him on the forehead. Just a thumb—that was all it took. Adam's eyes fell shut. He stood motionless, like a sculpture.

"What are you doing?" I screamed. "Stop touching him! Stop it! He doesn't know anything! I haven't told him anything."

Letting out a little sigh, Kurt stepped back. A small, sated smile played across his lips. I thought I heard Hayden apologize, but I couldn't be sure. Rushing filled my ears as ice touched my blood.

Hayden let go.

I staggered forward. "Adam? Are you okay? Adam, look at me. Open your eyes."

Adam blinked slowly, as if he was just waking up. First he looked at Kurt, then Cromwell. "Where am I?"

"Nowhere," Cromwell answered quietly. "You need to go home, Adam Lewis. Go now, before your mother worries."

"I don't want Mom to worry." He rubbed a hand over his forehead.

I pushed down the dread building bitterly in the back of my throat. Adam was fine. He just looked tired and confused, but okay. "Adam?"

Adam blinked again. "Who . . . who are you?"

My laugh sounded strange. "You know who I am, you idiot."

He fiddled with his glasses, pushing them up the bridge of his nose. "I have no idea who you are, but I've got to get home. Mom is gonna kill me." He walked past me, shaking his head. "Man, I'm in so much trouble."

I stared. He got back in the car, muttering the whole time. He slammed the door and turned the ignition. The engine roaring to life snapped me into action. I rushed to his car. "Adam, look at me. Please! You know who I am."

He jerked back from the window, frowning. "I'm sorry, but I don't know you. I don't even know why I'm here."

"Please, don't do this, Adam. We've been friends since I ate your lunch in kindergarten. You fell off your bike when you were ten and you broke your leg. Remember?" He continued looking at me blankly. Panic caused my voice to rise. "You have to sit next to Sheila Cummings in bio. You hate that, because she thinks osmosis is bad breath. Last week, she asked you if she was Jewish. Come on, don't do this to me. Please!"

"Ember," Hayden called out, his voice sounding ragged. "Just stop. Stop now. Please."

I ignored him. "Adam, come on. You are my friend—my best friend. You're the only one who was my friend after the accident. We . . . we . . ." We had sandbox love; didn't he remember that?

Adam started rolling up the window, brows raised. "I'm sorry. I don't know you."

Pain cut through me so sharply that it knocked the air right out of me. "No. No." I hit the window with my palm. It shook, but did not give. "Adam, please. Say my name. You know who I am. You have to!"

He shook his head, lips pulled back in a sneer—a look I'd never seen Adam give me. "I don't know you. Jesus. So stop being a freak."

My hand stilled against the window. I blinked, willing myself to wake up. Because this—this had to be a nightmare. Surely, this couldn't be real—the pain in my chest, the numb way my body felt.

Adam threw the car in reverse, shaking his head. Someone pulled me back before he ran over my foot. He left—really left. I wanted to run after him, but it'd be pointless. His face showed the same blankness Mom had whenever she looked at me.

I was dead to him, just like I was dead to Mom.

I could've stood there for hours. It didn't matter. My heart seized, then shattered, and with everything I'd learned to deal with, I didn't know how to deal with *this*.

Cromwell sighed wearily. "I'm sorry for your pain, but you left me no other choice."

My cheeks felt damp. My fingers came back wet. When I looked toward the house, I saw Cromwell go back inside. Mom thought I was dead. My sister chose toys and a pseudo-mom over me. Our house was gone. And now, my only link to anything had been wiped away.

Adam was gone.

8

"Desolation" wasn't even an adequate word. "Fury" didn't describe what I was feeling. Blindly, I turned around. Rage and sorrow swelled, wanting to swallow me whole.

"I knew this was going to be a mistake," Kurt said. "I told Jonathan we shouldn't have brought her here. The little one—whatever, but I knew this one was going to be a problem. Just look at her, she's getting ready to blow."

"Kurt, can you just shut up?" Hayden started toward me.

"You can't tell me you aren't worried about her being here. She's unstable right now. She's capable of anything. Are you seriously comfortable with her running around in your house?"

"She's not dangerous," Hayden said in a low voice.

"That's right. I forgot. You're blinded by your obsession with her." Kurt took a step forward. "Everyone knows. All those times you went back there. There was no reason."

"Are you finished?" Hayden asked calmly.

"No," he said. "She should've been wiped—"

I acted at the basest of instincts, the cruelest of desires. I dove at him, aiming for any part of exposed flesh. All I could see was him touching Adam, removing all traces of me. So that was his gift. For some reason, I felt like that should have been a more powerful realization.

But all I could think was that I kind of wanted Kurt to die.

Kurt's hand caught me in the side before I could even touch him. An explosive string of curses sounded, and then he pushed hard. Unable to catch myself, I fell backward and landed in the gravel at an awkward, hip-first angle. Pain flared, unexpected and intense.

Since I was on the ground, I didn't see how Hayden got to Kurt so fast. All I knew was that he did, and I could *feel* his rage in the form of a blast of red-hot energy. There was a smell in the air—almost like rubber burning. A snapping sound jerked my head up. A huge tree branch swayed and then broke free from the tree, landing between the two. Ignoring the pain in my hip, I scooted back.

"Don't ever touch her again," Hayden growled.

Kurt looked up, eyes wide. "Are you threatening me—over her? I'm like your brother, Hayden!"

"Not anymore."

Kurt blinked, a stunned look crept across his face. "She was going to touch me. I defended myself."

"I don't care. Stay away from her."

For a tense moment, they locked eyes—Hayden's the color of the darkest hour of night. The air thickened and snapped. I glanced up at the trees, half-afraid the whole forest would come down on us. Neither of them moved for what seemed like an eternity. Finally, Kurt spun on his heel and stalked toward the house.

"Are you okay?"

I stared at the branch. It was thick enough to crack a skull if it'd hit someone. "Yeah," I whispered.

Hayden unexpectedly reached out, grabbing my hand and hauling me to my feet. Stunned by the contact, I didn't pull away. He held on for seconds, but it equaled a lifetime to me. Without thinking, my fingers curled around his, reveling in the smoothness of his hand, the way his fingers seemed to bend around mine almost eagerly.

But then he dropped my hand as if it burned him. From what I'd learned from him before, a few seconds couldn't have done anything to him. Silence stretched out between us. I tried focusing on anything other than Adam, but Hayden just had to go there.

"Why did you lie to me yesterday?" he asked. "You told me you didn't tell him where you were. If you hadn't lied to me, I could've stopped this from happening."

"I didn't know he was going to come here. Adam didn't know anything. He never knew." I stopped, sucking air unsteadily. "Why am I even telling you this? It doesn't matter now. So I lied to you. You all have won, okay? I'm not going anywhere, because I don't have anywhere left to go. Olivia loves it here, and isn't that what you all wanted? To make sure she loved it here?"

"Ember, no one—"

"And now I have nothing." My voice broke. "So you've won. Aren't you happy?"

He reached for me again. This time his hand caught my arm. "This doesn't make me happy."

I looked down at his hand. His fingers, long and elegant, circled my covered arm completely. I glanced up; our eyes locked for one, two, three counts. Something intense flowed across his face, and he took a step forward—so close I had to crane my neck back.

"You hurting would never make me happy," Hayden said.

"You don't get it. He was all I had. Adam was it. That was it. And you all took it away."

He flinched and dropped my arm. "That's not true. I'm here for you."

Shaking my head, I backed up. "I don't know you, so that means nothing to me."

"Emmie? You sleeping?"

I opened my eyes, staring at the vaulted ceiling. "No."

Olivia was quiet. Seconds later, I felt her hoist herself over the edge of the bed. She crawled across and sat so her face was directly above mine. I closed and opened my eyes, but her face was still planted in front of mine.

"Why didn't you eat dinner?"

"I wasn't hungry."

She reached out and grabbed a handful of my hair. I braced myself, but she managed to not leave me bald this time. "Ms. Liz said you had a bad day."

That was the understatement of the millennium.

Humming softly, she separated the curls in her hands. I stayed impossibly still so her little fingers didn't brush my scalp.

"You mad at me?"

"I'm not mad at you."

"You sad?" She tugged a thick curl across her fingers.

I had no idea how she jumped from me being mad at her to me being sad. It hurt my head to even try to figure it out. "I'm just tired."

Straightening out several curls, she pulled my hair in front of my face. Her fingers smelled like Play-Doh. I loved that smell. The sudden rush of tears was unexpected. I squeezed my eyes shut.

She let go of my hair, giggling as the curl sprang back. "Emmie?"

"Yeah?" Even with my eyes closed, I felt her face in mine again.

"I love you lots."

Something was wrong with my eyelids. They weren't blocking the tears. I slid my hands between us and smacked them over my face. I bit down on my lip to keep the horrible sound from escaping.

Olivia tugged on my sleeves. "Emmie?"

"I love you too," I said thickly.

Eventually, she gave up on the tug of war. The bed dipped as Olivia shifted down and wrapped her arms around my waist. I didn't dare move until I heard Olivia's soft snore. I lowered my hands carefully to chest level.

Vaguely, I wondered when I'd turned into such a wuss. I had cried after the accident, Dad's death, and my own dying stuff, but I thought I'd used up a lifetime's worth of tears. But losing

Adam was just as painful—ripping open old wounds, creating new ones. I eventually caved to exhaustion.

My eyelids drifted shut and when I opened them again, Olivia was gone.

Crying always left my head feeling like a drummer had taken up residence inside my skull. I pushed off the covers and swung my feet off the bed.

Soft light from the bedside lamp cut away at the darkness. I found my way to the bathroom and washed away what remained of my tear-fest. Then I pulled off my hoodie and tossed it back into the bedroom. I refused to look in the mirror after that. With my current drama-induced freak-out, I would probably throw myself on the floor after one glimpse of my scars.

Unable to fall back to sleep, I sat down at the desk and booted up the computer. Hope sparked alive when I checked my email. There were old messages from Adam, proving that he had known me once upon a time, and the one Dad had forwarded to me before the accident, but nothing new.

I don't even know what I was thinking.

Out of boredom and a sort of desperate need to think about anything else, I Googled: "Gifted." Results were so not what I was looking for. Then I searched "special powers." Wikipedia brought the giggles, but since I didn't think I was dealing with the *X-Men*, I hit the backspace button.

Finally, I came across a website dedicated to real accounts of superpowers. Taking a deep breath, I clicked on the link and started reading. Things like clairvoyance, precognition, the ability to look into the past, rapid learning, super-speed, telekinesis, telepathy, pyrokinetics, memory removal, dream manipulation, and on and on. There was nothing on bringing back the dead or a "toxic touch" syndrome. All these years I'd never really considered the idea of Olivia having "superpowers," but there was no doubt she was gifted, and so were the other people in the house.

Me? I was cursed.

Yawning, I scanned the rest of the page. Curiosity got the best of me and I typed in "The Facility." After several pages of nonsense, I gave up. I don't know why I'd thought some crazy research-slash-kid-stealing institute would have a website.

Weary, I turned the computer off and picked up my sketch-pad. Several attempts at drawing ended in failure. Everything came across wrong, uneven. I ripped the pages off one by one and tossed them to the floor. All the while my brain kept spitting out questions that had no answers. Tossing the pad on the desk, I stood and glanced around the room. The drapes covering the balcony doors stirred as the air kicked on.

The flimsy material billowed out further. I reached out and caught the drapes. Outside, thick clouds rolled through the night sky. Only a fine sliver of moonlight hit the balcony, casting shadows of the nearby trees. But something looked strange about the shadows near the balcony door. Frowning, I leaned closer and peered through the glass.

One of the shadows appeared way too thick, too solid—and way too tall.

My fingers slid away from the curtain. Then the shadow moved.

I jerked back from the door, tripping over the chair I'd been sitting in. I caught myself on the edge of the bed, eyes glued to the door.

By the time I found the courage to look again, there was nothing on the other side of the door or anyone on the balcony. I double-checked that the door was locked—a pointless precaution, but it made me feel better. I climbed into bed and lay down on my side, clutching the blankets to my chin. My eyes stayed on the balcony doors.

It was a long time before my heart would calm down enough so I could fall back asleep.

9

I felt like a ghost.

Gabe, the blond guy who'd thrown me across the room tele-kinetically, left the room if I walked in. The twins, Phoebe and Parker, just flat out refused to acknowledge my existence. Never in my life had I felt more like a loser—and that was saying something. By the time Cromwell basically ordered me to the kitchen, I was grateful. At least *someone* wanted to talk to me.

Once there, I found myself sitting in the same spot I had two days ago, but this time Hayden was with us. He wasn't talking much since he was busy shoving a foot-long sub in his mouth.

"I wanted to discuss the school situation. You're already registered and set to go tomorrow," Cromwell said.

I watched Hayden. He ate amazingly fast, and he was sloppier than Olivia. Pieces of tomato and turkey fell to the plate, along with globs of mayonnaise and mustard.

"At no time are you allowed to discuss any of our gifts with the outsiders."

"Yeah, I think I already know what will happen if I do," I snapped.

Cromwell sighed. "Ember, I'm sorry about what happened to your friend. However, you left me with no other option."

"Adam didn't know anything," I said for the hundredth time.

Cromwell folded his arms on the table. "I will not continue to discuss this with you, Ember. But do understand—if I think you have told any outsider about us, I will do the same. Again."

"Or you could just ship me off."

He took a deep breath, visibly struggling for patience. "Yes, that is always an option. Do you understand, Ember?"

Hayden stopped eating long enough to hear my answer. "Yes. I understand."

"Good," Cromwell said. "I have some questions for you." I stared at him until his smile strained.

"May I ask how many times Olivia has used her gift? Besides the time she used it with you."

I thought about lying. "Only a few times since: a cat, a pigeon, and Squeaky. I've gotten her to understand not to do it, but I can't promise you that she won't if she sees a dead animal." I glanced over at Hayden. The sub was gone. Now he stared at me. "Olivia has a soft spot for animals."

"Squeaky? The hamster upstairs?" Cromwell asked.

I got a twisted amount of pleasure from seeing Cromwell's eyes widen with surprise. "Yep. Squeaky died. I buried him. Olivia dug him up. I woke up the next day with the thing sitting on my chest."

Cromwell blinked. "Oh. Okay. Well, most children her age usually don't attend public school until they have a strong grasp on their gifts. Over the past few days, I have seen no reason to believe that Olivia will be a risk in public school."

"What about the kids who *do* pose a risk?" I cut in. "Do they go to the Facility?"

"Someone has been listening to our conversations." Cromwell glanced at his son. "Yes. Children who could benefit from a more specialized school would attend there. Hayden went there for several years. He was taught to control his gift."

I stole another quick peek at him. "From what I overheard, it doesn't sound like a fun time."

Hayden's lips slipped into the half-smile, but he said nothing. Cromwell ignored me. "As I said, Olivia will do fine among outsiders. She is such a bright child. She has an old—"

"An old soul," I finished for him.

Cromwell's smile was real this time. "And that brings me to you, Ember. There are some reservations."

"Naturally," I muttered.

He ignored that, too. "Your inability to control it is a concern of mine."

"You know, I've lived two years with this." I started tapping my fingers on the table. "It's not like I run around and touch people. What happened with . . . Dustin will never happen again."

"That may be true, but there have been several situations of you losing your temper since you arrived here," Cromwell said. "That's a concern."

I snorted and continued to tap my fingers. I could tell by the way Hayden stared at my fingers it was annoying the crap out of him. "That should probably tell you something."

"It *has* told me quite a bit. When you're frightened or confused, you react violently. Unstably, even. Throwing you into a new school with new people may provoke the same reaction from you."

My fingers froze over the wood.

Cromwell's smile turned smug. Just for a second, but I saw it. "I know you would never want to hurt someone innocent, but I fear you just may not be able to control yourself."

I returned to tapping my fingers. I had no problem with Cromwell thinking that. Whatever. His opinion—

Hayden placed his hand on my arm. I shot him a dirty look, but when he released my arm, I didn't start back up with the tapping.

"That's why you need to do everything in your power to control yourself, Ember. I want to keep you with your sister, but if something happens I will have no choice."

"But she won't do anything. Will you?" Hayden asked, speaking to me for the first time since, well, yesterday. We'd crossed paths a couple of times today, but he'd ignored me, too.

"Um, I'm going to go with no."

"Then I'm relieved to hear that. You already have one strike against you, and I'm not playing baseball," Cromwell said. "You won't get three strikes with me."

It took everything for me not to roll my eyes—or laugh in his face. I doubted he'd appreciate either.

Cromwell stood and pushed his chair back in. "I'm glad we've had this conversation."

I slid Hayden a wary look as Cromwell clapped him on the shoulder before leaving the room. Alone, Hayden and I stared at each other. Growing uncomfortable with the awkward silence, I started to stand.

Hayden leaned across the table.

I jerked back, but he flashed me a lazy grin and wrapped his hands around a thick, brown candle. Immediately, the candle collapsed in on itself. The scent of maple and cinnamon permeated the air.

"Well, aren't you just special," I said dryly.

"Not as special as you." He leaned back. "Why are you so argumentative?"

"Were you on the balcony last night?" I asked instead.

Hayden draped his arm over the back of his chair. "No." His eyes dropped to where I fiddled with the button on my sweater. "But I was in your room last night."

It took me a minute to respond. "Look, I don't want you following me around anymore. Or whatever it was you were doing in . . . my bedroom."

He arched a dark eyebrow. "I wasn't doing anything in your room, Ember. Liz was looking for Olivia. I checked your room and found her."

"Oh." My cheeks flushed.

"Why do you ask if I was on the balcony?"

I shrugged. "I thought I saw someone."

"Well, did you?" .

"I guess I was seeing things."

He made some sort of affirmative sound and I looked up. His dark eyes were narrowed on the wall, the lines of his face tense.

I cleared my throat. "So, yeah, thanks for . . . um, getting Olivia."

His dark eyes swiveled back to me. Strands of hair fell across his forehead. "I think you can control your gift."

"It's not a gift," I blurted out. "It's nothing like you or Olivia. I'm just screwed up. That happens when you die, I guess."

"That can't be it, Ember. I don't believe that."

"Well, I don't know what to tell you, then."

Hayden stared at me silently, and I grew uncomfortable again. The way he did that made me feel like he could see right through me.

"I can help you," he said finally. "There isn't any action out there in the world that doesn't occur without a thought—a want or need behind it. If we can figure—"

"No." I shook my head. "You were told not to do this."

He sent me a sly grin. "I don't always do what I'm told."

"Neither do I, but it's *my* ass on the line. Not yours. I heard Cromwell. He'd send me away."

"We wouldn't get caught, and he wouldn't send you away. He was just saying that to make the others feel better." He paused as he saw my doubtful look. "Look, it wouldn't hurt anything. Don't you want to be able to touch someone? Hold your sister's hand?"

"It's not going to work, Hayden. I'm not like you."

He swung his legs around so he faced me. "So you rather not do anything? Just give up?"

"Why do you even care?"

"Do you want to be sent away?" he said, instead of answering my question. "Because there are some here who are hoping you do screw up."

"Gee, thanks."

"But if you could control your touch, then no one has anything to worry about." He shifted closer, his knees pressing against mine. My stomach went all fluttery. "I never thought I could control my gift, but I did. You won't know until you try."

"I don't want to try and fail." The words came out. I wanted to stop them, but couldn't. "And I couldn't deal with hope and then failure. You know? 'Cuz that's what's going to happen."

An array of emotions flickered over his face, his eyes swiftly turning from brown to black. He reached forward.

I scooted back. "Don't."

He stopped, one arm extended. The heat from his skin blew back at me.

"I don't want your pity."

"I don't pity you, Ember. If anything, I admire you. Not many people our age could deal with what you've had to. You know, my dad has always thought that Olivia was the amazing one, the one who has this remarkable gift. But I've always thought it was you." He stiffened and looked away. "So yeah, I don't pity you."

Blood rushed to my cheeks. Compliments nowadays were so few I had no idea how to act. Part of me warmed, and not in embarrassment. Hearing him say that didn't make me feel like so much of a freak.

I shifted awkwardly, and finally, I said something really stupid. "I'm remarkable because I can kill people. So I'd say you're obligated to say that. Or else."

Hayden gave that lopsided smile. A dimple appeared in his right cheek. I wondered if the left cheek had one, too. "It's not what you can do, Ember. It's who you are."

"But you don't really know me. Yeah, you saw me a couple of times. Whatever. But you don't know who I am. Or what I am. The whole dying thing took something from me, I think. And . . ."

"And what?"

"Nothing." Shaking my head, I pushed back from the table. "I don't know what I was saying. Just forget it."

He looked like he wasn't going to let it go. "Okay, but we are going to try."

I hugged my elbows. "But—"

"You have no reason not to. We won't get caught. You won't hurt me. I can control it. I'm like your kryptonite."

"I don't have a choice, do I?"

"Nope."

I let out a breath. "Why are you doing this? Why do you want to help me?"

Hayden's eyes locked with mine, and his had this weird, magnetic pull to them. "I'm doing it because I want to."

10

Some nasty-looking, dark circles had formed under my eyes—being held prisoner like this chased away any chance of sleep and left my thoughts in tangles. My eyes still felt swollen, and I was sure I had a zit the size of Canada on my forehead.

And I had to go to school—a new school.

Listing the ways my life currently sucked butt made me late. By the time I got downstairs, *Ms. Liz* had already taken Olivia to her new school.

Taking Olivia to school was *my* job—my responsibility. How dare she think she could take Olivia to school? To top off what was sure to be a wonderful day, Cromwell informed me I'd only have the keys to my car once I'd earned his trust back. *His trust*? Like I was the creeptastic person who whipped kids off the street and collected them like figurines?

What about my trust in him?

Give me the keys to one of the Porsches in the garage and I'd trust the hell out of him. Until then, he was more likely to have me call him "Dad" than trust him.

So there I stood on the porch—with my new backpack, wearing my new jeans and gloves and an old button-down sweater—waiting for my babysitter.

Hayden. Of course.

"You ready?"

I jumped at the sound of his voice. Turning around, I saw that he stood right behind me. I hadn't heard him come out of the house; he was that quiet.

He chuckled as he moved past me. "Come on. Even though we won't get any tardy slips, I guess you shouldn't be late on your first day."

There went my pretty pink collage for Olivia.

Groaning, I followed Hayden back to the garage. He opened the door of the Infiniti SUV and motioned me in.

I mumbled something halfway coherent and climbed into the car. Out of the corner of my eye, I saw Gabe and Phoebe jump into one of the Porsches. Gabe yelled something that earned a laugh from Hayden. Phoebe's eyes lingered a few seconds too long on Hayden as he made his way around the front of the car.

"Where's Parker?" I asked, curious.

"He's homeschooled." He backed out of the garage.

The way he said it left no room for questions, but I went there. "Why?"

"It's too hard on him." He went on before I could push for more information. "You look tired."

My pale reflection stared back at me in the side mirror. The pale blue of my eyes looked even more watered-down than normal. I sank down in the seat and faced forward.

"Have you've been sleeping okay?"

I nodded. The ride into town was one giant fail boat. Hayden tried to make small talk, but I ignored him and focused on my surroundings. Petersburg was the kind of town people missed if they sneezed. I spotted a McDonald's, a couple of pizza shops, several strip malls, and little else on the way to school. After I got over my self-imposed bitterness, I could admit the town had a cute look about it.

I broke the silence. "How did you guys end up here?"

"My father is originally from here, but I'm from Montana. He wanted to come back home and he gave me an option to come with him. I'm glad I did." He stopped as if he'd said too much. "I'm into hiking. The Seneca Rocks are a big thing around here. They're the mountains you can see from the house."

I shuddered. "I hate heights."

"I guess rock climbing is out of the question, then." He slid me a sly glance.

I ignored that. "What about the other kids?"

"Over the years Cromwell kinda found them."

"What? He found them? Like he found Olivia and me?"

Hayden frowned. "Yeah, just like he found you and Olivia."

"What about their parents?"

"They didn't want them, Ember. If they had, Cromwell wouldn't have taken them."

"So none of your parents wanted to keep any of you? All of you are adopted by him?" I paused and pictured parents throwing their kids out by the handful. To me, something wasn't right about that. "That sucks."

Hayden gave a low laugh. "When you say it like that, then I guess it does suck, but yeah, we've all been adopted by Cromwell."

"What can they do? I know what Gabe can do, but what about Phoebe and Parker?"

He nodded, his fingers tapped along the steering wheel. "Phoebe is an empath—she can sense emotions and sometimes control them. Parker is a telepath."

I scrunched up my nose. "He can . . . read people's thoughts?"

"When Cromwell first brought them home, Parker was a mess. Didn't talk to anyone and screamed when anyone came near him. He couldn't control it. Can you imagine always hearing people's thoughts? Never being able to shut it out?"

"No," I turned back to the window. "So that's why he doesn't go to school?"

There was a pause. "There are just too many people—classrooms so small and people crowding him. Liz is doing the whole homeschooling thing."

"And Cromwell is helping him control it? Like he doesn't do it all the time?"

"Yup. Parker still doesn't talk much, but he can block most of the chatter out as long as he's not around a lot of crowds."

I let out a heavy sigh. Cromwell was just super. "What is he anyway? What can Cromwell do? Walk through walls? Fly? Leap tall buildings?"

"We aren't superheroes, Ember."

"Then what is the point of gathering all of us together? What does Cromwell want?"

"He just wants to help us." A thoughtful look crossed his face as he concentrated on the road. "You're having a hard time believing that, aren't you?"

"Obviously," I said.

"Cromwell has psionic ability," Hayden said as the SUV slowed.

"What's that?" My eyes grew wide as the school came into view. The one-story, brick building was surprisingly large for such a small town and looked newly built.

He was quiet for a moment. "It's the ability to make some-one . . . believe what you want them to, among other things."

I twisted in my seat, facing him. "Are you kidding me?"

Hayden parked and cut the engine. "He doesn't use it, Ember. Not on us. If you doubt that, then ask yourself why you are having such a hard time accepting him. He could have easily changed that."

I admitted he had a point, but my stomach tipped over when Hayden opened the door. Cromwell was no longer my concern. School was.

Hayden dropped a crumpled paper in my hand. "I forgot. It's your class schedule."

I took it from him and looked over the schedule. It mirrored the one I'd had in Allentown. I clutched it to my chest and followed Hayden across the campus. Out of habit, I kept my eyes glued to the ground.

"You don't have to do that here," he said softly.

Flushing to what I was sure was an attractive shade of purple, I peeked at him through my lashes.

His eyes met mine. "You're going to do fine, Ember. I don't think you're going to run around and start throwing people into chokeholds."

Unable to help myself, I laughed at the mental image. "No. I guess not."

A wide, stunning smile appeared on his face. And there *were* two dimples. Impossible as it was, my cheeks grew warmer. "You should do that more often," he said.

"Do what?"

"Laugh."

I pressed my lips together and managed a weak nod. As soon as we crossed the entrance, the familiar smell of aftershave and too much perfume choked me. All around, people talked, laughed, greeted one another. Girls giggled with boys, and a few threw insults around. No one really paid any attention to me.

"I've got math in the other wing." He leaned over my shoulder, studying my schedule. "Your English class is down the hall and then to your right. It's room 104. Come on."

The old habit of staring at the floor was hard to overcome, but I managed to keep my head held high as I carefully navigated the crowded hallways.

"Here you go." Hayden propped himself against a locker. "I have lunch with you and bio in the afternoon."

"Okay." I swallowed, suddenly wondering how Olivia was doing. Then I thought of Adam. My throat closed up.

He leaned forward. "I'll see you at lunch, okay? You'll do fine."

Then he was gone.

Somehow, I found my way into the classroom. Taking a seat in the back, I discreetly studied everyone while I scribbled in my notebook and pretended I wasn't the new girl.

A clapping sound drew my attention. "All right kiddos, turn around. Time to get back to good old Holden Caulfield," announced a youngish teacher from the front of the classroom. "I know you guys have missed him over the weekend."

One of the guys up front snorted. "I wouldn't say we actually missed him."

A couple of kids laughed.

The teacher's smile was easy and friendly. "Now, come on. Everyone wants to catch kids as they fall off a cliff." His dark eyes drifted over the classroom, stopping on me, and his easy smile faltered. "Oh, we have a new student today."

With all those eyes on me, I slid down in my seat.

"Oh, yes. Ember McWilliams. My name is Theodore Greensburg. Please don't call me Theodore. I hate that. Also, the principal frowns on the first-name thing. So you can call me Mr. Theo." He winked. "Come on, class; let's give her a big old welcome."

Oh, no.

"Hello, Ember," said the class. Most of them said "Amber" instead.

Mortified, I mumbled thanks and shifted further in my seat while Mr. Theo rolled up his sleeves. Popping up on the edge of the desk, his gaze held mine a second longer before he cracked open a book and started reading from it. I found myself oddly enthralled with how passionate he sounded while reading— probably explained the infatuated looks many of the female students wore.

About forty minutes later, the bell rang and Mr. Theo slid off the desk, talking over the books slamming shut and feet hitting the floor. "All right, don't forget to read chapter four tonight." His gaze fell across the room, settling on me. "Miss McWilliams, can you hang out for a moment?"

As the other kids hurried from class, I was left standing in front of this Mr. Theo with no clue why he wanted to talk to me.

He dropped the book on the desk and folded his arms. "I always like to check in with my new students. I know changing schools—even at the beginning of the school year—can be hard. This is a new school for me, too." He smiled. "I just wanted to let you know that, if you need anything, you can always come to me or any member of the faculty."

A dozen or so snarky comments formed and they all disappeared the moment I met his eyes. My brain seemed to empty. I stared at the man like an idiot.

Mr. Theo smiled as if he was accustomed to such things. "I see on your transcripts that you transferred from William Allen High School. Your grades were outstanding."

I blinked a bit, relaxing in the familiar territory. My grades had been awesome—since I kind of had nothing else to do but study when I only had one friend. "Thank you."

"Got to give credit when it's earned. Especially if you see the grades I typically do."

Leaning against a desk behind me, I smiled.

"I hope you don't let those grades slip with the move and everything," he said. "It was an easy move, I assume?"

"It was . . ." Not an easy move, of course. And there was just something about his smile and the genuine warmth in his brownish-green eyes that I didn't have to second-guess. I wanted to tell him the truth.

"Was . . .?" he asked.

But I couldn't. What would Mr. Theo do if I told him the truth? He'd call the authorities like any good teacher would. I suddenly felt dizzy. "It . . . was very easy."

"Great. Well, I don't want to keep you from your next class." He turned back to his desk and sat. "See you tomorrow, Miss McWilliams."

I stood there for a moment, unwilling to leave. "All right, thanks . . . for the grade compliment thing."

Mr. Theo smiled. "Have a nice day, Ember."

Practically pulling myself out of his classroom, I hurried to find my next class.

In trig, I would have fallen asleep if it wasn't for the boy in front of me. Whenever the teacher turned to the chalkboard, he'd flip around and ask me a question. I was half-sure his name was Cory. He reminded me of Dustin—big and brawny, a square jaw and a charming smile, although without the doucheness. He didn't call me a freak, either. Bonus points there.

Toward the end, he grabbed my crumpled schedule. "Cool. We have bio together. Last period."

"Cool," I mumbled, knowing I sounded lame. Cory didn't seem to mind though. I noticed he had a slight accent. Almost like a southern drawl.

"So what's up with the gloves?" Cory asked after the bell rang and we were gathering up our stuff.

I felt my cheeks redden. "I was in an accident."

"Oh." Cory shouldered his backpack. "Are they messed up or something?"

The question wasn't asked in a rude way, but I still wanted to run. "Yeah."

Cory smiled easily. "Well, no big deal. See you later."

I watched him lope out of the classroom. The gloves were *no big deal*? Since when?

By the end of fourth period, the muscles in my shoulders ached, but some of the tension edged away when I spotted Hayden. He stood outside my history class, a half-smile appearing when he saw me. "You hanging in there?"

"Yeah." I fell into step next to him.

We headed into the cafeteria, and I grabbed what I thought was a slice of pizza and a soda. Then I turned toward the crowded room. Several students looked up, mostly girls—all staring at Hayden. He seemed to be oblivious as he pushed the tousled hair off his forehead.

I started forward, but he caught the edge of my backpack. "What?" I asked him.

"We don't eat lunch in the cafeteria."

"We don't?"

Hayden tipped his head to the side and laughed. "Follow me."

Following him didn't sound like a bad idea, but I had no idea where we were going. We ended up outside, cutting across the campus, heading toward the rear of the school. "Are we allowed to be out here?"

"No."

My pace slowed. "Are we gonna get in trouble?"

"Are you worried?"

I thought about that. "No, I guess not."

That seemed to amuse Hayden. "Don't worry. Teachers won't say crap to us."

"Why?"

He stopped beside the fence guarding the football field and faced me. "It's not like it was at your old school, Ember. Things are different here."

Several questions popped up, but I found myself smiling up at him instead. "That . . . sounds nice."

Surprise flickered across his face. Glancing away, he stepped back. "I don't think I've ever seen you smile." He started walking away.

For a heartbeat, I stared after him. "You really haven't been paying attention then." I had to walk fast to keep up with his long-legged pace.

"I guess not." He reached down, looping his arm through mine.

I stumbled.

Hayden grinned. "You're too slow, Ember. You could use some help."

He was a good foot taller than me, so I had to crane my neck. Right then, I forgot the last two years. Old Ember slipped through. "If I didn't know better, I'd think you wanted to hold my hand."

Hayden opened his mouth, but nothing came out. Then he laughed, and the sun broke free from the clouds, highlighting his hair with a dozen shades of red and gold mixed with the brown.

Laughter bubbled up and would have broken free if we hadn't rounded the corner. Sitting on an outcropping of several large, sandy-colored rocks were the gruesome twosome. Taking a deep breath, I slipped away from Hayden and ignored the urge to run in the opposite direction.

Gabriel spared Hayden a wave, but when he turned to me, his smile faded. I was sure he was picturing me flying back through the goal post.

Phoebe sat on a rock beside him, her hands balled into tight fists. "Hi," she managed.

Considering that was the first time she'd said a word to me, I thought she could do better.

Hayden elbowed me.

I exhaled slowly and glanced around. Tall grass covered whatever lay beyond the rocks. I sat down on a relatively flat surface. "Hey."

"Sometimes we eat out here," Hayden explained, "when the weather is nice."

"Or at the diner across the street," Gabe interjected. "Or wherever. Sometimes we go home for lunch. We don't always come back. Did you used to eat the cafeteria in your school? Like the rest of the Norms?"

"Norms?"

"Normals," Hayden sighed.

"Yeah, we weren't allowed outside." I placed my plate in my lap, ignoring the fact Hayden chose to sit on my rock.

"Neither are we," Phoebe said, her voice cold. "But it doesn't stop us."

They were talking to me only because they had to, I realized. Hayden had probably made them, but there wasn't an ounce of civility in their tone.

Hayden took a bite of his pizza. "Things were different at her old school, Phoebe."

Staring down at her nails, she shrugged. "Whatever." She nudged Gabe's arm and whispered something.

I nibbled on my pizza, keeping my eyes on the patchy field grass, trying not to show how uncomfortable I was with them.

"So what's it like to have the touch-of-death gift?" Gabe rolled up a wrapper and shoved it in a fast food bag.

"She's not gifted," Phoebe snapped before I could respond. "Not like us."

"Phoebe," Hayden warned.

"What? I'm just stating the truth. She died. We all know that. She wasn't born with a gift."

Between Gabe's question and Phoebe's obvious bitchiness, I lost the ability to speak.

"She's just like us, Phoebe. It doesn't matter how she got her gift," Hayden said. "Give it a rest."

Phoebe flicked her hair over her shoulder. "The only reason she's here is because of his failure. He's obsessed, like you. Do you think that's fair to any of us?"

Finally, I found my voice. "Whose failure? And how is it unfair to you?"

Phoebe wouldn't look at me. "None of us want her here, Hayden. Do you understand that? She's going to screw everything up—ruin everything."

Hayden's eyes snapped fire. "Phoebe, just shut up."

"Ruin what?" I asked, but no one was listening to me.

"Don't. Tell. Me. To. Shut up! You're the only one who wants her here!" She paused, finally looking at me. "Kurt should've wiped her."

Wiped me like he'd wiped Adam. Pure rage blasted through me. I shot to my feet. The moment her cockiness dried up and fear took over, a wild, vindictive smile spread across my face.

Moving lightning-fast, Hayden was in front of me. The heat from his body blocked the chill in the breeze. "Don't."

One word spoken so low, so powerful—everyone froze.

Then Hayden turned to Phoebe. "Get out of here."

Blazing green eyes locked onto Hayden's. "You're going to be sorry, Hayden. All of us are going to be." Then she grabbed her bag and stalked across the field.

Gabe stood, his eyes were wide and lips thin. "Well, this went just as planned, huh?"

Hayden whirled on the younger boy so quickly my head spun.

Gabe threw up his hands. "Don't blow anything up, Hayden. I'm just sayin'." He turned to me, actually looking sheepish. "Sorry. I think your little sis is pretty cool, but we all got a lot to lose."

I barely heard him. I was still fighting the urge to take off after Phoebe and sink my hands deep into her glossy black hair.

Lunch quickly fell apart after that. Gabe followed Phoebe; only Hayden and I remained on the rocks. Fury still radiated from him like gusts of hot air. I stared down at my half-eaten pizza.

"I'm sorry about Phoebe—about all of them."

Shaking my head, I picked up my bag. "What am I ruining being here? Like, is the world going to implode or something because I'm here?"

"No," Hayden said as he ran his hands through his hair.

"Why is she freaking out so bad?"

He pushed off the rock and folded his arms. "They're worried you're going to do something that will draw attention to us."

I stared at him. "Like what?"

"All of us have been trained to control our gifts, Ember, and Olivia's gift isn't dangerous, but . . ."

"But mine is?"

"They're afraid the Facility will come, and we'll all have to go to South Dakota—to the Facility. We like it here, and trust me, you wouldn't like it there."

A cold shiver lifted the fine hair on my neck. "What happened there?"

His face turned distant, cold even. "Nothing—it's nothing to worry about now. Look, all of our lives are affected. I mean, we all have to be careful."

"I don't get it. How am I supposed to care about the Facility if I don't know what or who they are?"

"Okay. The Facility is like . . . like the police of the gifted. I know that sounds stupid, but they kind of create the rules and make sure we follow them."

"What kind of rules?"

"There are a lot, Ember, but the most important is that we don't lose control of our gifts and expose ourselves to the outsiders."

I pressed my lips together. Looking at Hayden now, I wasn't too sure he had a firm grasp on his gift either. Even now he looked like he wanted to destroy an entire town.

"A lot is riding on you, Ember. It might not be fair, but if you can't control your gift, something *is* bound to happen," Hayden said. "And it's not just Olivia who'll be affected. All of us will be."

11

Pressure.

My palms were sweaty the rest of the day. Gross. I'd always thought my curse wouldn't affect anyone else as long as I didn't touch them, but I couldn't continue to hide from the fact one day I might zap someone again—by accident . . . or on purpose.

And that'd bring the Facility down on everyone.

All I knew about the Facility were the little tidbits dropped here and there. They existed somewhere in South Dakota. If gifted people acted up or did something that brought unwanted attention, they ended up there, and finally, the Facility took the gifted who couldn't control their abilities.

I did sound like a prime candidate when I thought about it, which put me in a fog the rest of the day. In bio, I got the seat next to Cory.

"How do you like it here?" Cory ran a hand over his cropped hair.

I stopped fidgeting with my pen and looked at him. He blinked and leaned back an inch or two. "It's really nice," I said.

"That's good." Cory looked to the front of the class and bit his lip.

"What's the teacher's name?" I asked, hoping that was a normal, appropriate question.

"Coach Ashford. He's a nice guy. Coaches the football team," he explained. "I'm the quarterback."

Go figure. I tried not to yawn in the guy's face. "Oh, that sounds interesting."

Cory nodded eagerly. "Yeah, I'm hoping to get a full ride at the University. Coach says I have a good chance as long I don't blow it." He laughed as if he thought that would be funny. "Gotta keep this arm . . ."

I zoned out at that point and stared at the front of the class. Actually, I stared at Hayden's back. His lab partner appeared to be just as talkative, but he did a better job at listening. And that kind of made me feel like a bitch, so I made myself focus on what Cory was saying.

Coach Ashford showed up late, immediately turned on the projector and sat behind the desk. Confused, I looked around and saw people hastily scribbling notes. All except Hayden. He looked like he was taking a nap. By the time I figured out we were supposed to write down the notes, Coach flipped to the next screen.

The rest of the class went like that. By the end, I was pretty sure Hayden had slept through most of it and that Cory suffered from some sort of hyperactivity disorder.

Hayden waited for me in the hallway after class. His eyes dropped to the load of books in my arms. "You're not taking all your books home, are you?"

"No. I have to go to my locker."

"Meet me outside?"

"Sure," I headed off toward my locker, which seemed strategically placed on the other side of the school.

I fumbled with the lock until it popped open on the third try. One of the books I tossed in slid out and hit the floor by my feet. It was my math book, ridiculously huge and unnecessary. I hated trig.

I bent over to pick up the book and froze. My mind rebelled. It must be a stuffed animal—someone's idea of a horrible joke. It just couldn't be what it looked like.

The smell of rust and death proved me wrong.

Lying at the bottom of my locker was a rabbit—a bunny rabbit, actually—the kind I'd wanted for a pet as a kid. It was the same kind Olivia would've loved to snuggle, all fluffy and soft-looking.

But the tuffs of white fur now were stained red.

Its stomach had been torn open; the insides looked jellylike. The rabbit had to be a fake, because this . . . *this* couldn't be real.

I covered my mouth, but it couldn't stop the horrified scream from escaping. Time stopped, and for the first time in my life, I wanted to have Olivia's gift. I wanted to reach inside that locker and bring the poor bunny back.

"Ms. McWilliams, are you okay?"

The voiced snapped me out of the daze. I jerked back from the locker, breathing heavily.

"Ember, what's going . . ." Mr Theo trailed off when his eyes fell into the locker. "Is this some kind of joke?"

Nausea built up in my stomach. "I don't know."

"Okay." Mr. Theo turned, about to place his hand on my shoulder, but he stopped short. He pulled back, shaking his head. "Don't look at it."

"Why would someone do that?"

"Has anyone been giving you a hard time here?" He looked back into the locker.

"No. I don't know anyone here." But I could think of three people right off who didn't like me. But did any of them dislike me enough to gut a poor rabbit? I shuddered. God, I hoped not. Whoever'd done this was messed up, really messed up.

I wanted to hurl.

"Are you sure, Ember? People, well, people just don't do that."

The sound of footsteps echoed through the empty hall, drawing my attention. Hayden stalked down the hallway. "What's taking you so . . ." His words faded off as he halted beside me. "Ember, are you okay?"

I pointed at my locker, pretty sure if I opened up my mouth I'd vomit.

"Holy crap." Hayden stepped forward, eyes narrowing. "You've got to be kidding me."

"Mr. Cromwell, do you have any idea who would do this?" Suspicion colored Mr. Theo's words.

Hayden's head snapped up, his eyes burning. I swore the temperature in the hallway skyrocketed. "No, but I'd like to know who did."

"As would I," Mr. Theo said.

"I want a new locker." My voice came out small, but it stopped both of them.

Theo cleared his throat. "That can be done. I'll talk to the principal and get you reassigned, but that doesn't address this issue here. Who would put this in your locker?"

I had my suspicions, but it wasn't like I could voice them— not with my English teacher standing there. Mr. Theo continued asking questions I didn't have any answers to, and all I wanted was to get away from the locker, away from what was in there.

"Can you take care of this?" Hayden asked. "I'd like to get Ember out of here."

"Yes, but I want to know if anything like this happens again," Mr. Theo said. I looked at him and nodded. "Okay. I'll get this cleaned up."

Hayden picked up my books and cradled them under one arm. "Let's get out of here," he said in the softest voice I'd ever heard.

We left Mr. Theo to deal with the rabbit. A few minutes later, we stood outside his car. The walk had been silent. In my mind, I kept seeing the poor bunny. What Hayden thought, I had no idea. Only after he'd dumped my books on the backseat and pried the strap to my backpack away from my fingers, did he speak. "Are you okay?"

What was I supposed to say? Yes. No. It wasn't every day I found a slaughtered white rabbit in my locker. "It's just so sick.

Who would want to do that to an animal? No one knows me here. I mean, at my old school, I'd kinda expect something bizarre, but here? No one knows me except . . ."

"Except us." Anger shone in his eyes like tiny flames. "Ember, I know what you're thinking, but none of us would've done something like that."

I slumped back against the car, staring up at him. "Then who would've?"

Hayden looked away, drawing in a deep breath. "Ember—"

"Kurt doesn't want me here. You heard him! And Phoebe hates me. Who else would want to do that? And why? To freak me out? Make me leave? Or draw attention . . ." I trailed off, heart dropping. "Oh my God, you can't let your father know."

"What?" He faced me. "We have to tell him. Someone cut up a rabbit and shoved it in your locker. He needs to know about this."

"No." I hugged my elbows, shivering. "Please promise me you won't. He'll think I said or did something. Then he'd . . . he'd send me off. Make me go away."

"Ember, he's not going to—"

I pushed off the car. "Please. Hayden, please don't tell him. I'm all Olivia really has. Please." My voice cracked, and I looked away, embarrassed. "She's all I have."

Hayden made a soft noise deep in his throat. Then he clasped my elbows and pulled me right up against him. His arms carefully snaked around my waist, trapping me in a hug.

It could have been the bunny. Hell, it could've been the last two years that suddenly made me want to stay in Hayden's embrace. Surely—*surely* not the way his heat thawed the ice encasing my entire body. Or how hard his chest felt under the sweater . . . or how perfectly I fit against him. And he was a chivalrous type of guy. Right? He wanted to help me control my gift, as ridiculous as that sounded. Comfort—he offered comfort, and I needed to remember that. His arms around my waist made it hard, really hard to keep that in mind, though.

"Okay." Hayden's breath stirred the hair around my ear. "Even though I think I should tell him, I won't. But I will figure out who did this."

"Emmie, I made this for you!"

I pulled my gaze from the television as Olivia shoved a sheet of construction paper at me. She'd done a drawing of what I assumed was her and me . . . and Ms. Liz. "Oh . . . this is really nice."

"This is you." She pointed at the stick figure with enormous red curly marks and blue eyes. "And this is Ms. Liz."

Did my hair really look like that? I ran a hand over my head, feeling a bit like Little Orphan Annie.

"See how we're holding hands?" she pointed out.

"Yeah."

"I see the three of us holding hands."

That was as likely as—I looked up, my fingers tightening around the paper. "What do you mean you *see* that, Olivia?"

Olivia pointed at the side of her head. "I see it all the time."

Any other kid saying that would have been chalked up to an overactive imagination, but coming from Olivia could mean just about anything.

She patted my knee, looking very mature. "I had fun today. Did you?"

I swallowed. Dead bunnies usually didn't equal fun—neither did the awkward dinner that every member of the Cromwell household attended that night.

During dinner, I'd wondered which one of them killed bunnies in their spare time.

"Yeah." I forced a smile. "Did you?"

Olivia crawled up on the couch and sat beside me. She launched into a list of all her new friends. She loved her new teacher—a Ms. Tinsley. They got naptime. I was so jealous of that. Then they'd watched a movie about manners.

I missed kindergarten. Things had been so much easier then.

Several hours later, Olivia drifted off to sleep with her head on my lap, and I found myself stuck to the couch—literally. I'd left my gloves in the bedroom, like an idiot. Absently, I flipped through the channels, totally screwed. And I was tired, ready to go crawl into bed after such a bizarre day. There appeared no way I could get her off me.

Another hour passed, and I worked out strategic plans in my head.

A blanket to pick her up would help, but none were close. Topple her off the couch, but that wouldn't be very nice. I glanced down at her. Thick curls identical to mine covered half of her face. She looked like a little cherub with her bow-shaped lips and hands folded under her cheek.

"What are you still doing up?"

I twisted around, spotting Hayden in the doorway. "Watching the . . . uh," I turned back, frowning at the screen, "the . . . way tigers mate." I sighed. *Damn you, Discovery Channel.*

He chuckled deep in his throat. "Didn't know that kind of thing interested you."

"Oh. Yeah, always wanted to know how they picked their boyfriends."

He sat on the arm of the couch and glanced down at Olivia. Understanding flashed across his face. "I see," was all he said. A minute went by. "I wanted to work on, you know, but after today . . ."

My features pinched as I focused on the screen, where one tiger chased another. "There's always tomorrow, I guess."

Nodding, Hayden stood and hovered there for a few moments. He raised his arms above his head and stretched like a cat would in the warm, baking sun. The pale-blue shirt he wore rode up his stomach, exposing a row of taut muscles.

I stared at him so long I felt my face flush. It seemed like such a natural reaction. My brain also chose that moment to remember how he'd looked shirtless. I turned back to the screen, wondering how I could ever look at him when I thought these kinds of things.

"Come on, let's go to bed." He bent down, and with surprising gentleness, picked up Olivia.

Immediately, blood rushed back to my legs and feet. "Thank you. Really, I mean it. I thought I'd be here all night."

"No problem." He cradled her in his arms. Olivia turned her head, drooling on the front of his shirt. "Uh, is that supposed to happen?"

I laughed, but was still unable to look him in the eye. "It means she likes you."

"What can I say?" He started out of the room. "Girls are always drooling over me."

"It must do wonders for your ego when it's a five-year-old." I trailed behind him, thinking Hayden *was* kind of drool-worthy. Okay. Not kind of. *Definitely* drool-worthy.

"They just can't help themselves." He sent me a grin over his shoulder as he went up the stairs.

Liz had prepared Olivia's bedroom with startling foresight. Olivia loved all things pink, and her entire room looked like someone had dumped Pepto all over. From the curtains and walls to the carpet and furniture, everything was pink.

It wasn't my thing.

Hayden carefully placed her on the bed while I searched for one of her stuffed animals. I came across a rabbit first and quickly decided against that one. After finding a stuffed monkey under the bed, I tucked it in with her. She wrapped one chubby arm around it and rolled onto her side.

I smiled faintly and left the room. "Thanks again."

He eased the door shut. "What did you do before?"

"Before what?" We started up the stairs, side by side.

"Before you had someone to get her off of you."

"I'd sit there until she woke up. Sometimes it would be like that all night, but I hated waking her up." My hand trailed along the banister, the wood cool and smooth.

"You have a lot more patience than me."

I lingered outside my bedroom door, drained but oddly awake. "It's been a weird day, huh?"

He shoved his hands into the pocket of his worn jeans. "Yeah, how are you hanging in?"

"I really haven't thought about it." That was a lie. I'd been thinking about it all night.

"Well, I have, and you know what I think? It could've been a prank."

"Stabbing a rabbit to death is a prank?" My voiced notched up.

A door swung open down the hall, revealing a disheveled Gabriel. His eyes bounced between us.

"Go back to bed." Hayden's voice was hushed, but the message came across loud and clear.

Gabe rolled his eyes and went back inside, slamming the door shut.

"He could've done it," I said. "Wouldn't even have to touch the rabbit or the knife would he? Not with his gift."

Hayden grabbed my arm and hauled me into the bedroom. "Gabe wouldn't do anything like that, Ember."

Even with my heavy sweater, I felt his hand burning through the cloth. Somewhat stunned by how easily he handled me, I stared up at him for a second. He really didn't seem afraid of accidentally touching me—he was crazy. I pulled my arm free and stepped back. "How do you know?"

"Because I've known him for years, and he's like a brother to me."

"Just like Phoebe's a sister to you?"

"Yeah, like that." He crossed his arms, his legs widespread

like a fighter. "And don't say you think it's her, either. Both of them were in class, Ember."

"They wouldn't have time to sneak out of class and do it?" I plopped down on the edge of the bed. "Just because you know someone doesn't mean they aren't psycho."

He crouched down in front of me, meeting my eyes. "Ember, you have to trust me when I say it couldn't be either of them."

"Fine." I rolled my eyes. "What about Kurt? He looks psycho, too."

"Kurt *does* look psycho, but he's not crazy."

"Then who do you think it could be?"

"I don't know." He ran his hand through his hair. "There's a chance it could be one of the kids at the school—an outsider."

"Why? They don't know anything about me."

"They don't have to. They could've done it just to mess with you. Some of the kids around here are really weird with new people."

A dozen or so stereotypes about West Virginians popped into my head. I'd watched the movie *Wrong Turn* with Adam. Hayden could have a point, and it was better than thinking someone I lived with could have done it. "You really think so?"

His eyes softened to a warm brown. "Yeah, I do. I'm sure you won't have any more problems. So don't worry, and get some sleep, okay?"

I nodded.

Hayden quietly closed the door behind him. Alone, I flopped back on the bed and rolled on my side. I wanted to believe it'd been some stupid prank, but the nagging worry in the pit of my stomach told me differently. People just didn't do things like that. Sighing, I wrapped my arms around the pillow and closed my eyes.

Visions of carved bunnies haunted my sleep.

12

Mr Theo delivered a few days later. "Have you had any more problems?"

I glanced down at the slip of paper that held my new locker assignment. "No. Three days without a single thing."

"I'm happy to hear that. I have to admit, seeing that rabbit even freaked me out a little bit. It made me question taking this job in West Virginia." He pushed his glasses up his nose, grinning. The act reminded me so much of Adam my heart clenched.

"Yeah, I guess it was just some sick prank to welcome the new girl or something."

"To be honest with you, I don't believe that was some kind of harmless prank." He met my eyes. "People just don't do that kind of thing."

It felt good to know someone else didn't appear as easily fooled or hopeful as Hayden. He, by the way, still refused to even consider that one of his adopted family members could have had anything to do with it. "I know," I finally said, "but nothing else has happened."

"Well, if anything does I want you to feel comfortable coming to me or another faculty member. Okay?"

The strange thing about Mr. Theo was that I did feel comfortable enough to tell him. Heck, I felt like I could confide in him. Which was odd, because who felt like they could talk—really talk—to any of their teachers? Maybe it was because he was so young, more like an older brother than an authority figure.

I shifted the backpack to my other shoulder. "Okay. Thanks again for the new locker. I really appreciate it." Something small and shiny caught my eye—a silver coin next to his grade book. I don't know what got into me. I never touched things on teachers' desks; there were rules against that sort of thing, but it was like I felt compelled. I picked it up, slowly turning it over in my hand. A carousel was imprinted on one side and the words *Ex mente* were engraved on the other. The coin felt heavy and warm in my hand.

"My lucky charm," Mr. Theo said, leaning back in his chair. "Not sure if it works, but I like to think it does."

"Oh." I flicked it over with my thumb. "What do these words mean?"

"The words are 'from the mind' in Latin. I believe all great things come from the mind." He opened his schedule planner, glancing up at me. "You can keep it."

"Oh, no." My cheeks flushed. "I couldn't do that. It's your lucky charm."

He waved his hand. "I don't need it. Take it. Maybe you could use the good luck."

I started to argue, but I realized I *could* use the luck. Hayden had said he wanted to start working with my . . . ability after school today.

I had no idea what he had planned, but I figured I could use all the luck in the world.

An abrupt wave of dizziness washed over me. Blinking, I took a step back and slid the coin in the pocket of my hoodie. I guess I was more freaked out about the secret training session than I realized.

"Thanks," I mumbled.

"No problem. Just take care of it." Then he turned back to his planner, checking off something.

I hurried to my next class, and the rest of the day kind of went like that. Every so often I'd feel dizzy and nervous. Hayden noticed, but didn't push it. I think he knew I was worried about tonight. He had this huge faith that my "gift" could be controlled.

He had no clue.

I shuffled into bio just as the last bell rang. From his seat, Hayden watched me with raised brows as I darted to my chair. I felt my ears turn pink.

"Pop quiz," Coach Ashford announced, handing out several sheets with the vaguest questions I'd ever seen. "Eyes on your own papers, kids."

"Quiz on what?" Cory muttered.

"I think the cell nucleus stuff," I said.

"Huh?"

I pointed at the last slide that was still up from yesterday. "I'm guessing that."

"What would I do without my new lab partner? I'd be lost." He grinned and nudged my hand with his pencil.

I jerked back so hard the chair screeched across the floor. Coach Ashford looked up with a frown from whatever sports magazine he had his nose stuck in. So did several kids from the front of the class.

Hayden sent me a puzzled look.

"Hey. Sorry. I didn't mean to scare you," Cory said.

I had to catch my breath. "Yeah, I'm a little jumpy."

"Hey! Hey! No talking or I take the slide down," Coach said.

Groans sounded and even a few death glares were directed at us. I started scribbling down answers as my heart thundered.

I had the gloves on, but it'd still caught me off guard. At my old school, no one casually touched me. It was like I was a carrier of the plague—at least up until the night Dustin had touched me outside the grocery store.

I shuddered.

Coach got up, walking down the aisles. "Time's up. Pass them over."

Cory reached over, almost brushing my arm as he grabbed my quiz. My anxiety level spiked through the roof. Clenching my hands, I glanced up and saw Hayden turned around in his seat, dark eyes fixed on me.

What? I mouthed at him.

He looked pointedly at Cory before he turned back around.

"We start a new section on Monday," Coach announced toward the end of class. "We are moving on to human—" He paused, glancing down at his notes. "Anatomy? Yep. That's it."

After the bell rang, I nearly tackled Hayden outside the classroom. "What's up with the look you gave me?"

His smile was dazzling, overly innocent. "What are you talking about?"

I struggled to keep up with his long-legged pace. "Did you think I was going to touch—?"

"More like, did I think Cory was going to touch you?" he asked as we stopped at our lockers. "Cory was getting way too friendly with those hands."

With a decent amount of dread, I slowly opened my locker. Nothing inside. Relief coursed through me. Day four and no dead things equaled awesome. "He tapped me with his pencil. I don't call that friendly. And I have my gloves on." I wiggled my fingers.

"Whatever." He slammed his locker shut, hands empty. He never took books home.

I wondered how, and if, he passed any of his classes.

Half an hour after dinner, Hayden led me outside through the garage. "Where are we going?" I asked.

"You'll see."

I raised my brows as he headed straight for the dense tree line. "We're going in *there*?"

Hayden chuckled. "Yes."

"Why?" I hurried to catch up with him.

"We need somewhere private, where we don't have to worry about anyone walking in on us."

My stomach went all fluttery. "There's, like, a hundred rooms in that house."

"There aren't a hundred rooms, and I don't want someone busting in on us."

The fluttering went up a notch. "We aren't going to get caught out here?" I shivered in my sweater while Hayden, in only a thin shirt, seemed unfazed by the brisk air. "Or attacked by Bigfoot?"

He laughed. "We aren't staying in the woods, Ember. We're going to the hunting cabin."

"Hunting cabin?"

"Yep. Some of the others use it, but I've pretty much taken it over. It's a good place to get away from stuff."

"Oh, well that—shit!" Not paying attention to where I was walking, I stumbled, my foot getting snagged in a gnarled tree root.

Hayden spun around and caught my shoulders before I ate dirt. He got me standing on my feet again, an uneven grin on his face.

"Thanks," I mumbled.

"You've got to be careful. There are a lot of holes and upturned roots in the ground."

"Now you tell me."

His grin spread, and I noticed then that Hayden was still holding me. And we stood so close my sneakers brushed his shoes. I lifted my head, bewildered by the sudden desire for him to pull me against him again. Our eyes met. There was a long stretch of silence as we stared at each other. What was I thinking?

And why wasn't I moving away?

A wild sort of smile appeared for a moment before he dropped his hands and backed off. "Come on. We just have a little bit more to go. I think you'll like it. No one but us knows it's even out here."

I shoved my hands in my hoodie, my fingers immediately finding the odd coin. I clenched it and ignored how fast my heart pounded. A good twenty minutes later, a cozy-looking log cabin came into view. Surrounded by tall trees and thick brushes, the cabin was even more isolated than the house.

Grinning, Hayden dug his keys out of his pocket and unlocked the door. A musty smell that reminded me of family camping trips and the aroma of coffee beans greeted me as I followed him in. He dropped the keys on a small table and started lighting candles with a lighter he pulled from his pocket.

"The cabin hasn't had electricity for a while." Hayden explained as the flame danced across his face. "I use the pellet stove if I'm here in the winter."

"Do you come here a lot?"

"Not that much lately, but I used to. It's quiet out here." He paused. "Anyway, what do you think of it?"

When he was done, soft light ate away at the darkness and revealed a rather large room outfitted with a small kitchen, an antique-looking couch, and a . . . a bed. Nervously, I turned away and folded my arms. The place reminded me more of a love-nest than anything else. Then again, the stockpile of rifles hanging on the wall kind of ruined the cozy feel.

"It's nice."

"Strange," Hayden moved past me, toward the bed.

My heart flip-flopped. "What?"

"Someone's been here." He stopped at the bed, frowning.

I didn't know what he'd seen that gave it away, but whatever. "Do you think someone will find us here?"

He glanced up. "No. Parker's the only one who ever really comes down here. Cabins aren't Phoebe's thing."

"What about Gabe?"

"No television means no Gabe." His eyes met mine. Midnight had nothing on them; they were that dark.

I bit my lip. "So what do you have in mind?"

His eyes still held mine. "I have a lot of things in mind."

All the air left my lungs. I felt dizzy. "Really?"

A wolfish grin flashed across his striking face before he turned and grabbed a potted plant. "Training, Ember. Grab a seat."

Feeling like an idiot, I opted for the couch while Hayden grabbed a wooden chair from the small table and placed it in front of me. Then he sat down, knees pressed again mine, plant in his lap.

"Take off the gloves."

I didn't want to, but I did. Taking a deep breath, I laid them next to me. "What do you expect me to do?"

"Just touch it."

Leaning back, I met his dark gaze. "Why?"

"Are you going to give me a hard time?" He sighed. "Ember, if we have any hope of getting this to work, you have to do what I say."

"*You* hope this is going to work. Not me. I deal in reality."

Hayden arched a brow. "Ember, you don't even know what reality is. You know nothing about gifts."

I rolled my eyes, but didn't say anything.

He looked sort of smug.

"Fine, then educate me. How are you the way you are—what makes you *gifted*?"

Hayden slid his palms over the ceramic pot. "A normal person uses only a small portion of the brain at any given time. *We* use all of our brain at once. Hook any of us up to an MRI machine when we are using our gifts, and it's like the Fourth of July. It's not the best evidence, but it's all they've ever been able to find. It's the only thing different between us and outsiders."

"Who's 'they'?"

The look on his face grew distant and cold—shuttered. "The Facility has searched for years to find out why we're gifted. So has my father, and even though the twins are both gifted, Cromwell has said it isn't typically hereditary."

Because if it was hereditary, then Cromwell wouldn't need to intervene with parents as often. My stomach twisted.

"Any more questions? If not, I'd like to see what we can get done tonight."

"Sure. Let's do this."

"Touch the plant, Ember."

I wasn't sure what the purpose of this was, but oh, well. I brushed my fingertips across the velvety leaf.

For a moment, nothing happened. Then the leaf shuddered. The outer ridges curled inward as the vibrant green faded to a dull, crispy brown. Death flowed through the rest of the plant, and within seconds, nothing was left but a dried-up stem hanging limply to the side.

There was a sharp intake of breath, and at once, I felt ashamed. Awful. Monstrous. "Okay," he said a few moments later. "What were you thinking?"

"I don't know. I really wasn't thinking anything."

"You had to be thinking something, Ember."

I shifted down, feeling for the coin in my pocket. Holding it in my hand was kind of comforting. "I guess I was thinking about what you wanted me to do."

"Okay. What else?"

"That's all. I mean, I could've been thinking about other things, I guess."

"Like what?" Hayden stood and walked toward the little kitchen area. In front of a large picture window, several plants basked in the fading sunlight. He picked a flower, one blooming with pretty, white and pink petals.

Closing my eyes, I forced myself to concentrate. "School. Olivia. The dead rabbit. Why Cromwell really has everyone here. Mom and Dad." I paused, sliding a look at the bed. *Never being able to touch someone. Dying a virgin. Was the pimple on my forehead still the size of a village?* "All kinds of stuff."

"Okay." Hayden sat back down, and his knees once again pressed mine. "That's a lot going on."

I snorted. "Sorry."

He grinned. "Try to empty all of that out. Get rid of it. When you aren't thinking about anything, touch the plant again."

I sighed. "It's such a pretty flower."

His lips twitched as if he fought a smile. "You ready?"

I shook my shoulders and tried not thinking about anything, but it was really hard. My brain spewed stuff out randomly, but I tried. When I thought my brain seemed appropriately empty, I leaned forward. The movement pressed our knees together even more. Crazy as it sounded, I swore I could feel the heat of his skin through the clothing, warming me.

"Ember?"

I ran my fingers over the plant. Like it was laughing in my face, the colorful blossoms went first. Pink and white petals broke off, and by the time they hit the soil, they'd turned brown. Ugh. I really was Death in sneakers.

"What were you thinking?" Hayden asked.

"Nothing."

"We always have something running in the back of our thoughts. What's running behind yours?"

Right now I was thinking about how nice his eyes looked, but I'd shave my head before I admitted that. "I don't know. Nothing's running in the background."

Hayden placed the plant on the floor. His knee slipped from mine and ended up against my thigh. Fine shivers coursed down my legs.

"Try to concentrate, Ember. There is always a thought to every action. Like something on repeat."

I really didn't want to share the thought I had on repeat right now. My cheeks felt on fire. I don't even know what was wrong with me, why I continued to think about him.

Hayden straightened, his knee sliding back. His eyes caught mine and sparked. "Let's do this again."

"Sure," I stuttered.

We went on like this for a while. I'd kill another innocent plant. Hayden would ask what I was thinking. His leg would flirt with mine. I'd tell him I wasn't thinking anything, and he would say something impossibly motivational.

A plant holocaust later, Hayden called it quits. "We'll try again tomorrow. You're doing really well."

From my slumped position, I raised my brows. "Oh, really?"

He smiled back at me, nodding. "You look tired."

Tired? More like exhausted, and I still had homework to do. Letting my head fall back, I closed my eyes. Minutes went by like this, and I only knew Hayden was still there because his legs pressed against mine. Maybe that's why I wasn't jumping to do homework.

"I really did try, you know?" I said.

"I know."

"I'm one giant fail. Maybe there isn't anything you can do. This is just how I'm gonna be, like, a 'you break, you buy' kind of thing."

Hayden's laugh rumbled all the way through me. "What?"

I opened my eyes and tipped my head forward. His smile was a big one—the one that reached his eyes, warming them into pools of liquid chocolate. Suddenly, it was like waking up or just realizing something huge.

But I had no idea what I'd realized.

He leaned forward and propped his elbows on his knees. Several locks of hair fell forward as he rested his chin in his hands. "You have to explain that one to me."

"You know how you go into stores and they have those signs

that say 'If you break it, you buy it'? I kinda live by that. If I touch someone, I kill them. So it's kind of the same thing."

He cocked an eyebrow. "You think the strangest things."

"You think so?" Out of curiosity, I mimicked his earlier movements. Our faces were merely inches apart. Anyone in their right mind would move.

Hayden didn't.

"What is it with you?" I asked. "You don't seem afraid to get close to me. Even people who don't know what I can do— outsiders—are afraid to be close to me. Like they can somehow sense I'm Death." I paused. "Or maybe it's my eyes. They freak people out."

The smile faded from his lips. "Why would I be afraid? I know you aren't going to hurt me, and if you did touch me, I could always stop it."

I made a face. "You said you wouldn't do that again."

He inched closer. "Yeah, I did say that."

"So you wouldn't flip it on me if I touched you right now?"

"No."

"For real?"

"Yup."

I moved one hand and brought it to his cheek. I didn't touch him, because seriously, I wasn't psycho or anything. I wanted to call his bluff. Any second now he'd jerk back, but for just a moment, I got to see his eyes do the color thing, and then he closed them. His face impossibly relaxed.

"Are you going to do it or not?" he asked me.

Dumbfounded, I dropped my hand. "You're nuts."

He opened one eye. "No. It would hurt eventually, if you held on. But you wouldn't hold on."

"You don't know that. Look at what happened to—"

"That wasn't your fault." Hayden shifted forward, wrapping his hands around my arms. "You know, I could say the same thing about you."

My gaze dropped to his hands. The brief moments that his skin had touched mine were too easy to recall, and now, his hands were so close to my bare wrists. "How so?"

"My gift will knock you off your feet, but I don't see you running for the door." His hands moved to cup my elbows. "You're not afraid of me."

"But . . . you wouldn't do that to me."

A small grin tugged his lips. "Ember, you don't know me as well as I know you." His hands drifted up to my shoulders before sliding back down to the cuffs of my sweater, as if he was trying to warm me up.

He was.

His touch, even though it wasn't against my skin, was doing strange things to me—affecting me in a way that created a warm flush all over my body. I struggled to find something intelligent to say. I came up with zilch. So I settled on a question that had been bugging me. "Why did you keep coming back to see me, Hayden?"

"You interested me."

"That's all? You traveled how many hours because I *interested* you?"

His lips pursed. "Because I knew what it's like to be an outcast. There was a long time when I was . . . alone. So I know how it feels."

To be lonely, I guessed. Something we had in common.

"And it was more than that." He paused, looking uncomfortable. "And I know it sounds creepy—"

"Yeah, total creeper."

He frowned, but it didn't reach his eyes. They seemed to dance. "You're not helping. I'm trying to admit something embarrassing here."

"All right, go ahead," I said, fighting a smile.

"Well, I was worried about you. I . . . wanted to make sure you were okay. There was just so much you were dealing with. I wanted to help."

Impulsively, I closed my eyes while he talked and allowed myself to enjoy the feeling of his hands running over my arms. There was no harm with this. A sweater separated our skin and I wasn't breaking my no-touch policy.

"Looking back, I'm sure there was something I could have done. Money or . . ."

"Or what?"

Hayden was quiet for what seemed like an eternity. "Find a way to make those kids pay for being so mean to you."

I shivered. Not because of what he said, but because, well, I was pretty sure there was something he'd wanted to do. Like, say, blow up their houses—or them. "Why did you finally talk to me the day in the library?"

"I don't know," he said quietly. "You just looked so sad each time I saw you. And I knew you'd seen me in the school. I just wanted to talk to you after that."

"You quoted Oscar Wilde." I smiled.

Hayden laughed. "Yeah, that was, like, the height of geekdom."

"No. It was kind of cool."

We lapsed into silence. He kept up the thing with his hands, repeatedly coming dangerously close to my skin. After a while, my arms tingled, kind of like when our skin had touched before, but not as overwhelming. When I finally reopened my eyes, Hayden had this serious look on his face. "What?" I murmured.

Shaking his head, he dropped his hands and stood. I felt the loss of him. "You know what the sad thing is? You trust me, and you don't even trust yourself."

I stared up at him. He was so right. "I don't trust your father."

"I know." A glimmer of a smile appeared. "But maybe one day you can learn to trust him . . . and yourself."

"Probably ain't going to happen." Hayden crossed his arms. "Why?"

I shrugged. The dude was his dad, so it wasn't like I could tell him that I thought Cromwell was skeevy. So I said nothing.

"You ready?" he asked, letting the subject fall to the side.

I nodded, and we made our way back through the dark woods in silence. At night, the forest took on an almost surreal atmosphere, one where all kinds of critters waited in the bushes. Needless to say, I felt ecstatic when we stepped into the house.

Hayden headed off to his room, but I stopped him with two words. "I'm sorry."

He flipped around, head cocked to the side. "Sorry about what?"

I bit my lip. "I'm sorry for what I said to you before. When you said you were here for me and I said that meant nothing."

He waited.

Flushing, I ran my hands over my arms like he had. The feeling was so not the same. "It was rude."

"You were upset." Hayden shrugged, a troubled look pulling at his face. "Adam . . . was everything to you."

I flinched. Adam was nothing to me now. "Anyway, I'm sorry."

Hayden nodded. "It's all forgiven, Ember. Friends?"

I felt my lips curve. "Friends."

13

Excitement hummed through bio—last class of the day, also Friday, and oh, yeah, Homecoming Weekend. Bor-ing.

"You really aren't going to the game?" Disbelief filled Cory's voice. As if nothing else in this world could be as important as "the game".

"Nope," I eyed Coach Ashford, who had his feet crossed at the ankles and propped on the desk. His head kept falling down, and then he'd jerk it back up and blink.

"And you're not going to the dance, either?"

I yawned loudly. "No."

Cory shook his head. "I thought you girls lived for that kind of thing."

We did—I did—but my date (if I had one) wouldn't live through the night, which kind of took the fun out of it all. "Just not my kind of thing."

"Oh." Cory twirled the pencil between his fingers and cleared his throat. "Billy is having a bonfire after the dance. You should come."

I simply stared at him. Billy McIntyre was in my English class. Nice kid, captain of the football team. I barely spoke to the guy.

Cory's cheeks turned a ruddy color. "Well . . . the other ones go—the ones you live with. They usually go—even Hayden. It's like tradition around here. Go out in the cornfields, get drunk, whatever. Anyway, you should come."

"Oh." I bit my lip. Hayden hadn't mentioned it. He also hadn't mentioned the dance, even though I'd overhead Phoebe talking about going. She had a date—some pensive-looking guy with dark hair and full lips.

I wondered who Hayden would take to the dance. I mean, he had to, right? Over half the female population stopped to drool over him when he crossed their paths. And why hadn't he mentioned the party? We were friends. Didn't friends tell each other about these things?

"Ember?" Cory said.

"Oh. Uh, I don't know."

Cory frowned. "Think about it, at least? It'll be fun."

"Sure."

Thankfully, the bell rang. A party sounded fun. So did keg stands. But if Hayden wanted me to go then he'd have said something, right? Of course, the moment Hayden and I walked to our lockers I had to open my big mouth. "Are you going to the bonfire Saturday night?"

Hayden palmed his bio book. "How do you know about the party?"

A frown creased my brow. "Cory invited me."

"Did he?" His voice was soft, deceptively quiet.

"Yeah, so what?"

We stopped at his locker. With one try, he popped it open and tossed his book inside. "I'm not planning on going this year."

"Why?"

He slid me a knowing look. "I didn't think you'd want to go."

"What does that have to do with you going? And why wouldn't you think I'd want to go?"

"Well, I thought we could work on the *thing* since everyone will be gone." He slammed his locker shut. "I also didn't think you'd be up for being around so many people."

"I like people. I like parties." We started down the hallway.

"I'll take you if you want."

I stopped and stared at my locker. Was he offering because he now felt obligated? "Look, you don't have to take me if you don't feel up to it." I finished dialing the numbers, gave the handle a tug, then sighed and started the combo over again. And then, I said something I had no intention of doing. "I can go with Cory."

His dark eyes flashed, like tinder igniting. "I want to take you. If I didn't want to, I wouldn't ask. You want to go, don't you?"

My tummy warmed for no reason.

Hayden leaned against a locker next to mine and sighed. "I don't dance—ever. An elephant has better moves than I do."

I kind of doubted that.

"I have no rhythm whatsoever. And I hate tuxes and stuff like corsages and really bad punch. Just thinking about all of that makes me want to gouge my eyes out."

"Okay." I laughed softly. "No dance."

"But I'm taking you to the party."

A stupid grin fought its way to my face. "Is that so?"

He nodded, a challenging look in his eyes. "So don't even think about arguing with me about it."

"Okay. I guess I can—" The locker finally swung open. The blood drained from my face, from all of me.

Hayden went rigid beside me. "What the hell?"

Sitting on the shelf was one of those model cars someone usually had to order and put together with glue and stuff. But it wasn't just any model car; it was the exact replica of Dad's Lexus: white, four-door, luxury edition. How someone knew that kind of detail amazed me.

But it was the driver's side of the model car that stunned me into silence. Someone had taken a hammer to it. The entire passenger side was untouched. They'd even gotten creative, drawing little red lines over the back, like thin rivers of blood. Scrawled across the side was a message. I got it loud and clear.

Dead things should stay dead.

Hayden reached around and picked it up. Fury rolled off him in heat waves.

"You gonna tell me now it's not one of them?" I asked, my voice wavering.

His eyes flicked up, and I took a step back. "We need to tell my father."

"No." I snatched the car back.

"He's not going to send you anywhere, Ember." Hayden's voice was barely a whisper. "He needs to know about this."

"No." I spun around and stalked over to the trashcan. Ignoring the curious stares from the kids lingering after class, I threw the model car into the bin. "Forget this."

Hayden had already shut my locker door. Rage pulled his face into tight, hard lines. Without warning, the garbage can turned over. I jerked back as the sides of the plastic can groaned, then split. Trash went everywhere.

The kids left in the hallway shrieked. Someone yelled for a teacher. A few hooted. Spinning around, I grabbed Hayden's arm and pulled him down the hallway.

"Whoops," he murmured.

I shot him a wide-eyed look. "Whoops? Wow. I wouldn't call ripping apart a garbage can in the school a 'whoops' moment."

He pulled away, shrugging. "It happens."

I didn't say another word until we sat in the car. "I want to go to the house."

The keys were clenched in his hands. I stole a quick glance at his face. He still hadn't finished reining in his ability.

"Why won't you let me tell my father, Ember?" he asked finally.

"I don't trust him."

His eyes widened. "You can't honestly believe he had anything to do with this!"

I flipped around in the seat and faced him. "It's not that. I don't trust that he won't send me away! I know he doesn't want me here, Hayden. No one but you wants me here! All he needs is a reason to send me away."

"Ember—"

"And yeah, I don't trust him. No one else would know, Hayden." I leaned away from him. "That car looked just like the real one. The damage done to it was like a perfect copy. So don't tell me it can't be one of them. Because, really, who else could it be?"

Hayden turned away, lips drawn.

"And who else would put a message like that on there?"

He shoved the keys into the ignition. "Even though I think it's stupid—and it's really stupid, Ember—I won't tell anyone. But if it happens again, that's it."

I flopped back in my seat, fuming. The tension and anger in his car were palpable. We drove for a while in utter silence.

Half the time I didn't want to be here, but I *was* here, and I wasn't going anywhere. And it wasn't even that I felt I didn't deserve this—maybe I did, like some kind of penance I'd have to pay for coming back from the dead and for what happened to Dustin. I was unnatural and wrong. I could understand why someone wouldn't want me here.

But Olivia was here, and that meant I stayed.

I didn't want to go to the party after the toy Lexus incident, but Hayden had insisted. "You need to do something normal," he had said after dinner. "Besides, I want you to go. With me."

Those two little words pretty much sealed the deal. So I tried to force it all out of my head as I dug through my closet. I decided on a jean miniskirt and black opaque tights that actually went with my chunky sweater. I also found a pair of totally ugly sheepskin boots, but they'd keep my feet warm.

Getting my curls to not look like one giant frizz ball took a good forty minutes, especially since Olivia dumped half the bottle of curl revitalizer on her own head.

"Mine." I snatched it from her and made a face.

Olivia sat on the edge of the bed, swinging her feet back and forth. "Why aren't you dressed like Phoebe?"

Phoebe had left over an hour ago, wearing a killer black dress that seriously pushed the dress code with its neckline. And she'd looked good.

I returned to the bathroom mirror and puckered my lips. Olivia giggled from the bed. "She went to a dance."

"Why didn't you go to dance?"

"Dances are lame, Olivia," I said, telling myself the same thing. Once I was satisfied with my curls, I tossed the bottle in a basket and twirled for Olivia.

She clapped a bit too enthusiastically. "You look pretty, Emmie."

"*Emmie* does look pretty."

The sound of Hayden's voice brought me to an abrupt stop. He stood in the doorway, dressed in a dark pullover, loose-fitting jeans, and a black baseball cap. Wisps of brown curled out from the sides, adding a boyish charm.

He also had his hands planted behind his back.

"Hey," I said.

Hayden gave me a lopsided smile before turning to Olivia. "Aunt Liz is baking cookies."

Her eyes lit up like someone shoved a diamond in her face. "Cookies? Coca-chip?"

"Uh-huh, but isn't it your bedtime?" asked Hayden. "You probably missed out on the chance."

"Nooo." She dragged the word out, eyes wide.

I shook my head, smiling. "So wrong."

He grinned at me. "Maybe if you hurry, you'll get to sample some before bed."

Olivia leapt off the bed and hauled butt out of the room. Coca-chip cookies were far more important than her sister. Her departure left us alone . . . in my bedroom.

Nervously, I picked up the coin and put it in my pocket. "You better hope there are chocolate chip cookies down there, or you'll hear screams in a minute."

Hayden laughed. "There are cookies down there. I may do a lot of things, but I don't lie to children."

I wondered what he meant by that. "What's behind your back?" He sat down on the bed. "Come here."

"What?" I sat beside him, smoothing my hands over the denim skirt.

He moved. A pair of cable-knit gloves lay in his hands, heather gray—always a good color. "I swiped them from Phoebe's room. It's going to be cold out there. You're going to need them. And they'll keep your hands warmer than the ones you normally wear. I just want you to have fun," he went on quietly, "and not have to worry about anything. You need to have fun tonight."

My eyes felt weird, like something had gotten stuck in them. I blinked a couple of times and ignored the way my throat felt tight. "Thank you."

Hayden nodded, not meeting my eyes. "Hold out your hands."

"I can do . . ." His eyes did meet mine. He had that look. Sighing, I held out my hands.

A ghost of a smile appeared. Hayden carefully tugged a glove over my right hand. The tips of his fingers just grazed the skin around my wrists, but it felt like a thousand shocks of electricity. The left hand followed next, and his fingers grazed my skin once more. Fine shivers raced up my arms, then down everywhere else.

I couldn't get over how reckless he was. Nobody in the house would even dare be so casual about accidentally touching my skin, not even Olivia.

Once he was done, his hands lingered a second or two before he dropped them. "Ready?"

I nodded, not trusting myself to speak.

Liz already had Olivia in one of the living rooms with a plate of cookies and milk. I wondered how she thought she'd get her to sleep now. The girl was about to have a wicked sugar high.

Thank God I wouldn't be here to experience it.

We almost made it out of the house without being stopped, but Hayden wanted to grab a bottle of water for the road. In the kitchen, Cromwell leaned against the counter, arms folded across his chest. At first he appeared alone, but then Hayden stiffened beside me.

Kurt sat at the table. The hairs all over my body bristled. Kurt tipped his head at us, a smug smile on his face.

"Where you guys heading off to?" Cromwell asked.

"A party one of the kids is holding," Hayden answered.

"Both of you?"

"Is that a problem?" I asked in probably one of my worst tones ever—the kind that used to earn me a stern look from my father.

Cromwell had the same look on his face, except he wasn't my father. So I didn't care. After a long stretch of silence, Cromwell spoke to Hayden. "Your curfew is eleven."

"What?" Hayden's eyes narrowed. "You've never given me a curfew before."

"You have one now."

Hayden's stance changed. His legs were spread, shoulders up. "Eleven is a ridiculous time."

Cromwell's gaze briefly flickered to my hands. "Midnight—no later."

It appeared that Hayden considered pushing the issue, but he just shrugged. He grabbed a bottle of water while I watched Kurt from the corner of my eye. Did he look like someone who'd carve up a rabbit and put a trashed toy car in my locker?

Yes.

I couldn't leave the kitchen quickly enough, but the deep, almost amused voice stopped both of us in the hallway.

"Have fun," Kurt called out. "Don't do anything you'll regret. That goes for both of you."

14

Sometime later, I sat surrounded by kids who looked familiar from the hallways at school and a few with whom I may've exchanged an entire sentence. Someone had shoved a red plastic cup in my hand as we'd arrived—cheap keg beer that tasted as bad as it smelled—but I drank it, anyway. Slowly.

Cory appeared thrilled to see me when he arrived from the dance, dressed in a full-out tux. He looked so silly, dressed so formally among the corn and battered lawn chairs. Thankfully, Hayden had thought ahead and grabbed a blanket. That's where I stayed, my legs curled under me and a cup of crappy beer in my hand.

And I was having fun.

Once the kids grew bored with the dance, they arrived by truck-loads. Girls still wore their pretty dresses, but most of the boys had changed. When I'd downed my first cup of beer, I refused a second. I was such a lightweight, and I was content watching Hayden interact with other people—outsiders. It fascinated me.

He was a natural. Charming and funny, and God, all the half-naked girls flocked to him, just wanting to talk to him, be next to him. The guys, well, that seemed a totally different story. They kept their distance, treating him with the kind of esteem that usually resulted from an innate fear. Even though Hayden mingled, he never roamed too far from where I sat, almost like he'd appointed himself my guardian or something. I'd be lying if I said I didn't feel flattered, but I also felt sort of bad. Was I keeping him from his friends?

Apparently, Gabe thought so.

"It's good to see him out." He dropped down on my blanket out of nowhere, still wearing his dress shirt, although he'd changed into jeans. A girl with brown hair and a god-awful purple dress that clung to her body waited nearby. "He's been up your butt since you got here."

I frowned.

"Not that it's not a nice butt to be up, but I mean, come on! What's he getting from spending so much time with you?"

My frown slipped into a scowl.

"Definitely not getting some, so what's the deal, Ember? What have you guys been up to?"

"Nothing that's any of your business."

Gabe tipped his head back and laughed. "You don't like me, do you?"

I thought that was a stupid question. "You don't like me."

"True." He laughed again, and then stood. A second later, Phoebe stood in his place. I sighed.

"Nice gloves," she said.

I glanced down at them. "Sorry. Hayden grabbed them."

"Did he?" She swayed to the left, a plastic cup dangling from her fingertips. "How nice of him, right?"

"Yeah, I guess so."

Phoebe took a step to the right, stopped, and then giggled as she bent at the waist. God only knows what the group of guys saw from their vantage point behind her.

I rolled my eyes, but Phoebe just shrugged. "Anyway, like I was saying. How nice of Hayden. You think he's like some great white knight, huh? But he's more like the black knight. Boy got damages. Yeah, he does."

My brows slowly inched up my forehead, the longer she talked. I wondered how many times she'd refilled her plastic cup.

"I bet he hasn't told you why he got kicked out of his parents' house, has he? Of course not," she slurred. "You don't know him like I do."

"Maybe you should stop drinking," I suggested.

"I have to pee," she announced to no one in particular.

"Good for you."

"You're supposed to come with, Ember. Girls don't let girls pee in the cornfield alone." She laughed and pointed the cup at me. I jerked back, narrowly missing a waterfall of beer. "Not that you'd know. I bet you didn't get invited to a lot of parties."

I looked around for Hayden, finding him with Gabe and a couple guys I didn't know. I noted he kept glancing over at us, but I was pretty sure he hadn't heard Phoebe. And I didn't want to bother him.

"Are you coming or not?" She hiccuped and covered her mouth. "Ugh, I think I just puked in my mouth a little."

"Oh, that's gross."

She giggled. "Yeah, it is."

I'd rather run around the party naked than take her to go pee, but a sense of girl-duty rose inside me. I shoved it down. It came back hard. The girl could barely walk straight. There was a good chance she'd get lost.

Not such a bad outcome.

"Ember . . .?"

Groaning, I stood. "Let's go."

Phoebe stumbled in front of me, but she made it to the edge of the cornfield. The further we ventured, the more the shadows consumed the fiery glow from the bonfire. I looked around, only able to make out the shapes of trees and bushes.

I shivered. "Is this good enough for you?"

"Sure. Whatever." Phoebe sat back. Well, she fell backwards, but managed to carry it off with the kind of grace I'd never have. Her dress rode up her legs, revealing several thin slices cut across her inner thighs. They were perfect straight lines, three of them, one after the other. Fresh wounds.

I squinted. There were more across her thighs. Some were older—pink fading into thin white lines next to the three angry cuts that bruised around the edges.

Even in her drunken state, she realized I knew. Slowly, she tugged her dress down and smirked. "Judge me. I don't care."

"I'm not judging you. Phoebe, you—"

"You don't know what it's like to always feel everyone." She slowly stood. "Being an empath sucks. Maybe not as bad as you, but sometimes I have to stop it. Okay? Pain stops it for a little while, but then it all comes back. Hate. Love. Lust."

"I thought Cromwell taught you how to control it?"

Phoebe snorted. "Yeah, sure. You know, I used to be able to get away from it at home, but I don't even have that anymore. Geez, it sucks. Why am I even telling you this? You don't know anything. You're not even *gifted*."

Whatever sympathy I felt for her started to slip away. "Just use the damn bathroom."

"You don't know anything. The accident?" She tossed the thick mane of hair over her shoulder, laughing. "That wasn't an accident."

My stomach clenched. A strange buzzing filled my ears. "What?"

"Don't be so dumb about it. They wanted Olivia. Not you. Not your family. So they went for it. No one knew she'd bring your ass back. I guess that screwed up their plans, huh?"

Her words hung between us. Everything else in the world came to a standstill. I felt hot, then cold. Surely I had misheard her.

She pointed at me. "You should see the look on your face."

"How do you know this?"

"Come on, it's obvious. None of our parents wanted us, or any of the other gifted. But yours didn't want to give her up." She glanced down at her drink, frowning. "My cup is, like, empty."

I wanted to shake her. "Phoebe, do you know who caused the accident?"

Phoebe lifted her head slowly. Some of the beer-fog faded from her face. "I really have no clue what I'm talking about. I don't even have to pee anymore."

My mouth hit the ground. "Phoebe—"

"I'm done here." She held up her hand. "Your freaking emotions are choking the crap out of me."

I started toward her, but she dipped around me. "Please. You can't tell me something like that and then walk away!"

"Look, I'm drunk. I don't even know what I'm talking about." She started down the dark path. Then she darted into the bushes, disappearing from view.

There was no way I was letting this drop. She obviously knew something. I rushed after her, hoping I picked the right bushes to squeeze past. Anger clawed through me. How could she say something like that, and then say she didn't know what she was talking about?

The further I went, the more the thin branches snapped at my hair and my clothing, but I caught sight of her slender figure rounding a tree.

"Phoebe!" I yelled, knocking a branch out of my face.

Thick underbrush made it hard to follow, and I wondered how Phoebe had gotten so far ahead in heels. I tripped more than once.

And then I was lost.

I stopped, hugging my elbows as I scanned the darkness. I couldn't even hear any of the kids anymore or see the bonfire. All that surrounded me were shadows. A shiver tip-toed over my skin. "Phoebe!" My voice cracked as my stomach hollowed.

Picking up my pace, I pushed through prickly bushes that grabbed at my tights. One of the branches snagged my hair again. I yanked to the side, losing a few strands of hair in the process. My heart tumbled over itself as I sucked in air.

"Crap," I whispered.

The shadows seemed to laugh at me.

Shivering, I started walking again. All around me, twigs snapped as *things* scurried along in the darkness. Pretty sure I was about to be eaten by a bear, I started running. The ground suddenly sloped upward in front of me. Stumbling, I fell on my knees. Pain shot down my shins, causing me to cry out.

The noise startled whatever was in the trees. Branches shook and leaves fell around me as birds—bats?—took to the sky, wings flapping.

Heart racing, I climbed to my feet and trudged up the slight hill. I let out a sigh of relief when I saw the highway Hayden and I had come down. Now I just needed to figure out if I should go left or right. I scoured the road for a sign, finally spotting a small green one I recognized.

Wheeling around, I headed right. When I got back to the party, I was going to find Phoebe, whip off my gloves and choke her. But right now I hugged myself and barreled down the side of the road. Cold air whipped against me, and I found myself wanting to be near Hayden. He always put off such wondrous heat, warming more than just my skin. Surrounded by the night and all alone, I could admit to myself that I was attracted to Hayden—like really, ridiculously attracted to him. A pointless attraction, but it didn't change how I felt.

Had Hayden even realized I was missing?

I forged ahead, relieved to see the shapes of cars parked at the entrance of the cornfield a ways up the road. A brutal gust of wind cut through my clothes, and once again, I pictured my hands wrapping around Phoebe's throat.

One of the cars parked on the side of the road flipped on their high beams, momentarily blinding me. I stumbled back a step, shielding my eyes against the intense light. Over the rushing wind, I heard the engine kick on, purring to life. It sounded nothing like the hunk of metal I used to drive.

I lowered my arm as the car pulled onto the road. A sliver of moonlight snuck out from the clouds, glittering off the car's black, glossy surface. Something about the vehicle triggered a memory, but it was too dark to really make out anything other than it was a coupe of some sort.

The car slowed down as I started walking faster. Watching it out of the corner of my eye, I realized the windows must've been tinted, like the Porsches in the Cromwell's garage. Black, two-door cars . . .

Without warning, the car sped up and veered to the right—toward *me*. Panic rooted me to the spot. I couldn't move—couldn't breathe as the car bore down on me.

15

Instinct propelled me into action. I sprang to the side, narrowly avoiding the bumper as the car flew past me, kicking up loose gravel. My footing felt off. I toppled backward, sliding down the incline. There was a screech as the car swerved back onto the road and roared down the highway.

I lay there, sprawled in the itchy grass, my heart pounding as I stared up at the cloudy, dark sky. It took several deep breaths to drag air into my lungs.

Numbly, I sat up and checked myself over. My legs curled inward, still working. I climbed to my knees and stood. The car was long gone, but my heart still thundered against my ribs.

I started walking toward the parked cars, reeling from what'd just happened. *It could've been accident. Kids were drinking. It was dark and they probably hadn't expected anyone to be walking along the highway.*

It couldn't be that someone had intentionally tried to run me over.

Every part of my body was shaking by the time I rounded the cars and spotted the glow of the bonfire. I hugged my arms close, but shudders racked my body.

Small clusters of kids hung out around the cars, laughing and having a good time. They were completely oblivious to me stumbling past them, didn't know what'd happened on the highway.

"Ember!"

I turned at the sound of Hayden's voice. He came out of the thick shadows surrounding the cornfield, the baseball hat sitting low on his forehead. I stared, unable to respond.

He grasped my arms. "Ember, where've you been? I saw you leave with Phoebe, but then she came back without you. Are you okay?"

"She left me in the woods." My voice was hoarse, shaky. "I got lost."

His grip tightened. "She did *what*?"

Suddenly, the whole incident with the car on the road wasn't important anymore. I remembered what Phoebe had said before she disappeared. I pulled out of Hayden's grasp. "Where is she? I need to talk to her."

Hayden grabbed my arm again, stopping me. "What's going on?"

"She said the car accident wasn't an accident." I wished I could read his expression. "I have to talk to her. Hayden, you don't understand. I have to talk to her!"

He leaned in, the hat casting deep shadows across his cheeks and eyes. "No. We need to talk."

Dread inched its way down my spine. "You know, don't you?" My voice had dropped to a whisper. "Oh, God . . . you already know."

Hayden studied me a moment, then his hand slid from my arm. Instead of letting me go, he threaded his fingers through mine. Even through the gloves, I could feel their warmth. "I don't know how Phoebe knew or why she said it like that."

I tried to pull my hand free, but his grip tightened. "Hayden . . .?"

Approaching footsteps and high-pitched laughter cut through the night. Without saying a word, Hayden pulled me toward the spot where we'd parked. "What are we doing?"

"We're going where we can talk in private."

I dug in my feet. "I want to talk now."

Hayden stopped, his hand squeezed mine gently. "I know this is important to you, but I don't want to stand out here in the open and talk about it." He lowered his voice. "We need to go somewhere private. Just trust me, Ember. You're not going to want to be around people . . . after this."

"All right," I whispered, "but I don't want to go back to the house."

"Why? It's the safest place to talk about this."

I thought about the car. It had been too dark to tell, but it could've been one of the Porsches. "I don't think so."

Hayden made an exasperated sound. "Okay. There's another place. We can go to the cabin."

"How are we going to get there in the middle of the night and still hit curfew?"

"You just need to trust me, Ember."

I did trust him. And I was probably stupid for doing so, especially when he'd followed me for years and I really didn't know a lot about him. But it didn't change that I felt safe around him. We didn't speak until we got in the car. He took off his hat and tossed it into the backseat.

Hayden ran a hand through his hair, glancing at me and frowning. "What is all over you?" He reached over, picking a crushed leaf off my arm and shoulder. His gaze met mine. "Were you rolling around in the woods? Something you want to tell me?"

"I was lost." I bit my lip, looking away. It seemed foolish to claim that it'd been on purpose. "I found the road and it was really dark. A car . . . almost hit me. I dove out of the way."

He went incredibly still in the seat beside me. "Are you okay?"

"Yeah, it just scared me," I swallowed hard. "I'm fine, though."

"I'm going to kill Phoebe."

My lips twitched. "Not before I do. Please?"

Hayden didn't respond. We drove in silence, his hands clenching the steering wheel until his knuckles turned a ghostly white.

I stared out the window, unable to quell the storm building inside me. I knew, beyond a doubt, that tonight would change everything.

We made it back to the house with time to spare. Cromwell had been waiting up, and I thought he looked seriously disappointed when he realized he couldn't bust us for being late. It took everything in my power not to rush him and demand answers, but I'd promised Hayden that I'd let him explain before I went to Cromwell.

Like Hayden had instructed in the car, I went straight to my bedroom and changed into heavy sweats and a hoodie. I put the boots back on even though I looked like a hot mess, but I figured the walk would be a cold one.

My stomach twisted and churned the entire time I waited for him. *That wasn't an accident.* Those words cut through me. I couldn't sit still and when I stood, dizziness and nausea swamped me. In the midst of all of this, Kurt's words came back to haunt me, as if he'd known something would happen that would irrevocably change everything. *Don't do anything you'll regret.*

Had he been the one driving the car?

As soon as that thought surfaced, I felt cold. There was no way to know whether it had been an accident or if someone had tried to run me down. And right now, I couldn't focus on that—not when I was about to find out if the accident that'd killed my father and me hadn't been an accident.

About an hour later, Hayden knocked softly on my door and I slipped the gloves back on. We snuck out of the silent house. Walking to the cabin in the dead of night wasn't my idea of fun. Every snapping twig or moving shadow caused my heart to race.

"This is so creepy." I scanned the surrounding dark for danger.

He grabbed my hand with his free one, giving it a little squeeze as the beam from his flashlight bounced over the terrain ahead. "Come on."

I did feel better with his hand wrapped around mine. About halfway there, something crashed through the bushes behind us, and my hand clenched his. "What was that?"

"Just a deer." By the time we arrived at the cabin, I'd about had five heart attacks and was already dreading the walk back. I waited by the table while Hayden drew the blinds closed and lit a few candles. Soft color glowed through the room.

Hayden slid past me, the scent of soap and fresh air momentarily enveloping me. I watched as he sat down on the edge of the bed. The cabin idea had been great back at the bonfire, but now I seriously wanted to kick myself.

What the hell had I been thinking? Sneaking out with Hayden and holing up in a cozy, little love-cabin? The spontaneous part of my brain spewed out all kinds of images, none of them even remotely possible in reality. He wouldn't have brought me out here for something like that. We couldn't even touch.

But we could, right? For a few seconds, maybe even more. I shook my head to get rid of the image that popped up.

"Ember, are you all right?"

Summoning up my common sense and purpose, I pulled off my gloves and dropped them on the back of the couch. Even though my hormones had totally picked a bizarre time to come alive, I wasn't here to drool over Hayden. "Tell me what you know," I said.

"The accident wasn't an accident, Ember."

My heart jerked. I tried to say something, but nothing would come out.

"You weren't supposed to know. My father thought it would be best if you didn't. No one wanted you to worry, to be scared. He thought it would be the best thing, but now . . ."

"What happened to my dad, to me? None of it was an accident?"

"All that we know tells us it was on purpose."

I lost it. "You knew this! Didn't you think I had a right to know?" My whole body tensed with emotions I couldn't even begin to name. "Someone killed my father? Killed me? And none of you thought you should tell me?"

Hayden shook his head. "You already had so much pain, I—we wanted to protect you."

"You don't know what's best for me, Hayden!" I paced to the side of the bed and stopped in front of him. "I can take care of myself."

He looked away. "What good does knowing do you, Ember? Doesn't it make it all the more painful? Does it change anything for you?"

"It changes everything!" I shouted. I was close to tears, close to breaking down. "Do you know who did this—did you have something to do with it?" As soon as the words left my mouth I wanted to take them back. The idea of living with my dad's murderers—my own murderers—was too much to consider.

I kicked the edge of the bed, but that didn't help. I threw myself at Hayden.

He must have expected it, because he caught me around the waist and flipped me onto the bed in one fluid motion. I reared up, catching him in the stomach with my elbow before he pushed my shoulders, pinning me down.

"Stop." He made a low sound in his throat as I continued to struggle. "We had nothing to do with it, Ember. My father is not about killing innocent people or taking children away from their parents. I know you don't trust him, but you trust me. I know you do."

I drew in several deep breaths and stilled under him.

"Ember?" he asked softly.

"If it wasn't your father, then who was it?"

His hands flexed on my shoulders, again and again. "We don't know. My father even went to the Facility to see if they had any ideas, but even with all their means of finding out things, they had no answers."

My hands curled helplessly at my sides. "Then how do you know it wasn't an accident?"

"We didn't. Not until we brought you guys here." He took another deep, steadying breath and tried to smile. "Liz has a unique gift. She can sense when a gifted is born—down to the exact location and time. But my father doesn't just swoop in and intervene. He checks it out first, and if things aren't right, then he tries to help out."

"I don't get it."

Hayden eased off me and sat. "We always knew about Olivia, because Liz sensed her. But then, two years ago, Liz felt a new gifted being born in the same location as Olivia, except she said it felt 'off.' She couldn't place what it was. Of course, that made my father curious, so he wanted to check it out. Kurt and I went along."

I made my way to the top of the bed and pulled my legs to my chin.

Hayden turned to face me. "The directions Liz gave us were to the exact intersection of the accident. We knew right off that something was very different with this. We hung around a few days. Then we saw a newspaper article about the accident that . . . killed a local doctor, and how one of the passengers had miraculously survived. The article listed the intersection Liz sensed. It got us curious, and we started watching, but we only ever saw you, then Olivia."

"Never Mom." I remembered how despondent she'd been. Mom had gone home, locked herself in the bedroom with Olivia, and shut me out. The last thing she'd ever said to me had been in the car, right before the accident.

"It took us a while to figure out what happened, that *you* were what Liz sensed. But my father thought that since your mom was alive, we shouldn't step in. It was the day you went to the bank that I knew something wasn't right."

I blinked. "You guys didn't realize my mom . . .wasn't right until then?"

"You've heard Kurt say it." He looked away then, his eyes downcast. "I kept checking in, even though they'd stopped. I knew something wasn't right, and when I told my father how you'd acted afterwards, he asked around."

And the rest was history, but it didn't answer one thing. "How do you know the accident wasn't . . . wasn't an accident?"

Hayden pushed off the bed and came around to where I was huddled. He placed his hands on each side of my legs. Candlelight danced across his features, softening his mouth. "After I drained your powers, Kurt found your mom. That was what he was trying to do when you came home. Once he saw her, he knew what'd happened."

Dread from earlier resurfaced, and suddenly, I wasn't too sure if I wanted to hear this.

"Your mom had been wiped, Ember. It had to have happened right after the accident, and it was a really bad job. It damaged her mind, destroyed her ability to process things properly. Kurt thinks whoever did it was interrupted, because she remembers Olivia, but she thinks you've . . . passed away."

And then it hit me. The day Adam had been wiped, the blank stare he'd given me—why it'd been so heartbreakingly familiar. The look had felt like a punch in the gut, only worse. Numbness settled over me.

"Ember, I'm sorry."

I scooted across the bed, but Hayden followed. "No." I held up my hand, holding him off. My whole arm shook. "I need a moment."

Hayden backed off, but I felt his gaze on me.

"Can it be undone? Can my mom get her memories back? Can someone . . . fix her?"

"No."

"Of course not," I whispered. My mind continued to spin, slow to process any of this. My dad was dead. Mom had been wiped. I was one giant freak. And all because of Olivia's gift?

Rage, hot and sweet, swept over me. For a moment—just a moment—I hated Olivia, hated her for something so beyond her control. Guilt was immediate, but it didn't dull the raw hurting. Or stop the rush of relief from washing over me.

My trembling hands moved through my curls, pulling them back. "I always thought she hated me, blamed me for the accident. And I'd hated *her* for it—hated that she pretended I was dead when I needed her. This whole time she couldn't help it. Why didn't you all tell me?"

Hayden rocked off his heels and sat down beside me, shoulder against shoulder, leg against leg. A muscle ticked in his jaw. "There isn't a good enough reason for not telling you."

The sound that came out of me sounded strangled. "Why? All of this because of what Olivia can do?" My hands fell to my lap and I stared at them. "They ripped my family apart. And for what? A gift—a gift that turns people into the Grim Reaper?"

He grasped my wrists and brought my hands to his chest, to where his heart beat under his sweater. "None of this is your fault, or Olivia's. There was no way you could know what had been done to your mom."

Another thought struck me. Pure ice flowed through me. "Do—do you think they wanted me dead, too? And Mom? What—what if they still want us dead? The stuff with the locker—"

"No. Don't even think that," he said.

My eyes met his for a beat, and I pulled back. "Kurt can wipe memories. How many others are like that out there?"

"There's no way of knowing how many share the same sort of gifts. We have a general idea how many gifteds have been born in the last few years, thanks to Liz's gift, but we don't know what they can do unless we investigate them."

I took a deep breath, but the air felt like it got stuck in my lungs. I flopped down on my back and stared up at the shadowy ceiling. "Do you think whoever was behind the accident may be behind the stuff in my lockers?"

"I don't know what to think." He looked away for a moment. "But I don't believe in coincidences."

I ran my hands over my face. If I'd learned anything in the last two years, I'd learned I couldn't change the past. I only had the future, no matter how craptastic it might seem.

"Are you dealing . . . with this?" His voice was so soft that I almost thought I'd imagined it.

I peeked through my hands. "I really don't know. I didn't think it possible to feel all of this at once. I'm torn up about my mom, but relieved that she doesn't hate me. I'm mad at Olivia, and it isn't even her fault. I'm pissed off, and I'm scared that whoever was behind the accident—the crash, they may—oh, God, they could still want Olivia."

Hayden shifted onto his side and pulled my hands back to his chest. "I'm not going to let anything happen. You don't have to worry about that."

I looked at him. Every cell in his body seemed perfectly controlled, and yet, there appeared a shadow of uncertainty in his eyes. "No more secrets. Promise me."

"No more secrets."

Silence surrounded us, and in the darkness, a determination sparked alive. "I want to find out who killed my dad." Fire burned in my stomach.

"I know."

"And Kurt is the likeliest bet. You know that."

"I don't know what to believe. I've known him for years,

Ember. And if it was him, then why? Why would he want Olivia?" Hayden asked. "He's been my father's partner a long time. He knows how hard it is for the gifted. It just wouldn't make sense."

"I don't know, but what about the stuff in my locker? It has to be . . . one of them."

He didn't answer. Instead, he eased himself down on his back, keeping a safe distance between us. Even after everything I'd learned tonight, my heart still pumped way too fast.

"We should head back soon," I said.

"We should."

But we didn't.

We talked—well, argued—about Kurt and his father. "We're never going to agree on this."

Hayden snorted. "And I still think we need to go to my father. This could—what's this?" He sat up, grabbing something small off the bed.

I had to lean forward to see what he held. Something small and round rested in his palm. Instinctively, I knew it was the coin. "Oh. It must have fallen out of my pocket."

He peered up through his lashes. "I can't make out what's on it."

"Nothing's really on it," I said, wishing I could take it out of his palm. "Can I have it back?" I held out my hand.

"Sure, but why do you have a coin in your pocket? I can tell it's not a normal one."

I shrugged. "I don't know. It's kind of like a good luck charm."

Hayden dropped it back in my hand. I could hear the smile in his voice. "Then you don't want to lose it."

"No." I put it back in my pocket and hoped it stayed there.

After that, we lapsed into silence for a while. Then I heard the soft, even breaths signaling that Hayden had fallen asleep. I envied him. My mind didn't want to shut down. At some point, I rolled onto my side and rose up on my elbow. I don't know what provoked me, but I studied him. I noticed things I hadn't before, like how thick his lashes were and how his brows seemed to have a natural arch in the middle. My fingers itched to draw the curve of his cheek, the line of his jaw. My gaze drifted down, over his parted lips, then further. His hands rested over his flat stomach. I found it strange that those long, elegant fingers held the power to hurt me.

Inspecting my own hands, I wondered if he ever looked at mine and thought the same thing. Though, my fingers weren't nearly as elegant as his. They always seemed stained with pencil marks, sometimes charcoal.

And my fingers killed—all because of Olivia's gift, all because someone had wanted her gift.

Slowly, I curled onto my side and watched the soft rise and fall of Hayden's chest until my eyes drifted shut. I fell into a deep sleep, the kind dreams couldn't even penetrate.

Mom looked different to me now—the thick locks of red hair didn't seem so dull, her face not so pale. Even the way she hummed didn't bother me like it used to.

I placed a mug of hot tea on the stand next to where she sat and backed off a step or two.

"Mom, I understand."

She continued to rock slowly.

"I know we fought a lot before the accident, but I always loved you. Did you know that? I probably didn't act like I did. I was just so stupid, and I wish you could really hear me now. I'm sorry for how I acted. I'm sorry for picking seafood that night, and . . . and I'm sorry for hating you this whole time."

I stopped and closed my eyes. The need to wait for a response evaporated in the silence between us. During the walk back to the house this morning, Hayden had explained that mind-wiping had to be done with a certain amount of finesse. "Like a fine art," he'd said. Done wrong, the consequences were terrible and the damage was almost always permanent.

Anger and a sense of helplessness rose. Mom hadn't deserved this. My nails dug into my palms.

"I know what happened to you," I said. "I know there's nothing we can do to change it, but I'm gonna make it right somehow. When I find out who did this, I'm gonna make them pay for this. I'll—"

Floorboards in the hallway creaked once, then twice. I whirled to the door, clamping my mouth shut. Crossing the distance, I peered out into the empty hallway. Not knowing if someone had overheard what I'd said, I pushed back from the door and turned toward Mom. My heart stopped.

She looked straight at me, her eyes unnaturally wide, the green hue surprisingly bright.

"Mom?"

Then I realized she wasn't looking at me, but behind me— toward the door, like she'd also heard someone in the hallway.

16

Self-reflection was like preparing for the SAT. I didn't want to do it, but I knew I had to. And when I did, it was going to suck butt—majorly. It was also going to take a while—mine took two weeks and a couple of days.

I guess I had Holden Caulfield to thank for it.

Mr. Theo sat on the edge of his desk, *The Catcher in the Rye* in his hands. He went on and on about how Holden had alienated himself as a form of self-protection, which led to his loneliness. And then something about loneliness being a form of security.

Whatever. At least Holden had had a choice in becoming an outcast.

But I had an epiphany while Mr. Theo's smooth voice read a line from the book. "'*The best thing, though, in that museum was that everything always stayed right where it was. Nobody'd move . . . Nobody'd be different. The only thing that would be different would be you.*'"

Mr. Theo cracked the book shut and peered at the class; his bright gaze seemed to zero in on me. "What does that mean to you?"

"The kid needed to get laid," Billy answered.

I ignored the laughter and Mr. Theo's response. I was way too focused on the fact I didn't want to be one of those statues in the museums—never moving, never changing—to forever be the girl who couldn't even touch a plant. I wanted to change—*needed* to change, but after two weeks of massacring every plant I'd touched, things weren't working.

Every evening, Hayden and I snuck off to the cabin and started with the plants. Afterwards, we sat on the couch and talked about anything. Sometimes we lay on the bed. On those nights, we usually fell asleep, and then snuck back into the house at the crack of dawn, praying we wouldn't get caught.

But maybe I wasn't trying hard enough. Maybe I was going along with the training so I could spend time with Hayden, because I liked falling asleep next to him. I liked being that close to someone.

The shrill sound of the bell startled me, and I almost fell out of my seat. Students shot to their feet, blinking away the dazed looks on their faces.

Mr. Theo dropped the book on the desk. "Ember, can you hold on a sec?"

Not entirely surprised by his request, I ignored the several "oohs" and shoved my book into my bag. Mr. Theo liked to check in every so often. I think he still felt bad over the dead rabbit.

He nodded at the last lingering student as he came around his desk. Once the room was clear, he smiled at me. "Anything going on?"

"No," I lied, immediately feeling like crap for doing so. I let out a sigh and dropped into one of the seats up front. "Well, there was a smashed-up doll shoved in my locker yesterday." I left out the noose I'd found the Monday after Homecoming. Mr. Theo already knew about that since he'd asked me to stay after class that day, too. For some reason, he'd looked surprised to see me in class that day, probably because I'd developed a nasty cold.

Hayden didn't know about either thing I'd found in my locker. I'd hidden them so he wouldn't blow up the entire school.

Mr. Theo shook his head. "Ember, I really think you need to speak to the principal. I've told you before, the faculty here does not accept bullying."

And I'd told him before that I didn't want to involve anyone else. I was about to say it again, when out of nowhere, I felt light-headed. "How is your home life?"

"It's . . . been okay." My head swirled a bit. I hadn't eaten breakfast this morning—bad choice. "Why . . . why are you asking?"

He folded his arms, looking uncomfortable. "I know I'm only your teacher, but I moved around a lot when I was your age. I know how hard it is to make friends with kids and to live with strangers."

"You do?" The lights seemed incredibly bright.

"My mother was very sick when I was growing up. We moved in with a lot of different relatives and friends of the family I didn't know well. I remember the other kids not being very friendly, pulling pranks." He took off his glasses, fiddling with them. "If it's one of them doing this, you need to tell someone."

I nodded slowly, and the truth—or what I believed to be the truth—was right there, on the tip of my tongue. I wanted to tell him everything, because maybe—*just maybe*—*he* would believe me.

"Ember?"

I snapped out of it. What would happen if I told Mr. Theo the truth? He'd either think I was crazy or he'd call the authorities. I doubted Cromwell would respond well to that. Look at what'd happened to Adam. I stood, swaying against the desk. "Everyone at home is great. I don't think it's one of them. Anyway, I'm going to be late."

A frown pulled at his lips. He slipped his glasses back on and nodded.

Guilt made me feel even worse. Besides Hayden, Mr. Theo seemed like the only other person who really cared. Maybe he felt obligated as my teacher, or perhaps he saw a little of himself in me; it didn't matter what his reasons were. I felt terrible. "Thank you for the offer, really, but everything at home is fine."

"No problem." He turned back to his desk. "Just don't forget you have people outside that house who can help you if you're having problems, Ember."

"Okay." I nodded, knowing I'd never tell him I suspected that Cromwell or one of his gifted kids was behind the stuff in the locker . . . and possibly something far more terrible.

By the time I left fourth period and Cory's never-ending talking, I'd forgotten about lying to Mr. Theo. Hayden waited by the door like he always did, and my stomach did a weird kind of shifting when my gaze settled on him—something I'd come to expect and be wary of. Today he wore this sweater . . . and it hugged his upper body like a second skin. With each move he made, the muscles stretched the cloth over his chest. Like now, when he reached up to brush his hair off his forehead.

"What are you doing?" he asked.

Since I was eye-level with his chest I was, well, staring at his chest. And it didn't take much for me to picture that chest naked. The image was forever branded in my memory.

Wow.

"Ember?"

I forced myself to look away. "Where are we eating?"

"Wherever you want." He grabbed my bag and slung it over one broad shoulder.

I shoved my hands into my hoodie while we shuffled through the crowded hallway. "Anywhere but the rocks is fine with me."

He gave me a sympathetic look. "Yeah. Yeah. How about the diner?"

"Sure."

We headed into the cool November air without a single teacher stopping us. At the diner across the street, I picked a booth by the window so I could see the trees outside. Their leaves were an array of brown, yellow, and red.

So beautiful.

"You seem quiet," Hayden commented after the waitress left our table. He'd ordered a grilled cheese sandwich with pickles. Gross. "It's not because of last night, is it?"

I turned from the window, cringing. Last night I'd taken out an entire family of cacti during practice. Not the prickly kind, but the pretty ones that sprout flowers in November. "No. I've just been thinking."

"About?"

Toying with the straw, I shrugged. "What did it take for you to gain control of your gift?"

Hayden rested his elbows on the table. "I had to figure out what caused it to happen when I didn't want it to."

"What was it?" I glanced up.

He averted his gaze. "It was a mix of stuff."

I frowned. No matter how private, Hayden usually answered any question I asked. But I must've hit a sore spot. Hayden had received a lot of training at the Facility, but out of all the time I'd spent with him and every night we'd fallen asleep talking, he wouldn't go there. And I must have unwittingly gone there.

"Forget I asked. It's nothing—not a big deal."

"Fear," he admitted, still staring at his hands. "Fear that I could never control it, that I would end up hurting someone."

Fear of hurting someone sounded all too familiar.

"It wasn't easy to get past it, Ember. I had to accept what I was, and for the longest time, I thought I could somehow hide it." Hayden peered up through heavy lashes. "Only when I started to trust myself—trust that I could control it—did I start controlling it."

"But your gift is natural, something you were born with."

Hayden sighed, wrapping his fingers around the cuff of my sweater. He had taken to doing that a lot lately. He never touched my skin, so I didn't mind. I liked to think he wanted to touch me. "You're not unnatural, Ember."

"Your father said what I could do was unnatural."

Anger flared in his eyes, sharp and fierce. "I'm sure he didn't mean it the way you're taking it." His voice dropped. "You have a gift, Ember. Just like me, like all of us. Don't you think the way you look at yourself is holding you back?"

"I don't know. I mean, you and I aren't the same. You're perfect at—"

"I'm not perfect." Letting go of my sleeve, he sat back against the red vinyl and stared out the window. His expression grew troubled, a look he got before drifting off to sleep, when I watched without him knowing. "All of us still struggle to control our gifts. I do. I haven't always been able to control it."

"But you do control yourself, and well, I admire your strength." My cheeks burned, but I continued, because I meant it. "I can't. Something is wrong with me."

Hayden rolled his eyes. "You have that strength, too. You're not evil, Ember. You're gifted, not cursed."

A shadow fell over our table, and I looked up, thinking it would be the haggard-looking waitress, but it was the last person I'd expected.

Phoebe appeared pissed off. "Gabe went home or something and I refuse to eat in the cafeteria. Move over, Hayden."

She still openly hated my guts, even more so after the bonfire. Parker had yet to say a word to me and basically avoided me whenever possible, but I kept reminding myself of what Hayden had said about him. Parker was like damaged goods, kind of like me. At least Gabe no longer looked like he wanted to toss me in front of a bus.

Hayden scooted over. "Are you going to play nice?"

Phoebe dropped her bag on the floor. "I'm always nice." She glanced over at me.

I raised my brows at her. I hadn't forgotten what she'd said at the bonfire. However, I was strangely grateful for her interruption. It took the attention off me, and she was good at keeping Hayden occupied. I was pretty sure Phoebe had a thing for him.

She toyed with the edge of her low-cut shirt, and then reached over and oh-so-casually brushed her hand over his while we ate.

Not that I could blame her. I'd love to do what she was doing.

Before the accident, Hayden wouldn't have been the kind of guy I went for. Watching him flirt with Phoebe, his hair constantly falling over his forehead, I realized I'd had no taste whatsoever before the accident. Now I wished I'd met Hayden before—back when we weren't each other's kryptonite.

It was a stupid, pointless realization.

I sank back in my seat and crossed my arms while they talked. Something unfurled in my stomach, killing my appetite. I refused to name the emotion.

When Hayden got up to take care of the tab, Phoebe and I drifted into an epic stare-down. As inconvenient as it was, that's when I remembered my self-reflection.

I broke the silence. "Look, I know you and I haven't gotten along."

She arched a perfectly groomed brow. "What makes you think that?"

I ignored that and tried to forget how she'd denied saying anything about the accident. "I'm not going to ruin things for you, Phoebe. I'm not going to touch someone. You don't have to worry about the Facility coming for you."

Phoebe glanced over to where Hayden waited for the cashier. When she faced me again, she bent forward. "You know what? I feel sorry for you. I feel sorry for your sister and your mom."

Geez, I think I'd rather be punched in the face.

"But most of all, I feel sorry for Hayden," she continued, her voice now laced with bitterness.

I leaned closer. "What?"

She looked at Hayden again. "Because for some reason, he's hooked on you like you're some kind of drug. I know he feels bad for you. I can feel it radiating off of him. I understand that. It's got to suck to be you."

I pressed my lips together, torn between wanting to smack her and wanting to beat the crap out of her.

"But don't confuse pity with caring, Ember," she went on. "Hayden's always had a soft spot for all things . . . lost and broken."

Later that evening, I shoved my homework off the bed and made my way downstairs to meet up with Hayden. A Friday night spent killing plants—couldn't get lamer than that.

At dinner, Gabe had tried to talk Hayden into going to the last football game of the season with him and Phoebe, but he'd passed. I think he was more dedicated to this training than I was.

I decided to grab a soda from the kitchen first, but it was occupied. Recognizing the deep rumble of Kurt's voice, I halted outside the entrance and tried to convince myself I had a valid reason for staying.

"He's making a mistake, Liz."

"Kurt." Liz sounded exasperated. "He knows what he's doing. You have to trust him."

"You are incredibly naïve if you think any of this is going to end well. You weren't around the last time. What it did to him when he failed. I can't allow this to continue."

Hairs on the back of my neck rose. Allow *what* to continue?

"I'm not naïve or stupid," Liz insisted. "He'll do the right thing."

"The right thing?" he repeated, sounding mystified. "Maybe you and I have two different views of what is right."

Water drowned out a decent part of the conversation. The next thing I heard was Kurt.

"You can't see past the little one, Liz. All you've ever wanted was a child, and now you have one. But she came with a price, and it's that *thing* walking around this house. If Jonathan knew what was best for him, Cromwell would send Ember to the Facility. Let her be their problem."

17

That thing walking around the house . . . I hated Kurt—hated how he consistently made me feel like a creep.

"You okay?"

I squeezed the coin until it dug into my palm. If Hayden truly thought I was lost and broken, then I would keep Kurt's words to myself. And Phoebe would know what he felt, wouldn't she? She's an empath. Empaths feel other people's true emotions. And what good would it do to tell Hayden what I'd overheard? Kurt didn't want me here. That wasn't big news.

"Ember?"

"Yeah, I'm fine." I gave him my best smile. "I just hate this walk. The chupacabra is going to kill us out here."

"Whoa. Chupa-what?"

I shrugged. "It's like Bigfoot, but it sucks goats."

Hayden's laughter broke apart some of the darkness around us. "You've been watching *way* too many cheesy sci-fi movies."

That might be true, but the chupacabra vanished from my thoughts when I laid eyes on the cabin. The soft glow of candle-light was unmistakable.

I halted, heart skipping a beat or two. "Wait. Someone's in there, Hayden."

"I know." Hayden stepped in front of me.

"But *someone's* in there." Wasn't he getting that?

"I wanted to try something different tonight. After our conversation in the diner, I think I know what's holding you back."

I shivered and huddled further down in my hoodie. "Okay. Then why can't you just tell me what you think it is?"

"I can't be sure." Hayden gave a soft shake of his head. "And I have a feeling you won't just agree with me unless you realize it, too. Sometimes it's hard to be aware of your own thoughts."

Suspicion sent me a step back from Hayden. "Who's in there?"

"Parker."

"What?" I nearly screeched. "What if he tells Cromwell what we're doing? Dammit, Hayden! You're going to get in trouble."

A strange look crossed Hayden's face. "Parker won't say anything, Ember. Of all people, he knows how important controlling a gift is. He won't tell a soul."

"Parker can keep this a secret until he dies—I don't care. He's not digging around in my head."

"He won't dig around. Parker will just be listening to your thoughts while you use your gift."

"That's digging around."

Hayden got the wide-legged stance—meaning he was in it for the long haul. "Ember, this is going to help you. If Parker can pick out what you're really thinking, then we can find out what's triggering your gift."

The idea of sharing my shame with someone else didn't tempt me. None of them knew how mortifying it felt not being able to touch something without killing it.

"Yeah, I'm not down for this," I said. "I've already told you what I'm thinking. It's not my fault it isn't working."

"I'm not saying it's your fault. I know it's not."

I shook my head. There was no way I was letting anyone in my head. That was too freaky, even for me. "No. I'm not doing this."

Hayden placed his hand on my arm and squeezed gently. "Em?"

No one called me that—no one but Adam. I started to tell him to never call me that again, that he didn't have the right, but the words died inside me. His gaze, so dark and intense captured mine. Everything else faded.

"I know you're scared. I know you think this is a huge invasion, and isn't right," he said. "But we have to find out what triggers your gift. He'll be in and out."

"It's not a damn gift." Didn't he understand that?

Exasperation twisted his lips, but his voice remained soft, understanding. "Don't you want to be able to touch people? Don't you want to have some sort of normal life?"

"Yes, but not this—"

"Remember what I told you at lunch?"

I remembered what *Phoebe* had told me at lunch.

"You asked how I learned to control my gift," he continued earnestly, "and I told you it was fear. You've got to let go of the fear, Em. Or you'll never get control of this. And you want that, right?"

Vaguely, I wondered if he had another gift hidden behind those dark eyes, because I found myself nodding, agreeing to submit to the mind-jacking.

Things kind of happened fast after that.

Parker waited for us inside. I was taken aback by how he blended into the darkness of the log walls, as if he was nothing more than smoke and shadows. He stood near the bed where Hayden and I had fallen asleep so many nights since the bonfire that it'd become a habit. I hated seeing Parker close to it. It was like this cabin was no longer a place for just Hayden and me.

It took me a moment to realize Parker held something—that something being a sweater of mine. "Why does he have that?" I asked.

"It's easier to get in when he has something that belongs to the person," Hayden answered. "Right, Parker?"

Parker nodded.

"Kind of like a psychic?" I asked, feeling dumb for doing so.

"Yes." Hayden brought a potted aloe back to the couch. He sat, keeping the plant in his lap. "You ready? It'll just take a few seconds. Parker will be in and out. It will be over before you know it."

My glaze flicked back to Parker. His bright, bottle-green eyes fastened on Hayden and me. As always, his pale face appeared vacant.

Hayden said a couple more reassuring things, and then it was time for me to do my thing. My fingers hovered just over one of the green stems, and it happened. It was like a whisper of air in my mind—a slow, purposeful brush behind my eyes that sent shivers through me.

Parker was in.

I touched the plant.

Immediately, my mind went blank. Then, like a switch being thrown, several thoughts rushed to the surface. I felt them being picked out, looked at, and then thrown to the side. During this, the thick arms of the aloe started to deflate, wither up. My scalp tingled, and then my head seemed to explode with information. My own thoughts and memories flooded me. I couldn't stop it, couldn't make sense of any of it.

A flash of bright light sent dizziness sweeping through me. It was like watching my life on rewind—not what I'd expected. My fear of being mind-raped, the conversation I'd overheard, lunch, my *Catcher in the Rye* epiphany, and on and on as Parker sifted through everything.

I think I started to stand at some point, because I felt Hayden reaching for me, calling my name. He just sounded so far away, unreal. Without any warning, the night of the accident came to life in startling detail. My eyes were open, but I wasn't seeing the room anymore. I was in *that* car, about to die again.

Dad had sat in the driver's seat, talking softly with Mom. No. Not talking. They were arguing again, fighting over Olivia. I hadn't understood why. I really hadn't even cared.

"You're saying her touch did that? Fixed it?" Mom asked, shaking her head.

"Yes," Dad snapped. "For the tenth time tonight."

"You shouldn't have ever involved them," she said.

I shifted down in the back seat and rolled my eyes. *Olivia. Olivia. Always about Olivia.* I was practically invisible to those two. So much so that last night I had snuck out and met up with Dustin. They hadn't even noticed. *Olivia. Olivia. Olivia.* I looked up and saw the stoplight turn from red to green. I was going to give Dustin the green light on Friday—the green light to go all the way.

Dad glanced back at me, forcing a fake, stupid smile. He hadn't smiled for real in a long, long time. "What do you want to eat, honey? Pasta or seafood?"

"I think we should just go home," my mom said. "I can make pasta at home."

I ignored her and picked what I knew Mom couldn't whip up. "I want seafood from Salt of the Sea."

He nodded and hit the gas.

Only a memory, but my heart raced. I felt sick. I stood in the cabin, but I couldn't pull myself out. I wanted out—needed out now before—before—

It happened.

A scream got stuck in my throat.

The headlights of the truck threw everything into a harsh yellow light, and then I was flying back in my seat. The collision knocked me into the door, spun the car around. The screaming and twisting of metal overpowered my mom's screams. Stunned and helpless, I felt the car whirl around and flip. Once. Twice. Glass broke, pain ripped through my stomach, and over it all, I could hear Olivia crying for Daddy, crying for me.

The impact was shattering, excruciating and terrifying—final.

"Nothing," I heard Parker speak for the first time. His voice strained, thick. "There's nothing."

The memory blinked out, flipped to the days after the accident. My mirror reflected an empty shell—a girl covered with scars and vacant, soulless eyes.

"No soul," Parker said. "Nothing but scars and an empty shell."

The image of me faded, replaced with several more memories. The first accidental kill, the first time I'd tried to touch Olivia, Dustin spasming on the cold, rain-soaked cement.

"No!" I jerked back from the couch, but Parker was still in, seeing everything. Panic floored me. The room spun around me. Parker let out a startled sound and pulled out all at once, but the room still spun. I felt sick, twisted.

"Ember? You okay?" Hayden said, coming to his feet. "What's going on? Parker?"

"I'm gonna be sick," I mumbled. I was too hot, too cold.

Hayden stood beside me, leaning down because I was bent over, grasping my knees. The dead aloe now looked like a skeleton to me. I stumbled back against Hayden, staring at Parker now.

His face constricted as he grabbed the side of his head, over his temple and winced. "She thinks she has no soul. It's always in the back of her mind. She thinks she has no soul."

The last thing I heard was Hayden yelling my name, and then nothingness closed over me.

Eventually I woke up. Shadows danced across the ceiling. My head felt fuzzy and sitting up didn't help.

"Ember."

The bed dipped beside me. Turning, I met Hayden's eyes. I was kind of struck by their color. They were brown, not black. Warm. Rich. So deep, I could fall into them and never come back out. Then I remembered.

I swung out at him, catching him in the shoulder.

"Hey!" Hayden said. "Take it easy."

I hit him in the chest, but it was like hitting a wall. "Damn you! You told me he'd be in and out! You said he wouldn't dig around in my head."

"He wasn't supposed to. I don't know what got into him."

"Whatever." I scrambled off the bed. "I want to go back to the house. Now."

Hayden arched a brow. "You won't go back through the woods without me, and I'm not leaving."

"You wanna bet?" I spun around and headed for the door.

Hayden jumped off the bed. In an instant, he was in front of me. The look he shot me was a pure challenge. "Not until we talk about what Parker saw."

Cursing, I looked around for another exit. There was a good chance I was being unreasonable, but I didn't care. There were things people never needed to know. Things I'd never wanted Hayden to know.

Again, he moved fast, way too fast. He caught me by the shoulders and turned me around. "You're not leaving."

I glared at him. "You can't make me stay here."

"You don't want to talk to me?"

"No! I don't even want to see your face right now."

He smiled—actually freaking smiled. "You're being a bit dramatic, don't you think? No one hurt you."

"Uh, I passed out! What do you call that?"

"I've never seen that happen before, but I guess going as long as Parker did made you a little lightheaded. I had to carry you to the bed."

I stopped trying to wiggle out of his grasp. Man, I'd missed him carrying me? "You carried me?"

He nodded. "I almost dropped you. Parker left after that."

"Gee, good to know."

"Em, we're not leaving this cabin until we talk about what Parker saw."

I pushed against his stomach, getting nowhere. Giving up, I went back to the bed and sat down. "Why did Parker go that far back? There were things . . . I didn't want him to see."

"You want to talk now?"

I glared at him. "I want to punch you. Just answer my question."

Totally unbothered by my threat, Hayden sauntered over to the bed and sat beside me. "I guess he wasn't getting the answer we needed." He paused, his earlier amusement faded. "Do you really think you don't have a soul?"

I stared down at my hands—hands that killed.

"Em?" He twisted toward me, his knees brushing my leg. "Parker said you think you don't have a soul."

"I don't want to talk about it, Hayden. Please."

He was silent for several heartbeats. Finally, he spoke. "There were other things that Parker said he saw."

I pulled on the hoodie's string and twisted it around my finger.

Hayden's gaze dropped over me. "Why do you always wear long sleeves? Is it because of what Parker saw?"

The string tightened around my finger until I thought it would cut the circulation. "He didn't tell you?"

"No. He only said you were scarred. At first, I thought he meant . . . well, something else, but then I thought about it. You always wear long sleeves, even to sleep in. I don't think I've seen your arms."

I shrugged.

He inhaled softly. "Do you trust me?"

I risked a quick look at him. "Why do you ask?"

"Do you?"

"I guess so. Even though I shouldn't after the crap you pulled, but whatever."

Hayden reached for me. Well, not me actually. He went for the hem of my hoodie, sliding his fingers under it.

My hands clamped down on his arms as the muscles in my stomach tensed. "What are you doing?"

"You said you trust me."

"That was before you tried to take my clothes off!" The moment the words left my mouth, a hot flush crept over me. Because, really, was that what he intended? Because . . . because I didn't know what to think about that.

He gave me a bland look. "You have a shirt on underneath. I can feel it."

"That's not the point," I sputtered. I actually had a tank top on underneath, not that it mattered. He wasn't seeing it.

"Em, you said you trust me."

My fingers curled around his sweater as my heart revved up to a ridiculous speed. "Hayden . . . no one—you wouldn't want to see this."

"I don't think you give me enough credit."

"It's not that. I do give you credit, but this—this is different." I stared down at his fingers. They were perfect, a far cry from what I looked like. "I . . . I died in that accident, Hayden. It wasn't my imagination. I was dead and there was a reason for it. I must've been really messed up."

"Do you think I'll look at you differently? That it would somehow change how I see you?"

He sounded kind of offended, and I had to look up; I had to see him. Our eyes met. There wasn't a challenge in them anymore. I don't know what I saw in them, but I felt my fingers relax and then let go.

Needing no other invitation, Hayden gathered the hem in his hands and began tugging it up and up. He pulled the hoodie over my head, exposing almost all my secrets.

18

I could feel his eyes traveling over my arms and across the swell of my chest. Hayden was checking me out, but not in a way I'd ever wanted a guy to look at me. I knew what he saw.

Angry lines slashed across my upper arms, and faint scars spread across my chest and disappeared under my tank top. They'd originally been red, but they'd now faded to white. Sometimes when I looked in the mirror, I thought the scars looked like someone had dropped a spiderweb over my body. The only parts of me not scarred were my legs.

A minute went by before Hayden spoke. "Does it . . . does it hurt?"

Opening my eyes, I stared into the dark corners of the cabin. I felt vulnerable, exposed. "No. It never hurt. Not when I . . . came back."

He let out a stilted breath. "But before?"

I forced a casual shrug and glanced at him. He wasn't staring at the scars, but at my face. "Yeah, it hurt. Can I have my sweater back now?"

"No." Hayden dropped it on the floor. "You shouldn't have to hide yourself."

"Doesn't it bother you?"

He frowned. "Why would it bother me?"

"Because . . . because it's ugly. I look like Frankenstein."

"You don't look like Frankenstein," he said, so softly I almost didn't hear him.

"Trust me, I know how I look."

"Okay. What do you want me to say? That I see those scars and wonder how badly it had to hurt to end up that way? Or how wrong I think it is that you let those scars take away from everything else?"

"Take away from what?"

"Em, the scars on your arms are barely visible. You could wear shirts without sleeves. No one would notice, and you . . . well, no one would pay attention to the scars."

I still wanted to jump up and grab my sweater, but I forced myself to stay put.

"How does it feel?"

"What?" I stared straight ahead, focusing on the darkness.

"To die."

Dying wasn't easy to put into words. "Nothing—it feels like nothing. One minute, there was pain, and then there was nothing. Just empty blackness and you're kind of aware of everything, but not. You kinda feel it here." I placed a hand over my stomach. "When you die you feel it empty and leave you."

"Feel what?"

I snuck a quick peek at him. He was watching me intently, his face soft. Before I lost my nerve or thought better of it, I reached out and placed my hand on his lower stomach. Even though he wore a sweater, I could feel the heat his skin was throwing off.

"Your soul," I said quietly. I knew I had told him I didn't want to talk about it, but here I was with a mad case of verbal diarrhea again. "You feel it burn itself out. Like a candle."

Hayden inhaled roughly. "You really think you don't have a soul?"

I pulled back and shrugged again.

"All because of your touch?" Hayden shifted and leaned on one arm. His breath danced over my shoulder.

I shivered. "Well, yes. That, and the fact that I felt it go poof."

"Em, you have a soul."

"How can you be so sure of that, Hayden? How many people die and come back?"

"No one dies and comes back. You did because of your sister, and you have a gift. Maybe that played a role in your coming back, but you have a soul. You aren't evil. There's nothing you can say that will make me think that."

I looked up and our gazes locked. "And there's nothing you can say to make me feel differently."

He lowered his eyes. Thick lashes fanned his cheeks. "I know you do, because I wouldn't want to . . . to kiss you if you didn't have a soul."

I froze. "You . . . you want to kiss me?"

His gaze lifted as he leaned in, placing his mouth an inch from mine. The air was sucked right out of the room, and I felt dizzy again. "Ever since I first saw you." He moved so that his mouth was angled with mine. "And right now I want to so badly it hurts. You have no idea, Em, but I don't want to hurt you."

My gaze dropped to his parted lips. What would it be like to feel them against my own? Unable to stop myself, I brought my mouth within a hair's breadth of his. "I want to kiss you, too."

Hayden made a soft sound in his throat. His breath moved over my lips, and I closed my eyes, imagining the way he would feel, taste. Then his breath warmed my cheek and each of my eyelids before it returned to tease my lips again.

I placed my hands on his chest, curling my fingers into his sweater. "Hayden," I whispered.

He answered by clasping my hips and pulling me into his lap. I wanted nothing more than to kiss and touch him. I lowered my cheek to his shoulder, squeezing my eyes shut as his caress drifted from my hips to the small of my back. Fine shivers danced over my skin, making me ache for something I could never have.

His hands traveled up my back, fingers pressing into my spine, bunching the thin material of my tank top, then back down. My body arched into the motion, and his hands shook. Each time his hands came close to my bare skin, it felt like every cell came alive only to slowly burn out. His breathing turned ragged.

I don't know how long we stayed like that, coming close to touching—to *something*—until Hayden drew in a heavy breath and lifted me off of him. "Enough," he murmured. "God, but it's not enough."

"I'm sorry." I lowered my chin, wishing I were someone else, someone he could kiss, he could touch.

Hayden leaned back, brushing a few of my curls back as his eyes met mine. "Don't apologize. I'm enjoying this. You have no idea how long I've wanted it to be like *this* between us and I don't want to stop, but . . ."

"But you're afraid you won't stop?" I asked, feeling my skin flush even more.

"Exactly." His smile was crooked as he lay back, patting the spot next to him. "Come here."

I raised my brows at him. Lying beside him was so not going to quell the fire burning in my blood. And a part of me couldn't believe what he'd admitted or what had happened between us. It seemed surreal, like a dream I'd never thought I could grasp.

Hayden's gaze fell to my lips.

My heart did a stupid little jump that made me all warm and fuzzy. He liked me—really liked me. Even after seeing my scars. It was like hitting the jackpot of awesome guys.

"Come on." He patted the spot next to him again.

"It's a Friday night. Shouldn't you be out having fun or something?"

One corner of his mouth tipped up. "I'm having fun here. Lots." He placed his hands behind his head. Straightening out his legs, he nearly knocked me off the bed.

I didn't have much of a choice. Carefully, I climbed over his legs and sat down on the other side.

"Lie down," he ordered.

"Hayden."

The smile grew. "Ember?"

I rolled my eyes, but did as he requested. "Happy?"

"Yep."

Tilting my head so I could see him, I smiled when he winked at me. "You . . . you surprise me."

Hayden rolled onto his side, propping himself up on one elbow. "How do I surprise you?"

I bit my lip. "You worry about hurting me, but you never seem to worry about me hurting you. And I'm the one with the killer touch."

"I don't because I know you won't hurt me." His gaze drifted over my face, then lower. He wiggled closer. Our knees pressed together, sending sharp tingles down my legs.

"Can I ask you something? Personal?"

He sent me a sidelong glance. "Sure."

"How old were you when Cromwell found you?"

His eyes moved back to the ceiling. The smile was gone. In its place was a dark, brooding look. "I was seven."

"Were you still with your parents?"

A shake of the head, a fine tensing of muscles followed. "No. I was in foster care."

I bit my lip. I didn't have any experience with foster homes, but it was a fear that'd driven me to do everything possible to keep Olivia out of them. "How did Cromwell find you?"

Hayden relaxed and tipped his head down. "He came to the foster home—the eighth one in two years." He stopped, laughed. "It was the beginning of summer, and he just showed up. The rest is history."

"What is it about the Facility? It's like they are so evil, but you've been there. It sounds like Cromwell worked for them. I don't get it."

"The Facility is complicated."

"Well, try explaining it to me. I may end up there one day."

Hayden frowned. "You'll never end up there, Em."

"How can you be so sure of that?"

He flipped onto his back, but somehow he was closer than before. "I'd never allow it. The Facility isn't evil, but they have their own methods of training. They're harsh at times, demanding. To them, being gifted is everything. Their motto, *'What lies behind you and what lies in front of you, pales in comparison to what lies inside of you,'* isn't what Emerson believed when he said those words, you know?"

"How long were you there?" I asked, not really expecting him to answer.

"I . . . I was seven when I got there. Eleven when I left. So . . . four years, give or take a couple of months. It was better than foster care, but in a way, it was also worse. There were a lot of rules. They monitored every single moment, so I had no time to myself. And there were a lot of tests. They liked to . . . push you to your limits. To really test your control and see what it took for you to lose it." He trailed off, staring at the ceiling. "Anyway, tell me something about you. Something I don't know."

There was a lot he wasn't sharing, but I let it drop. "I don't know. My favorite part of winter is the first snowfall. I . . . love the way autumn smells. I've never seen a shooting star."

"Really?" He sounded surprised. "I haven't, either."

I smiled a little. "I've always looked, but I've never seen one."

"I've never had a pet," he admitted with a low laugh. "Not even a goldfish."

"Goldfish don't count, anyway."

He laughed again and time slipped away from us. Only a pale slice of moonlight fell across the bed. At some point, while we talked, I forgot that he could see the scars and I actually felt normal. But every so often, he'd stop talking and would look at me, and I knew what he wanted to do.

"It's late," Hayden announced after dragging his gaze from me. "Do you want to leave?"

I thought about it. "No. I'm not tired yet."

"You wanted to leave earlier."

"I also wanted to punch you earlier," I pointed out. "You don't want to do either of them now?"

"No."

"Good. I have an idea," he said. "You game?"

A strange, intense feeling coiled in my stomach. "Sure," I breathed.

"Don't move." He sat up. "Don't punch me, either."

"No promises." Punching him wasn't what I had in mind.

"Just don't freak out, all right?" Hayden shifted down, and then I felt his hand slide through my hair. "Come over here."

At first I didn't get where "here" was, but it quickly became obvious. Somehow Hayden got me to put my head on his chest. Not that I needed a lot of urging.

On my side, my cheek lay against the soft material of his sweater and when he rested his hand against my lower back, I thought I'd die. This was almost as good as what'd happened earlier. Maybe it was even better, just lying there, concentrating on the steady thrumming of his heart and the wild fluttering of mine.

"Are you comfortable?" he murmured.

"Yeah," I whispered, closing my eyes. Truth was I enjoyed this way too much, but I refused to let myself dwell on it. Thinking was overrated. So was reality. In the dark, anything seemed possible. *This* was possible.

"Good idea, huh?"

I smiled sleepily against his sweater. "Yeah, it was."

He chuckled softly. The sound rumbled through me, curling my toes. Silence enveloped us and I started to drift off, content to just be this close to someone, to him.

Something jolted me straight up in bed. In the dark, I could make out the steady rise and fall of Hayden's chest. For a moment, I didn't know what bothered me.

Then it struck me.

Something in the memory of the accident Parker had resurfaced was really, super important. I couldn't believe I'd missed it.

My parents had known about Olivia's gift.

I turned to Hayden, needing to tell him. For a few seconds, I simply stared at him. Thick, sooty lashes fell against his cheeks, his lips parted with each deep breath he took. Asleep, the natural beauty of his face seemed even more alluring, more vulnerable. It was a shame to wake him up, to disturb him, but I figured this was pretty important. He'd want to know.

"Hayden?" I inched closer, resting on my knees beside his waist. "Wake up."

He didn't move; not even a lash stirred.

"Hayden, wake up. Come on, wake up."

Nothing.

I placed my hands on his shoulders and shook him. "Come on. I have to tell you—"

He shot up like a rocket, knocking me flat on my back. Then he was on me, sliding down my hips, straddling them, pinning my legs down. All of it happened so fast, was so unexpected, that I simply froze.

Holding himself up with his hands planted on either side of my head, Hayden lowered his. In that heartbeat, I didn't recognize him, didn't know the look in his eyes or the tense pull to his lips. He'd become a virtual stranger.

And I knew beyond a doubt he had no idea who I was.

"Hayden?" I whispered, putting one shaking hand on his chest. "It's me."

He blinked and inhaled sharply. "Don't ever do that again, Ember."

I stared up at him, my heart thundering in my chest. His eyes were darker than I'd ever seen.

"I could've hurt you."

Him hurt me? In any other situation, that might've been funny. It wasn't now. I swallowed. "Okay."

His chest rose and fell unsteadily above mine. His body threw off an amazing amount of heat. "I'm . . . sorry I scared you. There were too many nights in foster homes being woken up like that. It was never good."

I let out the breath I was holding, unsure of what to say. I could only imagine what he meant by that, and each idea grew more horrible than the last.

He closed his eyes, his voice ragged. "I'm sorry. This was a—"

"No. It's okay. You just startled me. I'm okay. You're okay."

Hayden opened his eyes. "Em . . .?"

His stare held so much intensity that I found it difficult to breathe. A look of yearning, of desperation, and he was studying me. Studying my face, the way my top had slipped down. And his stare was spreading a hot flush over my body.

Slowly, he dipped down, placing his weight on one arm. He brought his hand to the side of my face, his fingers hovering over my cheek. My own fingers curled into the sweater. God, I wanted him to touch me so badly. The need consumed me— burned like fire.

Hayden closed his eyes and let out a harsh sound before he pushed himself up on his knees. His hands fell harmlessly to his sides.

Disappointment crashed over me. I'd wanted him to pull me into his body like he'd done before, mimicking things we really couldn't do.

"So . . . what did you wake me up for?" he asked, his voice thick.

It took me a minute to remember what had been so important. "My parents—they knew about Olivia's gift."

He rolled off my legs and stood. I had a feeling he purposely put distance between us as he struggled to pay attention to what I'd said. "What do you mean?"

I sat up, forcing the thick cobwebs of half-sleep and something far more distracting from my thoughts. I fixed my top, flushing like crazy. "When Parker was in my head, I saw the accident again. I don't know how I missed it, but I guess I'd been so freaked out after everything, I just didn't think."

"Understandable." He ran a hand through his hair. "What did you remember?"

I told Hayden what my mom had said and how Dad had answered. While I talked, he shifted further into the shadows, where the dimming light of the candles couldn't reach.

"Olivia must have used her gift before she brought you back," Hayden said.

"Yeah, but who are 'they?' The ones who my mom said he shouldn't have told? Do you think he told the people who caused the accident?"

A full minute passed before he answered. "I don't know, Ember. That doesn't make sense. Maybe your memory is wrong."

"It's not wrong, Hayden. I know what I heard."

"Your parents wouldn't have known who to go to even if Olivia raised an army of the dead," he said. "We don't advertise what we are—neither does the Facility. We find the gifted; they don't find us. How would your parents have known who to go to?"

"I don't know," I said tightly. "They had to've known. Or maybe someone came to them first." An a-ha moment hit me. "You said before that Liz can sense the gifted—when they are born, right? And she sensed me when I came back?"

"Yeah."

"And she knew about Olivia, right? You said so yourself."

"So what? Just because Liz knew about Olivia doesn't mean anything. Wait. Do you really think my father—*Aunt Liz*, who doesn't even like to kill a mouse—would've orchestrated a car accident to get to Olivia?"

I scowled into the general vicinity of where I thought Hayden stood. "Yeah, I do. Or maybe Liz and Kurt did. They seem awful chummy with one another, and Liz treats Olivia like she's her damn daughter."

"That's because she cares for her." Hayden shook his head. "Look, none of this makes sense."

"Exactly," I said.

"It's almost like you want it to be my father or Kurt."

"I don't want it to be them, but who else could it be? My parents wouldn't have known who to go to, but they told some-one! Then Liz magically senses me coming back from the dead and look! Look. Olivia is here, isn't she?"

Silence greeted me, and I felt like doing a happy dance, because I knew I'd gotten Hayden thinking. But when he did speak again, it was a total letdown.

"We should head back, Ember. In the morning, we'll try to figure it. My brain is too fried right now."

My head jerked up. Hayden sounded different, off. I climbed off the bed and waited while he extinguished the candles. He kept his back to me the entire time, not speaking. My nerves were like a tight bundle in the pit of my stomach, unraveling with each passing second we didn't talk.

I pulled the hood up and hunkered down in the hoodie once we stepped out into the near-freezing night air. Overhead, the moon peeked through the naked branches while we headed back to the house in silence. Each glimpse of Hayden I snuck, my stomach rolled. His face was set in hard lines, closed-off and distant. He stared straight ahead, and never once did I feel his gaze on me. It was like those precious moments in the cabin, when he'd admitted how much he wanted to kiss me, hadn't even happened.

We stopped at the stairs, and I wasn't ready to let this go. "I want to talk about—"

"I know," he said, "but I don't want to. Not tonight. I'm beat. It's late."

"But—"

He stepped forward, tipping his head down as he did so. "We can't talk about this now. We'll wake someone up. Go to bed, Ember. We'll talk in the morning."

I stepped back, my heart twisting. "Okay. Tomorrow morning, right?"

He nodded, and before I could say anything else, he disappeared down the hall.

19

I didn't see Hayden in the morning or even that afternoon. Actually, I didn't get a chance to see him at all Saturday— not for more than five seconds. I was damn sure he was avoiding me.

By Sunday afternoon, the momentary satisfaction of casting doubt on Cromwell and crew soured. Hayden had always believed his adopted father's involvement with the gifted was to do something good, but whoever had wanted Olivia had killed to try and get her. And whether Hayden liked it or not, the evidence pointed to one of his family members—one of the people he trusted.

When I saw him climb the stairs to the front porch, I'd just finished braiding the hair on Olivia's doll. Racing out of the room without a word, I threw the front door open, almost plowing it to him. He stood, one hand outstretched and eyes wide.

Phoebe was behind him, a carryout box in her manicured hand.

"Hey," I gasped out, ignoring Phoebe's curious stare.

Hayden took a step back. "Hey."

"Can we talk?"

His lips pursed. "I have some things I—"

"*Please.*" I knew how I sounded and I didn't care.

Phoebe glanced between us, and then she slinked past Hayden. "I'll put this in the fridge for you."

"Thanks," Hayden answered, staring down at me. He inhaled and let it out slowly. "Okay, but I don't have long. Walk?"

I nodded, following him down the steps and toward the tree line. I couldn't believe it'd only been two days since I'd talked to him. It felt like years. Spending time with Olivia had been okay, but I missed Hayden. The moment we cleared the house, I opened my mouth.

"Are you mad at me?" I hadn't wanted to say that.

He stared straight ahead. "Is that why you wanted to talk to me?"

Okay. His voice sounded different—maybe even cold—but no big deal. "No, that's not what I wanted to talk to you about."

"Then what?"

My brain sort of emptied that moment. Hayden stopped walking, turned and faced me. His arms were folded across his chest and he waited. Waited for me to say whatever I wanted to say so . . . so he could *leave*. Well, this wasn't going as planned. Not that I had a plan.

"Did you go have lunch with Phoebe?" I stalled.

Hayden nodded.

A hollow feeling opened up in my chest. Stupid, but all I could think was that he never took me to lunch. Not when we were out of school.

"Ember?"

I swallowed. "I wanted to talk about what I told you in the cabin."

"The thing about your parents knowing about Olivia's gift?" He stared above my head.

"Yes. I've been thinking about it. A lot actually, and I know what I heard." I saw the moment he decided he didn't want to talk about this. It was in his eyes—they went all dark. I plunged ahead. "These things have to be connected. You believe someone caused the accident to get to Olivia. Now, someone is sticking stuff in my locker. Like . . . like they want me to leave or something."

"There's no way of knowing if those two things are related."

"You can't be serious! You know the two things are connected."

"What are you getting at, Ember? That my family is not only behind cutting up dead animals and leaving them in your locker, but also caused your car accident?"

"Yes."

He sighed and shook his head. "Look, I know that you don't trust them. I get that. Really, I do, but I know my family. *I know them.* They wouldn't do something like that, because they aren't horrible people. And what was done to your family—to you— was horrible."

"Then can you tell me who else to blame?" I practically yelled. "You said it yourself, Hayden. My parents wouldn't know who to go to."

"That doesn't mean it was my family."

"Oh. So the fact that you broke into my home, kidnapped us, and brought us here isn't at all suspicious to you? That no one was interested in Olivia until *Aunt* Liz sensed me? Bullshit."

"Ember."

"No." I pushed a hand through my hair wildly. I knew my curls had to be standing up every which way, but I didn't care. "The note on that toy car—'dead things should stay dead?' And then again on the noose—"

Hayden's eyes narrowed. "What noose?"

Whoops. I took a step back. "That's not important. What's important is how anyone else in the world could know about that."

"I've thought about this," he said after several long moments of silence. "It's not like I've ignored the obvious, but I can't—I *won't*— believe my family had anything to do with it. I'm sorry, Ember, but instead of spending time obsessing over how evil my family is, we could be figuring who really is behind this."

"Oh. Is that what you've been doing? Working to prove your family's innocence? Well, good luck with that."

The scent of something burning surrounded me, and Hayden's lips thinned and now his eyes were all black. I knew I'd struck low. "Are you done yet?"

"No."

"I am." Then he was walking away.

"Hayden!" I yelled, feeling the sting of tears in my eyes.

He stopped, but didn't turn around.

My heart leapt into my throat. "Do you regret what happened in the cabin?"

I didn't have to explain it any better than that. By the way he stiffened, he knew I was talking about his admission and how we had clung to each other, desperately wanting more.

"No. That's not what I regret," he said.

And then he was gone and I stood there, staring at the place he'd been—alone with the cold knowledge that things had altered between us and I had no idea where it left me.

Things just kind of sucked after that.

Hayden's and my drives to school were tense, and they usually ended with us arguing by the time we pulled into the school parking lot. I spent my mornings stewing over how adamantly he refused to believe his family had anything to do with what'd happened. They were all saints and angels in his book.

Even though I knew I needed to stop pushing it with him, I couldn't. I needed him—needed someone—to believe me. It wasn't like I'd imagined these things. It all seemed obvious to me, but they were his family. On a daily basis, I basically accused the people he trusted and loved most of murder.

I didn't even know why we bothered eating lunch together, because we argued then, too, but by Wednesday, Phoebe and Gabe joined us. It was almost like they'd sensed their presence had been needed. Either that, or Hayden had asked them to.

Phoebe struggled with lunch. Even I could see that. So I did try to cut back on my frustration when she was around. I don't know why I bothered. It didn't make her any nicer to me and it sure as hell didn't help things with Hayden. Our lunches usually ended with Hayden whisking off a pale, shaken Phoebe.

We tried practicing Monday night in the cabin, but that had ended in a spectacular disaster. Somehow a ceramic pot had crashed to the floor. We didn't attempt anything Tuesday or Wednesday night.

As if things weren't bad enough, I found spoiled chunks of hamburger meat in my locker Thursday morning. I started crying right then and there in the hallway, like a babbling idiot. Hayden had already disappeared, and I had to knock the globs of meat off my books and salvage what I could. My copy of *The Catcher in the Rye* was ruined and my math book smelled like decayed butt. I had to tell someone, because it needed to be cleaned up.

I spent the first half of the morning in the girls' bathroom by the gym. No one ever used it except the smokers. It smelled, but not as bad as my locker did. I couldn't remember the last time I'd cried that hard, and it wasn't till the beginning of third before I got up enough courage to find a janitor.

I found Mr. Theo instead.

"Ember, why weren't you—are you okay?"

"Yes. No." I wiped under my eyes with the sleeves of my hoodie. "I need to find a janitor."

His brows furrowed and his glasses slipped, and I thought of Adam, and then I started crying again. After that, I ended up in the principal's office. It was like a snowball rolling down a hill. Things just spiraled out of control from that point.

Principal Hawkes seemed like a nice lady, and Mr. Theo had been right. She didn't tolerate bullying of any kind, and when he told her about the other things in my locker, she called the guardian listed on my paperwork.

Jonathan Cromwell.

A couple of kids lingered in the admin offices, trying to find out why I was in the office. I ignored them, because I had bigger problems. Mr. Theo left during that time, and I really wanted him to stay through this, considering how he'd started it by telling the principal.

Cromwell showed up less than twenty minutes later. I'd stopped crying by then. I'd also stopped talking and started mentally berating myself.

He wore a business suit, his dark hair neatly in place and a tight smile on his face. He didn't look at me. I had no idea what they'd told him. "Principal Hawkes, how have you been?"

They exchanged pleasantries while I squirmed in my seat. I was very close to hyperventilating when the principal finally closed the office door and laid it all out on the table in a clipped, purely professional way: the rabbit, the dolls, the toy car, and everything in-between. I stared at her desk while they talked. Near her computer was a tiny coin, much like the one I had in my pocket. It couldn't be the same one, because I doubted Mr. Theo handed out lucky coins like candy.

I forgot about the coin the moment she stopped talking.

Only then did Cromwell look at me. I couldn't help it; I shrank back in my seat. "How long has this been going on?"

I didn't answer.

"Apparently since the first day she started," Principal Hawkes answered. "Mayor Cromwell, I want to assure you that PHS doesn't tolerate this kind of behavior. Nor have we ever, in the history of my career, had anything like this."

I felt his stare on me while he talked. "This is the first I've heard of this. I am . . . extremely disappointed that Ember didn't confide in me. Principal Hawkes, what are you doing to ensure this will stop?"

"She states that no one has been bothering her, so that gives us very little to go on. Although, I am not entirely inclined to believe her since this is the first time any of this has been brought to our attention."

I looked up then. That wasn't true. I'd told Mr. Theo and he'd told her. She had to have figured out that he knew, but then the next thing she said sealed my fate. I was a goner. No doubt about it.

"I don't mean this as any offense to you, Mayor Cromwell. As you know, I voted for you and you still have my vote," she continued. "But I am inclined to believe that this issue started even before she stepped foot in this school."

Cromwell stiffened beside me. "I'm not sure I'm following you."

She cleared her throat and nervously worked at the button on her suit. "How have her interactions been with the other . . . children living in your home? Are there any problems you may be aware of? It could be that—" She stopped talking. She stopped moving. Actually, I think she stopped breathing.

Holy crap.

Then I noticed that Cromwell was standing. "Nothing has happened in my house."

"Nothing," Principal Hawkes murmured.

"None of my children are involved in this," he continued, his voice surprisingly soothing. I found myself leaning toward him, listening. "In fact, you will forget we ever had this conversation."

Principal Hawkes nodded.

"Ember left her lunch in her locker. It spoiled. She panicked." I snapped out of it. "*What*?"

Cromwell ignored me, solely focused on her. "Nothing has happened. Ember is just sick. She will go home today. If anyone else brings this up, you will tell them it's being handled. And you will contact me if anyone comes to you about this."

"Yes. Of course. Yes." Principal Hawkes blinked. Then she looked at me, a fond, almost patronizing smile on her face. "Miss McWilliams, I do hope you feel better. And please remember to not leave your lunch in your locker anymore."

My jaw hit the floor.

Cromwell wrapped things up after that, and then we were walking out of the school and getting in his Porsche. My heart raced and palms sweated. I was screwed. And I needed to get out of here.

"I want—want to stay in school today. I have a test this afternoon," I told him.

He spared me a glance. "You can make up the test."

"But—"

"Who else knew about this, Ember?"

"No one," I stuttered, eyeing the door handle. I could make a run for it. I could also touch him.

"Do *not* lie to me. Who else knew about this?" he demanded.

"I'm not lying." My fingers clawed along the door. "No one else knew. I have to take a test—"

Cromwell pulled out of the parking lot before I could even open the door. "Why didn't you come to me about this?"

"I . . ." I couldn't think of a lie fast enough. Telling him that I thought he or one of his freaks was behind it wouldn't make anything better. So the next words that came out of my mouth even amazed me. "Why do you collect kids? What do you want from us?"

"I don't want anything from you. And I've already answered why I bring the gifted into my household. I will not explain it again for your amusement."

"It's not for my amusement! You want these kids for some bizarre reason." Another moment in my life where I knew I needed to shut up, but couldn't. "Just like you wanted Olivia— because they're all gifted. Why do you want their gifts?"

"I understand that you're upset, but you will not question my intentions. I'll determine who has been leaving those things in your locker whether or not you fess up to who's been bothering you. The next time—if there is a next time anything like this occurs—you will come to me. Do you understand?"

"A—Are you going to send me away?"

"Sometimes I want to, Ember. I really do. So don't push it."

My fingers opened and closed in my lap. "What are you going to do?"

"I'm going to take you home. You will go upstairs. You're grounded—"

"What?" I screeched. "How am I grounded? This isn't my fault! And grounded from what? I don't go anywhere."

"You're grounded, because you should've come to me. I could've stepped in before this—whatever this is—involved any of the outsiders. This is the second time you've let me down, Ember. I had to use my gift to manipulate someone. The last thing I need is the school administration prying around my home because they so obviously believe that one of my children has something to do with this."

"Go figure," I snapped.

"And trust that I will have a talk with every single one of them this evening."

"But I didn't tell any of them!"

Cromwell glanced in my direction. "I don't know why you think you can lie to me."

I didn't, either.

20

I kept waiting for Cromwell to change his mind, to storm into my bedroom and inform me that he'd contacted the Facility and they were coming for me. But as the hours passed and the light of the moon crept across the room, I realized I was safe for the time being.

My nerves settled down enough that I could get some semblance of sleep. I don't know what woke me near sunrise. Maybe it'd been a nightmare. I'd dreamt of shadowy figures following me, which probably explained why my heart threw itself against my ribs.

I sat up and tossed the covers off my legs. Climbing out of bed, I took a step, and then noticed a shadow against the door. And when it moved forward, I opened my mouth to scream.

"Ember, it's me."

"Oh, my God," I gasped, sitting down on the edge of the bed.

"Sorry. I didn't mean to scare you," Hayden said quietly.

I could barely see him. Once I felt sure I wouldn't pass out, I stood up again. "How long have you been in here?" *Watching me sleep?* Even though I didn't say that, it hung in the air between us. Instead of creeping me out, which it should have, knowing that he was in here made me feel weird . . . in a good way—a confusing way.

"Not that long. I was debating if I wanted to wake you up."

"Oh. Is . . . is everything okay?"

"I think that's a question only you can answer."

"I guess Cromwell talked to you last night."

"You guessed correctly."

I sighed and reached for the bedside lamp, but Hayden suddenly stood in front of me. I don't know how he moved so fast. Up close, I could see his expression, but couldn't gain anything from it.

"Why didn't you tell me about the other stuff?" he demanded, his voice low.

I should've known he'd be mad, but I hadn't been concerned with that last night. I started to turn, but he caught my arm. "We haven't exactly been getting along."

Hayden lowered his head, meeting my wide-eyed stare and holding it. "That's not a good enough reason, Ember."

"I know, but I didn't want to bother you with it. Anyway, it was just hamburger meat and I did overreact."

"What about the dolls and the noose? What about the fact that you told a teacher and not me, Ember?"

Well, apparently Cromwell had told him everything. "Mr. Theo—"

"The English teacher?"

"Yeah, but he knew about the rabbit. And I didn't mean to tell him about the rest, but he knew something was going on and—"

Hayden cut me off, eyes flaring. "You told him over me?"

His words meant something. It wasn't me telling a teacher over him. Or even a stranger over him. You told *him* over me. I recognized the look in his eyes, because I *felt* it whenever he left lunch with Phoebe. Not anger. Not even disappointment. "You're—are you actually jealous?"

"What?"

"You are! You're jealous because I told Mr. Theo over you." I yanked my arm back, but he pulled me right up against him. My legs were flush with his, our chests met. I could feel him take his next deep breath, and I forgot what I was saying.

The look of jealousy slipped away, replaced by something equally frustrating. His hands slid up to my shoulders, sending tiny shivers down my body. He backed me up until my legs hit my desk. "Can I?"

"Sure." I had no idea what I was agreeing to.

Hayden lifted me and sat me on the desk. His hands lingered on my hips, his touch burning through the thin cloth. A smoky scent, like a candle blown out, wafted through my room, but there was no source.

"What are you doing?" I asked, my breath hitching.

"I don't know."

"Hayden?" I whispered.

"Yes?" He shifted closer, his warm breath brushing the skin of my neck like the night in the cabin. This was *our* form of kissing—our soft, feathery-light kisses that never made contact.

My hand rose reflexively, wanting to touch him. I stopped myself a mere inch from his cheek. Helplessly, my fingers curled around thin air.

"It's okay." His hands were on the move again, sliding upward. When they circled my waist, all rational thought went out the window. His breath trailed across my throat, around my chin and stopped over my cheek. His fingers curved along my back as his soft breath hovered over my lips. "Do you know what you do to me?"

I think I shook my head, but I wasn't sure. All I could concentrate on was how exquisite, how right, how wonderful being this close to him felt.

His breath still lingered over my lips, and one of his hands drifted upwards, stopping at the collar of my shirt.

And then he touched me.

My eyes fell shut and a tiny sigh escaped me. Hayden moved the tips of his fingers across my neck, over my chin. They jerked more than once, but he continued until his entire hand pressed against my cheek.

"Tell me to stop," he pleaded hoarsely.

Any resolve I had shattered. I touched his face, cupped his

cheek. His skin felt just like I'd imagined. No. Better than I'd ever thought. His skin was hot, smooth, and inviting. Maybe even as hot as I felt and I was tingling all over.

Hayden let out a ragged sound. Seconds went by, and just our breathing could be heard. His thumb traced a broken circle over my cheek. He couldn't keep his hand still. Whatever poison was in my skin affected him, but I couldn't pull my hand away.

I inhaled once, twice. The scent of smoke and spice filled me.

He moved his other hand to the nape of my neck, his fingers spasming as they made contact with my skin. A startled sound escaped me. My brain couldn't process one logical thought other than how wonderful he felt—how beautiful, how alive.

"Ember . . .?" His voice felt like a whisper against my lips.

He was going to kiss me. I knew it. My entire body tensed in anticipation, my pulse hummed deliciously. But on the fringes, things start to blur. Even as I felt like I would burst through my skin any second, my head started to swim. Then he pulled away so fast I nearly fell off the desk.

Panting heavily, Hayden stepped back and stared. "I'm sorry. I shouldn't have done that."

"Did I hurt you?" I asked, surprised by how husky my own voice sounded.

He looked at me like I'd grown a hand out of my head and it'd wiggled fingers at him. "I was hurting you, Ember. I could feel it."

"No," I said slowly. "I was just a little dizzy. You didn't drain anything, right?"

"I wanted to." He looked away. "Don't you get it? I did. I could feel it happening and I would've held on. I would've done it."

I wished he'd pull me back into his arms. I liked it there. And I didn't see what the big deal was. "It's okay. Nothing happened." I sounded a little disappointed.

"I could have seriously hurt you." He ran a hand over his head, clasping the back of his neck.

"Do you realize how weird this is? I'm the one who could've *seriously* hurt you. You can make me dizzy and maybe, worst-case scenario, put me in a coma for a few days. I can *kill* you. So who has the bigger right to freak out here? I'd say me."

"You wouldn't hurt me. I haven't told you this, but my gift would kick in before you did any serious damage. I don't think I'd even be able to stop it from doing so."

Well, that was good to know. But it didn't bother me. It actually made me glad that he was protected in that way. I chewed on my lower lip and watched him. Regret strained his face. That kind of stung. This probably explained why I asked the next question. "Are you still mad that I told Mr. Theo and not you?"

Hayden took a step back, eyes narrowing. "I think it's ridiculous that you'd confide in a complete stranger. I thought you trusted me."

"I do trust you, but Mr. Theo isn't a stranger." I hopped down from the desk and brushed past him. "I'm sorry I didn't tell you. I thought you didn't want to hear about it anymore. That you were done dealing with it."

"What?" He spun around. "Why would you think that?"

"I don't know. I just didn't want to bother you." I folded my arms. "I just thought it would make us argue more."

Hayden shook his head. "I don't understand you sometimes. If you could just let go of how you feel about my family for two seconds—"

"Not going to happen."

He groaned. "Do you know—do you even care how disappointed he was in me? What that meant to me?"

My head jerked up. "What? You didn't tell him you knew about the stuff in the locker, did you? I told him I didn't tell anyone, Hayden. Oh, God."

"He didn't appreciate the fact that I'd been hiding what was happening."

"Then why did you tell him?"

"I needed to tell him the truth, Ember!" he said, equally frustrated. "It's bad enough that I've been lying to him about helping you."

"I never made you help me! You pushed it on me!"

He stared at me for what seemed like forever. "My father was on the phone with every contact he has ever made in the last ten years after he reamed my ass out last night. He sent Kurt to find out who's behind the stuff in your locker."

That meant nothing. I'd do the same thing if I was guilty and wanted people to believe I wasn't, but the look on his face stopped me from letting those words get past my lips.

"And I know none of that means anything to you."

I flushed. There was no point in denying it. I folded my arms and glared at him.

"But I wish it did. Then you could see that my family isn't against you." He stepped forward, catching the edge of my sleeve. Only the tips of his fingers brushed my skin, but it felt like a thousand touches in one. "They've been watching over you for so long. My father wants to help you. He'll do everything and anything to keep you and your sister safe."

I unfolded my arms, and Hayden let go. He didn't step back. My hands found the sleeve of his shirt. Mimicking his early movements, the tips of my fingers brushed the skin of his wrist. I closed my eyes, but I could tell the shadows in the room were breaking apart as the sun started to rise over the mountain.

"Please. Ember, you have to trust him. Trust *me*."

The moment I opened my eyes, Hayden knew. Neither of us spoke. There was just too much that pointed at Cromwell for me to ever trust the man, and Hayden would always remain loyal to him.

Our eyes connected for the briefest moment. Then he left without saying a word. I turned to the balcony. The sun had crested the mountain, casting an orange, fiery glow over the woods, and in that second, everything burned.

★   ★   ★

"I spoke to Principal Hawkes," Mr. Theo said, eyeing two students in the hallway who had their tongues shoved down each other's throats. For a teacher, he didn't seem to mind the PDA like every other adult did. "She said everything is being taken care, and you shouldn't have any more problems."

Feeling a strange pain in my chest, I pulled my gaze from the couple. The ache transferred to my temples. "Yeah."

He looked at me sharply. "You don't sound too convinced of that."

I squeezed the coin between my fingers, wondering how things had gone from Hayden almost kissing me this morning to not even speaking to me. We'd argued before, but they'd been different. "I'm just tired."

Mr. Theo turned and faced me. "You left school early yesterday. Was it because you wanted to, or were you made to?"

His question caught me off-guard, and between the pain in my head and lack of sleep, my brain wasn't up for the challenge of lying or talking in general. I just wanted to finish this day and go to sleep.

"Ember?"

I blinked. "No. I think I'm coming down with something."

"Well, at least you have Thanksgiving break to rest up and feel better."

Yeah. A whole week of being stuck in the house with people who hated me sounded like a restful experience. "I hope you have a nice break." I could hear the emptiness in my own voice. No emotion. I was that tired. Or maybe it was something else. I pushed away, swinging the bag onto my shoulder.

"Ember?" he called out. I'd gotten about a yard away before twisting back around. "Take care of yourself."

21

I stared down at my cup of hot chocolate, watching the darker chocolate swirl. She might be an evil child-stealer, but Aunt Liz could make some kick-ass hot chocolate. Setting the mug aside, I picked up the pad of paper and turned to a blank page. My mind wandered as I started etching lines across the paper.

Liz had taken Olivia to the library after lunch and they had yet to return. I'd been invited to go, but I'd turned them down. Stupid. I needed a new copy of *The Catcher in the Rye*. And since Olivia was the only living thing in this house who wanted to be around me, I should've gone.

So I sat outside on the porch, huddled down in a corner so the chilly breeze couldn't reach me, waiting for Olivia to come back. Or, at least, I kept telling myself it was because of Olivia. I was totally not waiting for Hayden to come home, hoping to catch him. I'd seen him leave with Phoebe and Gabe a little after noon. I hadn't been invited.

The pencil slid over the page, a line here, a stronger line there.

The breeze picked up, scattering the dull brown and yellow leaves across the porch. They came to a rest around my sneakers. My mind wandered away from Hayden, right back to another string of thoughts that started a low burn in my stomach.

There wasn't a part of me that doubted that someone in this house had something to do with the "gifts" in my locker. Pressure built in my chest when I thought about the possibility I could be living with the person responsible for the accident.

I stopped drawing, pushing back a wayward curl as I stared down at my sketch. The marks were unmistakable. *He* stared back at me, a lopsided grin on lips that were fuller on the bottom. I let out a disgusted groan and slammed the sketchpad shut just as the front door swung open.

Parker.

He stopped at the top of the steps and turned, his gaze settling on me. Sunlight sliced across his face, but it didn't warm his expression.

I tucked the pencil inside the sketchpad and started to stand, but what was I trying to run from? Parker knew everything.

He let out a sigh as he glanced down at the keys in his hand. "I'm sorry about that night in the cabin."

Struck dumb, I simply stared. Parker never talked to me. Ever.

Clenching the keys in his hand, he inched away from the steps and stopped a good six feet from me. "Sometimes when I read people, I get sucked in. I can't stop." He stared off into the woods while he spoke. "And you were especially hard to read. There's a lot going on in your head."

I wasn't sure how to respond to that. Should I apologize? But that didn't seem right, so I said nothing.

Parker appeared okay with that. "It's hard to block people like you out. People whose brains are always working at something, their emotions always on broadcast." He paused, finally looking at me. "Phoebe told me you saw."

"Oh," I said, knowing he meant the cuts Phoebe had made along her thighs.

"It's hard for her to block you out, to block out Hayden. It gets to her."

Somehow, I knew Parker was apologizing for Phoebe's behavior, explaining why she hurt herself. "I understand it's hard for her, but she shouldn't be hurting herself. Someone should do something. Get her help."

He tipped his head to the side. "Phoebe's fine."

"People who are fine don't cut themselves."

"Most people don't believe they're soulless," Parker raised his brows. "Nor do they believe they actually want to hurt people. Do you think you're fine?"

My jaw hit the floor.

"Isn't that how you deal with your gift? You believe you can't help it, that your touch is beyond your control. So you've convinced yourself that you are soulless, evil. In a way, it takes the responsibility off you."

"That's not true."

"Phoebe cuts to distract herself from other people's emotions. I stay away from people so I'm not tempted to get in their heads." Almost like he needed to prove his words, he took a step back. "Gabe is the lucky one; he doesn't have to deal like we do."

"What about Hayden?" I asked before I could stop myself.

A cynical smile twisted his lips. "Hayden's learned to be comfortable with his gifts. Out of all of us, he knew how to deal. He did deal."

"You say that like he doesn't deal anymore. I don't believe that. He's so . . . strong."

Parker shook his head. "Hayden shows you what he wants you to see. You don't know Hayden. He's never in control, not when he's around you."

You don't know Hayden.

With my sketchpad and lukewarm mug of hot chocolate in hand, I went back inside after Parker left. I shivered in spite of the toasty warmth of the house. Why was I even thinking about Hayden? We weren't even friends anymore. And besides, according to Phoebe, he had a thing for lost and broken people.

That didn't flatter me.

I didn't need him to help me get control of my touch. I didn't need him to believe that his father had anything to do with the accident. But what about all the other stuff—the things we shared that had nothing to do with my touch or the accident? His friendship, the way he could get me to talk about almost anything? Or the way he looked at me, the way I felt around him?

Coming to a stop in the foyer, I wanted to kick myself. I hadn't needed any of that stuff for two years. Surely, I didn't need it now. What I needed to do was forget about Hayden, because right now, he wasn't important. Finding out who'd been behind the car crash was.

The more I thought about it, the more I wondered why someone would want Olivia badly enough to kill. And come on, kill me, too? When I'd been just a kid? Or maybe they'd planned to wipe my mind—erase all of our memories of Olivia—but when she brought me back with a new "gift," they changed their plans. Maybe they wanted to see what I could do, see how I progressed on my own.

I just couldn't figure out the "why" behind it all.

Tucking my sketchpad under my arm, I rubbed my temples. Ugh. Lack of sleep mixed in with learning someone might've wanted me dead could cause one hell of a headache.

I headed into the kitchen to dump my hot chocolate and found Cromwell at the table, several newspapers spread in front of him. I couldn't make a hasty retreat before his gaze flicked up from the papers.

"Hello, Ember."

"Hey." I ambled over to the sink and dumped the mug, feeling his heavy stare on my back the whole time. It took everything in me to not fling accusations at him. When I turned around, Cromwell leaned back in the chair. "Can I ask you something?"

He nodded. "You can ask me anything."

"Is it possible my parents knew about Olivia's gift? Before she did anything?"

Cromwell glanced down at one of the papers. "It's possible, especially if Olivia wasn't the first one in the family to have a gift."

"You're saying someone else could've had the gift? In my family?"

"The ability to have gifts hasn't been proven to be hereditary, but there've been several instances in which more than one member of a family has shown a gift. Just like Phoebe and Parker."

"No way," I murmured. "Mom and Dad were super-boring and ordinary."

"Not your parents, but perhaps your grandparents, an aunt, or a cousin?"

My entire family was boring. "No, I don't think so."

"I admit I had looked into your family tree a bit when we first brought you here. Mostly for my own curiosity."

I came closer to where he sat. "Did you find anything?"

He hesitated. "No."

"Are you sure?" I asked quietly, finding it hard to maintain eye contact with him.

Cromwell smiled evenly. My insides went cold. "I'm a hundred percent sure."

Beyond a doubt, I knew he'd lied. He'd found something— something he didn't want to share. Cold crept over my skin, leaving little goose bumps behind.

He stood. "Can you follow me, please?"

I was more willing to walk off a cliff, but I didn't have much of a choice. "Sure."

Cromwell gave me a look like he knew what I thought, and I'd swear his lips curved into a real smile for just a second or two.

I ended up following Cromwell to his home office clear on the other side of the house. Located in the right wing, a part of the mansion I rarely ventured to, the study seemed sterile and lifeless.

Cromwell went behind his desk while I hovered in the middle of the room, unwilling to get any closer. I couldn't help it. When I looked at him, I saw my dad smiling at me before he hit the gas and crossed the intersection. A shudder of revulsion crawled over me.

"Cold?" Cromwell asked as he pulled out a ring of keys. "It's drafty in this part of the house."

I didn't answer.

He turned toward the credenza and plucked a key from the ring. "Your sister is convinced this part of the house is haunted. I'm almost positive that Gabe is behind it. He's quite the prankster."

I inched closer as he opened up a drawer and thumbed through several files. Craning my neck, my eyes brushed over the name on the first file: "Kurt Lagos." It was pretty damn thick. So was the file behind his. At first, I didn't register who it was because I only knew him as Hayden Cromwell. Not Hayden Gray. And then, files marked with the twins' names, then Gabe's, and finally, his nimble fingers skimmed over Olivia's and mine.

Before he could catch me watching, I whirled around and pretended to study a painting on the wall. With its rolling green hills and pastel colors, it reminded me of something I would've drawn before the accident, but I didn't give it any more thought. My brain focused on why Cromwell had files on all of us, and what could be in those files.

A sudden desire overcame me. I wanted to run over there and knock him over so I could get a look at the file. I had a right to know what was in my file, as well as the others. Okay, maybe not the others, but at least Olivia's and Kurt's.

And Hayden's.

"Ember?"

"Yeah?" I turned around.

"I think you might like this." He held a black album. Resting on top of it was a silver frame.

Coming up next to him, my chest tightened as I saw what was in the frame. It was a picture of my family before the accident, happy and smiling. Dad had his arm around my shoulders and Mom held a squirming three-year-old Olivia in her lap. I reached for them wordlessly, wrapping my fingers around the edge of the album. My eyes remained glued to the picture in the frame. It'd sat beside my bed, and I'd believed that these pictures—these memories—were forever lost.

"Liz went through the boxes we had in storage and gathered up the pictures," Cromwell explained. "She put them in this photo album for you and Olivia."

My hands shook as I brought the album and frame to my chest, holding them close. Slowly, I lifted my eyes and met his. Cromwell smiled tightly and looked away. "Thank you," I whispered, voice hoarse.

Cromwell nodded.

There was nothing else to say. I turned and carried my precious bundle upstairs. I set the picture on the table beside the bed, my fingers lingering on the polished silver for a few seconds. Sitting cross-legged on the bed, I opened up the album and started thumbing through the innocent, joyful years captured in the images.

Some of the pictures made me smile, like the ones of baby Olivia with her face beet-red, lips pulled open in a silent wail. And the ones of Dad and me making funny faces at the camera. Or my mom trying to cook, which always had been a humorous endeavor. But the photos also opened up a raw ache deep within my chest. I came to another picture at the back of the album and a burning rose in my throat. It was just the three of us: my parents and me, sitting in a pile of golden leaves, smiling blissfully.

We'd been a real family once. Sometimes I forgot that.

I slid the picture out of the clear plastic film, running my thumb over my dad's ruggedly handsome face. The burning in the back of my throat took over and tears spilled down my cheeks. Holding the picture close, I curled onto my side and tried to remember why we'd been so happy in those pictures.

A few hours later, I dragged myself to the sink and splashed cold water over my face. Tears still lingered in my eyes, but I drew in a deep, steadying breath as I pulled my hoodie on and tugged my hair back into a messy ponytail.

Downstairs, I searched for Olivia. After viewing those pictures, I kind of wanted to spend some time with her. The low hum of the TV drew me to the largest of the recreation rooms in the mansion. My steps were slow and light as I treaded to the archway of the room.

No one saw me from where I stood, and I was relieved. I couldn't even begin to imagine what my face looked like. Gabe sprawled across one of the recliners. Just the top of his curly head was visible. Parker sat across the room, reading a book, as usual. Curled on one side of the couch was my little sister, sound asleep.

And even though I felt sure that my heart couldn't sink any lower, it plummeted all the way to my sneakers.

On the other side of the couch were Hayden and Phoebe. Nestled between Hayden's legs, Phoebe lay still, eyes closed. One side of her face was pressed against his chest, and one of Hayden's arms was thrown over the back of the couch. The other was wrapped around her slim shoulders, his hand resting against her cheek.

Hayden murmured something against the top of Phoebe's head, and she smiled slightly.

An icy rush of air went down my throat, stealing my breath and freezing my insides. All of them looked so perfect together. Then, as quickly as the chilly feeling came, a red-hot surge shot through my veins.

Phoebe flinched and opened her eyes. They were glossy, stained with tears.

A frown pulled at Hayden's lips as he moved his other hand to her forehead. "What is it?" Concern deepened his voice.

I sucked in a sharp gasp, realizing Phoebe was sensing the wild crescendo of emotions inside me. Mortified, I backed up and spun around. I headed for the front door. My stomach twisted into knots as I opened the door.

Cool air eased my burning face as I rushed down the steps and across the driveway. Tears filled my throat, threatening to choke me, but I refused to let them fall. I shoved my hand into the pocket of my jeans, squeezing the coin until it bit into my flesh through the gloves.

I didn't know where I was going, but I had to get away—far enough that I could put distance between the humiliation of the raw jealousy I felt and its source. Seeing all of them together was like a punch in the face, but worse. It wasn't just Hayden and Phoebe cuddled together, holding one another like lovers do. That *did* sting. But it was more like lancing open a wound that had just healed. They'd looked like a family. And my own sister, softly snoring among them, was a kick in the gut.

I wasn't a part of their mismatched family. Once, Hayden had tried to include me, but he, too, had given up on that. Their bonds—their gifts—linked them all together, while I existed on the outside.

Everything crashed together: the accident, what'd happened to my mom, those two years struggling to keep our heads above the water. And then being brought here, thrust into a world I didn't really understand, surrounded by people who not only feared me, but possibly wanted to do me real harm.

I walked along the road from the Cromwell mansion, slowly shattering with each heavy step I took. Hugging my elbows close to my chest, I stopped as I reached the end of the private road. I hadn't realized I'd been walking that long. Tipping my head up, I watched the sun make its descent over the ridge of the Seneca Rocks.

Part of me never wanted to go back to that house, to have to see Hayden and Phoebe like that again. I rubbed the heel of my hand over my chest, taking a deep breath. I hadn't really thought there was something between them, but they had been spending a lot of time together.

My chest squeezed as I turned around and shuffled off the road. There were trails all through the woods, areas where I imagined Hayden and the others had worn the pathways into the ground over the years. My feet carried me deeper into the woods. The temperature dropped as the sun fell and thick shadows descended under the trees.

Finding a fallen log, I sat on the edge and pulled off my gloves. Gray smudges marred the tips of my fingers. They weren't as elegant as Phoebe's or as strong as Hayden's, but their hands didn't kill. Although, I guess Hayden's could, if he held on long enough.

But his hands were beautiful, anyway.

I dragged my fingers over my head, catching the curls that had escaped my ponytail. My heart was doing this weird achy thing that made me question my sanity as I thought about the last night we'd spent in the cabin. If I tried hard enough I could remember how it had felt to be in his embrace, feeling his heart beat under my cheek.

The same thing Phoebe was feeling right now.

Air caught in my throat, and I wiped my hands over my damp cheeks. My watery gaze fell to the log. A weed poked through the bark, springing up with green, spindly leaves.

Squeezing my eyes shut, I dragged in a deep breath and forced my mind to go empty—to let all the hurt wash away, to stamp down the fear that settled in the back of my throat. If I could just touch something and not kill it, then things would change.

They had to.

Slowly, I held my breath, reached and brushed the tips of my fingers over the velvety leaves. The weed shuddered once under my fingers. The soft leaves turned rough and crispy. I squeezed my eyes shut and bit my lip. When I did open my eyes, the weed lay limp against the bark. Dead.

"I really am Death," I muttered. Then I hiccupped as another salty tear rolled down my face.

A popping sound followed, and then something whizzed by my head, slamming into the tree behind me. Tiny pieces of bark splintered and shot through the air, raking the back of my head.

My heart jumped into my throat as I pivoted, grabbing the edges of the dead tree. An arrow was thrust deep into the tree, still quivering. Vaguely, I realized it was one of those arrows professional hunters used. My dad had owned a set.

"What the he—"

Searing pain lanced through me, stealing my breath. The force of the blow jerked me around and I toppled over the log. The back of my head cracked off a rock. Light burst behind my eyes, and then darkness pulled me under.

22

When I opened my eyes, it was dark and there was a raccoon digging at the ground by my face. I drew in a deep breath, whimpering as pain shot down my arm and through my skull.

The raccoon froze, and its ears went back. A heartbeat passed, and then it scuttled off.

Groaning, I sat up slowly and touched the top of my arm. The material was ripped and felt sticky. I pressed harder and yelped. In the dark, my hand and the sleeve of my shirt looked like they had been dipped in oil. A few feet from me, where the raccoon had been, an arrow lay nestled between two rocks and a patch of grass.

I'd been shot by a frikkin' arrow. My God, I had the worst luck known to man.

I rolled to my feet, swaying as a wave of dizziness nearly brought me to my knees. Placing my hand over the wound, I ignored the bite of pain and pressed down. Blood seeped through my fingers.

Things were foggy as I stumbled back through the woods. Luckily, I'd managed to stay on the trail and reached the road leading to Cromwell's house. The bad news was that the hike was mostly uphill from here, and I seriously doubted I was going to make it. I forced myself to put one foot in front of the other, stopping every once in a while to wipe the clammy sweat dotting my forehead.

Every few seconds I had a moment of clarity. Had someone shot me on purpose or had it been meant for a deer? But those questions slipped back in the haze. I was exhausted, legs shaking as I climbed the road.

Out of the darkness, a yellow light cut through the night, and then a voice, "Ember!"

I started walking faster, tripping over my own feet. "Hayden . . .?" My voice came out hoarse, weak. I doubted he heard me.

"Hayden, I can feel her. I think . . . I think she's hurt," I heard Phoebe say. "Her emotions are off, tainted somehow. She's in the road."

There was a muffled curse, and then the sound of pounding feet. The light swayed erratically, passed me and then swung back. A few seconds later, Hayden was running out of the darkness and grasping my shoulders.

I cried out as pain shrieked down my arm.

Hayden pulled his hands back. "What happened?" His gaze dropped. "Jesus, you're bleeding! Are you okay?"

"I was shot . . . by an arrow." Those words sounded bizarre even to me.

His response was to move in, sweeping one arm under my legs, and then I was up, my cheek resting against his pounding heart. "Phoebe, run back and tell them to meet us halfway."

All I heard was her lighter footsteps rushing off. "I can . . . walk. I'm fine."

"Being shot with an arrow does *not* equal fine." Hayden started back, his long strides eating away at the distance between us and the house. "We've been looking for you for the last hour. Do you know what happened?"

Each step jarred the wound in my arm. I wondered how deep it was. Another scar, I realized dully. I told him everything, skipping over the part where I'd seen him cuddled on the couch with Phoebe.

"Jesus, you could've been killed," he said. I opened my eyes, but the hard lines of his face gave nothing away. He looked down, his eyes drifting over me. "Does your head hurt?"

"I'll survive." Assuming someone didn't shoot a rocket at me next.

A car roared down the road, coasting to a stop in front of us. Kurt jumped out of the driver's seat, spinning around to open the back door. "Put her in here."

"When . . . when did he get back?" I asked.

"An hour or so ago," Hayden replied. "He's going to take you to the hospital."

I clenched his arm, not wanting to go anywhere with Kurt. "What about you?"

"I'm coming with you." He placed me in the back seat. "Don't worry."

"No." Cromwell turned around in the front passenger seat, his eyes coolly assessing everything. "I want you to go back to the house, Hayden."

"But—"

"I need you to make sure everyone stays calm, Hayden. I need you here. We can take care of Ember."

I shuddered as my eyes bounced from Kurt to Hayden's father. I had a death grip on Hayden's arm.

Hayden looked reluctant to let me go. He watched as Kurt climbed behind the wheel. Pressing his lips together, he faced me. "It's going to be okay." Then he was letting go and closing the door. His pale face filled the window.

Kurt tore off, leaving Hayden behind. I turned to the front of the car, my eyes meeting Cromwell's as I held my injured arm close to my side. Balls of ice formed in my belly.

"Tell me everything," he said.

I told him the same thing I'd told Hayden, and the whole time I felt Kurt's eyes watching me from the rear view mirror. The balls of ice grew, drenching my veins. It sort of struck me then. Nothing in the past had been an accident. Why would the car the night of the bonfire—or this—be an accident?

I hadn't been in a hospital since the night of the car crash, but this by far won for the most bizarre hospital visit ever. Cromwell stayed by my side, using his Jedi mind tricks to make sure the nurses and doctors gloved up before ever coming into contact with my skin.

Ripped and soaked with blood, my favorite hoodie was toast. The arrow had caught the upper part of my arm, digging deep enough to require stitches. Watching the blank-faced doctor suture my skin was an event I never wanted to experience again. I kept waiting for his fingers to slip.

The nurse returned halfway through the procedure, wearing the same indifferent mask as the doctor. She handed me a small cup and a couple of pills.

"What's this?" I asked, glancing at Cromwell.

"It's for the pain," she replied. Her slight southern drawl was flat. "The local anesthesia will wear off and you'll be aching for sure."

The tugging on my skin stopped and the doctor studied the x-rays they'd taken of my head. "It looks good, Mayor Cromwell. No signs of a concussion or serious injury."

Cromwell nodded. "That's a relief to hear."

Swallowing the pills, I sort of doubted that. I handed the empty cup back to the nurse. The numb part of my arm already tingled pins-and-needles around the edges.

"I'd keep an eye on her for a few days. If she experiences any dizziness, memory loss, abnormal fatigue or behavioral changes, I want you to bring her back in here." The doctor stood, moving to the trashcan as he peeled off his bloodied gloves. Facing me, he smiled weakly. "The woods this time of year can be danger-ous. It's bowhunting season."

Unwillingly, my gaze went to the massive man slouched in the corner of the room. I wondered if Kurt did any bowhunting. Could it only be a coincidence that he'd returned at the same time someone had tried to make a shish kabob out of me? And the car that'd almost run me over could've been one of the Porsches sitting in the garage.

Kurt arched a blond brow at me.

My lips twisted into a semblance of a smile. I waited until we were in the car before I gave him the third degree. In the back of my mind, I wondered if the pain pills had given me a form of chemical courage. "So, where've you been?"

He glanced at Cromwell. "On business."

I leaned forward, planting myself between the two front seats. "You have a job?"

Cromwell raised his brows at me. "Perhaps you should sit back and rest, Ember."

"I'm not tired." I stared at Kurt. "What kind of job do you have?"

He looked at Cromwell again, who sighed and shook his head. "I work for Jonathan."

"Really," I said. "And what kind of work is that?"

Kurt looked like he was fighting a smile. "Whatever he asks me to do."

I started to fold my arms, but felt the stitches pull. "So, you'd put stuff in people's lockers?"

He laughed. "What?"

"How about slicing up bunnies?"

His jaw tightened. "Not lately, princess."

I made a face. "So, when was the last time you did it?"

"Are you high?" asked Kurt.

"Maybe," I admitted. "But you didn't answer my question."

Cromwell turned in the seat, clearly not amused. "You've had a very stressful evening and are probably under the influence of strong narcotics. That's the only reason why I'm tolerating what is coming out of your mouth at this moment, but please let me make myself clear. One more insinuation and I may do something I'll regret later."

My eyes narrowed on him. "Like what?"

He held my stare. "Did I not make myself clear?"

I flung myself against the back seat, wincing at the dull flare of pain. "Yeah, you're crystal clear, boss."

Kurt snorted. "I kind of like her like this."

"Why does that not surprise me?" Cromwell said, sighing.

Thankfully, Kurt drove like he was in NASCAR and we pulled into the garage in record time. Not waiting for them, I yanked open the handle and stumbled out of the car.

"Hey, you might want to take it a bit easy. You're going to pull your stitches out." Kurt was a step behind me.

I glanced over my shoulder. "And you'd care? Really? Didn't you try to tackle me in my house?"

A wry smile pulled at his lips. "Didn't you hit me over the head with a lamp?"

"*And* I knocked you out," I added.

Cromwell pinched the bridge of his nose.

Before Kurt could respond, the door to the garage flew open. Hayden's dark eyes focused on me. "How are you?"

"Lovely," Cromwell muttered. "Hayden, could you please get Liz? She can help Ember get cleaned up and ready for bed."

I brushed past them all, promptly tripping over the raised doorway to the kitchen. Incredibly fast, Hayden snagged me around the waist and set me on my feet. I shrugged his arm off. "I can clean myself up, thank you."

"What's wrong with her?" he asked, following me into the kitchen.

"Pain pills." Kurt laughed. "She's definitely not a happy pill user."

I spun around, using my good arm to point at him. "I'm not happy because someone is after me! There are creepy and gross things in my locker!" I stepped to the side, tugging on my ruined hoodie. "And I can clean myself. I don't want *her* to help me. I want my mom to help me."

Hayden's expression softened as he caught my covered wrists. "Ember, you don't want to do that." He moved my hand away from the hem of my hoodie. "Let me take you upstairs."

I stared into his deep brown eyes. They were so beautiful, so open. It took me a moment to remember why I was angry with him. I pulled away from him. "I saw you," I whispered.

His brows rose as he whispered back, "Saw what?"

"With her." I lowered my eyes, letting out a shaky sigh. All my anger suddenly vanished. The cockiness dried up. I just wanted to sit down. And maybe take a bath. Sit first, though.

Confusion faded from his face. "Ember, that's not—"

"I wanna see my mom." I turned away from him, realizing then we had company.

The twins stood in the doorway, flanked by the cherub-faced Gabe. They all stared at me.

"What?" I grumbled.

Gabe's lips pursed. "You have blood all over your left cheek."

Hastily, I used the good sleeve of my hoodie and swiped it over my face.

Hayden caught my arm, pulling it down. "It's okay. Gabe, where's Liz?"

"She's with Olivia." Gabe folded his arms as he shifted his weight to his other foot. "Olivia wanted Liz to stay with her until she fell asleep or something."

My shoulders slumped. Olivia hadn't asked me to do that since we'd come here.

"So . . . what happened?" Phoebe asked quietly.

"She thinks I slice up rabbits." Kurt pulled out a chair and dropped into it. I scowled as he stretched out his legs. He winked. "She thinks I'm your run-of-the-mill psychopath."

Phoebe's eyes went wide.

"Kurt," Hayden warned softly.

"You are a psychopath," I said.

"Ember, what did I tell you in the car?" Cromwell grabbed a water from the fridge. "You've had a troubling evening—"

"You can't tell me these things aren't related!" I backed away, hitting the edge of the counter. "Y-you just expect me to think all these things are coincidences?"

Phoebe crossed her arms, stricken-looking. "Oh, damn . . ."

"What?" asked her twin, frowning. Then his eyes narrowed. "What did you do?"

Those words had a stilling effect on everyone in the room, probably because Parker rarely ever spoke. I'd forgotten how soft and melodious his voice was.

Phoebe rubbed a hand down her face. The kitchen light caught and reflected off the deep purple nail polish. Suddenly, she whirled on her twin. "I know," she hissed. "I'm fucked up. Don't you think I know that?"

"What's going on?" Cromwell demanded.

Parker shook his head. "Tell them, or I will."

I leaned against the counter as Hayden stepped forward. Compassion marked his gaze as he approached Phoebe. At once, I had a feeling I should be sitting down.

"Phoebe? You can tell us." Hayden took her hand. "What did you do?"

I squeezed my eyes shut. He cared for her. It was so evident; probably everyone in the room could sense it. How had I missed it? Because I was a glutton for punishment, I opened my eyes in time to see Hayden pull her against his chest. Had I really meant anything to Hayden? Or was Phoebe just more broken than me?

Then Phoebe started crying. "I'm sorry. I really am." Her voice was muffled against Hayden's sweater. "I just couldn't take it."

Cromwell walked around the table, placing his hand on Phoebe's back. His eyes met Hayden's as he spoke. "Couldn't take what, Phoebe?"

"Her," she said. "Her emotions are all over the place, and they're dark. They keep pulling me in!" She tore away from Hayden, whirling on Cromwell. "You brought her here without any regard to us! How it would affect any of us!"

I felt my stomach sink, and then Kurt was beside me, guiding me into a chair. "You look like you're going to fall over."

Phoebe wiped the palms of her hands across her cheeks. "I just wanted her to leave, so everything could go back to normal. Then I'd be able to come home and not have to rely on Hayden to take the edge off everything!"

"Why didn't you say something?" asked Cromwell. "We could've been working on your blocking."

She laughed, and suddenly, she was composed—only her wet lashes gave an indication that she'd been crying. "It was me. I did it."

The room tilted a bit as I stared at her.

Hayden took a step back. A muscle feathered along his jaw. "Did what?"

"I've been the one putting stuff in her locker," she said. Kurt swore under his breath, but everyone ignored him. "I just wanted her to leave. And I thought it would scare her enough to make her go away."

I was out of the chair before I realized it. "I never did anything to you!"

Hayden was fast, positioning himself between the two of us. Cromwell just looked shocked, and Gabe's eyes were wide.

"You came here!" Phoebe screamed.

So much anger welled up, boiling over. "You killed a rabbit! And shoved it in my locker! What is wrong with you?"

"The rabbit was already dead. I'm not a freak."

"Really? You aren't?" I started around Hayden, but he blocked me. "You did everything else! How did you know what the car looked like?"

She was watching Hayden now, her lower lip trembling. "I saw the pictures Jonathan had of the accident."

I wanted to hurt her.

"Phoebe," Hayden said so softly. There was such disappointment in his voice. "You should've told us it was bothering you so much. There was more I could've done."

She laughed. "Like what? You can't just keep draining my gift all the time."

Part of me could understand how much my mixed-up emotions messed with her. Hell, they got to me. But still . . . "I don't want her around my sister." My voice shook. "Anywhere near her."

Phoebe's mouth dropped. "I wouldn't hurt your sister!"

"You're crazy!"

She started crying again.

Cromwell took Phoebe's arm. "We need to talk in private," he said to her. "Parker, please come with us." He turned to me, his expression blank. "You need to get some rest."

Tears burned my eyes as it all settled on me at once. Phoebe hated me so badly—it was an ugly feeling that slid over my skin. The three of them left the room, with Kurt trailing behind them.

Gabe slowly backed out of the kitchen, hands raised. "Wow. That takes family drama to a whole new level."

Hayden stared at him.

"And I think I'll go to my room now," Gabe said.

I watched him disappear down the hall. A numb feeling settled in my bones.

It'd been *Phoebe* this entire time.

"Ember . . .?"

Slowly, I lifted my gaze to Hayden's. "You didn't believe me."

He opened his mouth, but closed it.

I laughed, but it sounded harsh. "What will Cromwell do with her?"

"I don't know." He ran a hand through his hair. "I don't think he'll send her to the Facility, but I'm sure he'll work with her more to help her block . . . everything."

"It's not my fault."

His gaze fell to my face. "I know it's not."

"Your girlfriend is pretty messed up, you know that?"

Hayden frowned. "Phoebe's not my girlfriend."

"Yeah." I waved my hand, too tired to argue with the obvious. "I can't believe she . . . she hated me so much that she would take it that far."

"She has . . . problems, Ember. Her gift is difficult."

"And mine isn't? I don't use my gift as an excuse to terrorize people." I felt my face pale. "Is me being here really that bad? That I would drive someone to do those things? Am I that bad?" My voice broke, and I choked back a sob. "I can't help what I am."

"Ember." Hayden reached for me, but stopped short. "None of this is your fault. And you're not a bad person."

I drew in a breath, but it got stuck in my throat. "But you don't even want to be around me anymore and no one—" I bit my lip to keep from crying. "No one wants me here."

"That's not true."

Everything I felt started to boil over again. I pressed my lips together, but they still trembled.

"I'm sorry," Hayden said. "I didn't want to believe that it was someone in my family. I should've believed you." He ran his hand through his hair, clasping the back of his neck. "When I saw you tonight and realized you were bleeding? God, it scared me. Em, I don't like this."

Which part didn't he like—the arguing between us, the tension in his family, people possibly trying to skewer me in the woods . . . or both of us wanting something we couldn't have? I didn't know where that last part came from. Most of the anger drained out of me. "I don't like this, either."

"Then why are we doing it?" Hayden asked me, stepping forward. Less than a foot separated us and he reached out, not stopping this time. His hand circled my uninjured arm. I thought he was going to pull me to him like he had in my bedroom, and something in my chest fluttered. "Em, I don't want to—"

"Gabe said I was needed to help Ember," Liz called from the entrance to the kitchen. "Or are you helping her?"

I hoped he'd say that he was. That way he'd spend a little more time with me and we'd pick up where we'd left off. I'd apologize for blaming his entire family—no one else had known what Phoebe had been doing—and he'd apologize for not believing me and say everything would be okay.

Hayden dropped my arm. Those dark eyes lingered for a second and then he turned around. "No."

My heart sank all the way to my stomach. He didn't even look back, not once—which probably was a good thing because I was sure the disappointment I felt was written all over my face.

23

I spent the entire next day in my room, trying to sketch, but I couldn't commit anything to paper. Everything I drew looked bleak and boring. By dinnertime, the floor of my bedroom was covered with crumpled balls of paper.

Mr. Cromwell insisted on family dinners. They were always awkward, but tonight, with everything that had happened, that hit an epic high. A thick tension clung to the entire table.

"Yuck." Olivia pushed the peas around on her plate with her fork.

I sighed and wondered if blowing chunks across the table would get me excused. Olivia had been kept in the dark about last night's events, which was the only thing Cromwell had done I could agree with. My chunky sweater covered the bandage around my arm.

"Peas *are* gross," Gabe said.

"Gabriel," Liz warned. "Peas are not gross, Olivia. They help you grow up to be big . . ."

I blocked her out at that point and tried to manage what I hoped would be an inconspicuous glance across the table. Except, when I did look, Hayden stared right back at me, slouched in his chair, jaw clenched. He hadn't even touched his plate. Averting my gaze, I accidentally settled on Phoebe. Her hands clenched the edge of the table. I couldn't believe that she still sat here, at dinner, after everything she'd done. Stupidly, a part of me felt bad for her, and I hoped someone would get her help.

Parker, as always, had his nose in a book. He hadn't even looked up when Olivia knocked over her glass of milk when I tried to get her to not throw her peas.

I sank in my seat. This dinner couldn't get any worse.

"Peas!" Olivia flicked a spoonful toward Gabe. In turn, Gabe threw a biscuit at her plate. She took a bite and erupted into giggles, chunks of bread falling from her mouth.

Cromwell lured Hayden into a discussion about which football teams would be playing on Thanksgiving Day while Olivia and Gabe continued their food play.

"Can we go like we did last year?" Phoebe asked Hayden. "We could leave Wednesday afternoon and stay over."

My ears pricked up. They were talking about the parade in the city—the big one. Would Cromwell let her go after everything she'd done?

Hayden's eyes flicked away from his plate. "I don't know. I don't really feel up to it this year."

"Come on. It'll be fun." She pouted. "I could really get away."

I tried to act like I wasn't listening, but the moment I looked up, Hayden and I locked eyes. He was the first to look away.

Finally Cromwell seemed to hear what Phoebe was suggesting. "I do not believe that will be possible this year, Phoebe."

Phoebe opened her mouth, then clamped it shut. Her gaze, full of accusation, drifted to me like I was the reason she was in trouble.

I wanted to throw *my* peas at her.

My stomach twisted as I poked a lump of meat around my plate, and I couldn't sit here anymore. Pressure built in my chest. Without looking at anyone, I pushed away from the table and headed out into the hallway. No one stopped me. I think, if anything, the stress around the table lessened. It was like I was the one who'd been doing crazy things, not Phoebe. It blew my mind.

Drawing in a deep breath and letting it out slowly, I stopped in the foyer outside one of the dark sitting rooms. No matter how many times I did this, the walls still closed in around me. Minutes ticked by. I just stood there, staring into nothing.

"Are you okay?" Hayden asked me. "Your arm?"

I closed my eyes. "Yeah, my arm is okay."

"You didn't eat anything."

A snappy retort died on my lips when I faced him. He stood so close that I could smell his aftershave. "You didn't, either."

Hayden shoved his hands in the pockets of his jeans. "What are you doing?"

"Nothing. You?"

"Nothing." He nodded, then pulled his hands out of his pockets and ran one of them through his hair. "Em?"

"Yes?"

A moment passed in silence, and then Hayden shook his head. A tight, tense smile appeared on his face. "Never mind, I'll talk to you later."

Then he was gone, and I stood there, wanting to cry.

"You need to stay away from him."

Startled, I spun around. Kurt slouched against the wall, the strands of long blond hair practically obscuring his eyes. I had no idea how long he'd stood there. Obviously it'd been long enough. "Are you following me?"

"I'm not the one who's been following you, and I think you know that." Kurt pushed off the wall. "You need to leave Hayden alone. You're not good for him."

My hands balled into fists. "I'm not bothering Hayden."

"He loses sight of everything when he's around you."

I frowned as I rubbed the itchy skin around my stitches. "It doesn't seem that way."

Kurt tipped his head slightly. "You've been dealt an unfair hand in life. I can see that. Everyone can see that." He stepped forward, clasping his hands behind his back. "But so have Hayden, Gabe and the twins. And so have I. The only difference is that we've been able to see past all of that. You haven't."

I opened my mouth, but he cut me off.

"What Phoebe did was wrong, but can you blame her for wanting you to leave? What you feel must choke her. And your presence has affected Hayden since he first laid eyes on you. If you cared about anyone—your sister—you'd leave here. Leave your sister so she can have a real chance at life, and leave Hayden before he does something that all of us will regret."

His words struck a chord. Anger sparked and fired through me.

"And I think it would be best for you, too. You don't trust us." Kurt smiled. "We don't trust you."

"Where would I go?" I asked. "Live on the streets so I'm not your problem?"

If he was surprised, he didn't show it. "I don't care where you go. Money won't be a problem. How much do you need?"

"Are you serious?" He couldn't be, but the look on his face said he was. "You know what? I don't care what you think or what you want. The only way I'm leaving without Olivia is if you drag me from here. And I'd like to see you try."

Kurt opened his mouth, but closed it. I got the satisfaction of stunning him into silence. Spinning around on my heel, I left him standing in the foyer.

My run-in with Kurt empowered me. Instead of hiding in my room to sketch or forcing Olivia to entertain me, I started practicing with the plants on my own. Each night I crept downstairs once the house was silent and painstakingly carried a plant back to my bedroom. With my bum arm, I could only carry them one at a time. A garden of dead plants littered my room, serving as a painful reminder that I had yet to figure out how to control my touch.

If control was even possible.

The evening before Thanksgiving, I sat on the floor with a plant in front of me. Six withered plant corpses filled the pots in the corner. I stared down at the new one—the live one—then closed my eyes and tried to clear out my mind. Hayden had said it had to be one thought that triggered it. He'd tried to use Parker to get to that thought, but everything had turned to crap after that.

Parker—something Parker had said to me.

I wrinkled up my nose and held my breath. What had he said? Something about how we all coped with our gifts, everyone except Gabe. But it had nothing to do with Gabe, because he didn't have to cope. Neither did I, right? I didn't cope with it because I always believed there was nothing I could do.

I couldn't help what I did.

Like when Dustin had touched me in the grocery store parking lot. I couldn't have helped what'd happened. I had no control over it. It wasn't—

My eyes popped open and I exhaled. *That* was it—what Parker had said. I'd convinced myself that I had no control so that I didn't have to deal or have any responsibility.

And oh shit, maybe Kurt had been right—kind of. I had wallowed in my self-pity for two long years. If wallowing were an art form, I'd be on a gallery wall.

I placed my hands on the cool ceramic. Could that really be it? Was control over my fingers of death really something as simple as actually believing I had control? Taking responsibility for it—for my gift?

No. I don't have a gift. Olivia has one. Hayden has one. I don't have—

"I'm doing it," I said out loud. "I'm doing it right now."

What about my self-revelation courtesy of *The Catcher in the Rye*? I'd decided I didn't want to be like those statues in the museum, but I was. My thoughts worked the same. My actions did, too. I'd tried everything except believing I wasn't a freak of nature.

Because it wasn't that I didn't have a soul. I mean, there were minutes when I truly wondered—when I thought about what'd happened when I'd died and how I'd felt afterwards—but I didn't want to hurt anyone. What'd happened to Dustin had been an accident. I hadn't wanted to hurt him. I never wanted to hurt anyone—not really. I'd had moments when I'd entertained the idea, deep down, times when I'd felt threatened, but I didn't want people to be afraid of me.

It was more than that.

I didn't believe I was gifted, but maybe I was. Maybe my gift worked differently than the rest—like something had to trigger it to become active. That something had been dying. Who knows, maybe I would've come back anyway, even without Olivia. Dying could've been a part of the great plan or something.

"Okay, now I sound crazy," I muttered, running my fingers over the rim of the pot. "Like I walked into a cheesy sci-fi movie, but it's something. I think. I guess."

I dragged the pot into my lap. Earlier, I'd changed into linen shorts and a long-sleeved shirt. Both were thin enough to sleep in, if I ever decided to go to bed. It was well into the early morning hours. Everyone else had gone to bed hours ago . . .

And my brain was rambling again.

I made a face at the plant and sank my fingers into the rich, soft soil. Well-hydrated—Liz took good care of the plants here. I'd come to believe her other gift was a green thumb, because all of the plants grew so beautifully.

Until I killed them, that is.

"So I have a gift. A gift—not a curse—and the gift is the fingers of death, right?" I asked myself, feeling stupid when I waited for an answer. "Think about how badass that would be if I could control it." I stopped there. Thinking about that inevitably led to what could happen if I could control it.

Touching, holding hands, kissing . . . Hayden.

Not the most helpful train of thought.

I focused for hours on telling myself I did have a gift before I finally felt confident. Only then did I pull my dirt-stained fingers out and took a deep breath.

Now or never. I focused on the plant. It was dark green, and on the tall, slender stems there were marks much like the skin on a snake. It had become my favorite of all plants, because it looked so weird.

I took a deep breath and tried to speak in my most confident tone. "I have a gift."

Slowly, I brushed my fingers over one smooth stem, then jerked my hand back and waited.

A few seconds went by, then maybe a minute. Then five, and holy crap, nothing happened.

I started to stand, but my legs gave out. "No," I whispered, clutching the pot until it chafed my skin. My heart sped up until a faint buzzing filled in my ears. This could've been a fluke. There was only one way to find out.

I needed to touch it again.

Calming down took a few minutes, but when my heart did beat somewhat normally, I touched the plant again. It moved under my fingers. It didn't die. Not for ten minutes or twenty.

Around the twenty-five minute mark, I think I started crying. My cheeks were wet so, unless it'd rained inside, I guessed they were tears.

I *had* to share this with someone.

Jumping to my feet, I rushed across the room and yanked on the door with my good arm. In my excitement, I forgot I had locked it. My fingers were shaking so badly it took me a few tries to open it, but once I did, I raced down the hallway and prayed Hayden hadn't locked his door.

His room was three down from mine, and I stopped in front of his door. What if he didn't care? I'd be crushed. I turned the knob and it gave way. Breathing a sigh of relief, I eased it open and let my eyes adjust to the darkness.

I could barely make him out sprawled across the bed, but he was there. Remembering his last reaction when I woke him unexpectedly, I resisted the urge to pounce on him. I felt along the wall until I found the switch and flipped it. Bright light flooded the room. It didn't faze Hayden, but it stole my breath. I stood there, unable to tear my eyes away from him.

The blanket twisted around his narrow hips, one muscled arm thrown over his head, and he was naked. Okay, at least from the navel up.

Snap out of it, I ordered myself. "Hayden? Wake up." I inched closer, raising my voice. "Hayden! Wake up."

His arm dropped from his face and he blinked several times. Slowly he eased himself up on his elbows, squinting.

"Good." I swallowed and tried to smile. "You're awake."

Hayden frowned.

"You have to get up! I need you—"

He threw the blanket aside, revealing that, in fact, he wasn't completely naked. He wore flannel pajama bottoms. "What is it?" He came to his feet. "Are you okay?"

"I . . ." I could only stare. My memories of how he looked shirtless hadn't been burned in my mind like I had thought. I had missed little details—the line running down his stomach, the muscles that popped near his hips.

"Ember, are you all right?"

"Yeah." I closed my eyes and turned around. "I have to show you something."

"Show me something? Ember, it's almost morning. Can't it wait?"

His lack of interest stung, but I persisted. "No. Just come on. Then you can go back to bed. Okay?"

Hayden muttered something as he grabbed a shirt off the floor and tugged it over his head. Silently, he followed me back to my bedroom. I shut the door behind us and led him to the other side of the bed.

"You wanted to show me your bedroom floor?"

I exhaled slowly. "No. I wanted to show you this." Without looking at him, I sat down and pulled the plant into my lap. "You ready?"

"Yeah," he said quietly, sitting on the edge of the bed. "Ember, why are there a bunch of dead . . ." Realization dawned across his expression, and in that pause, he looked sad—disappointed. Not what I expected.

"Hayden?"

"I haven't been working with you," he said.

"I know, but—"

"You've kept up on it."

"Well, not until recently."

"Em, I'm sorry. I've let my own problems—my own mixed-up feelings—get in the way."

I stared at him, growing impatient. "Hayden, it's okay. All is forgiven, but can you just look—"

"It's not okay." He dropped his arms over his bent knees. "You've been at this all alone and why? Because of . . . well, whatever."

"Hayden." I leaned forward and wrapped my hand around the closest thing I could reach—his calf. He stiffened, but didn't move, although I think his body gave off more heat than normal. "It's not your responsibility to fix me. I'm not your science fair project. You don't owe me an explanation."

"Em, I don't think of you as an experiment. I don't think of you like that at all."

I wondered how he did think of me. "Okay, fine. But can you just watch me for a second? I have something I want to show you."

Hayden nodded.

I let go of his leg and closed my eyes. Concentrating with him in the room proved harder than I'd thought. When I felt sure I had that "I have control" mantra on repeat, I cupped the slender stem and ran my hand up it.

Hayden's startled gasp caused my eyes to flutter open. The snakelike plant remained whole and healthy.

"Em." He dropped to his knees beside me, eyes wide. "Did you see that?"

I grinned. "Yes."

"How—how did you do that?"

"I've been practicing, but it hadn't worked till tonight."

"Okay." He picked up the pot and placed it aside. "Touch me."

"What? I don't think that's the next logical step, Hayden. This is the first time I haven't killed a plant. Let me soak in that victory for a bit, first."

He smiled, momentarily stunning me. It had been ages since I'd seen him really smile, the one that showed those dimples. "What did you do differently this time?"

A hot flush spread over my cheeks. "It was something Parker said, actually. That I'd made myself believe . . . the whole soulless thing so I didn't have any responsibility or control, but it's more than that."

Hayden shifted closer. "What?"

I swallowed. "I told myself, I had a gift . . . I'm not cursed, you know?"

"I know—I've always known that. I guess you just had to believe that."

My eyes fell to where his hands rested. Out of everything to ask and be concerned about, I went with the entirely ridiculous. "Why have we been mad at each other?"

"Mad at you?" Hayden rocked back. Three counts went by before he spoke again. "I haven't been mad at you, Em."

There was no turning back now. I was probably going to regret this. "But you haven't really talked to me or . . . spent any time with me. Not since that night in the cabin when I told you that my parents knew about Olivia's gift . . . and I thought, after what you said when I woke you up . . . well, I don't know what I thought."

He took in a deep breath and let it out slowly. "It's been hard. I didn't want to believe that anyone I knew was behind the stuff in the locker, and you were right, but it's more than that. I just need— *needed* some time to sort it all out."

I came to my feet, wiping my hands over my shorts. I felt his gaze inching over me. I realized then, he'd probably never seen my legs before. He didn't say anything as he stood. "What is it?"

He looked like he was about to retreat, shut back down. Watching the war of emotions battle across his face, I had a burst of courage. "I'm not mad that you didn't believe me when I said it was one of your family members doing that stuff. Okay, I *was* mad, but not anymore. It's done now."

"I should've believed you, though. The evidence was pointing at one of them. I shouldn't have doubted you."

But he'd had reason to doubt me. They were his family and Phoebe was important to him. If the situation had been flipped, I'd have had a hard time accepting what was in front of my face, too. "Can't we just move past this?"

Hayden stared, eyes darkening to a shade of night.

Frustrated, my arms dropped to my sides. "Don't you like me anymore?"

"Yes," he said immediately. "Of course I do."

"Then can't we be friends?"

Hayden moved his hand to his chest, rubbing a spot by his heart. "Em, it's hard being friends with you."

My stomach dropped. Not a pleasant feeling. I thought of my effect on Phoebe and winced. What had Kurt said? I was getting to Hayden, too. "I . . . well, wow. I have no idea how to respond to that."

"I don't mean it the way you're taking it." He glanced around the room, sighing. "Look, I'm not explaining this right. Aren't you tired?"

I shook my head. "Are you?"

His dark eyes flicked to my face, impossible to read. "I'm wide awake now."

I admitted to myself right there, I had no idea where this conversation was going. "Um, you can stay—if you want to."

He stared at me in silence, and then headed over to the balcony doors. Somewhat mystified, I watched him draw the shades over the door. There was a barely there smile on his face when he locked the bedroom door.

"I doubt anyone will check on you, but better be safe than sorry." He gestured at the bed. A faint blush tinged the tips of his cheekbones. "You first?"

I hurried to the bed and scooted to the far right side, suddenly nervous. My eyes felt impossibly wide as I watched him come back to the bed. "Do you want to practice with the plant some more?"

Hayden made his way to the side I'd escaped to and sat on the bed beside me. "No."

"Oh." I bit my lip, racking my brain for something to say. I came up empty.

"There are a couple of things I want to clear up." His eyes found mine and held them. "Phoebe and I aren't seeing each other. In fact, there's never been anything romantic between us."

A ridiculous amount of elation swelled in my chest, but I pushed it down. "But I've seen the way she looks at you. And the night of the arrow accident, I . . . saw you two together in the living room."

"Phoebe may've had a . . . crush on me at one time, but she knows I'm not available." He leaned over me, placing one hand on the bed beside my hip. We were so close I could feel the heat rolling off of him. Shifting closer, he picked a strand of hair off my shoulder and wrapped the thick curl around his finger. I froze. "And you misinterpreted what you saw. Her gift . . . well, you know it's been getting to her. I was draining some of it so she wasn't feeling everything. I've done it for years."

"But you guys were so close . . ."

"Yeah, but it wasn't what you thought." His lips formed a crooked smile. "She's not the one I want to be close to."

I sucked in a deep breath. Confused, I pressed my hands against his stomach. I wanted him . . . to touch me like he had in the cabin, but he'd said it was hard to even be friends with me. How was this making it easier? But I couldn't—didn't want to stop him. Hayden's warm breath danced over my cheek and his eyes held a lot of depth. I thought I could probably get lost in them if I wanted to.

"And it's been hard being just friends with you when I want to be more than that. Seeing you every day, wanting to touch you . . ." He stopped, looking thoughtful.

"What are you thinking?" I breathed.

"Well," he drawled. "I'm thinking something really crazy right now."

"What?" I moved my lips closer to his. I'm not even sure if I was aware of doing it.

"I'm thinking about kissing you," he said, "and touching you. It's all I can think about. It's why it's been so hard being around you."

My heart jumped in my chest, and then sped up erratically. The thick tension hit a new all-time high. Surprisingly, I found that I still had the ability to speak. "That's really crazy."

"Yeah." He dropped my hair. "Crazy stuff."

"You should really think about something else," I advised, even as I moved my hand up the front of his shirt, stopping over his heart.

Hayden placed his hand on the small of my back. That touch wiped away the logical part of my brain. "What are *you* thinking about?"

He was close, way too close. The scent of soap and spice filled my senses. I let my eyes drift shut. "Kissing you," I admitted in a low voice.

"I wish you hadn't said that," he said, unbelievably still.

"I know, but you started it." I took a deep breath and opened my eyes. "We shouldn't do this. I don't know if I can."

"You didn't kill the plant, Ember."

"But that's just a plant. It's different. I can't—"

Hayden kissed me.

24

His lips barely brushed mine, as if he wanted to test out what would happen. I didn't dare move. Because nothing happened, he pressed forward. Gentle and soft, then hard and hungry as the kiss deepened.

My world exploded.

Little shivers of pleasure and panic shot through me. I needed to stop, but I couldn't pull myself away, couldn't focus on anything other than how wonderful his lips felt against mine.

And when he pressed me onto my back, I was lost in this madness. Any memories of kissing were blown away. My body sparked alive; my heart swelled and thundered. Blood flowed to every part of me.

A fine tremor shifted through Hayden, but he kept kissing me. His hand slipped to my shoulder, slid down to my hip. I wasn't thinking anymore, just acting. My hand crept from his chest to the back of his neck. I pulled him closer.

He made a strangled sort of sound against my mouth and jerked. A heart-stopping second, and then all the strategic parts of our bodies met, and whatever control I had left snapped. Both of his hands had dropped to my hips and I wrapped my legs around him. My pulse pounded and my skin burned, but I didn't mind.

Twenty seconds of kissing, of touching, maybe a little more.

Then it happened.

Hayden tore his lips from mine and reared back, breaking my hold. Veins bulged and pulsed on the exposed expanse of his neck.

"Hayden . . .?" My breath came out in short gasps.

He shook his head and rested his hands on his knees. "I just . . . need a minute, okay?"

I nodded and wrapped my arms around myself. The poison in my touch still had gotten to him. Plants were one thing, but humans must still be up in the air. Then something else struck me. "Why didn't you drain my touch?"

His hands unclenched. "I won't do that . . . again."

"Dammit, Hayden. I could've killed you!" I came to my knees in front of him. "God, I'm . . . sorry. I shouldn't have let you do that."

"No. Don't be sorry. I'm not. We . . . we just have to be . . . more careful."

"You want to kiss me again? After that?"

"Yeah, I want to do it again. This . . . all of this is progress." He stopped, a small smile spreading across his face. "Maybe I could. I mean, it took a while for your touch to kick in. And you didn't kill the plant."

"Well, I could concentrate *then*."

Hayden laughed softly. "Maybe one day you'll be able to."

Concentrating on anything other than kissing him while, well, kissing him, didn't seem likely.

"Anyway," he said, grabbing my arms and pulling me right up against him, chest to chest. "For now, we'll just work around it."

Before I could even ask what that meant, Hayden kissed me again. This time he pulled back every couple of seconds, leaving me breathless. Soon, I realized he was timing the kisses, pulling away before my touch kicked in. He exhibited far more control than anyone, including himself, ever gave him credit for.

Hayden sat back, pulling me into his lap. "This is working."

I looped my arms around his neck, careful to not touch his skin. "Mmm-hmm."

He chuckled deep in his throat, and then put his mouth on mine again. He pushed it to the limit, stopping only after the first tremor racked his body, and God, it was like sweet torture. Just when I thought I'd come right out of my skin, he'd pull back, breathing just as heavily as me.

"Em, do you know how long I've wanted to be this close to you—to kiss you?" His voice was rough, thick.

I pressed my cheek against his chest, inhaling his scent. "As long as I have?"

"Longer," he murmured, working his fingers into my hair and tipping my head back. "You're so beautiful to me."

"Beautiful?"

"Yes," he said so seriously. "Your lips, your cheeks, your eyes . . . I find everything about you beautiful. Your strength, the way you care for your sister . . ." His gaze dropped, and I shivered. "I admire your control. Your willpower. Everything. I wouldn't change a thing about you."

My heart seemed to take over everything. I crushed my mouth to his, immersed in the thrill of his lips against mine. I don't know how long we did this or how many different places his lips touched before he'd pull away, take a moment, and then start all over. I felt feverish, alive, and . . . and something far, far stronger than anything I'd ever felt in my life.

Sometime later, I was wrapped in the bed sheet and Hayden lay beside me, that clever mind of his finding a way to hold me without really touching. He stayed above the covers, one arm and leg thrown over me. Every so often, he'd brush my hair back and I'd snuggle in closer.

"Ember?"

Tipping my head back, I opened my eyes so I could see him. He looked terribly serious. "What?"

"I really am sorry for not believing you," he said quietly. "I won't doubt you again."

"It's all right. It's over now." But it really wasn't over. Phoebe may've been responsible for the stuff in the locker, but she hadn't been behind the accident that started all of this. But right now, curled up in the closest thing to being in Hayden's arms, I didn't want to think about that.

"When's Santa coming?" Olivia asked for probably the hundredth time in the last hour. Phoebe glanced up from her magazine, actually smiling.

I yawned. "At the end of the parade, Olivia. You know that. It's the same every year."

She walked her Barbie doll over to where I sprawled across the floor. "I wanna see Santa now!"

"So do I." I picked the doll up and inched it back toward her.

"Have you written a list for Santa yet?" Gabe asked, surprising the hell out of me. "You know, telling him what you want?"

Olivia whirled on Gabe, launching into a rather detailed description of the toys she wanted while I closed my eyes and replayed last night over and over again. Nothing could take the smile off my face or stop the somersaults that kept occurring below my navel.

Last night had been wonderful. Perfect.

And apparently, the happy feeling clouded any sense of judgment I had, because when Liz asked me to help her with the stuffing, I agreed.

We stood side by side at the kitchen island. I wished I'd had the forethought of tucking my hair back before sinking my bare hands into the mix of bread, egg, butter, and milk.

"Did you used to do this with your mother?" Liz asked after a couple of minutes.

I squashed my hands around, feeling egg ooze through my fingers. "Yeah, but we . . . we used to do it the night before."

"And stuff the turkey then, too?"

I nodded. "I used to eat the stuffing when Mom wasn't look-ing, but the last time—when I was fourteen—she saw me eating it. Said I'd get salmonella or something."

She laughed softly. "Do you think it needs more onions? Bread?"

"Sure." Not that I had a clue, really, but I think she asked to make me feel like I'd contributed.

Liz reached into the bowl—carefully avoiding my hands—and plucked out a small ball of mixed stuffing. She raised her brows at me.

"Want some?"

I stared at her a moment, then decided *what the hell*. I opened my mouth and she tossed the little ball. I missed the first one, second, and third. By the fourth try, when the ball actually went into my mouth, we both were laughing and stuffing slime covered my chin.

"You know," Liz said, crumbling up chunks of bread and adding them in. "I think your mother hears you when you talk to her."

I looked up from the bowl. "How do you know I talk to her?"

She smiled, fine lines spreading out from the corners of her sloe-colored eyes. "I've heard you a few times. I think it's good you do that. She's still in there."

"Do you really think so?"

Liz nodded solemnly. "Yes, I do."

"Think what?" Hayden asked, sauntering into the kitchen.

I froze beside Liz; all rational thought flew right out my head. I didn't even need to look in a mirror to know my cheeks were turning a bright red.

"Nothing, just me running my mouth," Liz said, laughing softly. "We're making stuffing. Want to help?"

Hayden propped himself against the island, close enough that I could *feel* him smile. "I think you guys got it handled."

I stole a quick glance at him. He wore a simple, black shirt and jeans, but he looked amazing. He nudged my leg with his, earning a grin.

A sudden squeal broke the silence, followed by, "Santa! Santa!"

I turned back to the stuffing, mashing it together. "That would be Olivia."

Liz laughed. "I have to see this. Do you think you can finish it up?"

"Yes." I nodded and blew a curl out of my face. It fell right back.

She hurried from the room, wiping her hands on her apron. My eyes followed her, silently acknowledging that she really did care for Olivia. "As much as it pains me to say this, she really is good for Olivia."

"And who is good for you?" Hayden asked, moving behind me, trailing quick kisses over the curve of my shoulder.

My breath caught. "I think . . . you know the answer to that."

Hayden placed his hands on my hips, pulling me back against him. "Hmm, maybe you should show me?"

"I'm making stuffing, so you better—" He placed lips against the side of my neck, then behind my ear. "*Oh* . . ."

He laughed and pulled away, leaving one hand on my back. "Need help?"

"Sure."

"Good." Hayden tucked a strand of my hair behind my ear.

We finished up with the stuffing, laughing and talking about nothing in particular. Every so often, Hayden became distracted. He'd stop, give me a quick kiss or brush my hair back. I think it took us a little longer than necessary to get it in the turkey.

I was washing the gunk off my hands and Hayden sat on the counter beside me when his father walked in. If anyone could kill my buzz, it was Cromwell.

"Liz tells me you two are making the stuffing. I really didn't believe it."

"What? I have a bit of the chef in me." Hayden smiled.

Drying off my hands, I turned around. "He was helping."

Cromwell raised a brow. "You can't even boil an egg, son." He paused. "Or toast bread without burning it."

I couldn't help it, I laughed. "Nice."

Hayden frowned at me. "I can toast bread."

"You tried to shove a fork in the toaster to get your bread out—that was only a few years ago."

"Oh. Wow." I grinned at Hayden.

"Thanks, Dad." Hayden pushed himself off the counter.

Cromwell smiled at him as he walked to the oven, and I seriously believe he was checking out the stuffing.

Hayden tugged on my sleeve and nodded at the back door. He mouthed *outside.*

I nodded, immediately looking away when Cromwell turned around. "So, what are you two getting yourselves into now that you've proven you both can cook?"

Hayden shrugged. "I think I'm going to take a nap."

"Up late last night?" he asked innocently.

My eyes widened as I stared at the floor, but Hayden sounded unfazed. "Yeah, I stayed up late watching TV."

"What are you doing, Ember?"

"Huh?" My head jerked up. "Oh. Now—I think I'm gonna go sketch."

"Well, we have dinner at three. I expect both of you to be here." His gaze fell on Hayden. Cromwell smiled, but it never quite reached his eyes. "Before you run off, Hayden, I'd like to talk to you for a moment."

I headed for the door, worry gnawing at my stomach. As I went to my bedroom, I could hear Liz and Olivia's giggles mingling in with the male voices. I pulled on a hoodie and a pair of gloves before grabbing my sketchpad and a pencil.

Taking the route farthest from the kitchen, I slipped out the front door. I felt a little bit guilty about not spending time with

Olivia. It used to be just us, and for two years, there wasn't the smell of turkey or so much laughter.

I convinced myself she was okay while I waited in the chilly air for Hayden to appear. He showed up five minutes later, a wide smile across his face. Bright sunlight broke through the trees, casting a halo around his head.

"Aren't you cold?" He hadn't even put on a sweater.

"Nah." Hayden held out his hand.

I stuck the sketchpad under my arm and took his hand. "Where're we going? The cabin?"

"I thought we could take a walk."

"Okay." I let him lead me into the woods. A chorus of dead leaves crunched under our feet. "What did Cromwell want?"

"He wanted to know what we were up to." He held a branch back.

"What? Does he know about . . ." I couldn't say "last night."

"No." He sent a reassuring smile over his shoulder. "He just wondered what was up, I guess. I told him we were making stuffing."

"He still doesn't want you around me, does he? He's worried you'll get hurt."

Hayden looked away. "I don't think he really thinks about it anymore."

I raised my brows.

"Seriously, I think he knows I like you and nothing is going to change that. He's coming around. So it's nothing to worry about."

"Are you sure?" I didn't believe him, not in a million years.

"Yes." He squeezed my hand. "Let's not worry about him right now, because later—after dinner—I'm seriously going to take a nap."

"It's something in turkey," I told him.

"Tryp-a-something, right?"

We'd stopped walking, and I wasn't sure how far we'd gone. The sun barely broke through the canopy of branches out here, if that was any indication. Hayden circled his arms around my waist and pulled me forward. I came all too willingly.

"So why did you want to come out here?" I asked.

Instead of telling me why, he showed me—with his lips, his hands. And eventually we were on a pile of fallen leaves, testing just how far we could go. Breathless and a bit dazed, I rested atop his chest, running my fingers down the side of his face.

"Take off the gloves," he demanded.

"No. It's too much." That was something we had learned last night. If a lot of skin touched, then, well, my gift went into overdrive.

He tipped his head back and sighed. "Later, then."

I smiled and dropped a kiss on the middle of his throat. "Can I ask you something?"

"Sure." He snuck a hand under my sweater and splayed it across my shirt. "Anything."

"What made you decide last night to be okay with . . .?"

"I like it when you blush. Brings out your eyes."

I rolled my eyes. "Shut up."

He chuckled as he tucked a strand of my hair back with his free hand. "I realized I wouldn't lose control. Not with you. I . . ." He stopped, smiled slyly. "I just wouldn't want to hurt you."

I could tell there was more to it. "And you believed I wouldn't hurt you?"

"I never believed you'd lose control, Em." He reached up and threaded his fingers through my hair. "You're good inside, better than any of us."

Tears sprang to my eyes. I looked away, not wanting him to see how hearing him say that affected me.

"Hey. You okay?"

"Yeah," I said, chewing on my lip. "It's just that . . . that was really nice."

His hand drifted out of my hair and fell to my hand. "Will you answer a question for me?" When I nodded, he continued. "What do you draw? Can I look?"

I rolled off him and grabbed for my sketchpad, but Hayden was just so much faster. "Hayden—don't—you—dare!" He had the creased pad in his graceful hands—hands I had sketched. *Oh, God.* "Don't open it!"

He glanced up with a grin. "What's in it, Em?"

"Just stuff—look, no one has ever seen my sketches."

"No one? Then I'd be honored if you'd let me see."

Groaning, I ran a hand through my hair. "I suck. They're really bad. You don't want to see it."

"Your cheeks are blood-red again," he pointed out, settling back down on his arm.

"Yeah, well, then you shouldn't look at it."

"If it really bothers you, I won't look at them." He offered me the pad.

I stared at it. One last secret—maybe, and what? Our eyes met as I took it back from him. My drawings were private stuff, like a reflection of my innermost thoughts. Allowing someone to see them was like standing naked in front of a crowd, opening up in a way I've never considered. Then I remembered how he'd looked when he'd seen my scars for the first time. He hadn't stared at them. He looked at my face, and not because he couldn't bear to look at them, but because he hadn't cared. They hadn't mattered to him.

Making up my mind, I thumbed open the sketchpad after a few tries. The gloves made it difficult. "These . . . these were before the accident. Flowers, landscapes, and this was Sushi."

Hayden sidled over to my side at some point. He peered at the mashed-up nose and squinted stare. "Wow. That *was* an ugly cat."

I laughed softly, flipped to another page. "Dad."

He stopped my hand before I could turn the page. "He looks like a kind man."

I traced my fingers over the picture. I had drawn it from memory and it'd taken several tries to get the line of his jaw correct, and the slight bump in his nose. "He was."

"Em, I'm really sorry about your dad."

Swallowing, I nodded and turned another page. "This, of course, is Olivia and Mom. These are—"

"Seneca Rocks, Em, you're really good. I mean it."

"I don't know. The edges could be softer, not so bleak and hard."

He reached across me and turned the pages. He'd make a comment, brush his fingers over the drawing, and then flip to another page. When he came across the sketch I'd done of his hands, I don't think he realized who they belonged to, but there was no stopping him.

I closed my eyes as he turned to the first sketch of him. He didn't say anything. I don't even think he breathed. All I could hear was the sound of him slowly going from page to page.

"When did you draw these?" he asked, his voice rough.

"The first one a couple of days after getting here, and the rest were over time." I rubbed my hand under my chin and finally looked at him. He had this awestruck look on his face. His eyes were wide and bright, lips parted just enough to show a bit of teeth. "What?"

"I didn't expect that."

"It's kind of creepy, huh?" I closed the pad and tossed it aside. "I don't mean for it to be. You just have this face that's all lines and curves. I . . . I had to draw it. I hope—" His mouth cut me off, stopping whatever lame excuse I was about to give. He leaned into me, deepening the kiss until I swam in the ecstasy of his mouth.

Hayden broke away reluctantly, easing down on his back. He stared up through the branches, his expression oddly pensive.

"Are you okay? Did . . . did I hurt you?"

"No," he said quickly, finding my hand and squeezing it. "Do you want to know why I trust my father so much? Why I know he could never do anything to hurt you?"

Not the conversation I really wanted to have right now, but I nodded. "Okay."

A brief smile pulled at his lips. "When I say he saved my life, I'm not exaggerating. Not just once, but twice. The first time was when he found me in foster care. If he hadn't found me, I don't think I would've survived."

I sat back, still holding his hand. I didn't dare speak, giving him the opportunity to continue.

"Things were bad. There were days when I didn't get to eat. And if I was caught sneaking food? The beatings were . . . intense. And at first, things were better—so much better—at the Facility. Then they started this thing called the Assimilation Program, and I was a candidate for it. At first, Cromwell didn't know all that the program entailed. It was headed up by Doctor Ishtar." He paused, eyes squinting. "They used every possible method you can think of, Ember. Exposure therapy at its finest."

"Exposure therapy?"

He nodded. "Because kids like me were having trouble controlling our gifts when we were, well, just about any time, the doctors would create high-stress scenarios that would provoke our gifts over and over until we became desensitized to the triggers. Some of the things they did would blow your mind."

I wanted to ask what. Maybe it was just morbid fascination, but somehow common sense prevailed. "How long were you in the program?"

"Long enough," he answered, sliding his hand out of mine. "When my father saw what it was doing to me—literally driving me crazy—he pulled me out and we came here. Since then, the Facility and Dr. Ishtar swear they've changed the program. I know he said he'd send you there, but, Ember, he never would.

Even though the Assimilation Program works, it's horrible. The things I had to do . . ." He trailed off for several long moments. "Anyway, he would never do that."

"How can you be so sure?"

Hayden tipped his head toward me and smiled. "Because he knows if that happened to you, it would hurt me."

"I'm sorry you had to go through all of that, Hayden. It doesn't seem right."

"Well, it's over now." His smile slipped away and he reached for me. "How much time do we have until dinner?"

"About two and half hours."

"Hmm." Then he tugged on my sweater, pulling me down so his mouth could reach mine. "Not enough time at all."

25

The rest of Thanksgiving break didn't seem real—everything was great. It was like I was in some fictional dreamworld and in the morning, I'd have to go back to my real life. And in a bizarre twist, on Sunday morning, Cromwell handed over the keys to my Jeep.

I lifted my head and stared down at Hayden. My fingers itched to touch him, but he looked so content in sleep I didn't want to bother him. So I brushed my fingers over my lips instead. They felt swollen and plump. We'd kissed a lot before he carefully tucked me against his chest, a sweater and a sheet separating our flesh.

We'd been kissing a lot. It seemed like that was all we did. Oh. Well. We didn't *just* kiss.

We did other things. Like talk. Touch. Practice with plants. Kiss. Eat. Sleep. Practice with plants some more. Every night he snuck into my room, kind of like the way things had been in the cabin.

Ah, I did miss the cabin.

Hayden shifted, his arm curling around my hips, pulling me closer. I placed my hands on his chest so I didn't topple right on top of him. Not that I would've minded, but we couldn't go longer than a minute. Which was an improvement over twenty seconds, but who knew if it was Hayden's gift that had added the additional time?

There was no way to really test it unless I touched someone else.

"Out of the question," I murmured, placing my cheek against his chest, where his heart beat. I closed my eyes and let out a little sigh.

The only thing we hadn't done was talk about the accident. And I didn't want to bring it up. My mind went back to the files in Cromwell's office. I had no plans to tell Hayden about them. Things were just too perfect right now to ruin them. Well, almost perfect.

If only I could get rid of the nagging thought that when things are this perfect, they usually come to an end in one big, messy ball of flames.

"What have I learned from *Catcher in the Rye*?" repeated a student from the front of the class.

Mr. Theo pinched the bridge of his nose. "Yes, that is the question."

The same student leaned back in his seat. "Well, I've learned I'm probably going to fail English this semester."

An eruption of laughter followed. Mr. Theo looked like he was nearing the end of his patience, showing a splinter in his easy manner. He'd looked that way since class had started.

A smile cracked my face even though it felt like someone was pounding an ice pick into my temple. When the bell sounded, I think Mr. Theo and I both breathed a sigh of relief.

I coasted through the rest of my morning classes. My chest swelled unexpectedly when I spotted Hayden slouched against my locker, waiting for me. Like it was nothing, he dropped his arm over my shoulder and grazed his lips over my temple.

Several kids glanced at us—mostly girls who looked like they'd trade their knock-off Prada shoes to be in my position.

"Hungry?"

"Always." I tucked my hand into my sweater. "Diner?"

"If you don't mind that Phoebe and Gabe join us?"

"That's cool." Not a total lie, but it also meant we had to act like we weren't doing whatever we were doing. It wasn't like we'd become official or something.

Then again, Hayden hadn't skipped the PDA a few seconds ago.

Phoebe and Gabe were already at the diner when we walked in. I slid in first, then Hayden. The entire length of his thigh pressed against mine. I pulled a curl from behind my ear and started fiddling with it.

Phoebe's bright gaze slid between us before settling on Hayden. She and I still weren't talking, obviously. And I was making it a habit to not feel anything when I was around her. I wasn't sure if it was working or not.

"Are you going to Charleston with Jonathan tomorrow?" she asked. "Parker's going with him."

"Nah, I'd rather sit in class." Hayden stretched and dropped his hands in his lap.

"I think I'd skip class." Gabe frowned at the menu.

"Is he going to be gone all day?" I asked, visions of files dancing in my head.

"Most of the day," Hayden answered. "Probably won't be back till late evening."

"Oh." I took a drink of my soda. Hadn't Olivia mentioned at dinner that Liz would be going to class with her tomorrow? Something about a field trip involving a play. That meant no one would be home.

Gabe said something, but I'd stopped listening and was suddenly cold—shivering beside a boy who threw off boiling-level temperatures. Tomorrow would be perfect. No one would be home besides my mom— and let's face it, she didn't count. Who knew when I'd find another opportunity to see those files?

But did I want to know what was in them? What if I found something that changed everything? What if there was evidence that Cromwell had been behind the accident?

Hayden's hand on my thigh brought me out of my thoughts. I kept my face straight and kicked him under the table. He squeezed in return.

If I did this—which I already knew I would—I needed to prepare myself for the possibility that Hayden would hate me forever for outing his father or another member of his adopted family. Phoebe's locker stuff hadn't done it, but this would be different, worse.

I glanced at Hayden, and a small, secretive smile graced his lips. That kind of smile usually set my skin aflame, but ice was building in my stomach.

Later that night, I talked things through with Mom. That went well—meaning I had a twenty-minute long conversation with myself—but I no longer held it against her. This wasn't just about my dad, or me, or even Olivia.

Mom would never talk to me again. She'd only see Olivia, and from what I understood, she hadn't been doing much of that lately. Olivia didn't understand why and honestly, neither did I.

Before supper, I drew with Olivia. Besides absolutely refusing to stay on the paper, the kid had talent, more than I'd had at that age. Then again, Olivia's talents were more than just her gift. She was sort of perfect.

I checked my email, more out of habit than anything else, and straightened my room while I waited for Hayden to show up. Yesterday, he'd removed all the plants from the room, except the snake one. I kept that one on my desk as a reminder of my success.

It still hadn't died and well, I sort of loved that plant.

The soft sound of my door brushing over the carpet drew my attention. I turned off the computer and swiveled around in my desk chair. My stomach did the weird fluttery thing at the sight of his lopsided smile.

"No plants?" I asked.

Hayden shook his head and shut the door. "Thought we'd do something normal for a change." He pulled a DVD out of his waistband and tossed it to me.

I caught it and flipped it over. "Didn't this just come out in the theaters?"

"I cannot answer that question." He tugged off his hoodie with a sly smile and dropped it on the floor. The long-sleeve shirt he wore underneath rode up a couple of inches. "Em, if you keep looking at me like that, we aren't going to watch any movie."

Blushing, I jumped up and busied myself putting the DVD in. It wasn't my fault that I stared a little. He had that kind of effect. We started off watching the movie—honestly. But it was way too hard to pay attention from the moment Hayden tugged my ponytail down and started messing with my hair.

"I like your hair down." He twisted his fingers through the curls.

My eyes drifted shut as I relaxed next to him. "It's a mess. I need to get a haircut."

Hayden's fingers stilled. "No. You shouldn't cut your hair. It's beautiful."

I would never cut my hair. Ever. "Pay attention to the movie."

"I am."

No, he wasn't. He left my hair alone, only to circle his arms around my waist and tug me back against him. I let my head fall back against his chest and tried to focus on my plan. "Can I ask you something?"

He made some sort of affirmative sound. His breath stirred the hair at my temple.

"Do you mind if I drive to school tomorrow?" I held my breath.

"No." His arms tightened. I warmed in a lot of places.

"I thought I could drive myself, you know? I haven't in a long time and I thought it would be nice to do it . . . by myself."

Hayden turned me around in his arms in about a nanosecond. I put my hands on his shoulders to steady myself. He
looked incredibly serious. Oh no, this didn't look good. "What?"
I asked, a bit transfixed by how the different colors from the TV
swayed over his face.

"If you want to drive yourself to school, Em, you don't have
to ask for my permission," he said, tucking a curl behind my ear.
"You can do whatever you want."

"I know. I didn't ask for that reason." I felt terrible for lying.
Terrible for what I planned to do tomorrow. Terrible that everything could change if I found something.

"Okay." His dark gaze searched my face. I felt my stomach
drop. "Em, do you like this? I mean, we haven't really talked
about this." A faint blush stained his cheeks. "You know, about
what we're doing."

Relief swamped me, but then I realized this was also a serious
conversation. Like, *the* conversation. Were we moving to "title"
territory? Somehow that seemed just as important as the files in
Cromwell's office.

I sat back. "What are we doing?"

Hayden ran a hand over his head, and then dropped his arm
to his knee. "I really don't know how to put what we're doing
into words."

"Me, neither."

"You know I . . . like you?"

"Like" was such a lame word. "Yeah."

"For a while now, and well, I don't want how I feel about you
to influence how you feel about me."

I frowned. "Uh . . ."

A tiny grin appeared. "What I mean is—I don't know what I
mean." He laughed self-consciously and shook his head. "I'm
not very good at this. I guess what I'm trying to say is, I don't
know if what we have between us is because you can touch me,
or something else."

I'd never really looked at it that way, but I could see how he would. My options were painfully limited. "Hayden, are you asking me if I only like you because you're the only guy I can touch?"

His gaze flicked off my face. "Yeah, I guess that's what I'm asking."

I scooted closer. "I like you because I can touch you."

Hayden's head jerked back to me. He opened his mouth, but I held up my hand. "Wait. It's more than that. When I first came here, I didn't trust you—trust any of you, really. But out of everyone here, you were nice to me. You talked to me and you . . . you believed in me. You didn't treat me like a freak."

"Because you're not a freak," he said seriously.

"I've felt like queen of the freaks for two years, but I never felt that way around you. Anyway, you're funny and you're nice. And you're smart. I trust you—obviously. I've told you and showed you things that not even Adam knew about." I shook my head. "And you're—"

"Hot?" he asked with overt innocence.

I laughed. "That too, but it's more than all of that. And I like you. I really do." Even that sounded stupid to me. "I don't know." My pulse picked up, and my palms felt gross. "Does that tell you anything?"

"Yes," he said softly.

"I don't know what any of it means. I'm . . . not used to any of this, but yeah, I like you."

Hayden scooted down, wrapping his hands around my arms. "You know I think you're amazing."

I knew my face was on fire. I think I nodded.

"And I don't feel this way," he brought my hands to his chest, over his heart, "about anyone else." Hayden locked eyes with me, and I really felt on fire then. "So where does that leave us?"

"We're . . . dating?"

"No." His expression was full of desire, along with another emotion, one that thrilled and frightened me. "'Dating' doesn't sound right."

I swallowed, unable to look away. "Then, what?"

"I think you know." Hayden pulled me forward as he lay back, his hands spread over my back. "Do you want me to say it?"

"Yeah," I breathed.

"Come closer."

I lowered my head. "Close enough?"

Hayden closed the minute distance between us and brushed his lips over mine. It was just a touch, but I stopped breathing altogether. When the kiss deepened, I lost track of the world around me, and the fact that he never answered the question. Not that he needed to. This kiss was beyond silly titles. This kiss was something—I pulled back when I felt Hayden's fingers spasm. We'd gone too long. Both of us were breathing heavily, and a sudden realization floored me.

This could be the last time I ever kissed him. A sharp, stabbing pain sliced through my chest. Would Hayden forgive me for exposing Cromwell?

I didn't think so.

And I didn't want to waste another moment with him. His hands spread up my back, over my shoulders. When he put some space between us, I made a sound of protest. But then his hands were on the move again, stealing down the front and under the hem of my shirt. His knuckles brushed close to my navel. At once, fire and ice coursed through me.

Somehow my shirt ended up on the floor, and I should've felt embarrassed. I'd never been this exposed with a boy before and with the scars . . . but in the soft light and under his intense stare, I'd never felt more perfect in my life.

His shirt stayed on, and so did the rest of his clothes. Obviously, we could only take this so far, but I could still feel the heat through his clothes and it felt amazing—especially when his hands grasped my hips and he held me close, our lips touching every so often, our bodies rocking together.

It was the simplest of touches that got to me the most. Just being able to be this close to him felt a thousand times better than anything I could ever imagine—like lightning shooting through my veins each time he whispered my name.

Amidst all these wonderful sensations, my heart swelled so big I was sure it would explode from my chest. I knew what it was. I knew what I was feeling.

I was in love with him.

My stomach twisted and turned from the moment I stepped into the shower until I climbed in my Jeep. Instead of focusing on the huge part of me that wanted to forget all of this, I set my plan into motion. A nervous sort of excitement thrummed through my veins and so did a measure of dread, but I felt kind of badass.

Like a spy or something.

I'd patiently sit through three of my morning classes before skipping out. Waiting any longer would be risky. I ended up getting to school way too early. The corridors were unusually silent, and my footsteps echoed down the hall. As I made my way toward my locker, I couldn't help but feel a little creeped out. I half-expected the lights overhead to flicker out and a gruesome one-handed, one-toothed janitor to jump out at me.

I didn't feel so badass then.

I shook my head in an attempt to get rid of the image and focused on my locker. Even though I knew there wouldn't be anything in it, the locker still filled me with unease. Phoebe had officially traumatized me when it came to lockers.

Drawing in a deep breath, I closed my eyes and unlocked it. A couple of heartbeats went by, then maybe a minute, and I pried one eye open. It was, of course, empty.

By the end of English, I started to feel queasy and my temples felt like they were about to explode from the pressure in my head. My nerves were getting to me and I knew I was going to chicken out if I waited as long as I'd planned. When the bell rang at the end of second period, I gathered my stuff up in a rush and hurried from the classroom.

I stopped at the front doors. Fat raindrops splattered against the pavement. My hair was about five seconds from turning into a giant frizzball. Chewing on my lip, I glanced over my shoulder and about fell over.

Mr. Theo stood by the entrance of the admin offices, chatting with another teacher. If he turned his head, I was so busted. Then he did look up, right at me. I started to back away from the door, but he raised a brow and smiled, then turned away.

I couldn't believe it. And I couldn't stand here any longer. I pushed open the doors just as the skies ripped open and sleety rain poured. It felt cold enough to snow.

Navigating the rain-slick streets with bald tires proved harder than I remembered, but around forty minutes later, I parked the Jeep in front of the Cromwell mansion.

Soaked to the bone, I went in through the garage and made sure all the cars were gone. Then I shrugged off my wet sweater and hung it on the back of a chair in the kitchen. Even my thin shirt underneath was damp, but I didn't have time to waste changing.

From there, I half-ran, half-slipped over the hardwood floors. Statues and paintings seemed to watch me as I entered the right wing. I came to a halt outside Cromwell's study and sucked in air. There was a chance the door would be locked—if so, a waste of a good hair day.

A little nagging voice whispered in my head that what I was about to do was wrong. I'd be prying around in other people's personal business, but my reasons for doing so were far more important than a silly little thing like privacy. Right?

I reached into my pocket and ran my fingers over the coin. This was supposed to be for good luck. Well, I needed some luck now. I pushed on the door. It creaked open and a blast of frigid air hit me.

Clamping down on the voice that screamed moral outrage, I headed for the glossy oak desk. Geez, my conscience acted like I planned on doing something terrible. Where was that voice when I cheated on tests and at computer games?

Not the same thing, I guessed.

I yanked open one drawer. No keys. I moved to the second, third, and finally, the middle drawer. The key ring gleamed up at me. I grabbed them and whirled around.

The keys felt strangely heavy in my hand. After several false starts, I found the right one and yanked open the drawer in the credenza. I hesitated a moment; the little voice was back again, whispering I might not like what I found.

I ignored it and grabbed Kurt's file first, having no idea what to expect.

The first pages consisted of basic information: birthdate, hometown address, and a brief outline of his gifts. From what I read, he had extensive abilities in the mind-wiping field, able to remove certain memories while leaving others intact. Adam had been a perfect example of that. He'd remembered everything— except me. But Hayden had said whoever had done the sweep on Mom hadn't done it right. Looking at the file on Kurt, I doubted he'd mess up so badly. I assumed whoever was behind the car crash would've also wanted Mom to believe Olivia had died, too.

Pushing the hair out of my face, I flipped to the second page. Bingo.

It wasn't a criminal record—not a formal one, at least, but Kurt had quite the history in his younger days: B and E, robbery, and assault. All before the age of twenty-one, which I didn't think was such a big deal—people change. But the psych eval on the third page caught my eye.

Kurt was described as exhibiting malignant narcissistic personality traits paired with antisocial and paranoid tendencies from onset "G." I assumed that "G" stood for "Gifted." I didn't need a degree in psychology to know some of the words didn't bring the warm and fuzzies, but nothing pointed to him being a full-out psycho-killer.

Disappointed, I shoved his file back in and picked up Parker's. As I read through his stuff, I began to wonder why Cromwell even had files on them. Why did he keep this information? Cromwell was a mayor, not a psychologist, and stuff like this belonged in a clinical setting.

Parker's personal information didn't come as a surprise. Cromwell commented on his inability to block out other's thoughts, which led to antisocial traits. Phoebe's had the same stuff about controlling the empath in her, and there was a recent note about her reaction toward me and a treatment guide outlining blocking techniques that Cromwell wanted to work on.

Gabriel's file didn't mention much of anything.

Olivia's included a bio with all the normal stuff: our parents' names and whatnot, but just one word about her gift: "Miraculous." I stared at it for a while, and then I shoved it back inside and moved to grab mine.

But I saw another file labeled "T.G." and nothing else. Curious, I grabbed that one and cracked it open. The first page had been blacked out the same way I imagined they did with classified papers. I flipped to the second page, then the next. *Everything* had been blacked out. Frowning, I put it back in the drawer and pulled my file out.

I prepared myself for the worst, figuring I'd see things like "bad-mannered" and "ill-tempered" as character traits. So I was surprised when I found nothing on the first page. Not a damn thing—no bio, no birthdate, just the date Hayden and Kurt had shown up at my house, the day they'd relocated me. Weirded out by that, I turned over the page, already cringing at what I would see. And God, did I want to go find Cromwell, rip off my glove, and choke-slam him.

I didn't even have a freaking name. The sporadic notes referred to me as "Project E."

Project E has an unstable gift. The ability to disable and even kill with a touch proves to be reminiscent of Project J. Project E is also a candidate for the Assimilation Program. At current time, there has been no evidence that her gift can be controlled. Caution must be exercised.

My fingers curled around the paper until I heard the pages crumple. Assimilation? For me? He could assimilate my foot up his ass. And when did he start believing I had a gift? If I remembered correctly, the last thing he'd called it was *unnatural and wrong.*

I slammed my file back down, and because I couldn't help myself, and because I was mad and confused, I picked up Hayden's file. I sat down and cracked it open. Immediately, my eyes scanned down the page. Just like Kurt and the rest, there was a full bio and I knew the good stuff would be on the second and third pages.

Don't do it.

But I wanted to do it and I needed something to distract me from my desire to burn down Cromwell's office. There was a lot about Hayden's gift that I hadn't known. Being an ener-path, he could manipulate almost any form of energy: use air to crush a house, create fire out of the electricity in the air, and even move the ground like a mini-earthquake. It was all pretty amazing . . . and frightening. I flipped the next page over and flinched.

Once, twice, three times—that was how many times I read it before my brain accepted the words written there. "Oh, my God," I whispered.

Hayden hadn't been removed from his parents' home because they'd been afraid of him, but I could understand the lie. The truth would hurt too much—provoke too many questions, too many memories.

He'd just been a kid—God, only five. Way too young.

And he'd killed his entire family.

26

An old newspaper clipping, dulled to faint yellow, had been shoved between page two and three, detailing the horrifying events without a trace of the heavy emotion involved.

The house had burned. It'd started in an upstairs bedroom, spreading downstairs and engulfing the entire home. There had been only one survivor—Hayden.

I wiped under my eyes with the back of my hand and started to close the file. But toward the end of the page, I stopped. The times Hayden struggled for control flashed before me. The day Kurt had pushed me, and when I'd found the car in my locker and the trashcan had exploded. The times we'd argued and I smelled the distinct odor of smoke—like the smell of ozone burning—not fire. Had that been one of the reasons he'd backed off from me? Maybe it hadn't just been my suspicions. Maybe he feared losing control again because of me, like both Parker and Kurt had warned me.

I swallowed past the lump in my throat and closed the file. Sorrow burned through me. I couldn't even begin to understand what he'd gone through—was still going through. My heart felt like it would rip open. The guilt I carried with me over Dustin's death was nothing compared to what he must feel.

After reading about Hayden, I didn't care what Cromwell thought about me or the Assimilation program. If anything, it gave me more reason to figure out a way to control whatever it was I had. I'd always thought I had it bad—that what'd happened to me was the worst thing ever. Now I knew that wasn't the case.

God, I felt like a douche.

Leaning forward, I put Hayden's file back and started to close the drawer when I saw another file labeled only with initials: "J. G." I pulled it out and flipped it open. There was a picture of a girl about my age, but the photo looked old and grainy.

Whoever she was, she'd been a pretty girl with long brown hair and glasses resting on the tip of her nose, but the photo also captured an intense, frightened look in her eyes. Now even more curious, I shuffled through the file, stopping on a paper with notes written in Cromwell's hand. Most of it, like the chick's full name and any info that would reveal her identity, had been blacked out like in the other file. There was still enough left for me to read, and what I learned shocked and confused the hell out of me.

Cromwell had really, really lied to me.

This girl had been a part of the Assimilation program, which had turned out to be a complete failure. She'd been unable to control her gift and had committed suicide at the Facility.

She'd only been sixteen, and she'd been able to kill with a touch.

I closed her file, hands shaking. I really didn't know how to process that. Someone else had been gifted like me? She'd killed herself because she couldn't control it? I started to put her file back, but a cluster of papers slipped out and fell into my lap.

Just like with Hayden's file, I didn't really believe what I saw at first. But then, like everything else, it sank in slowly. Dizziness and nausea rushed through me. I dropped the file.

Newspaper clippings about Dad and his work at the hospital before the accident, articles I couldn't bear to read after he'd died. A schedule was attached to the clippings—my sophomore year class schedule. But that wasn't all; there were directions to my house, to Dad's hospital, and . . . *Oh, my God.*

Attached to the newspaper clippings was a menu to Salt of the Sea, the restaurant I'd insisted on the night of the accident. Scribbled on it were several dates—the last of them, the date of the accident, was circled. Realization crept over me like cold fingers tracing down my spine. The papers slipped from my fingers.

Static filled my ears. For several long minutes, I couldn't move, couldn't even breathe as my world fell out from underneath me.

No, no, no.

The handwriting—all of the stuff written—looked like Hayden's scribble. He'd been watching way before he'd admitted—he had written the schedule, the directions, the date of the accident. It hadn't been just Kurt or Cromwell. It'd been the three of them, maybe all of them.

Time seemed to stop, and then I sprang forward and gathered up the papers. My breath came out in short, little gasps. I needed to get out of here—get Mom, find Olivia. The buzzing in my ears made it hard to think, but all I knew—

"What are you doing?"

I shrieked, jumping to my feet and spinning around.

Hayden stood in the entrance of the study. Little streams of rain dripped from his hair, traveling down the side of his face. The ends of his hair curled around his temples and cheeks.

"Ember?"

My heart pounded so fast I swore my shirt fluttered.

"What are you doing in my father's office?" He took one step into the room, then another. "Why did you leave school?"

I eyed the door behind him and tried to nudge the drawer shut. It wouldn't budge. "I . . . I'm not doing anything."

"Call me crazy, but I don't believe you." His gaze dropped over me, then behind me. His eyes narrowed. "You went through my father's files?"

"N—no," I stammered.

His eyes flicked up and bore into mine. "You went through our files, didn't you?"

I didn't answer, because really, what could I say at that point? So I stepped to the side, gauging the distance between the door and Hayden. I doubted I'd get past him.

"I wish you hadn't done that." There was controlled anger in his face, but there was also disappointment.

I needed time. I needed to ignore the way my heart was cracking open. The way I wanted to sit down and cry, because none of that would help. "Why does he even have files on all of us? Is that something normal? Is that what people do?"

"Do people skip school to snoop through stuff that isn't theirs?" The coldness in his voice shocked me. Nothing reminded me of the boy from last night, the one who'd held me and kissed me like he . . . loved me the way I loved him.

I stepped back.

"Ember, what's behind your back?"

I shook my head. Hayden stepped forward and I made my move. I don't even know why I tried. I made a leaping run for the door, but Hayden caught me by the waist and hauled me back. "Let go of me!"

Capturing my wrists, he backed me against the wall and pinned me there, our bodies flush. The papers—the evidence—fluttered to the floor once more. "Not until you hear me out."

"I don't want to hear anything you have to say!" I struggled not to let the tears fall, but they kept building and building. The sense of betrayal, the hurt, cut so deep I couldn't breathe. "How could you?"

"Listen to me." He pressed forward and dropped his head. "I could never hurt you. Don't you understand that?"

I clamped my lips together and turned my head. He *had* hurt me. He'd ripped me apart.

"Em—"

"How could you?" I whispered. "How could you do that?" A muscle ticked in his jaw. "It was an accident, Em. I didn't understand what was happening—"

I pushed off the wall, but he pushed back.

"Listen to me, Ember. I couldn't hurt you. I can't." Hayden settled his eyes on me. They were softer than I'd ever seen. "I love you—I've loved you since the first time I saw you." I froze. Only my chest moved as I dragged in heavy gulps of air.

"I'd convinced myself for the longest time that concern drove me to keep checking in on you. Each time I left Allentown, I told myself I wasn't coming back. But I did. I couldn't stay away. For two years I kept coming back. I had to make sure you were okay." Hayden's eyes drifted shut. "Dealing with your sister and your mom all alone, but you were so strong and so determined to make it. And the day—the day you went to the bank, I wanted so badly to talk to you—to hold you."

My heart felt like it was breaking and swelling all at once. It left me reeling.

"I know— *I know* how crazy it sounds, but it's like I came to know you. I knew you sketched when you were upset. I saw how much you loved your sister. How brave you were to keep going to that damn school. And all those times I watched you, I grew to know every one of your fake smiles. I never even heard you laugh. All I've ever wanted to do is help you, because maybe then, you'd smile once and really mean it."

I shook my head, willing him to stop— *just stop*.

"I thought being around you would make it easier, but once I got to know you, really know you? I thought I'd loved you *before*." He pressed his lips together, but he never looked away. Not once. "I had no clue. Everyone knows. My father wanted me to stay away from you, because he knew how I felt. And Kurt thinks my judgment is skewed—that I'll lose control again."

Had I misread the conversation I'd heard between Kurt and Liz? I'd assumed Kurt had been talking about Cromwell, but he only mentioned his name when I stopped listening. Did it matter?

"But I realized I'd never lose control, because of you—because I love you. That's what I was trying to tell you last night, Ember. I love you."

"Don't," I whispered, pleaded really. "Don't tell me that."

"But it's true. It's always been true." His fingers flexed around my wrists, inching the sleeve down and exposing my skin.

"Hayden—"

"I've killed," he said, his face constricting. "You have to know the truth, Em."

I let out a sob. It had been him, always him.

"You can hate me forever, but it won't change how I feel."

His mouth came down on mine so hard, it stopped whatever I was about to say. This—this was so wrong, but when he released my wrists, I didn't touch him like I should have. A speck of illogical trust flared alive in me. I grabbed a fistful of his wet sweater and pulled him to me.

Hayden made a low sound in his throat before his lips suddenly found mine again. His hands slipped to my hips, under my shirt. Desperately, the smart part in my brain screamed that this was wrong, but I pushed myself closer instead of away.

Then, when I thought I'd seriously lost my mind, his fingers brushed over the scar above my navel. It was a like a bucket of ice water thrown on me. I pushed—pushed hard.

"No—stop. I can't do this."

Hayden was breathing heavily. Although he didn't look like he wanted to, he let go and stepped back. "Em—"

"Don't. I can't do this!" I screamed, surprised by how pathetic I sounded. "You can't love me. Do you know how twisted this sounds?"

He looked like I had physically wounded him, but it was nothing compared to what I felt.

"You need to let me leave here, Hayden. Please."

Hayden shook his head. "You have to let me explain—"

"Explain what?" I cried. "You killed my father—you killed me, for chrissake!"

"*What*?" he gasped.

"I saw the papers, Hayden! I saw them. And you've basically admitted to it."

His brows furrowed. "I have no idea what you're talking about. I never admitted to causing that accident because I didn't! How could you even think that?"

God, he sounded so honest, so genuine, like the words were tearing him apart. But the evidence—the evidence was right on the floor.

I dropped to my knees and grabbed for the menu, planning to shove it his face. "This is the menu to . . . to—I don't understand." I turned the menu over.

"It's a menu to the Smoke Hole diner. And no, I don't know how it got there."

"No, no, no. This wasn't a menu to the diner!" I flipped it back and forth. "This is—was a menu to Salt of the Sea."

"Obviously, it's not, Ember."

I looked up, shaking my head. Hayden's arms were folded across his chest and he looked angry. "No. There were dates written across the menu! The date of the accident was circled. It was in your handwriting! There were newspaper articles about my Dad, my school schedule—" I made a grab for them, only to find out that they, too, weren't what I'd previously seen.

The article clippings were of Cromwell's election. The schedule was council meetings. The directions were to Morgantown. "I don't understand. This isn't what I saw!"

"I didn't touch those papers."

"I know—I know you didn't." I dropped them and sat back. Hayden hadn't been talking about the car crash when he'd said he'd killed people. Oh, God. He'd been talking about the fire and . . . and I'd yelled at him—demanded how he could've done that.

"Ember, what's going on with you? Dammit, was this why you wanted to drive to school by yourself today? So you could sneak through our stuff?"

I dropped my head into my hands. None of this made sense. I know what I saw and yet, it wasn't there.

"And still after everything, you don't trust me. You really think that I would have ever hurt you or your family? That I could have done something like that?" He gave a harsh laugh. "Wait. What am I saying? You read my file. You know why I was in foster care. So yeah, I guess you'd think I'd murdered your father, too."

"No." I moved my hands away from my face. "You didn't murder your parents. It was an accident. You didn't know how to control your gift. You're not a killer, Hayden."

He stared down at me silently.

"I . . . I think I'm losing my mind. I really am."

The anger faded from his face, replaced by concern. He crouched and gently grasped my shoulders. "Ember, what's going on?"

"I'm sorry," I whispered. "I'm sorry I said those things to you. I don't know what I was thinking. I know what I saw, but it isn't there anymore. I'm sorry—I'm sorry about what happened to your family. It's not your fault."

"Forget about that. Are you feeling okay?"

I laughed, because honestly, I felt funny. My brain was processing everything wrong. I was far from being okay. Either my mind had played a horrible trick on me or I was crazy.

"Em?" He ran his fingers over my cheek. Just a simple, gentle touch and it pierced my heart. How could he ever forgive me for this? "Em, you don't look so good."

"I have a headache." In fact, I'd had a headache ever since English class. "I want to leave. Can we just leave?"

Hayden stared a moment, then nodded. We stopped long enough to change into dry clothes before climbing into his SUV. He leaned forward, running his arm over the fogged windshield. "Em, did you feel anything strange before you looked at those papers?"

"No." I stared out the window. "Just a headache, but I haven't eaten."

Hayden stopped at the end of the driveway. "Do you want to get something to eat, then? We can talk about what you saw."

I nodded. We traveled down the rural highway in silence until I couldn't stand not knowing what he thought or apologizing to him again. "Hayden, I'm sorry. I shouldn't have read your file. That's your personal stuff."

"I would've told you, Em. I just didn't know how to. I thought you'd—Shit!" He slammed on the brakes.

I jerked forward. There was a black car—two-door. Not a Porsche, but it looked familiar, and it was right in the middle of the road.

The tires slipped over the rain-soaked road, losing traction as Hayden whipped the steering wheel into the spin-out. We'd been going too fast to stop so suddenly. The car spun into the other lane, going up on two tires and we sort of hung there in the air for a second. In that pause, my brain flipped back two years.

I heard Hayden curse.

And then we were flung to the side as the SUV rolled. An explosion of white and dust threw me back into the seat. My heart stopped and my lungs seized the moment we came down on the driver's side, then the roof, then my side. The crash jarred every bone in my body. The air flew from my lungs and my head hit the window with a disgusting thud.

A crack sounded as the SUV took another nasty flip. I couldn't even scream. It was like being trapped in haunting memory that wouldn't relinquish control. My head slammed into the window again and this time the glass shattered under the impact.

Something metallic ripped and pressed into me as we skid-ded off the road and slid across the field, finally coming to rest on the driver's side.

I remained still for minutes, stunned and barely able to breathe. Blood, wet and warm, trickled down the side of my head. Something poked into my right leg, leaving it numb. I tried to look around, but the movement hurt. Over the radio, I could hear the tires spinning.

Miraculously, I was still held by my seatbelt and I was alive, I was— *Hayden*. I didn't hear him, couldn't see him.

Frantic, I ignored the waves of red-hot pain and pushed at the airbag until I could see around me. The driver's airbag had deflated. Hayden lay against the crushed door, motionless and covered in blood.

And through all that blood, he was pale so, so pale.

"Hayden!" I pitched forward, but the seatbelt yanked me back. "Hayden! Wake up! Please—oh, God. Please be alive." My fingers, drenched in blood, slipped over the latch.

He didn't move. I couldn't even tell if he was breathing, and I couldn't get the seatbelt undone. Panic poured through me, screams filled my ears. Someone had to help us, right? Hayden had to be alive— *he had to be.*

This couldn't be happening again. No. No, not all over—

The passenger door yanked open, startling me. I stopped struggling, stopped screaming. Someone was here to help. Everything was going to be okay.

Arms reached down, wrapping around my waist while a hand felt for the seatbelt. I was too relieved to even think about what would happen if they touched me. I couldn't tear my eyes off Hayden to even look to see who was pulling me out of the car. I was hoisted into the air for a second, and rain beat down on my face, mixing with tears. "Please help him! Please!"

Then nothing was holding me.

I hit the wet, unforgiving ground hip-first. Fresh, new pain stole my breath. I rolled onto my back, squinting through the sheets of icy rain at the dark shadow towering over me. Slowly, I lifted my head. I recognized the body—the face—as someone I trusted, someone who would help us.

"Please help him," I whispered, crawling onto my knees.

Without any warning, a booted foot connected with my head. Everything went white, then black.

27

When I came to, I noticed two things immediately. I was freezing—so cold my teeth chattered and I couldn't feel my toes. And I couldn't move my arms.

I opened my eyes to see nothing but darkness. It was hard to distinguish anything until my sight adapted. Once it did, I delved headfirst into freak-out mode, which didn't help the pounding in my skull.

I was in a cellar of some sort—an old one used to store things no one wanted. The walls reflected a slimy sort of surface. It took me several seconds to realize water dripped down the blocks, pooling along the floor, soaking my jeans. The thin tank I'd thrown on before leaving the house now clung to me like an icy sheet. I had no idea where my hoodie was.

I really started to spaz out then.

Kicking my legs up, I tried to stand, but couldn't get my arms out from behind me. They were tied to something—a thick, cold pipe cut into my back. Metal sliced my wrists as I struggled wildly to get them undone. All I succeeded in doing was tearing the skin open, spilling more blood.

A squeaking noise came from one of the dark corners, then the sound of something scurrying across the room.

My heart lodged in my throat. I stopped moving, staring blindly into the shadows. Two beady eyes became visible. I shrieked and yanked my legs up, knocking my shins against something—several coarse, hairy little bodies.

Rats.

I screamed, really screamed, until my throat felt like it'd ripped open. Rats hurried back to the corners, their claws clicking across the cement. I pulled against the pipe, thrashing until my fingers turned numb. Terror consumed me, eating away at the thin grasp I held on sanity.

Time came and went. I lost track. My throat was so hoarse my screams sounded more like moans. I peered into the gloom, sure everything moved—the rats, waiting until I passed out to start nibbling on my skin. A hysterical laugh escaped me—little did they know that the first bite would kill them. My mind started playing tricks on me. I was sure I heard movement above me more than once, but no one answered my cries. No one came. Was this how I would die? By rats or blood loss? Or by freezing to death, because I was pretty sure hypothermia was setting in. At one point, I swore the shadows whispered my name— called to me like some sick chorus of death.

Above me, a door opened. With the sound of a thrown switch, a bulb overhead came on, sparked once, and then dimmed. Footsteps came down the stairs. Boots first, then jeans, leather-covered hands, a heavy sweater rolled up to the elbows . . . and then any hope I had that this was a good thing crumbled and died.

I squeezed my eyes shut and pretended to be asleep—or dead.

The footsteps neared, stopped, and poked my curled toes. "I know you're awake."

I didn't move, didn't dare breathe. Not even when the buzzing droned to an intense pitch.

A sigh came. "Ember, I can read your thoughts. I know you're awake. Don't make this harder on yourself, or me."

My eyes snapped opened then. I hadn't realized how close the monster was to me, but only inches separated us. "Why?" My voice came out hoarse and weak.

Mr. Theo gave me a smile—the same one he wore when he lectured in class. "I'd think it would be obvious at this point."

But it wasn't. "I don't understand."

"Sorry to make you wait so long. I had to finish up school." He picked up a rat by its tail. "Dirty little things."

I swallowed back the taste of bile. His words gave me a hint at the timeline. Hours had passed if he was done teaching.

"You look cold."

"I . . . I am," I whispered.

He tossed the rat aside and rested his hands on his knees. Theo sighed. "You could've avoided this. I tried to make it fast before."

My gaze fell back to him. "I don't understand. I thought . . . I thought you liked me. That—"

"That I related to you? With my sad, sad story about a sick mom and kids who hated me? Sorry. Not particularly true. My mother was a cold-hearted bitch who thought her kids were nothing but freaks. She shipped me and my sister off to the Facility when I was only six. Really, this—all of this—isn't anything personal."

"It's not?"

His brows furrowed and he removed his glasses, putting them aside. "I tried the night of the bonfire. You would've been another teenager killed by one of their drunk friends, but you moved out of the way. Then the night you went walking through the woods, it seemed even more perfect, especially after all those nasty things were left in your locker. I figured they'd blame the empath, but once again you survived and no one blamed the other girl."

My brain slowly worked though the sludge of fear and confusion. "You won't get away with this."

"I won't?" His tone relaxed. "The last time I checked, Hayden was in the hospital and, thanks to your plans to snoop around, I know Jonathan Cromwell is out of town. By the time either of them realizes what's going on, it'll be too late."

"No—no, you're wrong."

"The sad thing is that they *could* find you if they cared. Phoebe could trace your feelings. Parker could get in there just like I have so many times and figure it out. But I must say, I don't think *they'll* put too much effort into it."

Right now I could care less about them, but I knew to keep him talking. That's what they did in the movies. Maybe I'd get lucky and he'd launch into an evil villain speech, and then . . . what? I'd freeze to death. That sounded like a better alternative to whatever he planned. I twisted my wrists. Blood, water, and cold sweat coated the cuffs. There was a chance I could slip out of them. Maybe, but not likely.

He rocked back on his heels and reached into his pocket. Withdrawing a tiny silver coin—my coin—Theo held it up. "Ah, I see you recognize this. It's the same coin I gave you. After all, how else could I get into that little head of yours? I either needed something of yours or you had to have something of mine."

It all started to click into place. The times I'd started to feel dizzy in his class or sick to my stomach when I talked to him. He'd been in my head, messing around. And when Parker was reading my thoughts, he'd held a sweater of mine—a connection to me.

"You're a telepath."

Mr. Theo reached out and patted the top of my head with one gloved hand. I winced. "Good girl. I also can put thoughts into other people's heads. Make people believe whatever I want them to."

"And—and the papers I found? You made me think I saw the articles and the menu—because I had that coin?" I would've smacked myself if I could get my hands free. "Why did you make me see those things?"

"Because I knew that was your worst fear—and what you already expected. I figured you'd run away at that point, giving me my chance to swoop in." He leaned over, plucked up another rat and threw it. The soft thud and shrill shriek made me shudder. "When I saw you leaving school, I followed you. I should've expected Cromwell's little prodigy boy would follow you. I've seen how you've spent your Thanksgiving break, you naughty, naughty girl."

I felt sick knowing he'd been peeping in on my immensely private thoughts.

"But it's all okay now."

"I don't understand why you're doing this." I hated the way my voice broke, the way my whole body shook.

"You know, telepathy isn't my primary gift. None of the mind tricks are. I picked up a few new talents at the Facility." Catching my reaction, he smiled. "Oh, yes. The Facility did come in handy. You see, those who are gifted—like us—are able to obtain more gifts under the right cultivation. But my first gift? Well, why don't I just show you?"

Morbidly fascinated, I watched him tug one glove off his hand. Still smiling, he picked up one of the dead rats. Within seconds, it started squirming and squeaking. My mouth dropped open as my heart thudded painfully fast. "You—you can bring back the dead."

"Just like your little sister." He threw the rat into the wall, making a sickening crunch. It didn't move. I felt sick. "You and I have a lot in common."

"No," I whispered.

Calmly, he pulled his glove back on. "But we do. You see, I'm like your sister—"

"You are nothing like her!" I screamed.

"And *you* are just like *my* sister." Slowly, the smile faded from his face. "All of this started over ten years ago. And it's funny how small the world is." He brushed a clump of damp hair off my forehead. I tried not to flinch, but I couldn't stop the reaction. "I work—well, *worked* for the Facility. Not anymore."

"Really?"

Theo's hand snapped out and circled around my arm. "You can stop struggling. You're not getting out of this."

I bit down on my cheek. "Please let me go."

Theo glanced down, frowning. "What a nasty cut on your leg. No wonder the rats are circling us."

My stomach churned. I couldn't afford to think about that. "Why are you doing this?" My voice rose to a hoarse whine. "Who made you do this? Cromwell? The Facility?"

He looked up, meeting my eyes for the first time. "Actually, your father."

My heart skipped, missed a beat. "No."

"Your father wasn't a good man."

I started pulling against the pipe, whipping my head from side to side. "No! You're lying. No!"

"Now, stop. You're only hurting yourself." He grabbed my arms. "You wanted the truth. I gave you the truth. Your father was a money-hungry bastard who would've sold his soul if it fattened his pockets."

I kicked out at him, missing by a mile, but my lack of coordination didn't keep him from getting pissed off. He grasped my leg, digging his gloved fingers into the cut. I opened my mouth to scream, but all that came out was a tremendous sob.

He slammed my leg back to the cement floor. "Your father was going to sell Olivia to the highest bidder. How do you think the Facility even knew about her? It's a more common practice than you think. Parents love their kids—even if they are giant freaks—but money always talks."

"You're lying. My dad never would've done something like that."

"You have no idea. Did you know your great-grandmother was gifted? No. I see that you didn't. She was a healer and not afraid to use it. Your father did a lot of research on gifts. He learned that the trait is typically passed down, and those newer generations sometimes are even stronger—look at me when I talk to you!" He pressed into the gash until I did as he ordered.

I bit down on my lip until I tasted blood.

His grip relaxed. "He knew there was a good chance that his children would be gifted. I think he hoped it would be you. Yes, he was in contact with us long before Olivia came along, but as you grew older and showed no gift, he needed another kid. He didn't understand that he just needed to wait a little longer on you."

My heart was breaking, even though my mind rebelled against what he said. And then it happened. I felt a subtle brush behind my eyelids. Nothing like Theo's barbaric mind-reading skills, which made me want to vomit. I thought I imagined it, but the presence remained, lingering on the fringe of my consciousness.

Parker?

I couldn't be sure, but I freaking hoped so. I started mentally saying Mr. Theo's name, and that I was in some kind of basement. Hoping and praying that Parker—not Mr. Theo—was tinkering inside my head . . . and that I wasn't losing my mind.

"I don't know what he planned to do with your mother. Maybe she was in on it. But did you know what he wanted done to you?" He turned my face so I had to look at him. "He wanted someone with my . . . gifts to handle the transaction. Your father was supposed to hand over Olivia for quite a bit of money. He wanted me to make you believe Olivia had died."

"No, no, no." I twisted away from him, tears of anger and fear rolled down my face, mixing with blood. This couldn't be true. It just couldn't be.

"Yes. I came to handle the transaction, but your father had a change of heart. He didn't want to give her up, and I don't think he planned on your mom putting up such a fight over it. Either way, it didn't matter in the end."

I stilled. "The accident . . . it was you."

"The accident was just an accident."

"No. It wasn't. Cromwell—"

"Cromwell is a liar! The accident was just that—an accident. A freak accident that I *had* thought would've worked in my benefit since your father was no longer a part of the picture. I hung around after the accident, waiting to see what the Facility wanted me to do. You see, they hadn't told me what Olivia's gifts were, and at the time, I didn't care. And then I saw Jonathan Cromwell snooping around."

"Sucks for you, huh? He ruined the Facility's plans." I gasped out, hating this man with every fiber in my being.

He smirked. "You have no idea, do you? I couldn't care less about Olivia and her gift. And I care even less about the Facility. I don't work for them anymore."

I stopped struggling. "What do you mean?"

Theo's stare met mine, and I shuddered. I'd always heard about people looking crazy, but I'd never seen it—not until now. "After I saw Cromwell hanging around, I knew something was up. Then when his boy kept coming back, I grew even more curious. This was my chance. See? I didn't really have any loyalty to the Facility. I only stayed with them so I could keep an eye on Jonathan. Once I saw his interest in you, I left the Facility and got a job up here, where I could keep closer tabs on him. You'd be amazed at how far you can get with a little bit of mind control. Then you showed up. Perfect."

"Why?"

"My sister was older than me. So bright and beautiful, but she was gifted with a terrible curse."

Ice slithered through my veins.

He leaned in so close we almost touched. "She could kill with a single touch of her hands. Julie never wanted to hurt a single person, but she couldn't help it. She never could."

"Oh, my God," I murmured.

"Did you think your desire to see those files was all you?" he asked. "I put that need in you. I wanted you to see—*to know*— *what* they did to my sister." He paused, and my temples started to pound. "Of course he scratched out everything about me. Couldn't live with his greatest failure."

"Get . . . out." I struggled for air. My head felt like it would explode. His lips twitched, and the pressure eased off. "I can't let him succeed. Not when he failed my sister. That's the why of it, Ember."

"Cromwell? But he didn't have anything to do with the project!"

Theo barked a short laugh. "Cromwell lets you know what he wants you to know. It's always a half-truth. That's all he deals in. Cromwell was assigned to my sister at the Facility. He was responsible for her treatment—her Assimilation. He allowed my sister to die. Do you even know the kind of horrors they subjected her to?"

I tried to think quickly. I had a feeling I was running out of time, which wasn't helping.

"They would make her touch things—living things, Ember. Animals. People. Do you know what that did to her?" he asked. "It slowly killed her. Day by day, *they* killed her. And Cromwell stood by. He allowed it to happen. So think of this as me doing you a favor."

"You're going to kill me so I don't kill myself?" I pulled against the pipe again. "Do you know how insane that sounds?"

He stood slowly. "I gave you the coin so I could keep an eye on you. See what Cromwell was doing with you."

I dragged in deep, musty air. "Why are you going to do this?"

"I'm going to kill you because Cromwell has always wanted a gifted who could bring death—one who could control it. Do you know what kind of power someone could wield with that? But he failed my sister. He's not going to have you."

Wincing, I continued to pull away from the pipe. "Cromwell will know this was you. He'll figure it out."

He cocked his head to the side. "Really? You think so? Cromwell was so wrapped up in my sister when we were at the Facility, he never looked twice at me. He didn't even know about my gifts. Only the higher-ups knew what I could do, and it was kept secret. And we've passed each other several times. He's never recognized me. Not once."

I dragged in deep, heavy breaths. "You're crazy."

"Crazy?" he repeated. My eyes followed his movements. He was digging around for something. "Maybe I am. My sister was everything to me. Cromwell took everything. Now I'm going to take from him."

I laughed, and it did sound a bit insane. "I don't mean anything to him. He doesn't even like me."

"No. You mean a lot to Cromwell. You'd thank me if you knew what the future held for you."

Something metal glinted in the light. Terror rolled through my stomach. "Then tell me! Tell me!"

Theo straightened and sent an amused glance over his shoulder. "Can I ask you a question?"

Panic clawed its way through me. "Sure. Ask away."

"How does it feel to die?"

"Let me go and I can show you."

He laughed at that, genuinely amused. "You've got spirit. I like that." He came back to me, his hands behind his back.

"Wait. Wait!" I stalled. "If the accident was just an accident, what happened to my mom? She—she was wiped. Who did that to her?"

"Your mom? I don't know. Does it matter? She already thinks you're dead," he said. "So are you going to answer my question?"

"Go to hell."

Theo crouched beside me. "Are you afraid to die—to really die—this time? Because there'll be no Olivia to bring you back."

Nothing short of fear gripped me, because yes, I *was* afraid to die.

"Wait. I still—"

"Ah, I can tell you are. I've been debating how to do this. I could let you stay down here. Eventually you would slip away, either from hunger or the cold, but that seems unnecessary and cruel." He shifted and moved his arms.

I saw it at once. It was the only thing I could see.

Theo held a gun in his right hand.

Instinct took over. I kicked out wildly. Instead of hitting his hand, my leg smashed into the side of his face. Startled, he recovered all too quickly. Rearing off the damp cement floor, he swung the gun around, pointed right in my face.

I didn't want to die in this cold, hellish place. Not before I got to tell my mom and Olivia goodbye. Not before I told Hayden that I loved him—

His finger moved to the trigger, and I knew I was going to die, for real this time. "Nothing personal."

"Please! Wait—" My voice cracked with panic. "Don't do—"

A bright reddish, yellow spark blinded me, and I waited—waited for the inevitable feeling of metal tearing through flesh and bone.

Except the pain never came, and the screams tearing through the cellar weren't mine.

Mr. Theo spun away from me, falling to the floor as flames engulfed the lower half of his body. Transfixed by the disturbing dance, I watched until he dove into a puddle large enough to extinguish the flames. He didn't move after that.

"Ember?"

Hayden stood at the bottom of the stairs. He looked rough—torn sweater, dark splotches staining the front. I think there was a hospital bracelet on his wrist. What looked like dried blood covered half of his face and his hair was matted to his forehead.

But he was, in that moment, the most beautiful thing I'd ever seen.

He was at my side before I could even respond. His expression held a striking mix of terror, pain, and relief. Hayden grasped my face. I didn't even care that it hurt. "Ember, oh God, Ember, please say something."

I started to cry and blabber at once, telling him things I was sure he already figured out, while he shrugged out of his sweater and tried to tuck it around my shoulders. Beyond him, I saw Kurt in his cowboy duster poking at Theo with his booted foot.

"Holy shit," Kurt muttered, shaking his head. "Isn't he an English teacher at the high school?"

Hayden peered behind me and swore violently. "Kurt, get over here. Em, just hold on a little while longer and we'll get you out of here."

"How . . . how did you find me?" I asked, shivering uncontrollably.

"Parker traced you, with Phoebe's help." His breath felt exquisitely warm against my chilled skin—something I thought I'd never feel again. "When I woke in the hospital and found out you weren't there—that you weren't even at the accident—I knew something was wrong. I got ahold of the twins, who called Kurt. They picked me up and we started driving around until they could feel you."

"Jesus," Kurt muttered again. "These are metal. There is no way we're going to get them off." He slid out of the duster and dropped it over me. "Jesus. Ember, stop shaking. You're ripping the skin off your wrists."

"I . . . I c-can't help it."

"It's okay." Hayden tucked the edges of Kurt's coat around me. He stroked my face and my forehead with quick brushes of his fingers. A strong shudder ran through me as he brushed back my hair. "Em, I need you to open your eyes and look at me."

I didn't realize I'd closed them.

"I need to melt the metal to get you free." He paused, his eyes sharpened by a protective shine. "I need you to be perfectly still."

"O-Okay."

Hayden glanced over at Kurt and nodded. "Make sure she doesn't move."

"You got it." Kurt shifted closer and groaned. "Dammit—rats. I hate rats."

"M-Me too, b-but I think they h-hate me more," I said.

Kurt laughed, a real honest-to-God laugh. "Trust me, that's a good thing."

I rested my head against Hayden's chest as he felt around behind me. His body heat felt marvelous, so much so that I ignored the first flare of intense heat, but then I felt pain. Real pain.

I stiffened.

"Don't move," he whispered. "You helped us find you, did you know that?"

I flinched and squeezed my eyes shut. I should've thought about it more when he said he needed to melt the metal. The kind of heat needed to do that had to be ridiculous. My wrists felt like they had been shoved in an oven. Pressing my face into his chest, I whimpered.

"Em? Did you know?" he asked again, coaxing a response from me."

"N-No."

"Yeah, you kept thinking about Mr. Theo and being in a basement. We wouldn't have known to check down here if it hadn't been for you. You did really good, Em."

Searing, red-hot pain shot through my arms, but I managed not to move. Melting metal stung like holy hell. But it was working. The cuffs were already loosening.

"It'll be just a little bit more, and we'll be done."

"She's pretty messed up, Hayden," Kurt said, like I wasn't right there. "You need to hurry up. Her leg is bleeding real bad."

Probably due to my heart rate skyrocketing. Between the burning around my hands and everything that'd happened, I was pushed to my limits, but I needed to make sure that, if they failed, they wouldn't take me to my sister. "P-Promise me, you won't take me to Olivia. If t-this doesn't work—"

"This will work," Hayden said. "And if it doesn't, I'm not losing you."

"Y-You can't use Olivia again. I-I won't allow it."

"Dammit, don't argue with me about this!"

In that instant, I realized Hayden would risk anything—anyone—to make sure I lived. But I couldn't expose her to this. Not again. The handcuffs melted enough that, with Hayden and Kurt's combined efforts, they broke apart. My muscles screamed in protest, but I ignored them.

I grabbed Kurt's hand, the raw flesh around my wrists bubbling. His mouth dropped open, a mixture of fear and disbelief crawling across his face. "Don't let Olivia see me like this. D-Don't let her touch me. Please."

Kurt's gaze bounced to Hayden, then back to me. "Okay. Okay."

"Dammit, Kurt," Hayden roared. "I won't let her die!"

But Kurt was on his feet the moment I let go of him, digging in his pocket. "Jonathan has connections at the hospital, Hayden. He's already on his way. I'll call him."

The heat of his anger poured off him. "If anything happens to her . . ."

"I know. You'll kill me." Kurt pulled out his cell and cursed. "I have to go upstairs. I'm not getting a signal."

"I'll get her. Just go." Hayden turned back to me, already dismissing Kurt. His gaze traced every inch of me, enduring every cut, scrape, and bruise. His voice turned husky. "Em, I thought—I thought I'd lost you."

"N-No, I'm here."

Hayden leaned in and brought his mouth down on mine. I sank into him—his warmth and his love. When he pulled back, his eyes shone in the dim light.

"I want to go h-home."

"Hospital first," he said. "Then we go home. Together."

My eyes fell around the dark recesses of the cellar—the area I'd thought would be my final resting place. They roamed over the damp walls covered in mold and over Hayden's shoulder where I saw Mr. Theo—on his feet, gun in hand.

"Hayden—watch—"

But it was too late. Hayden gasped and shifted as if he planned on shielding me with his body. I broke into a wild struggle, so powerful that Hayden jolted to his left just as the gun fired.

Mr. Theo missed, but he was aiming again.

Using the last of my strength, I pushed hard. I heard Hayden yell my name, but I focused on Mr. Theo. He fumbled with the gun. With all the burns, he moved in halting jerks. Anger and desperation propelled me across the slick floor. The pain didn't matter—nothing did but stopping Mr. Theo.

He leveled the gun, not at me, but at Hayden. I stretched out, running my hand under the hem of his charred pants and circling the sticky flesh of his ankle. He jerked once, twice. His entire body went rigid, even his fingers. The gun slipped from his hand, hitting the floor with a sharp rattle of finality. I held on.

Mr. Theo dropped to his knees, arms splayed out like some kind of fallen angel. A grayish color raced over his skin, veins bulging and darkening as if someone had taken a charcoal pencil and traced the fine lines. He turned his head and stared down at me, mouth gaped in a silent scream. In that heartbeat, our eyes met.

I felt my lips spread into a smile.

A great and terrible spasm rolled through his body, then his eyes rolled back and he fell face-first into a cold puddle. Mr. Theo didn't move again.

Over the next couple of hours I slipped in and out of reality. When I woke in a warm place, I reached for Hayden. My fingers curled into the empty air until someone gently guided my arm back.

Cromwell moved into my line of vision. "Hayden's all right. Just getting checked over again."

I blinked and my head rolled in the other direction. A white curtain fluttered and a machine beeped. There were voices far away. Or were they close? Things were kind of foggy from there on out. Someone in medical scrubs shot a syringe into the IV tube snaking from my arm, which didn't help with my observation skills at all—not to mention I felt like I was floating halfway off the bed.

"Don't touch her skin, whatever you do." Cromwell—I was pretty sure that was Cromwell. Talking to the doctor, I guessed.

I couldn't open my eyes again. I felt pleasantly numb. Detached. A door opened and closed. I hoped it was Hayden. I held my breath, waiting, hoping, waiting, floating some more.

"So this is Project E?" said a female voice I didn't recognize.

"Yes, this would be her."

"Do you want us to take her? We have a place for her immediately." The woman's voice was soft and melodious. She sounded like Mom. I liked that.

"No," Cromwell answered after a stretch of silence. "She's one of mine now. And she's very important."

"You should take better care of her, then. It would be a shame to lose this one, too."

Then I floated up and up, past the ceiling and into a bright, warm nothing.

"It hurts. I can fix it."

"No. Olivia, don't touch it." I pushed at the arm hovering way too close to the side of my face. "It's fine. I'm fine."

She sat back on her heels, dipping the bed. "Emmie, why are you hurt?"

I turned my head slowly and stared up at the ceiling. How could I tell a five-year-old that my crazy English teacher had wanted to kill me? I couldn't. So I settled on the same thing I'd told her ever since I'd woken up with her next to me. "I was in an accident."

"With Hayden?"

My heart squeezed. I'd only been awake for a little while, and Olivia was the only person I'd seen. "Yes, with Hayden." Her lower lip trembled. "I don't like accidents."

"I know, honey, but everything is okay now."

"You promise? No more accidents?"

I smiled, but it was more of a wince. When I'd first woken up, I'd hobbled into the bathroom and gotten a good look at myself. Half my face looked like someone had pummeled it. I had a knot the size of a golf ball on the side of my head. Even now, every inch of skin hurt, every muscle felt torn, and every bone ached, but my leg and wrists had suffered far worse. Olivia said I had over a hundred stitches, so I deducted eighty from that. I couldn't see most of my hands; they were wrapped in heavy gauze.

"Emmie?"

"No more accidents. I promise." I started to sit up, but a wave of dizziness forced me back down. I hit the pillow, grimacing. I felt out of it, tired and so damn thirsty. "Olivia, want to do me a favor?"

Her head bobbed eagerly.

"Can you get me something to drink?"

"I can get you juice. I can help."

"Juice would be great. Olivia—" She was already off the bed and at the door. "Olivia, I love you."

"I love you, Emmie!" Then she took off flying from my room. I could hear her little footsteps all the way down the stairs.

Slowly, I tried to push myself back up again. It didn't work. I stared at the ceiling until my eyes started to drift shut. The next thing I knew, Cromwell was pulling my desk chair across the room and sitting by the bed.

"Where's Olivia?"

"You were asleep when she brought the juice up." He motioned at the bed stand. There my juice sat. My mouth watered. "She's with Liz. Do you think you can sit up?"

With his careful help, I was able to sit up long enough. My throat burned, but I downed the entire glass before lying back down. "I feel . . . weird."

"You were given some pain medication at the hospital, and again this morning. You don't remember that?"

I frowned. "No." All I remembered from the hospital was floating through the rafters. I must've been really high.

"I need to talk to you. Do you feel up to it?"

"Okay," I said, but there was something about the hospital I thought I should remember. It was there, on the very edge of my memories, hazy and out of reach.

"Parker and Hayden filled me in on most of what happened. I can understand your distrust of me and my intentions, but I hope you have learned that's not the case."

I thought that was a very smooth way of asking if I'd learned my lesson. "Parker was in my head again?"

"We thought it would be easier than making you relive everything."

I guess that made it okay—sort of. "So, you worked with his sister."

Cromwell let out a soft breath and nodded. "It was a very long time ago, before Hayden and the others. Theo was a child, and I had no idea his gift was like Olivia's. His sister had a remarkable gift."

"Remarkable?"

"She was the first, Ember. No one before her had ever showed that type of gift, and no one after her—until you. With what happened to her, I didn't want to attempt the same thing." He paused, a small smile appeared. "I never intended to send you to the Facility. I didn't want you to have the same fate she did. I don't expect you to believe me, but you have no idea how her death ate away at me. She was why I started searching for others, hoping to get to them before the gifts became too much to control."

"But . . . you worked with her? In the program?"

"I did," he admitted. "It was a long time ago, Ember." And that was all he would say about that. His next words distracted me, anyway. "From what I could gather, it appears that Theo did tell you the truth about your father. He was going to transfer guardianship of Olivia to one of the doctors at the Facility. I'm sorry. I know that isn't what you wanted to hear."

No. It wasn't. I didn't even know how to deal with that—what to think or where to begin. All I could acknowledge right now was the sick twisting of my heart.

"I'm really sorry."

It could've been the drugs, but he actually looked sympathetic. "Isn't someone going to do something to stop them? They can't do this to people, let parents sell their children."

"The Facility never used to be like this, and trust me, something is being done about them," Cromwell said, anger sparking deep in his eyes. "But it's not something you need to worry about right now. I know it's hard for you not to focus on it, but you need to get better."

What I needed . . . I didn't even know what I needed.

"There's one other thing I want to talk to you about." He took a deep breath. "I know you've been working with my son. We had a very long talk last night."

"Oh," I whispered.

"I always knew he wouldn't listen to me when it came to you. I'm just surprised by how far he disobeyed my wishes."

"He . . . he just wanted to help me."

Cromwell raised one brow, and the bland expression on his face slipped a degree. "It appears Hayden had his own motives."

"I don't understand."

"Ember, I know you and Hayden are . . . involved with one another. I'm going to be honest with you; I'm not thrilled. Among other concerns, you both live under my roof, but I suppose it's a good thing he didn't listen to me."

"It is?"

"Kurt told me you grabbed him in the cellar, and that your touch didn't hurt him. It seems I should've supported Hayden when he first asked to work with you."

"I can't touch . . . for a long period of time. Maybe a minute."

"But that is miraculous, considering where you were before."

That same word from Olivia's file popped in my head, but I decided to let it go. "I guess so."

Cromwell leaned forward and held out one hand. "I need to see if it's true."

"Are you serious?" The look that he gave me said he was. I sighed, too tired to argue. "If it doesn't work, well, I guess you'll know." Then I touched my hand to his. His fingers felt smooth to me, like the man never used his hands for anything other than pushing a pen. A couple of seconds passed, maybe about thirty, when he seemed satisfied.

"Miraculous," he murmured again. He stood. "We'll talk more later. Get some rest."

"Cromwell?"

He stopped at the door, twisting back. "Yes?"

"Is . . . is Theo dead?"

"Yes."

I let out an unsteady breath. "I don't know how to feel about that."

Cromwell came back to the bed, studying me a moment. "Do not think for one second that Theo wasn't going to kill you. He saw you as having the future his sister should've had. And you defended yourself, but you did more than that." He sat down on the edge of the bed and smiled.

I think it was the first time he ever truly smiled at me like he meant it.

"Hayden may not be my biological son, but he means the world to me. If you hadn't stopped Theo, he would've shot my son. You saved Hayden's life."

Something awful shifted in my stomach. "But I killed someone. Again."

"The first was an accident, Ember. And this? Well, it's not something you will ever get used to. However, in time, you will come to accept what you have done. Get some rest, Ember." He left without so much as a look back.

I thought he sounded like someone who knew what it felt like to kill. Then again, that could've been the pain meds. I couldn't be sure.

Silence settled in around me and I shifted uncomfortably. That awful feeling kept worrying me. Yes, Theo had planned on putting a bullet in my head—Hayden's, too—but I'd killed him. And I was pretty sure I'd smiled while doing it.

That couldn't be good.

What would Olivia say if she knew? What would my mom say? I'd killed twice now, but this one—this kill was different. I'd *wanted* to do it. I squeezed my eyes shut. I already knew what Hayden would think. Maybe that's why he hadn't checked in on me yet. He had once said I was good inside, better than all of them. I doubted he thought that now.

I lay there for a little while, trying not to think about anything, and eventually slipped back into sleep. When I opened my eyes again, night had fallen.

"Ember."

My heart skipped a beat or two at the sound of his voice. The bed dipped. Fingers brushed my hair back, lingering as long as possible. *Hayden.*

"Hey there," I whispered.

"How are you feeling?"

I tested sitting up. "Not so woozy. Better."

"Good. I've checked on you several times, but you've been sleeping. I didn't want to wake you."

"I wish you had." Hayden smiled. "Miss my face?"

My eyes fell over him, checking for wounds. "Are you okay?"

"I'm a hundred percent."

I stared at him, wanting to memorize every inch of his face. "You're really here, right? I'm not having a drug-induced dream, am I?"

His brows furrowed. "No. I'm here."

"I . . . I didn't think you'd want to see me after everything."

"Em, sometimes you think the weirdest crap."

My lips twitched, but I sobered up pretty quickly. "I'm sorry for everything. For the thing with the files and . . . and what I did. I never wanted to kill someone. And I've done it twice." I wiped under my eyes, feeling on the verge of coming apart. "I'm sorry. I didn't want him to hurt you. I didn't know what else to do."

"Shh, don't." He pulled me to him, cradling me against his chest so gently. "I don't care about the file thing anymore. Do you think that's even important to me now? After all you've been through?"

"But . . . what I did to Theo."

"You did what you had to do. It doesn't change anything about you. How beautiful you are inside. How good you are. Or what I think of you."

Heavy tears rolled down my cheeks. Hayden held on until the panic and fear slowly eased off. My grip on his sweater loosened and when I lifted my head, he swooped in and dropped a sweet kiss on my lips, silencing my worries and doubts. With that one simple touch, I knew I was going to be all right.

"Do you remember telling me what you loved most about winter?" he asked me.

"Yeah, I think so."

His smile turned beautiful. "Let me help you stand."

Hayden also helped me limp to the door. There, he grabbed a quilt and wrapped it around me. "Close your eyes."

I raised my brows, but did as he asked. I heard the door open and cold air washed over me. Then, without any warning, I was swinging off my feet.

"Keep your eyes closed, Em."

"Hayden, what are you doing?"

"Carrying you," he said, laughter in his voice.

"Yeah, I gathered that."

He held me close to his chest as he carried me out onto the

balcony. I felt his lips brush my forehead. "All right, open your eyes."

I did, and in that moment, I was blown away by the beauty of the place I had once found terrifying. Flakes of falling snow glistened in the moonlight like a thousand glittering stars. They came down fat and thick, placing a heavy blanket of white over the branches of elm trees, already softening the sharp peaks of Seneca Rocks.

"It's . . . it's beautiful."

"I thought you'd like it." His arms tightened.

"I love it." I tipped my head back. "Hayden."

"Hmm?" He lowered his head, the edges of his hair brushing over my forehead.

It felt like silk on my skin—like his voice, his gaze. I felt close to tears again, but the happy kind, and even though I thought it would be hard to say these words, they came out easily. "I love you."

Much like the look he got when he saw my sketches of him, wonder flickered across his face. "You have no idea how long I've waited to hear you say that."

My smile spread. "Two years, give or take a week?"

Hayden grinned, his dark eyes like pools of the night sky. "Yeah, that sounds about right. Do you know what I want to do now?"

"Kiss?"

And we did. Our lips touched. The world simply faded away, and it was just Hayden and me. We parted only after we had to, at the very last second.

"I love you, Ember."

Resting my head against his chest, I smiled and sighed a little. Beyond the edge of the balcony, through the snow-touched trees, and over the rising slope of the mountains, a star broke away from the sky and fell to the earth.

ACKNOWLEDGEMENTS

I would like to thank Kate Kaynak and the wonderful team at Spencer Hill: Rich Storrs, Patricia Riley, Kendra McCormick, and Laura LaTulipe. Also a shout out to my agent Kevan Lyon and foreign rights agent Taryn Fagerness. A big thank you to those who helped shape *Cursed* into something readable.

Julie—you'll always be my rockstar.

Cindy and Carissa, you guys are always there with feedback.

To all my friends and family, thank you for supporting me. And to all those who read my books and those who blog about them, I can't express how much I appreciate every one of you.